OBSESSION

A DARK ROMANTIC SUSPENSE NOVEL

JANE HENRY

SYNOPSIS

They call him the executioner.

Some say monster.

Dishonorably discharged from the military, he runs a highly secret, clandestine operation, and has everything I need to find the justice I crave.

Power players at his disposal.

An insatiable hunger for justice.

A reckless disregard for the law.

I offer him my skills, but that's not what he wants.

He wants me.

And Cain Master always gets what he wants.

CHAPTER ONE

Violet

THE DRIVER PULLS OVER by the side of the road. "Here you go. Pay on the app."

I look at the GPS and note we're still a mile away. We drove by the wooden placard that read *Welcome to Salem,* complete with the obligatory golden witch on a broom, half a mile ago.

"Uh, this isn't it. Still a mile up ahead."

The kid driving the car's about twenty years old, clean-shaven, and he wears glasses perched on the end of his nose. He looks over the wire rims and frowns. "This is as far as I go, lady. Do you know who lives up that hill?"

"I do." I barely control my temper. "It was the address I gave you when you agreed to drive me, remember?"

He blinks. "I didn't recognize the address. Would've turned down the job if I had."

Lovely. Does everyone know the man I'm going to see, and I've somehow lived in ignorance all this time until yesterday?

"Soooo?"

"I won't go up there. I don't have a death wish, lady. I won't charge you for the rest of the trip, only this far," he says, as if somehow that makes it all better.

"How kind of you." I can't hide my disgust.

"Out," he snaps.

"Fine." I grab my bag, a beat up black leather crossbody I picked up at a thrift store, and sling it over my shoulder. I really should maybe find something a bit nicer for times such as these. "Thanks."

I slam the door harder than I need to and frown at my choice of footwear. I have exactly *one pair* of heels in my closet, and it figures today's the day I'd decide to wear them. I could call for another ride but that risks another rejection, and the truth is, I don't have time. I've got to be at work in two hours, and I have no idea how long this—interview?— will take.

So, I do what I must. I take a deep breath and begin walking toward the house.

I fume the whole way. If Mr. Master's asshole employee hadn't totaled my car, I wouldn't be walking alone to the ridiculously huge mansion a mile away on the hill. I wouldn't have this massive headache or bruises either.

I also never would've discovered Cain Master or have an excuse to visit him.

The summer heat's cooler by the seaside, yet it's still nearly eighty degrees with no breeze. I'll show up sweaty and disheveled, no matter how slowly or carefully I walk.

My head hurts from the injuries of the night before, but I'm otherwise alright. I used a little bit of makeup to cover the bruises, and even ran a mascara brush through my lashes. But the makeup was old and dried up, and I'm afraid I look like a little kid playing with her mom's lipstick.

Normally, I prefer to mask my eyes—they're a vivid violet that unfortunately is hard to hide—but today I decided it couldn't hurt to accent them a little. Or... whatever. I don't know what else people who know about these things would call it. Shades of purple make my eyes stand out.

The dress I chose is one of the few I own. A pale lavender number in a cotton blend, it dips in the front while still being professional, the hem hitting mid-thigh. Combined with a nude pair of pumps, the dress is professional and simple, suitable for a job like today.

It's odd that while I was able to find out Cain Master's history, including the cases brought and accusations made against him, I wasn't able to find a birth date or a single picture anywhere. It's disconcerting, honestly.

Cain Master is insignificant in the eyes of the American public... but it's a lie.

A part of me wonders if hiding damn near everything about him online was intentional. Or did he have an identity before this one? Another name? Is this one given to him by the government, or one he chose for anonymity?

I bet he isn't as quick as he once was, his wits dulled over the years. He's wealthy enough, that I know from just a cursory glance at his home. But does he even own that? I spent my time researching his history and background and haven't looked into his personal assets.

I'll get there.

He has no family to speak of, not even so much as an ex-wife.

I know enough. Sometimes it's better not to know more than what's directly in front of you.

I twist my foot on a rock and stumble but throw my arms out wide and catch myself before I fall. If I hurt myself now, I'll have to head home and cancel this mission altogether.

I carefully take off my heels and begin to walk along the side of the road. It's cooler here, under the shadows of the large, stately maples that offer shade and shelter. I'm physically fit, but panting from the heat. I blame last night's accident.

The call of a seagull over the water catches my attention. Even from here, I can see the blue-green depths of the ocean bordering his house. What would it be like to live in a place like this? I'd hazard a guess the view isn't the only reason he lives here, though.

His house is far enough off the beaten path to deter strangers from visiting—at least, most of them. No little girls in uniforms would make this walk to peddle their Girl Scout cookies, no Jehovah's Witnesses would come knocking to save his besmirched soul. It's almost a fortress of sorts, set far from the main roads, but not so far that a twenty-minute ride wouldn't bring you into the city to get food or gas.

The closest Air Force base is in Hanscom, only thirty-two minutes by car. I checked.

Here, in the light of day, when I'm not compromised and as badly injured as I was when I first arrived last night, I note things I didn't see before—a large, sunny porch that overlooks the private beach, immaculately well-kept and homey, and a pathway lined with brilliant white rocks that leads to the front door. It's like a trail to the gingerbread house, set just far enough back to beckon unsuspecting victims.

I always did have an overactive imagination.

The last time I came here, he wasn't home, and I was injured. I missed lots of details.

Here in Salem and the surrounding cities, it's unusual for a home this close to the water to be much bigger than three or four bedrooms. Small colonial homes are the bedrock of the North Shore. Much larger homes are rare and cost a small fortune.

As I draw nearer, I note a four-car garage, a large, paved, circular driveway, and two main entrances, both bedecked with large but simple wreaths. The landscaping's immaculate, well-groomed and maintained, and if I peek a bit to the right of the main entrance, I can see into a rock-lined garden that overlooks the sea. Is that a barn or a shed out back? I also catch glimpses of a heavy gate and fence and another glimmer of water. A pool?

The owner of this home favors privacy.

A brisk wind kicks up as I near the main entrance. Here, right by the water, the temperature's dropped by at least ten degrees.

I'm not alone. There's someone in the side yard tending the garden, humming as they pull weeds. A small pile of drying dandelions sits beside him. Someone else is rummaging around in the garage. I'm guessing the people I met last night aren't the only staff he employs.

At least I should be able to get someone's attention.

I walk up to the closest entrance, draw in a deep breath, and square my shoulders. The front entryway's swept neatly, and a large potted plant stands to the right. Everything's masculine and utilitarian, no welcome mat by the door, nothing flowery or bright. I ring the doorbell.

The clanging of the bell reverberates inside, a deep, musical baritone. Footsteps sound on the other side of the door, and I see a tall, thin man through the rectangular windows that flank each side of the double doors.

I let my breath out, then draw in another to steady my nerves. From here, I can see the kitchen entrance where I went in last night and the sitting room where I saw the doctor. No sign of the master of this house.

He's in there, though. I know it.

Will he see me?

When the door opens, I notice a uniformed guard standing in the shadows to the right of the doorway, armed and ready. His face is set in stone, his eyes staring at me unblinking from the shadows. Now that's a sight you don't see every day.

My pulse staggers.

I wonder if the guy at the door's a daytime butler, or house-keeper or something. He's older than I am, pale, with a receding hairline, but he's wiry and strong. When he looks at me, only one eye is seeing, the other is dull and lifeless.

He gently bows his head in greeting, and when he speaks, he has a gentle southern accent. "May I help you?"

I clear my throat. It's make-or-break time. I give him what I hope is a disarming smile, but I'm rusty with such formalities and only manage to bare my teeth at him. *Cringy.*

Step one. Confirm the name of the owner of the house. Say it with confidence.

My voice rings loud and clear. "I'm here to see Mr. Master, please."

He nods. *Check.*

"Do you have an appointment?"

I briefly consider lying just to get inside, but quickly dismiss that idea. It could backfire too quickly.

I shake my head. "I don't. Is he in?"

He holds my gaze for a moment before he responds. Is he sizing me up? He quickly schools his features and gestures for me to come in.

"I'm not sure if he is in or not, but please, have a seat and I'll find out. Your name?"

I don't believe him. He knows exactly whether or not he's in, he just doesn't want to tell me until he knows if Mr. Master's entertaining visitors.

"Violet."

"Last name as well, please, miss."

"Violet Price." The name I adopted when I turned eighteen.

He nods. "I'll be right back, Miss Price." As he walks away, he takes a phone out of his pocket and begins to type. Texting.

The guard looks at me, immovable and serious.

"Hey." I give him a little side-wave.

He doesn't even blink.

"You come here often?" Funny, Vi. Real funny. He just stares at me without responding, a real-life stoic. I sigh and turn away.

I take the opportunity to observe more details. The interior of Cain Master's home is simple yet elegant and updated, coupling the charm of an earlier time with the technological advancements of the twenty-first century. Hardwood floors line the entire house. The walls and trim are clean and off-white, the furniture both sturdy and understated. A large, wide-screen TV adorns a wall along with what looks like state-of-the-art intercom and alarm systems. In the kitchen, light blue and white tiles line the backsplash, setting off large stainless-steel appliances, while a massive digital calendar occupies one wall of the uber masculine room.

Fancy.

Every detail speaks of wealth and comfort. It's exquisite.

But the truth is, I'm more interested in the titles of the books on the shelves I see when I wander into the sitting room, little clues into the character of Cain Master. Most of these are in English, though I catch a few foreign titles. Many are the types of books you'd expect a well-read retired army general to read.

The Art of War.

Elemental Strategy.

The classics, some titles a bit surprising.

The Adventures of Tom Sawyer.

Cold Mountain.

Pride and Prejudice.

I've seen libraries like this before, outfitted with popular titles for show. But if you take a book off the shelf, you'll find the spine's never been cracked, the poor books left to collect dust. Not these, though. They're well-worn and clearly loved, every one of them bearing marks of repeated use.

Interesting. No e-book readers for Cain Master. Does he occasionally eschew modern technology, then? Or is there another reason for the volume of print books?

Footsteps sound in the foyer outside this sitting room, and I pause in my perusal. Is it him? But the footsteps retreat, along with the sound of a deep, masculine voice.

My pulse races. I don't recognize the voices as being from the night before, and for some reason, my intuition tells me they aren't the man I've come to see.

I twiddle my thumbs, read every title I can see in front of me on the lined shelves, then sit down and begin counting to twenty in every language I know. I'm at number ten in Hindi when footsteps approach, heading this way. I get to my feet. I know who it is.

A shadow precedes him. I still at his breadth and height just before he enters.

I know before he speaks, by the way the air seems thinner and the furniture somehow smaller... this is the master of the house.

He's taller than I am, by a full foot or more. Thick, dark brown hair just a touch longer than acceptable military length frames a ruggedly masculine face, his square jaw lined with stubble that underscores harsh, brutal beauty. If not for the cut of his jaw and the harsh lines of his face, he'd be too pretty.

He's younger than I expected. At least... physically.

His eyes tell another story.

They spark with latent energy and power. His posture commands respect, and swift, blind obedience, like the kings of old. I can't decide if I expect him to pull a sword out of a stone or bare his teeth with a show of fangs.

I meet his gaze, which is harder than it sounds, as it takes an act of sheer will not to look away. Stark, naked cruelty lies in the savage sapphire depths. Barely civil. He holds me in the power of that gaze for one wild, terrifying moment. A mere glimpse of the ferocious honesty in his eyes shows a world of barely contained fury and power, as if the blood of an unnamed god thrums in his veins, demanding homage and obedience before he snaps his fingers and orders destruction.

A shiver skates down my spine.

Heavy, dark brows slant over his eyes, and his mouth is a harsh slash softened by full lips. He stares at me, unblinking, his hands on his hips.

"May I help you?" I nearly startle at the rumble of his voice, as the polite words he's chosen bely a savage intensity I feel from across the room. He wears faded jeans and a black Henley, but the simple clothing doesn't hide the resilient cords of muscle that outline the column of his large neck and run down the nearly graceful slope of his powerful shoulders to the sleeves stretched tight across the carved biceps of his arms. His is a body perfected and honed for the sole purpose of harnessing a human's full potential.

I realize I'm not breathing, but it's his fault. He took all the air out of the room when he entered and barely left any for me. No fair.

He clears his throat, the polite veneer quickly vanishing, and I suddenly feel as if I've done something wrong. Have I? I suppose coming into his presence unbidden may qualify as unacceptable. Perhaps I was supposed to wait for a summons.

I brace myself, but he pauses, leaning casually against the side of an armchair. His voice drops an octave in warning. I haven't replied to him yet. Oops.

"Who are you?" His tone is accusatory, as if he only talks when necessary, and it's my fault I made him do it.

"Violet." I blink in surprise at myself. No one unnerves me. Why does he? With a deep breath, I stand taller and remember who I am. I square my shoulders and steady my voice. "Violet Price."

He doesn't respond. Normal people would say something forced but polite, like, "Pleased to meet you, Miss Price." But it seems he's already used up all his politeness for today.

"And?" His gaze no longer polite, his eyes scour the length of my body, lingering at the show of cleavage at my chest, moving quickly down my bare legs, then back to my face. He doesn't even pretend he didn't sneer at the dust on my shoes or my worn bag, or even bother to hide the fact that he just undressed me with his eyes, like it's his right because I'm standing on his property.

I should be offended. I should be angry that he just... *stares* like that. But I'm not. Instead, the deep, dark recesses of my mind beckon with a whisper.

God, what a man like him could do to a woman like me.

What I could do to bring him to his knees.

I don't like sex and never have, and yet...

Something tells me, he'd teach me how to enjoy it.

My cheeks feel hot. I clear my throat. It's time for me to take back control of this situation.

"Are you Mr. Cain Master?"

He nods, one brief jerk of his head. "I am." The sound of his voice feels like a liquid, sensual caress that skates across my naked skin, gently barbed with a prickle of heat.

I take in a deep breath. If he can skip the formalities, I can, too.

"Last night, my car was hit by someone I believe works with you. He totaled my car."

No show of surprise or reaction. No apology. He knows, then.

"Right," he says with a bored sigh. "You'll be fully compensated for any damages to your car or medical bills." He pushes off the side of the armchair and turns away from me. "Please leave your contact information before you leave."

I'm... dismissed?

He's given me the small amount of time he's reserved for interruptions, and now he has to go do manly, important, adult things.

How dare he?

"While I thank you for that, Mr. Master, covering damages caused by the guilty party is a given, and certainly not worth my time in coming to see you. Clearly, you're a man who values his time, so I won't waste it. That's not why I'm here."

He turns back to me, that fiery anger stoked in the depth of his eyes again with a warning I should heed. But there's something else I see that keeps my feet locked in place, holding me back from sprinting right out that door and leaving the way I came before he skins me alive.

He's curious.

Danger, my mind warns me. The man probably has enough room right here on this property to bury my body, and no one would ever even know.

Yeah, my mind went there, but after reading what I have about him, I can't help it.

His voice is a low rumble that borders on a drawl, challenging me.

"Then why are you here, Miss Price?"

The better question is, why does the way he says my name, drawing each syllable out like it's an act of foreplay, make liquid heat pool at my core? My skin shouldn't feel this tight. My breath shouldn't be this ragged.

"I looked you up when I got home. It started because I wanted more information about the man who hit my car, and what I found out about him led me straight to you."

Is that a glimmer of amusement in his eyes? No... it leaves so quickly, I wonder if I imagined it.

I clear my throat. I have his attention, so it's time I stop circling around him. It's time I go in for the kill. "And you're the man who could help me."

As he turns more fully to me, I watch the way his muscles bunch with tension. He raises his brows, a physical admission that I've interested him. When he crosses his arms over his chest, I realize he has muscles in places I didn't know even had them.

"Could I?" A low, lazy drawl.

This could be my only chance. I say it all in one breath, unblinking as I speak to him.

"I need your help to find the people I'm after."

God, I could've done better than that. They make it look so easy in the movies.

He cocks his head to the side, all traces of humor gone from his face. "And who are you after, Miss Price?"

I lower my voice as I stay my course. I've never been in the military, but something about his presence makes me speak to him as if I were. "That's a conversation for a much more private audience, sir." Though we're alone here, we both know anyone could walk in on us at any moment.

I want to bite the little nail of my pinkie on my left hand or tug a lock of my hair and fiddle my worry away, but I force myself to stand still and wait.

Several beats pass before he responds. Outside the window, his gardener walks by with a trowel and a rake. Far in the distance, the tide goes out behind him. I can almost hear the waves lapping at the shore.

"Let's take a walk." My heart flutters in anticipation. I'm a drowning woman, and he's thrown me a length of rope.

This is what I wanted, privacy with him, but a little warning voice in the back of my head tells me I should tell him no. I should talk him into speaking with me in his office or someplace neutral.

I came here for a reason, and I don't take no for an answer.

I go against my every instinct and follow him.

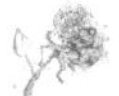

CHAPTER TWO

IT ISN'T until we walk into the kitchen that I notice there are a lot more people here than I initially thought. Somehow, it helps me draw in a breath. They're just quiet, their presence and work seamless in the background. Two more of his staff are in the garden, and only paces away from them, four strong men dressed in military attire look like they're doing... drills? It's hard to tell from here, but it's clear they're training.

The guard at the door inclines his head at us as we pass, and Cain holds his palm up when he begins to follow us. Either he has guards outside as well, or he trusts that I'm not here to ambush him.

Maybe he shouldn't be so trusting.

The side door leading to the garage opens, and a portly, middle-aged Latina woman with pretty brown eyes and short brown hair enters, her arms heavily laden with brown grocery bags. Cain pauses, his hand on the door to exit, when he sees her coming in.

"You know better than to carry those in yourself," he scolds, clucking his tongue at her as he walks over to her. "Alma, why didn't you call me?" Reaching her, he plucks the bags out of her hands before sliding them onto the countertop.

She smiles at him. "Eh, thought you'd be busy, and it's good for me to still do things sometimes, *señor*," she says.

"And you're no good to me laid up in bed because you threw your back out again," he mutters, rebuking her. I nearly cringe at the sharp edge in his tone, but she only winks at me.

The door shuts behind us. The warm summer air tickles my skin.

"Mr. Master—"

"Call me Cain."

Skipping the formalities so soon. Interesting. "Cain. That's a unique name. I've only known one other man with a name like that, but he spelled it differently." The son of one of my foster parents.

"You've looked up my name."

"Of course." I am not going to lie to him unless I have to.

A shadow crosses his features for a split second before he grows serious. "You don't hear the name Violet every day either."

"My name was supposed to be Angela, but when my mother saw my eyes, she changed her mind."

"You were born with eyes that color, then?"

A curious question. It shouldn't please me that he's noted the color of my eyes. Everyone notices them, but *he* seems the type that only notices you if it matters.

"Yes."

We walk in silence down a path made of stones that leads past the garden to the barn or shed or whatever it is.

"I'm not going to waste your time, Mister—Cain. You own a private investigation agency."

He walks with his hands in his pockets, which might look casual but really only serves to make the muscles along his arms and neck bulge that much more. *God.*

"Depends on who you ask."

I have to walk faster to keep up with his long strides. I'm falling behind him. For one brief, crazy moment, I'm tempted to smack his back and tell him to slow down. "What do you mean?"

He shrugs a large shoulder and scowls at the path in front of him. "I don't advertise."

"And yet, I'd hazard a guess you're booked through next year."

"And then some."

We walk in silence for another moment while I try to formulate a plan to tell him what I need.

"I don't have the kind of money you'd ask for, but... I could barter."

Why did it sound so much better in my head?

He stops walking long enough to give me an amused smirk. "I don't need homemade soap or homegrown tomatoes." Another rude glance down at me. "And you're right. You can't afford my company." I know he means I can't afford to hire him, but the way he says it makes it sound like I'm not worthy of being in his presence. I bite the inside of my cheek so I don't tell him off, grounding myself in the stab of pain.

Deep breath in. Deep breath out.

My cheeks heat. I decide the best course of action is to ignore the taunt. "We could help each other. A mutually beneficial situation. I mean, I—I have talents and skills that could benefit your organization, and I could benefit from what you have to offer as well."

He sighs. "Don't waste my time. To be honest, I'm not even sure this consultation is something you could afford, but it's warm out and I needed some fresh air. I'd be charging most people by the hour for this discussion alone, but I'm taking pity on you." He looks down at my crumpled dress and faded purse. My skin prickles uncomfortably, but before I can respond he continues. "You're already talking about collaboration, and I don't even know why you're here."

I won't rise to take his bait, I *won't*. But God, my temper's a beast, and it's hard to keep it on a leash sometimes.

"I—I need help finding a few people, and I believe you could help me."

Still scowling, he doesn't respond, so naturally I feel the need to keep talking, because that always helps.

"I'm skilled in martial arts. I'm reigning champion on the East Coast—"

"In the women's division," he interrupts with an impatient sigh.

Does he know that? Does he know anything else about me, or was it just a guess about an obvious fact?

My blood begins to go from a simmer to a boil, and I slow my pace. "Excuse me?"

"In the women's division," he repeats with a casual shrug, hands still in his pockets. "Means nothing when you're up against a man."

"Oh, is that right?" *Chauvinistic prick,* I mentally tack on.

I imagine drop-kicking him right here. A swift kick between his legs would incapacitate him enough for me to move quickly.

He doesn't bother to hide the disdain in his tone. "Of course. I'm sure you could drop a pussy on his ass, but it means jack shit unless you're fighting a real man."

He's dropping all semblance of professionalism, and another warning bell chimes in my mind.

We've made it to the edge of the garden. A brisk wind carries warm air from over the sea, white-capped waves crashing in the distance behind him. A gull caws overhead, but I hardly hear it. The blood pounds in my ears with my rising temper. A corner of his beautiful, perfect lips quirks upward. Mocking me. "Got under your skin. Want to prove me wrong?"

I'm already in a fighting stance, my shoes kicked to the side like so much baggage. My hands clench into fists at my sides. I don't care who he is, he just tossed the gauntlet down and I *do not back down.*

"Of course I do."

Stop, the little inner voice of reason warns.

I never did like that voice.

And suddenly, it doesn't matter that I'm wearing a dress, that he's a hundred pounds heavier than I am, and I'm trying to convince him to hire me. All I see is a brawny sexist who needs to learn a lesson.

I've spent years perfecting the double-leg takedown, a move that works in the ring or on the street. If he was unaware, I might be able to take him down. He's prepared though, and way too big.

All I want to do is level him. I could drop him to the ground, without actually causing injury. I've done the move a thousand times. Though he's bigger than I am—by a lot—I'm smaller and more agile, giving me a decided advantage. But while it might be satisfying to drop a man of his size to the ground, that's just the problem—he's fucking huge, and I'm not, and that really fucking matters.

"No." With effort, I drop the fighting stance, and shrug my shoulders. I walk casually over to him. "You're too big for a girl like me," I say with mock humility. I wait until he resumes his casual walking. "I couldn't possibly—" He looks away from me, a strategic error and my only chance.

Thwack. I kick my leg out so fast I register surprise in his eyes, but he's even faster than I am. Instinctively, he deflects, and instead of striking back, ducks. When he's bent over, I shove, pushing him off-kilter.

For one second, one glorious second, I've got him as he's taken by surprise and falls. I quickly pin him down. Victory courses through me, and I can't stop the grin that sweeps over my face at the surprise in his eyes. But the moment's short-lived.

Fuck.

His eyes darkening to gray blue, he coils his body, and the next thing I know, I'm soaring through the air. There's an audible sound of a tear, and then... he's immobilized me.

No.

He's on top of me, and I'm pinned beneath him.

"You think you need to show me who you are?" he asks. Just to show off, the bastard's got both my wrists in one huge hand, and I can't move.

I realize three things at once.

First, my dress is torn. The ripping sound was the neckline. A flap of fabric moves in the breeze, baring my bra-clad boobs to him. *Great.*

Second, his... *body is on top of me.*

And he's... large, and strong, and masculine, and really smells a lot better than any man ever should. Images of the two of us naked flit through my mind because I'm not a corpse, and other than us not knowing each other, being outdoors where anyone could see us, and fully clothed... what's to stop me from mentally going there?

Third... he's furious. A vein throbs in his temple, and his nostrils flare. I can tell he's holding himself back from really hurting me.

My throat tightens with the sudden knowledge that once again, I've let my temper get the best of me and probably just ruined *everything*.

Again.

He won't let me stay now. I know he won't. Only a fool would.

"You were saying?" His eyes spark at me like flashes of flint.

"I can fight," I say through gritted teeth, my voice shaking.

"Of course you can." He spits out the words like venom. I feel momentarily vindicated. He doesn't wonder if I can fight. "*That* was never in question."

Wasn't it? Did he bait me? If he did, I leapt to it like a goddamn fish to a worm-covered hook. His admission that I can fight takes a bit of the wind out of my sails.

If I wasn't fully restrained under him, I could reach out and touch that rugged stubble along his jaw. There's a silvery scar near his left eye I didn't notice before, weirdly similar to mine. Huh.

"You listen." His voice is a deadly purr, like the growl of a mountain lion warning its prey. He lowers his face to mine so we're only inches apart. I can't believe I thought he had an ounce of softness in him just moments ago. He's nothing but hard lines and angles, as flexible as steel. A bead of sweat runs down the side of his face, but his eyes are cold as ice. "Do not *ever* do that again."

"Do what?" My voice is barely a whisper.

He leans in closer, the muscles along his neck taut. He bares his teeth, his voice no more than a growl. "Try to fight me."

He doesn't even say *fight me,* but *try.*

Ouch.

Okay, so I'm getting off with a warning? If he wanted to throw me off his property, he wouldn't use the word "again."

Would he?

He's got me in an expert submission hold, more skilled than most I've fought before.

I came here to suggest a business proposal and he's served me humble pie.

Good one, Vi. I stifle a sigh.

"Tell me you won't ever even think about fighting me again, Miss Price."

"I won't fight you." My voice is clogged with emotion. I don't concede often, and when I do, it's under duress, just like this. I don't make any promises beyond that, though.

There are many, *many* things I could do that don't fall under the umbrella of "fighting."

"Why are you here?"

"You're still on top of me."

"I'm aware." He doesn't budge.

I won't sugarcoat things. I won't pretend I'm here for any reason other than my true purpose. I draw in a breath and hold his gaze, unblinking, my tone of voice firm and confident despite my compromised position.

"I need you to help me find the people who killed my parents."

Still holding me beneath him, he gives me one short nod before he releases me. I get to my feet, shaking a little, and fruitlessly try to hold the flapping fabric against my breasts. My hands shake.

He reaches for the hem of his tee and yanks it up over his head before he tosses it in my direction.

Numbly, I catch it mid-air. It's soft and warm and smells like him, spicy and virile and all male.

I look at him and blink.

"Put it on."

I look down at my bare chest and ripped dress, then back like an idiot to the bunched-up fabric in my hand before I realize he's standing bare from the waist up in front of me. As he turns away from me, I tug the tee on quickly, to block my view of his perfect, chiseled back, crossed with the same silvery scars as my own.

For some reason, that makes me want to cry. No one has scars like that without a story. No one.

His tee swims on me, and I feel like an utter fool, the edge of my dress peeking out underneath the hem of his shirt. But I came here with a purpose, and I'm not leaving until I tell him more. So, I ignore the burning in my throat. I ignore the way his tee feels on me, too soft for a man like him, so warm it's a comfort. I ignore the way my body responds to his.

And I take back an ounce of control. I can either walk around here like a little kid wearing her brother's oversized tee, or I can own this.

I reach to the back of the dress, ignore the pain in my arm from the awkward position, and tug the zipper down. I shimmy out of it, and the ripped fabric pools around my ankles. I bend and lift it, so I'm wearing nothing but his tee like a dress.

If he's surprised, he doesn't show it, only crooks his finger at me. I follow.

I read once that in the animal kingdom, a female can't control the innate biological desire to mate with an alpha male. Instinctively, she knows he would protect her and their offspring

I comfort myself with the knowledge. Visceral attraction to an alpha male is an instinct, not a choice. It isn't my fault.

"Come with me." He jerks his chin forward and begins to walk. I'm not really a fan of being bossed around, but I think I've pushed my luck enough.

With his shirt flapping around my body, I follow him to the fence at the edge of his property. From here I can see he has a pretty, curved pool with a small waterfall cascading into it from the left. Adirondack chairs line the sunny perimeter, a perfect retreat.

"Sit."

He folds his bulk into a large chair by the poolside and jerks his chin at a chair opposite him. I choose a chair as far away from him as I can get. Here, I'm in direct sunlight and blinded, unable to stare at his muscled shoulders, the dog tags that swing around his neck, or those washboard abs I would drink shots off of and not regret. Even while staring at his eyes, I'm aware of a faint smattering of dark hair across his chest, the way his waist tapers to faded jeans that hug his waist right where... I swallow. And block out everything I can to focus on him.

I've studied neurolinguistic programming, among other brain tricks. If you train yourself hard enough, you can erase bad memories, traumatic events, and replace them instead with a flash of white or a happy thought. It takes practice, but it can be done. In a split second, I mentally block out his masculinity and focus on his eyes, the rest of him bathed in imaginary bright white.

"Tell me everything."

"About what?"

"About what you need from me."

I take a risk and push him a little.

"You've already decided I can't afford your services and you've already decided I'm of no use to you. So why tell you?"

A slight narrowing of his eyes tells me he isn't used to being questioned. "Did I say I have no use for you?"

Did I—does he mean—no. *God*, no. Again, I want to run, and again, I make myself stay before my mind thinks of the very many ways he can use me. "No, sir. You didn't."

"Then tell me. Let's just say I'm curious."

I know without explanation that the only way I'll ever get his cooperation and help is to do exactly what he's asking.

So, I do. I give him the bald, honest, painful truth. I tell him quickly and succinctly, so I don't waste his time or mine.

"When I was four years old, my father worked as an assassin. My mother did not know this, and it took me a full decade after I put my mind to it to find out the truth. One night, they were pulled from their beds and executed."

Anyone else would be surprised by this. It's not exactly a story you tell when you first meet someone. It's not a story *I* tell anyone.

I register no surprise in his eyes. He's heard accounts like mine before.

It's why I'm here.

"Whoever it was never came after me. We lived in a cramped apartment, and my makeshift room was a closet. My mother must've shut the door when she heard intruders."

"Sloppy work."

"At the very least, hasty. I spent the rest of my childhood in foster care until the moment I turned eighteen. I've been piecing things together about their death since my earliest memories, and I've reached an impasse."

"How old are you now?"

"Twenty-four."

He holds everything I've said for a moment and doesn't respond.

I watch as he crosses his ankle over his knee and leans back, lacing his fingers behind his head. I make my eyes look away from the rippling muscle he effortlessly flaunts when he leans back.

"And what will you do when you find them?"

"The same thing you would."

It's a bold move, to assume I know how he'd behave.

I brace myself for his anger, or outrage, or a command to leave. Maybe he'll even call someone to come and escort me off his property. How far is too far to push a man like him?

He does none of those things.

"And what is it I would do?"

I squirm but don't look away. "You'd kill them."

He doesn't deny it.

"I don't think you're capable of murder, Miss Price."

So, we're back to formalities. I can play that game, too.

"That's only because you don't know me, sir."

"And if I did?"

I swallow before I draw in a deep breath. "You'd know that there's nothing I won't do for the people I'm loyal to."

He slowly nods. The hint of approval fills me with pride.

Run, my instinct warns. It's dangerous to value the opinion of someone like him.

"That's closer."

"Closer to what?"

"Convincing me to hire you."

CHAPTER THREE

Cain

SHE'S HERE. I've waited for this. I've planned this. And everything I've orchestrated led her here, but she can't ever know that.

I'll kill Armand for the way he did this. Fucking hit her car to get her attention, planted bits and pieces of information for her to find us. But it was too damn risky, the son of a bitch.

I look at the way she sits, her back ramrod straight in one of the pool chairs, my tee melting against her curves like a seductive tease.

It's a mistake to hire her.

I don't hire impulsive, headstrong people for my team.

Ever.

But that's not why I wanted her here.

She can't know why I'll hire her. Not now. Not ever.

I want Violet Price so close to me I could touch her. I know every goddamn thing about her. If she knew who I am and why she's really here, she'd run. Maybe even change her name again.

I've been obsessed with her for six months.

Who was the woman with the mesmerizing eyes? The first time I saw her, I wanted her. I had to have her. And I haven't gotten her out of my mind since.

I saw her in one of our surveillance videos. We were monitoring a local shopping mall, and her studio was doing a demonstration. Then there she was. Violet eyes staring at our camera as if she knew who we were, that we were watching her. We were trailing one of the parents in her youngest class, not her, and later found him guilty of cheating on his wife. The man was dumb enough to bring his girlfriend to a jewelry store at the mall. We pocketed half a million for that one.

We got what we needed the first two minutes into the surveillance footage. It was crystal clear. Yet I played that video over, and over, and over again until I could recite every line she said, make every move she made.

And I was obsessed.

I spent the next week learning everything I could about her, and finally had Armand put up video surveillance where she worked out. We stayed out of her home until last night.

I noted the way she held herself. When she wasn't throwing punches or kicks, she assumed a fighter's stance, light on her feet, knees slightly bent. The only move she made with more effort than the rest was blocking. *No one* hit her. Ever. She was a master at self-protection.

It wasn't until after my initial... obsession... that I unearthed her skillset.

Small and lithe, she's a fighter to the core. She can hold her own when she needs to, and she fucking will. Skilled in multiple languages, indefatigable, her only real flaw is disrespect for authority. It only draws me to her more, because I'll teach her that skill. On my terms.

With the exceptions of our doctor and on-site chef, every member of my team is ex-military. Dishonorably discharged. I like it that way, and I have my reasons. I, of all people, should know what it's like to have to defend your honor and fight for respect. I give my team that chance, and because I have, they're loyal to me.

Violet isn't.

How would I keep her loyal to me? She tells me she is, and I believe her. But talk is cheap. She'll have to show me with her actions that she means what she says.

I've never hired anyone like her, someone ruled by emotions instead of intellect.

But I'll make an exception for Violet.

It's her fire that fuels her, and *that's* what she'll learn to harness. To use. To finely tune into a weapon.

I planned it this way, her coming to me for help. I need what she has to offer, but on my terms and my terms only.

I push myself to standing from the chair, and I don't miss the way her eyes go a bit wider with fear, a sort of desperation surfacing that I know too well. She knows I'm about to dismiss her. That our meeting is over.

I have to. It's the only way to get her buy-in, to make sure she's as committed to our team as everyone else. If her place here is hard-won, I've got one more chance at ensuring her loyalty.

"Go home, Miss Price. Send a formal resumé to the address I'll give you. I have your contact information because of the accident. Now if you'll excuse me—"

The T-shirt of mine she's wearing billows in a gentle breeze from the water. She's a woman cut from marble and tough as nails, somehow made vulnerable in borrowed clothing. A gust of wind whips her hair around her face, the windswept look nearly shaking my resolve to dismiss her.

I don't want her to leave. She belongs here.

She shakes her head at me.

I blink in surprise.

"No?"

I don't realize I'm clenching my fists until I see her eyes quickly dart to where my hands curl by my sides.

"No, sir."

I'm so surprised I don't respond at first.

No?

I fully expected her to push back, to fight for what she wants. Hell, it's exactly why I'm giving her shit. But I didn't expect flat-out defiance. My voice sharpens.

"I don't hire people for my team who don't know how to respect authority, Miss Price."

I take a step toward her, and to her credit, she stands her ground.

"I know how to respect authority."

The waves behind her whip in a frenzy, whitecaps rising and crashing against rocks. Clouds roll in, the sky quickly darkening. A storm's brewing.

I don't have the time or patience for this.

"Bullshit. Words are cheap, Miss Price. You don't know the meaning of the word respect."

Her lips thin, as a wispy piece of hair crosses her vision. She pushes it impatiently out of the way. "I respect the authority of the people who earn it, Mr. Master."

Ah, so we're playing *that* game.

"If you think this is how a job interview is conducted, I'd suggest you go back to school."

"Job interview?" She shakes her head and actually laughs. "That was never in question. I'm no one's employee, Mr. Master. I'm suggesting I work for you as a paid contractor. Barter and trade, the very building blocks of modern-day free enterprise."

Well played.

She wears her defiance well, and it makes me goddamned hard.

What I wouldn't give to strip that all away from her, one stroke at a time.

I will.

"No."

She shakes her head from side to side. "No, what? No, bartering isn't a cornerstone of free enterprise? No, you won't work with me?"

When I was her age, I'd kill a man for less than this. I was paid to. I built my business on the back of those early days.

"Come here, Miss Price."

I don't forget the way it felt with her wrists trapped between my fingers, her pulse racing. I loved the feel of her beneath me, pinned under my weight and heaving for breath. She thought she'd best me, and she did catch me off guard, but not for long.

The first time I saw her, I knew that she was the one we're after—no, the one we *need*. I need. It was written in the way she held herself, in the rigidity of her spine, the tightness in her jaw.

I watched her fight.

Her hair caught back in a tight, merciless bun, she wore little to no makeup. It didn't matter. I knew I was looking at a goddamn masterpiece.

There's a slight scar across her left eyebrow, the only imperfection on her otherwise flawless face, the type of scar one gets from a street fight. There's a story behind that scar. I mean to find it out.

Violet Price is five foot even and one hundred ten solid pounds of muscle. Petite, but powerful, like tightly packed dynamite.

My T-shirt blows about her slight frame. The cool breeze from the ocean warns us a storm is coming, and fast, but she ignores her hair whipping around her with wild abandon. Her stunning eyes, a deep, mesmerizing hue, are like nothing I've ever seen before, so much more brilliant when I see her up close.

I want her closer.

Violet.

Amethyst caught in light. The color of magic.

It's both her name and her most distinguishing characteristic.

One of the few colors labeled by Newton when cataloging the spectrum of visible light, violet's the rarest of any eye color, so rare many believe violet eyes to be mythological. But no. Her violet eyes, those singular gems of beauty, are no myth, and they're staring straight at me. "Yes?"

It's on the tip of my tongue to offer half my kingdom for *one night* with her. One blessed, glorious night, and she'd be mine. All mine.

"You have a look on your face I'd pay good money to decipher," she says in a voice so low it's as if she's talking to herself.

Words spoken before a storm like this feel stealthy and classified, like the first brisk wind will sweep them away.

"Not sure you'd want to hear what I'm thinking right now."

"I definitely do, Mr. Master." She takes a step closer to me, her voice low. "Try me, sir."

"I'm thinking of the terms of our contract, the types of terms that professionals would never consider."

A beat passes. I watch as her tongue darts out and runs across her chapped lips. "Perhaps professionalism is overrated."

A whistle blows three times in succession. The spell is broken. My breathing stills. Even the breeze over the water seems to cease. I whip my head around to look at the house.

"It's an alarm," she says. "Isn't it?"

I don't respond.

The heavy sound of feet running toward the house comes from the training area. I listen, braced for the second alarm as I do a mental tally of all staff on hand. My men in training. Joe, Claude, Henri.

Violet.

The back door's yanked open, and Joe stands, barely visible under the shadow of the awning.

"What is it? Who sounded the alarm?"

"I did. When you didn't answer your phone, sir. It's Skylar."

Skylar? I can't be hearing him right. *Skylar?*

I know the answer to my question before I ask it. I'm not sure why I do. "Is it urgent?"

He winces, as if recoiling from an invisible blow. "She's missing, sir."

Storm clouds break open, and a torrent of rain sweeps down. I run for cover and barely catch myself from grabbing

Violet's hand to tug her along with me. She doesn't need my help, but it's tempting. The only woman in my life who means something to me is in danger, and the frantic need to control something consumes me.

Violet isn't mine.

We're soaked before we get to the door.

I turn to Violet and note the desperation in her eyes. She wants this so badly, she's trembling.

I grab a fistful of dish towels from the kitchen drawer and toss them at her. Not missing a beat, she wipes her eyes and pushes wet hair out of her face. The straps of her heels are slung around one finger, and as we walk through the kitchen, she shoves her torn dress in the trash bin.

Change of fucking plans. If my sister's at risk, I need Violet's help, and I need it now. I wanted to recruit her for a purpose just like this, because I needed a woman on my team who could get shit done, and her list of qualifications outnumbers everything else.

"When can you start?"

She blinks. Her reaction will be telling. I note a flash of alarm that quickly fades to eager excitement. "Immediately."

"We negotiate terms of your contract with me today."

She nods eagerly. "Yes, sir."

"You start now, Miss Price."

CHAPTER FOUR

Violet

SKYLAR. I know enough about body language to know Skylar is someone who matters to him. He moves like he's at war, preparing for an ambush, and whoever's responsible for hurting Skylar's going *down*.

Yikes.

Who is it? An ex? I doubt she's a current girlfriend or significant other. He's the type that would want a woman who mattered to him nearby, under his protection and watchful eye. I haven't missed the way his team trains right here on his property.

I go through a myriad of feelings at once.

Elation—*he hired me!*

Fear—*will this go the way I planned?*

Panic—*what does this mean? What's happened to Skylar?*

He walks at a clip I have to run to keep up with, either oblivious or unconcerned with my trailing behind him. I don't mind it, though. Moving fast burns the adrenaline that courses through me like fire.

When we reach the house, a tall, lanky man with a shaved head comes out. Two meaty pit bulls circle Lanky Man's legs, prowling as if they smell the blood of someone new in their territory.

My heart swells. God, I love pit bulls. What most people don't know about them is that they used to be nanny dogs, hired to watch over and protect babies and small children. A cross between terriers and bulldogs, pit bulls were once used as symbols of American strength during the First World War.

They're fiercely loyal and protective to a fault, though. And once trained to guard illegal activity, drug dealers and the like used them for their own benefit. When they attack, they don't let go. They'll bite to kill. And while that might've once kept children safe, pit bulls have gotten a bad rap in recent years.

I love them. I want to kneel in front of them and nuzzle their chocolate-brown necks and scratch their perky ears.

I've always been attracted to powerful, lethal creatures.

"JUST GOT A CALL FROM LOTTIE."

Cain nods. "And?"

"Said she never came home last night. They expected her at

midnight, and when she didn't show, they figured she was spending the night with her date."

His jaw clenches, but he doesn't otherwise react. "And?"

"And when she didn't come home this morning, Lottie got scared. Said she didn't know what to do or how to reach her, and thought you'd want to know."

"I would've wanted to know last night," he says through gritted teeth.

I'm glad I'm not the one on the receiving end of that anger. It boils at a low simmer, threatening to scald and eradicate anything it touches.

"Right, sir, but you were traveling, and not even due back until today."

Cain curses under his breath, then turns and jerks his chin at me. "You. Come with me." Like I'm going anywhere else? I'm wearing his damn T-shirt, and he just hired me. If he gave me a cot to sleep on, I'd camp right here.

I thought there were a lot of people around his house before. Now, it seems like people that work for him come out of the damn woodwork. Big, muscled guys. A few in military fatigues and others in civilian clothing mill around the large house, talking in hushed tones. None of them speak to Cain, and it takes me a minute to realize the reason they don't is because they're waiting for his command.

"Who's Skylar?" I ask, panting as I follow him up the steps two at a time.

His jaw tenses before he responds.

"My sister."

Oh, wow. Shit. Now *that* didn't show up in the search history. And why is a part of me relieved she's family, that she isn't a woman he has romantic ties to? My gut reaction spells danger, but I shove it down. I'll deal with that later. Now, I've got shit to do.

His sister... Has everything I read about him been a lie? Do I really know anything about him at all?

He shoves open the door to his office, and I'm not surprised by the way it looks. His desk is large, sturdy, and intimidating, a paragon of masculinity... just like him. Massive windows look out at the pool below, and on another wall one overlooks the waterfront view. Storm clouds gather to block the sun, darkening the room even though it's still daytime. He flicks on a switch, and bright overhead lighting illuminates the room.

"Sit."

He gestures for me to take a seat across from him.

Why me? Why now? Doesn't he have anyone else that works for him that could do whatever it is he wants me to do?

Lanky follows us into the room.

"Joe, meet Miss Price, our new hire."

I give him a little wave. "Hey."

Joe takes a seat beside me and leans forward, elbows on his knees.

Cain pulls out his phone and swipes. A grid shows up, with a little squiggly arrow, and he curses under his breath. "It shows her home, and it shows she hasn't left since Wednesday. That can't be right."

Joe shakes his head. "I was worried about this."

Cain blows out a breath. "Cut the shit, Joe. You don't have to be polite. You not only worried about this, you warned me about this. Said she wouldn't go for it."

I gather up my courage and clear my throat. They both look at me. "If I'm working for you, it would be helpful if you could fill me in a little?"

Joe looks to Cain for permission, and when he gets it, he nods. "Skylar's his younger sister."

"Got it. How old is she?"

"Only eighteen."

I cringe. Anything could've happened to an eighteen-year-old. She could've hung out at some guy's house and drank the night away, be still wrapped up in his sheets and not bothering with the time. She could've lost her phone or hooked up with someone and decided a trip to Vegas would be a smart idea. Really, anything goes.

Joe continues. "We put tracking software on her phone, because Cain wanted to keep an eye on her."

"Are you her guardian?"

A muscle tenses in his jaw. "No."

"Does she know you track her?"

"Found out two weeks ago."

"And lemme guess. Wasn't too fond of her big brother keeping tabs on her anymore?"

He huffs out a breath. "How'd you know?"

I nod. "It's kind of a given."

"Yeah, so she took all tracking off her phone..."

"But you're not dumb enough to really not keep tabs on her."

People frown all the time, a common facial expression one might say. When Cain Master frowns, the temperature in the room shifts, and my skin prickles. "Of course not."

He flips open his laptop, and the screen flashes to life. Cameras outside of a coffee shop show people entering and exiting with paper bags and steaming cups of coffee. Another camera shows the inside of a typical college kid's apartment, complete with beer cans stacked in blue plastic recycling bins, empty pizza boxes, and about ten pairs of shoes scattered haphazardly around the couch.

"Her place?"

"Yeah."

"She know about those cameras?"

He scowls at me. "What do you think?"

It's a rhetorical question, but I want in on this case, so I jump right in as if he really wants to know what I think. "I think you need to talk to her roommate and get everything she knows. Find out where she was last, who she was seeing, if she had plans. And I think you need to call the police."

The last suggestion was a test.

"You were spot on until you got to the police."

He passed the test. Still, I need to needle him a bit to get to more of the truth.

"You're not going to report a missing person?" *Le gasp. Oh, my, Mr. Master, are you above the law? Don't trust our criminal justice system? ::Hand to brow::*

"Lottie already did," Joe says with a scowl. "Police say she's not a missing person until she's been gone for twenty-four hours and wouldn't listen to her impassioned plea about why this was a special case."

"Right."

He scrubs a hand across his brow and shoots Cain a furtive glance before he looks back at me. "And if you're working with us, you might as well know as soon as they find out who she is, they won't touch it anyway."

I exhale. They don't know Candi, but something tells me I should tell them. "Just so you know, my best friend's an officer."

Again, no register of surprise. Either the man has an iron-clad poker face like nothing I've ever seen before, or he already knows what I'm telling him. Great. Not a big fan of either of those options.

He's back on his laptop, swiping at the board. "I'll fill you in as quickly as I can. There will be time for more questions later, but we don't fuck around with this."

"Understood."

"Skylar was my mother's youngest child. My mother remarried when I enlisted in the army."

If he enlisted right out of high school, that puts him probably somewhere in his mid-thirties. My instincts tell me that if he'd reached seventeen or eighteen years of military service, he'd be almost untouchable, and very unlikely dishonorably discharged.

He pushes up from the table and stalks over to a large, framed print on the wall. He moves it to the side magically, like it's cast beneath a spell, before he punches in a code.

"Under normal circumstances, we'd have a training period, then initiation. No time for that, so you'll work with me and I'll fill you in as we go. We have an armory here at the house, but I keep some things personally locked up. My team knows I have this here and has the code. No one else knows and I'd like to keep it that way." He pauses, glancing at the ragged, soaked tee that clings to my body like plastic wrap. I nod and will myself not to be embarrassed by my total lack of clothing. I need gear.

He spits out words like they're bullets. I know he's concerned about his sister but I can't help wondering if I bring out his anger, too. "You're part of the team, but you'll have to earn your place. Going forward you'll keep a change of clothes on site. Am I clear?"

That gets my hackles up, and I inwardly cringe. Earn my place, like a dog begging for his table scraps? We'll see about that. I play nice, though. "Yes, of course."

I watch as he slides a handgun into a concealed holster at his waist.

"Do you know how to use a gun?"

Shit. My silence is response enough. He curses under his breath.

"You may be a skilled fighter, Miss Price, but you'll need something to keep you safe at long range. For now, you'll stay with me and have a guard on you, but you'll join me at the shooting range when they open tomorrow morning."

"Which is...?"

"Five o'clock."

"In the morning?"

He gives me a withering look and doesn't reply.

Five in the morning?

"How did you get here?"

I have a sneaking suspicion he knows but wants everything out in the open.

"I got a ride." I bite my tongue so I don't snap back to remind him it's his employee's fault I don't have a car.

"Right. I'll make sure you get one back, and you'll need a car."

Wow, okay then. "You don't have to give me a car as part of our arrangement—"

"I do. All my employees need reliable transportation. It's for my own peace of mind more than anything." His voice sharpens. "I won't have people that work for me taking a fucking Uber to work."

Ouch.

I need to remind him of something, though. "I'm not your employee, Mr. Master."

He purses his lips and doesn't reply, but I can feel the judgy judgment in the air. *Grrr.*

We're walking at a good clip, and he shouts out commands as we go. He tells one guy to run surveillance at the college (I'm guessing the one his sister goes to?), another to load "Goldie" with ammo (Who is Goldie and why does she need ammo?), and a third to keep a watch on all video surveillance of Skylar. Joe takes off.

He pulls out his phone and barks out a few commands.

As we walk through his house, as people dressed in fatigues start moving and calling him *sir*, it doesn't feel like a home but a compound or a military base.

At the door, Joe comes up to us with a folded pile of clothing and hands it to me.

"Take those with you," Cain orders.

With me? What the hell?

He looks up at Lanky—er, Joe. "Have Claude track my location and copy everything we say and do. No one follows us. I do not want backup until I call for it, is that clear?"

"Yessir."

He clicks a key fob, and bright lights and a beep light up a truck a few yards away from us.

Oh my God.

When I was a teen, I had a few friends who got their licenses, and everyone wanted a car. Some just wanted a set of wheels to get from point A to point B, some freedom and independence. Some wanted a nicer car that would take them to job interviews or on road trips.

I wanted a truck. Specifically, a Toyota Tundra 4WD with a crew cab and thirty-eight-inch mud terrain tires with eighteen-inch Rockstar rims.

Cain Master drives my dream truck.

His truck's like him, sturdy and fearless, a veritable force of nature. The wheels alone come up to my chest. *Good God.* Two-tone black rawhide leather seats with red inlay matches the candy blood-red paint job, and if it wasn't for Massachusetts' insanely strict gun laws, this baby would house a gun rack in the back perfect for a twelve-gauge shotgun or semi.

And is that... *no.* Behind this truck, in the back, there's an even bigger truck.

"You do not drive a Ford 650!"

He gives me a curious look. "I do, but it's too big to take tonight."

"Will you let me touch it? Please? I just want to touch it, just once."

Cain's lips twitch, and he mutters, "That may be crossing a line, Miss Price."

I don't dignify his response with a reply, and don't speak because I don't trust my voice.

"Not now." He's right, I know he is. We have to get moving. Still, one day I just want to sit in that beautiful truck.

I hoist myself up on the metal platform of the Toyota. I want to get into the cab before he notes how small I am compared to this thing and decides to do something drastic and chauvinistic like touch me and help me in.

He's your boss, I remind myself. Your ridiculously hot, very scary, very dominant alpha male boss who just joked about...

No, wait. Not boss. *Not boss.*

Business associate or...something.

Whatever.

I hop in so quickly I manage to smash my shins on the unyielding metal step. Fuck, that'll bruise. I don't wince or say a word but silently slide onto the passenger seat. He, naturally, swings himself in with one smooth motion like this truck was custom-built to accommodate him.

I take a quick look at the clothes in my hands. Some kinda faded khaki pants that could be men's or women's, but there's an adjustable waistband and elastic to help them fit. A small black tank top, pair of socks, pair of boots.

He stares down at the boots. "Those are the smallest size we had, but something tells me you'll still have to stuff them."

"I'm not *that* small."

It's a stupid thing to say when I'm sitting next to a man so big he could double in Green Giant ads. His hands are three times the size of mine, his arms bigger than my thighs, and *those* aren't even the most intimidating things about him. Normal humans are composed of skin and tissue and strung together with muscle. Cain defies normal human body structure, because every inch of him seems to be nothing but raw, corded muscle. If we broke down, I feel as if he could hitch this truck to his shoulders and haul us home without breaking a sweat.

"I'd guess you're five feet tall, just over a hundred pounds."

"Didn't anyone ever tell you it's rude to ask a woman her weight?"

I sigh. Exactly one-ten the last time I checked.

"I'm not asking. My point is, you're small. Pointless trying to argue."

He revs the engine, and heat pulses low between my legs. If this truck proposed to me, I'd accept. *Gah.*

"It can come in handy, you know," I say in protest.

"What can?"

"Being small."

He shifts in his seat and mutters to himself, "Could be a fuckin' issue, too."

"Not like I can help it."

He doesn't respond but launches straight into giving me more details about his sister. "Things to know. Skylar has the shittiest taste in boyfriends and won't ever bring them to meet me for dinner or anything before she dates them."

"Does that surprise you?"

He pauses, flicking on his directionals before he takes a turn, then cruises back up to a breakneck speed. I guess not only does he not have a use for the police, but he obviously seems to think they can't touch him.

"No."

"If I had a brother like you, I don't think I'd bring my skinny little boyfriends home to roast marshmallows by your bonfire either."

A glimmer of something like amusement flits across his face, but he quickly goes back to the scary mask.

He grunts. "Especially the kinds of assholes she dates."

"Okay, so this is important information to note if I'm going to help you with this investigation. Little sis dates assholes."

He nods. We've left the shore and are heading into the heart of the city. I love Salem, with its aged houses and history. As we leave the shore, we draw closer to the historical parts of Salem—the Witch House, other museums, and the House of the Seven Gables.

"Skylar wrote to me when I was stationed in Europe and didn't travel much. Didn't like coming home, didn't prioritize it."

Why didn't he like coming home? My radar pings again, adding to my growing list of *things I need to find out about Cain Master.*

"Well, I know how that goes," I say softly, almost to myself. I do. Some of us would give anything to never come home again. "You and Skylar. How close are you?"

"Pretty close. She wrote to me constantly when she was a kid and I was deployed. Slowed when she got older, but I still have those letters."

I nod.

"Right. When I got back… she lived at my place for a time. She got tired of finding my mom passed out on the couch or her flavor of the week in her bedroom. I was beyond done with it. She stayed here a few months. She needed some structure, guidance. I gave her that."

Yeah, I *bet* he's good at giving people structure and…guidance. I stifle a shiver.

I note how he chooses his words carefully but doesn't sugar-coat a thing, a master at precision in his speech.

"She wanted to date." He spits out the words like they're distasteful. "She was old enough to. Let's just say we didn't see eye to eye when it came to who she chose to date."

I nod. "Let me piece this together, then. She's raised by a mom who let her do whatever she wanted. Doesn't get what she needs. You went off and enlisted which gave you the structure and accountability *you* needed. She had none of that, so when you came back, you did your best to provide that for her." He nods. "She wasn't too fond of your rules and expectations, but she was maybe grateful for a roof over her head and a large, scary big brother who'd keep her safe."

He draws in his breath with practiced patience and gives me a look I can only classify as a warning. "Yeah."

"So she rebelled. On the one hand, wanted your protection and everything you could offer, but on the other, didn't like being treated like a child and wanted you to damn well know that."

"Right."

"So at the first chance she got, when her friends got an apartment, she took off. Maybe checked in with you from time to time but didn't do much more than that."

"Very good, Miss Price."

"I got the basics then."

"Enough chitchat. That more or less brings you up to speed. Two boyfriends ago, she dated a guy who told me, I shit you not, that he was leaving that night to go become a vampire. And the next one after that came wearing a fucking cape and black boots. In July." Something tells me he wouldn't forgive black boots and a cape even in the dead of winter.

"We *do* live in Salem."

He huffs out a breath.

"And… let me guess… she didn't bring anyone else to see you after that?"

He grunts like a caveman. I'd pay good money to hear what he said to those two boyfriends.

"Cape. Boots. Salem. Is your sister involved in anything with witchcraft? Wiccan?"

His back goes so rigid, I could trace a straight line from the top of his spine to his seat. "Yeah."

But he doesn't offer any other details.

"How so?"

"What do you mean?"

"Is she actually Wiccan?"

I watch his reaction. He looks like he wants to wince, but he catches himself. Instead, his fingers tighten on the wheel, his knuckles white. He does not like that his sister's involved with the crowd she is, not one little bit.

"Involved in witchcraft?" He makes a face like he just ate a rotten apple. "She's got friends that do it, but…"

Aww. Is the big bad alpha too scared to admit his sister's involved in something outside his control?

"Are you in denial about her involvement, Cain?"

His eyes narrow on the road ahead of him, but he still manages to give me a brief sidelong look. "Be careful, Miss Price."

Something in me thrills at the warning he gives me, my skin prickling with heat. His voice has dropped, and is it my imagination, or has the inside of this car just heated up about twenty degrees?

"Careful about what?"

"Treading into areas you know nothing about."

I release a breath patiently. "Mr. Master, if I'm going to work with you, it doesn't make sense for you to hold anything back from me."

He gives me a sharp, sideways glance before he looks in front of him again. "You'll help me find my sister. You'll help me make sure she's safe and that the idiots she shares living space with haven't done something brainless like sign her up to be sacrificed to their fucking gods for the summer solstice."

"They can't do that."

"Why not?"

"It's August. Summer solstice is in June."

I think I actually see little tendrils of smoke come out of his ears.

Easy, Violet. Don't poke the bear too hard.

"You think you're clever, don't you?" He shakes his head as he flicks on his directionals again and takes a left so hard, I swear the tires leave the ground for a fraction of a second, a hard feat considering what this monstrosity weighs. When my stomach settles back to where it should be, I remember to protest.

"I—"

"You think you have it all figured out. I'm an overprotective brother who doesn't know jack shit about teens and boyfriends and how to *relate*."

Well... If the shoe fits...

"What you don't know is that I goddamn know what it's like to be the ostracized freak who can't rely on his parents. I know what it's like to want to fit in, to find a peer group you can socialize with who'll value you for who you are, not what you do."

Oof.

"So yeah, maybe it looks like I don't have a lot of respect for this witchcraft thing. And maybe I don't. I value what I can see. What I can hold. What I can touch."

I nod. It takes me a few seconds to realize I'm clutching at my neck, like he's a vampire who's going to bite me. My blood thrums through my veins, hot and visceral, and my skin feels too tight. I have to get control of the situation. He continues.

"I don't have a lot of use for bullshit. I will find the truth if I have to hunt it into dark valleys and hold it at knife point. Do we understand each other, Miss Price?"

I draw in a breath and release it slowly as I unfold the clothing in my lap. "Perfectly, sir." I cast a glance around the small interior of his truck. "Now where am I supposed to be getting dressed?"

CHAPTER FIVE

Cain

"RIGHT HERE. I'M NOT LOOKING."

Like fuck I'm not. I notice everything about her, from the way her fingers graze the pulse at her neck, to the wispy ringlets of hair that cling to her temple, still damp from the sudden summer shower that caught us unawares. I'm aware of her delicate scent, clean and fresh yet feminine, like moon-kissed dew. I'm aware that despite her training and level of fitness, of how easily I could hurt her.

I remember the way she felt pinned beneath me, how I held my weight above her so I wouldn't hurt her, both wrists gathered in my hand.

I remember how I liked it.

"Be quick about it, we're five minutes out."

"Not a problem."

She unfolds the tank, then wriggles it through the collar. Holding my T-shirt over her like a tent, she shimmies and wriggles and huffs into the clothes. If I wasn't so pissed and ready to kill, I'd find it amusing. Less than a minute later, she tosses the wet tee on the dash. I glance at her. She's dressed, and the clothes don't fit her well, but they'll stay on her for now. Next, she pulls the socks and boots on.

"We'll arrive in two minutes. We'll question everyone who's there and get all the details we can. What languages do you speak, Miss Price?"

"I'm fluent in French, Italian, German, and Japanese. I can get by in Portuguese and Russian, though don't ask me to write either."

She's being modest. She also knows passable Greek and Hindi as well.

I'm fucking hard just listening to her list some of her many talents.

"Noted. We'll get into why I hired you later, but for now I want you to know that I needed a woman on my team. There are places a petite woman like you can fit a lot more easily than a man like me or many on my team, and your skill set will also come in handy."

She nods.

"When you're proficient with a gun, you'll conceal and carry."

"Don't I need a license?"

"I'll take care of it. For now, if we get into a dangerous place, you'll use the skills you already have, but only at my command. You do *not,* under any circumstances, act without my permission."

"I thought we were just going to investigate."

"We are. I like to be prepared. Lesson one, Miss Price. Investigations can turn sour, and easily."

She nods, frowning as she looks out the window. "Why are the streetlights on during the day? That's odd."

I look to where she does. Each streetlight glows with a dim yellow light. I mentally commend her for noticing a detail I didn't. One of the reasons I hired her.

I flick a button on my phone. Joe answers immediately.

"Boss?"

"Check the electric grid between North and Downey Road. See if you notice any unusual activity."

I hang up the phone. I turn to Violet and point toward a sheathed knife on the console. "Have you ever used a knife?" I know for a fact she has, it's one of the many skills her studio has taught her that they don't advertise.

Though she doesn't answer me at first, I can tell just by the way she takes the ankle sheath she's skilled in knife use. In seconds, the sheath's safely secured under her pant leg, but easy to retrieve at a moment's notice. Throwing knives are long and sharp, and this one is no exception.

"Knives and I are BFFs, you could say."

We'll work on honesty, a two-way street. Eventually I'll tell her exactly why I've watched her and looked into her past.

My reasoning is pretty simple and honest, but I know that if I tell her too much too soon, I could push her away. I can't risk that, not now.

I try to discreetly watch as she gets out of the cab of the truck, but I had nothing to worry about. She swings herself down like an expert, with grace and fluidity. Perfect. Something tells me I won't regret hiring her.

We walk at a good clip to Skylar's apartment building, but Violet pauses just outside the door. "Wait!"

I tamp down irritation. I don't like waiting, and I want to get this done. But she's fallen to one knee outside the door. She reaches out, fingering something I don't see right away.

"What is it?"

She shakes her head. "Flowers."

"Right. I'm sure there are flowers everywhere. I don't want to waste any—"

"No. No, listen." She stands, holding a delicate spray of tiny white flowers. "Baby's breath. I found the same flowers outside my car yesterday, these and a little purple one. Before I got into the accident."

"Coincidence?"

Her gaze is troubled when she looks at me. "Could be. We should note it, though."

"Noted. Now can we move on, please?"

My phone rings. Joe.

"Yeah?"

"Someone fucked with the electricity on that block last night. There are reports of the lights going off from dusk to this morning, and since they're set on auto, they came back on this morning when they don't usually."

"Thanks." I tell Violet, who only frowns but nods.

"Do you have like a special bag or something to hold evidence? We should maybe—"

I do not have the time or patience for this.

"For fuck's sake, stuff them in your bra if you're that worried." I turn to the door and push the doorbell. Out of the corner of my eye, she makes a gesture that *could* be flipping me off, but when I look sharply back at her, she shrugs her shoulders at me innocently. Probably just as well. Hauling her over my knee to teach her respect probably wouldn't go over too well right now.

The flowers are gone. I wonder if she took my advice. I imagine them pressed up against her perfect breasts, and with effort, pull my mind back to the job.

I turn back to the door at the sound of footsteps heading our way. Like many apartment buildings in downtown Salem, the door and stoop are aged with time and wear. A potted plant, the leaves dried and dead, sits to one side of the stairs. Below us, on the ground, my eyes fall on a crumpled condom. I hate that Skylar lives here.

Someone speaks to us through the door. "Who's there?" Lottie.

"Cain, Skylar's brother. Open up, please." The *please* is an afterthought. I try to remember my manners. Manners can sometimes get you places, but they're damn inconvenient.

Hushed voices rise and fall on the other side. Violet and I look at each other in silence as the door stays shut.

She shakes her head. "Now remember, you can't just go in there and kill them," she says in a whisper so soft I can barely hear her. I didn't even realize my hand was already grazing the butt of my gun. It's a little scary how she reads my mind.

"Why not?" I whisper back. I've killed for less than this, and I'd do it again. This is my sister we're talking about, my goddamn sister, and if anyone hurts her—

"Laws," Violet whispers. "You're no good to your sister in jail or dead yourself."

"Fucking logic." She can try all she wants, but she won't stop me if anyone's hurt Skylar. No one will.

I turn back to the door and raise my hand to knock, when I hear the clicking of metal, and the doorknob turns. Lottie, my sister's roommate and best friend, stares at me with wide, haunted eyes behind thick glasses. Her purplish black hair's in braids on either side of her head, and she wears a black cape with a black and silver dress over her curvy body. Someone I've never seen before—man or woman, I don't know yet, dressed in drab black clothing with long dark hair — stands next to her.

Lottie's voice is pained. "I didn't do it, Mr. Master. I had nothing to do with it."

Never a good way to begin a conversation.

"Do what?" I just want to get inside so I can ask some questions. I take a step toward her, and she steps back. Violet watches us both curiously.

"Any-anything." She's terrified of me.

Sometimes, that works against me. Sometimes it's in my favor.

I consider shoving past them to get inside, demanding answers to questions and scouring the place for clues, but I know that brute force isn't *always* the best response.

I look to Violet, and with subtle eye movements and a slight jerk of my head, silently ask her to get us in here without someone shitting their pants.

She steps forward, a smile on her lips.

"We didn't think you were to blame." Her voice exudes confidence and grace. She looks so small, so wholesome, no one would realize how quickly and easily she could cut or maim them. Her voice gentled, she stands close to me, as if showing with her physical presence that she's with me, and we mean no harm. "We're concerned, though, and want to help. Let us in, please?"

Lottie releases a breath, steps aside, and beckons for us to go in.

The sweet, nearly acrid smell of incense hits me when we set foot inside. It's hard to tell it's daytime, with the blinds drawn and nothing but candles lighting our way. Several cats curl around my ankles before gracefully gliding away. I take in every detail I can. Skylar's never invited me, but I've had surveillance on it since she came here. I know the basic layout, but now I'm looking for other details.

It's a small, crowded apartment. Two bedrooms? The kitchen sink is tidy but cluttered, dishes stacked on a drying rack that's nearly bursting. Beside the dishes there's a stack of coffee mugs, Zodiac signs engraved on the outsides of them. A velvet cushion lies on a table to the left, and several long, carved sticks that look like wands sit atop it. A carved structure featuring three women in dresses, holding hands around a white candle base, sits to the left of the cushion with the word *goddess* engraved below, and beside the candle a long incense burner casts smoke heavenward. The scent grows stronger.

On one wall several silver pendulums hang on a silver peg, and in the living room, there's a stand with a large, clear sphere. A crystal ball? Several dragons are displayed on the walls, some carved in 3D and some flat prints. The door to one bedroom's ajar, revealing an unmade bed and a large stack of unfolded laundry in a wicker basket. One of the cats walks into the room, quickly swallowed up by darkness.

"Miss Price, meet Lottie. Lottie, Miss Price. Lottie's Skylar's best friend and roommate."

"Pleased to meet you." Violet sticks her hand out, but Lottie doesn't take it. She stares at her, untrusting.

I turn to her companion. "And you are?"

"Haven, my boyfriend," Lottie says. He gives me a jerky nod, then steps back, falling into the shadows. Can't speak for himself? Interesting. I turn back to Lottie.

"You called us. What has you concerned?"

Lottie wrings her hands and paces in front of me. "Skylar had a date. Someone we met at a local gathering."

Gathering. What exactly is a gathering? I do my best to reserve judgment, but it's hard, seeing the dark, cramped apartment my sister shares with her friends, knowing I'm fully capable of putting her in a bigger, better place.

"They were supposed to go to dinner," Lottie says. "They had plans, and she even told me where they were going." Tears brim behind her glasses.

"Where?"

"Bubbles and Broomsticks." Pretty common name. In a city like Salem, over a quarter of the local establishments features names playing off some variation of the word "witch."

"She went to meet him, and she came home earlier than she expected. She'd texted me that the guy creeped her out."

"Did she give you specifics? What exactly creeped her out?"

I fucking hate that my sister went out on a date with someone she didn't trust and I didn't know.

I pace in the kitchen, trying to ignore the way I want to break things. My hands clench, and I try to steady my breathing. I hate this. If they hadn't tampered with anything, I'd have gotten full footage of everything. "And I have no idea where she is because you two thought it smart to remove all surveillance."

Violet places a gentle hand on my arm. My skin heats where she touches me, and I take in a calming breath. My fingers unclench, relaxing by my sides.

I didn't know she'd have that effect on me.

Lottie doesn't respond but plays with a silver lip piercing, her brows drawn together over her large glasses.

"What happened after she came home?"

"Well, about an hour later, I heard the front door open and close again. I yelled after her, but either she ignored me, or she didn't hear me. Honestly either could've happened."

"Did you see her?" Violet asks.

"When she came home?"

"Yeah."

Lottie shakes her head.

"So she didn't respond, and you didn't see her," Violet says. "Is it feasible that it was someone else who came into the house and left again?"

Lottie's magnified eyes widen. "Oh. Oh, God, I didn't think of that."

"Do you lock your door?" Violet asks, shooting me another look as if to warn me not to lose my shit.

"Well... sometimes, yes, sometimes no."

Even Violet looks frustrated at this point. "Lottie, this is important. Did you lock the door last night?"

Lottie winces. "I have no idea."

Violet's lips thin. I run my thumb over the metal handle of my gun to calm my nerves.

"So she probably didn't come home," I supply.

"No."

Lottie's companion shifts on his feet, as if enduring something uncomfortable.

Violet keeps her voice gentle. "What makes you think she didn't just go back out with him? Why call us?"

She turns to face me. "She left her phone here. She didn't tell me where she was going. And that on its own might not have really concerned me. But we have a rule, we always tell each other where the other's going."

The one smart fucking thing she's told me today.

"I'm going into her room," I tell Lottie over my shoulder, halfway in.

"Mr. Master, I don't think that's a wise idea—"

I ignore her. Violet walks in behind me and voices my thoughts when she looks around the room.

"Oooh. Oh my."

The gauzy black curtains are drawn over the windows, but it isn't dark enough to hide the large, king-sized bed decorated with a circular, plush blanket in purples and blacks, the skeletons that dance along every flat surface in a macabre display, or the feathery dream catchers that hang from the ceiling. That isn't what's got my attention, though, nor Violet's.

A curved, black leather chair sits in one corner of the room.

"Is that what I think it is?" I say out of the corner of my mouth to Violet.

"A chair designed for tantric sex and multiple positions or partners?" Violet responds. "Ohhh yeah."

I curse under my breath. "And you know this because..."

"I believe that question violates our confidentiality agreement, Mr. Master."

"We don't *have* a confidentiality agreement, Miss Price."

Her tight-lipped smile makes me want to smack her saucy little ass.

She steps further into the room and looks around. "Something for sure's off," she says. "Look."

She points to where Skylar's phone sits, plugged into the wall. Her laptop's beside it, and the little bowl for her cats is empty. "No way she'd leave without putting fresh water and food out for her pets."

Lottie stands in the doorway. "And you called the police?"

"I did." She sighs. "They won't touch the case. They said that she hasn't been missing long enough and we have no evidence."

What she doesn't say is that knowing I'm Skylar's brother doesn't help the situation.

Violet's frowning, my sister's phone in her hand. It's password-protected, and she hasn't gotten far with it.

"We're taking this with us," she says. "I'm sure I'll be able to get in."

Lottie doesn't protest.

Moons line every surface of the room. Half-moons pinned to the wall with Latin phrases I don't know, a full moon framed in silver above an end table that's actually a half-moon shape.

"Why all the moons?"

Violet frowns, her eyes quickly flitting over every detail. "You said she was dating a vampire?"

"Miss Price, there's no such thing as fucking vampires."

She nods. "Look, there may not be in our world—in the practical world we both inhabit—but in hers? There are. And it's noteworthy."

I give her this and don't argue again.

After scouring Skylar's room and the rest of the apartment, I get directions for Bubbles and Broomsticks. Back in the truck, Violet frowns as she fiddles with Skylar's phone. She's tried her birthday, her astrological sign, every obvious password she could think of, and finally locks herself out of it for fifteen minutes.

"Damn it," she mutters, scowling. She takes her own phone out. "Have you noticed that your sister's companions are all sort of outcasts? You've got Lottie, who's sweet but wears glasses, is overweight and dresses in costumes. Probably not the most popular girl in her class. Were all her friends sort of unpopular?"

"Mhm."

I flick on the directionals and take a left.

"Like... the boyfriend who's essentially androgynous, and I bet if we investigated her other friends, we'd find something similar."

I nod, not sure how this has anything to do with the case.

"Our goal right now is to bring back everything we can to my men. Tonight, we'll go over every detail and see what we can piece together."

"Your men. That sounds so…" Her voice trails off.

"So what?"

"Like, masculine."

I grunt. "What should I call them? My employees?"

She shrugs and gets a little haughty. "It's just that they're not all men anymore."

I look at her full breasts, her petite little body, and those pursed lips I want to kiss. "They're definitely not."

I pull up onto the highway, twenty minutes out from the restaurant we need to investigate. A car whizzes past us so closely, Violet screams. It hits my left tire, ricochets forward, and I have to slam on my brakes to keep it steady.

Violet gasps. "What was that?" I'm already accelerating, following the small black Mazda.

"Are you road raging after them?"

"Me? Road rage? What makes you think I have road rage?"

I'll fucking kill them.

"That was not an accident," Violet says. She's sitting straight up next to me, hands on the dash. "They so did that on purpose."

I'm gaining on them, as they take a sharp right and exit the highway.

"Uh yeah, no reason," she says with a grimace as I follow them off the highway. Horns blare as the light turns red and I plow through it, gaining on them. Someone flips me the bird. The truck's too big to chase them too closely.

"Get the plate," I tell her.

"On it."

The car zigzags in and out of traffic, way too quickly for my huge truck to follow them. I curse under my breath.

"This is not a good getaway car," she mutters.

"No, but it off-roads like a motherfucker and there isn't a better place to be when the shit hits the fan." The glass is shatterproof, the wheels reinforced and nearly invincible. I could mow down a goddamn semi if I had to.

"You can't chase them now, though." She mumbles something under her breath.

"What was that?"

"I said, 'thank God,'" she says loudly. "Not sure what you'd do to them in your present state of mind."

"You work for me now. That means accepting anything and everything that working with me entails. Under any and all circumstances. Understood?"

She nods. "Yes, of course. Why do you think they would hit us?"

"Isn't it obvious?"

"It is, but I want your take. No stone unturned and all that."

"They hit us because they have something to hide. They don't want us on this case. It was a stupid, pussy threat."

I hate that someone basically assaulted us and got away with it.

I call Joe. "Run this plate." I repeat the plate number Violet gives me.

We're going to get answers, and we're going to get them now.

CHAPTER SIX

Violet

SOMETHING'S definitely not right here, I know it in my gut. My mind wanders to the flowers squished against my breast, the phone and cats left unattended in Skylar's room, and the little car that just tried to run us off the road.

"Please tell me the truth," I say to Cain. "Is it more likely that someone has a beef with Skylar or with *you*?"

He clenches his jaw. "Me."

"Thought so. And do you think there's a chance they'd come after her to get back at you?"

He curses again. "Yeah."

I pull up my phone to Google some facts when I remember something. "It's a full moon tonight."

"And?"

I remember Skylar's fascination with moons. I take her phone and type in *full moon*. Nothing.

"Can you name the phases of the moon?"

He gives me a quizzical look, but nods. "Full moon. Waxing crescent. Waning crescent. Waning gibbous... waxing gibbous..." He strokes his chin, a surprisingly masculine move that makes me look away because he's my boss—*correction, no he is not, we work professionally with each other*—and I will not look at how sexy those fingers are rasping against the stubble on his jaw *goddammit*.

I type *waxing crescent*. Nothing. With a sigh, convinced this isn't going to work, I type in *waning crescent*.

Her phone unlocks. I pump the air.

"Got into her phone."

The streets are quiet, the oppressive heat and humidity of late August making the air around us shimmer with haze. Cain guns the engine, as if reminding the universe that he's coming for his sister. "Good work."

I suspect it isn't often that he commends someone who works for him, and his praise sends a warm flicker of pleasure through me. I ignore it. I don't like that I want his praise.

I focus on scrolling through her phone for some clues. I'm violating her privacy, I know I am, but we have to find something that can help us. If we let the police department take their time, it could be too late. I feel sick.

"So, your sister only has like twenty contacts."

"And?"

"Well, it's pretty unusual. The average person has... I don't know, I'd guess hundreds. Huh." I shrug. "That'll make it easier to go through."

"Okay, good."

"But... well, that's not a lot. Is she sort of a loner?"

"Yeah, you could say that."

Bingo. I read a text on her screen that pings my attention.

"She has a text from a guy she's named 'Cowboy.'"

"Cowboy." He frowns. "That's not usually her scene."

It's definitely not.

"Yep."

I flip through the phone. "They met... a week ago... online. He asked her out for drinks and they agreed to go out last night." I don't say anything for a minute, because I'm not sure he wants to hear what's going on in these texts.

"Oh. Oh wow. Then there's a text here, she says, *Don't call me back. I don't ever want to hear from you again.*"

"I want his address."

With the tone he uses, he could replace what he said with *give me the coordinates so I can bomb his ass.*

"And then it looks like there might've been more communication between them, but maybe it was a phone call or several because there are no more texts."

"And there's nothing else?"

I sigh. "I don't see much of anything. She's got some social media stuff... but even that.... Well, there's just Wiccan stuff."

I don't tell him what. He's obviously not a fan of her lifestyle, and I don't know how much is relevant anyway. I scroll through text after text, and it makes me feel shitty. I don't like invading her privacy like this.

But I share his concern. She's in danger, and we need to find her. I look for something, anything at all that will clue me in.

On a whim, I pull up a browser and scroll through her history. Now this is starting to feel more invasive. I ignore the growing unease.

My cheeks scald at the first dozen or so searches.

Doggy style

Reverse 69

Best tantric sex moves

Cowboy

"You're blushing, Miss Price," he says, as he flicks on the directionals and gets off the highway.

"She, uh... not sure how much you want to know. Let's just say I think I know why she calls him Cowboy."

His jaw firms. "Fuck."

"There are maybe some things you don't need to know about your sister."

With a grimace, he shakes his head. "Everything. I need everything."

"She... had a pretty rich sex life, it seems."

He looks like he's just bitten into a lemon. A rotten, mold-covered lemon.

"Sorry."

"Don't be."

I scroll a little more.

"Oh. Oh, wow."

"*What?* Will you please stop that?"

Fuck, I need to find a better poker face.

I shake my head. I will not tell him I had no idea *that* was a position one could put themselves in. I mean, honestly... someone would have to have... like a really, *really* big... in order to fit that way...

"We aren't going to work together if you're hiding things from me."

"I just don't know if you want to know what I'm seeing over here about sexual positions, Mr. Master."

He clamps his mouth shut.

"Some of these are—" I stop talking, as a cold shiver runs down my spine.

Baby's breath.

She has six search histories involving baby's breath and three more with purple irises.

Why?

He pulls into a parking spot outside the restaurant. I remind myself to tell him about the flower search history later.

I need to call my bestie Candi but have to find a way to do it without him knowing, since he doesn't want to involve the police.

I pull out my phone and shoot her a text.

> Babe, off record. You were telling me something last night about a recent string of sexual assault victims… what can you tell me about it?

No response. I tuck my phone in my left pocket and Skylar's in my right. He parks the car. I pull up my pants leg to make sure my knife's secured, inwardly groaning when I see the purplish bruises along my shins from getting into his truck. I look like I fell off my bike when my mom took my training wheels off. *Great.*

I don't miss the way people look at us, and I don't think it has anything to do with my odd choice in attire. I can tell that people recognize him, and those that don't, notice him from afar. He's large and intimidating, but that isn't what garners attention so much as the way he walks.

Some people walk like they know you're watching them. Others walk timidly, as if they don't want to step on toes or offend you. Cain walks into the restaurant as if he belongs here and anyone who doesn't ought to fuck off before he makes them. His confident gait and the take-no-prisoners steel in his eyes are silent declarations that he isn't afraid, that if anyone does something dangerous, they'll deal with him. He drips arrogance and violence through his goddamn pores, something that should turn me off.

It doesn't. It doesn't at all.

A few women vaping to the right of the entrance look him up and down, and one even hands her bag to her friend and steps toward us. She gives me a quick look and easily dismisses me as someone who isn't competition, because she doesn't even bother to hide the fact that she likes him, thinks he's hot, and wants to sleep with him, probably right this very minute.

Without missing a beat, Cain slides his large, warm hand along my lower back, curves his fingers around my side and pulls me to him. His eyes are glacial, a man on a mission, but my body doesn't seem to care. At the feel of his hand on me, my blood heats, an electric current coursing its way straight through me. I can't help but step closer to him. I like the way my body tingles, as if every nerve knows this is a man who knows how to treat a woman's body.

The woman heading toward us halts mid-step, then shoots me a scowl. I don't know if I want to stick my tongue out at her or punch her.

We step further inside, and a waitress hands us some menus.

"Do you still have wings on the menu? Babe, you remember those wings you like?"

Babe? Wait, what? Cain Master's just staked his claim on me, and I have no idea why. But when the woman who'd been heading toward us steps to the side, it's starting to become clearer.

I draw in a shaky breath and laugh. I could get into this. "I do. You're the best, honey." *Gag. Me.*

A glimmer of a smile crosses his lips, like a particle of sun breaking through clouds before they swallow it up again. "Anything for you."

This is a front. Nothing more, nothing less.

"Let's sit at the bar," I suggest, gesturing toward the bar.

"Sure thing, baby."

God! He's really pushing this. I make gagging motions with my finger down my throat, then slice my hand in the air in front of me. *Stop!*

He mouths, "*Nope.*"

Argh!

I hop up on a bar stool, but he shakes his head at me. "Scoot over."

"You wanna sit here?"

"I do," he says through tight lips. He's the boss, and he has his reasons, so I move to the left and let him take the seat I was in. "I can see all exits this way."

I'd be pleased if I felt he'd made this move to protect me, but I don't romanticize shit.

The bartender, a thin, kinda young ginger with a scraggly beard and piercings all along each ear and his eyebrow welcomes us. "Can I get you two a drink?"

His eyes linger a little longer on Cain. He recognizes him, I think. Hard to forget a guy like him.

"Soda water with lemon," I order. Cain gets a soda.

"I know you," the bartender says to Cain when he hands us our drinks. Bingo.

"Yeah?" Cain takes a sip of his drink and places it back on the counter. His eyes flit over my shoulder, scanning the entrance, before he looks back at the bartender. He folds his arms across his chest, and his muscles bulge. I don't know if he's trying to intimidate him on purpose, but the bartender takes a step back. "How do you know me?"

"On second thought, not sure I do. You remind me of someone."

He turns to walk away.

"He's Skylar's brother," I say loudly enough to get his attention. "Do you know her?" I keep a close eye on the people watching us. Does anyone look guilty? Curious? Does anyone know her?

Cain shoots his eyes to me, the quickest glance. I pull out my phone and open up a picture of her.

"We're actually looking for her," I say casually. "Have you seen her recently?"

The bartender wipes down condensation from my glass, then slides it over to me as my phone beeps. "Haven't seen her."

He doesn't make eye contact, though, and as soon as someone else comes to the bar, he walks away from us to take their order.

"He's lying and avoiding us." I sip my soda and check my phone.

"Agreed. The question is, why?"

There's a string of texts from Candi.

Where are you? No one's seen you at work and you never miss.

I'm doing a job. I can't tell you any more right now.

Are you safe?

I look at Cain. Am I safe? Hell no, I'm not safe. But he's likely not going to hurt me in the next few minutes, so I can lie for now. I have to.

Yes.

What did you need to know?

You said there was a rise in sexual assault cases lately. What did you tell me about flowers?

It's his signature move. He leaves flowers for his victims before he rapes them. Why do you need to know?

I don't reply.

The baby's breath at my breast feels suddenly hot, burning against my skin like a brand.

I try to reason with myself. Not every flower is a sign.

I'm going crazy.

Half a minute later, another text comes in.

Hey. You're nowhere to be found then the next thing I know, you're asking me about active cases. Way to freak me out. What the hell is going on?

I don't know. I'm safe.

I glance at the monster of a man sitting beside me and release a breath.

Two

Fuck.

I have some research to do tonight.

Cain's scowling at his phone, too.

"Anything important?"

"Yeah. They got the details on the car that hit us, but the car was stolen so there's no way to tell who was driving."

"And the lights?"

"Someone reconfigured the timing grid at the intersection."

Also notable.

I have to find out more about the missing women and the surviving victims. I open my phone again, and I Google shit I *never want to Google* until I've got a list of details involving the rape crimes around here lately. I do not tell any of this to Cain quite yet, because I have to find a way to do it without giving him a coronary.

I make notes on my phone.

Tonight, I'll look up every detail I can until I have a better idea of what's going on.

I slug the rest of my drink and raise my hand for another, just so I can get the bartender to come over.

He glances from me to Cain apprehensively. "Need a refill?"

He nods.

I watch as the bartender fills both of our glasses. He jerks his head behind him. "Be right there."

He's just trying to get us to not ask questions, I know he is, because I see no one has called him, no one who's waiting for him.

I turn on my most charming smile. "Oh, hey," I say, crooking my finger at him to stay before he goes off again. "I actually have a few more pictures of the girl we're looking for." I try to keep my tone casual, my body language relaxed. I wish I could send a message to Cain to lighten the hell up, because he's definitely not contributing to the casual, relaxed vibe I'm going for here.

The look the bartender shoots Cain is nothing short of terrified, but I talk quickly so he doesn't look at Cain and looks at me instead. "I've got a few more pictures for you." I pull up the pictures I swiped from Skylar's social media. "It's really, really important we find her. Are you sure you didn't see her? She was here last night on a date."

The bartender rubs a hand across his face. I read once that touching one's face is a classic sign of guilt or nerves, and I note this carefully. My guess is he didn't have a direct hand in taking her, but somehow helped the people who did or at least knows who they are.

Son of a bitch.

I glance at Cain, narrowing my eyes to tell him to stop looking like the Grim Reaper, then quickly glance at the bartender.

Cain leans forward on his big, beefy arms, his voice a low drawl. "I'd be very pleased if you could help us find her. Like she said, she's my sister." *Implication: And I'll be pissed if you don't.*

"Right." The bartender's words are barely above a whisper.

Cain flashes a disarming grin that somehow makes my nerves stand on edge. There's something about that smile I don't trust. There isn't an ounce of humor in his body right now. "I'm not sure we've met before?"

He extends his large hand out. It's then that I notice small tattoos along the inner side of one hand. I can't see what they are yet, but there's a lot of them.

"Name's Cain Master."

Now this time, there's nothing left to the imagination. The bartender pales, and only after prompting from Cain, reaches out and gingerly takes his hand. "I've heard a lot about you, sir."

Cain shrugs. "Eh, people like to embellish facts. I bet half of what you heard isn't true."

And the other half is.

The bartender doesn't reply at first. Then he clears his throat, and when he speaks, it's in a low whisper. "Meet me by the dumpster out back. We can't talk here."

Cain slowly picks up his drink and sips. I take inventory. There's one more bartender near the dishwasher, unloading clean, steaming hot glasses and placing them on a rack. A few people glance our way, but most are drinking or dancing, and in one corner of the room, some people play pool. A waitress sidles past me with a tray of pizza that looks so good my mouth waters.

Damn, this place is teeming with people, from young adults to teens, and I'm starving. I haven't eaten in way too long.

"Finish your drink," Cain says in a low whisper. "Then follow me."

The bartender wipes down the space in front of him, turns, and leaves. He walks down a hall that leads to a door, a broken *restroom* sign leading his way. The door shuts behind him.

A minute later, Cain gets up from his seat, tosses a few bills on the bar for the tab, then goes out the door the way the bartender went. I follow. Someone crosses in front of me, putting more distance between me and the guys.

Before I can reach them, an alarm goes off. White lights flash. The wail of a siren goes off and sprinklers water down on us.

"Everyone evacuate!" someone shouts, just as the smell of acrid smoke reaches me.

Utter chaos erupts.

You don't realize how crowded a place is until you all try to evacuate at once. One minute ago, the place was relatively calm, save some voices and laughter. Now, it's a zoo.

People shove past me. Some scream, and others have the rabid look of someone being chased. I might be small, but I won't let myself get trampled. Someone in front of me shoves me back. I throw my shoulder, knocking them down.

"Hey!" her boyfriend says, and the dumbass thinks he's somehow entitled to hit me. I duck his hand, and in one quick movement, sweep his leg. With the crowd pushing on him, it's the most effective way to make sure he stays down. His girlfriend screams. I take the opportunity to run.

I'm small, so it's easy to dodge the melee of people around me. I wonder where Cain is, but I'm not too worried. Something tells me he can take care of himself.

I get to the exit when someone grabs me from behind. I feel strong fingers at the nape of my neck. On instinct, my hand flies up to block the touch just before I bend and strike at the torso behind the grasp.

I gasp when I see Cain doubled over, the people around us swarming past, oblivious to us. Shit! Sirens scream, coming closer.

"Fuck," he pants, still doubled over. "It was a set-up. And Jesus, look before you fucking strike. Come with me."

It's then that I realize there's blood dripping down his forehead and a gash on his upper left arm, and neither one of those were because of my self-defense moves.

"Are you alright?"

"I'm fine. Follow me." He sidesteps people left and right, then ducks down behind a barrel. He tugs me down beside him. Fire trucks come down the street, their sirens piercing the air. Our hiding space is so small, I'm right up against him, my back against his thighs. I keep myself very, very still.

His voice is a low vibration in my ear. "Stay here. We're waiting until this has all died down. He pulled the fucking alarm trigger thinking it would scare us off."

"Asshole. I don't scare off that easily."

"Good," he says from behind me. His voice is a low rumble, his warm breath on my neck. "I don't either. And now, we wait. The son of a bitch set me up."

I would *not* want to be that bartender right about now.

"How do you know it was a setup?"

"The second I stepped outside of the bar, he was gone, the alarm went off, and when people poured out of the bar, I was attacked."

I suspected he knew something. This only confirms it.

"Who attacked you?"

"Couldn't see. Someone hooded, and they took off the second the place evacuated."

"Son of a bitch." I wobble in my crouched position, and without a word, he wraps his hand around my waist to steady me. His hand's large enough that his grip on one side rights my whole body. My skin seems to flame beneath the heat of his touch. I force myself to stay focused.

The firefighters come, finish evacuating the place, and put out a small kitchen fire. I look in every direction to see where the bartender might have hidden. I pull up the bar website and look for everything I can find. They have a profile page with the name of everyone who works here. I get to work.

By the time the crowd's dissipated, I've got everything I need to know about the bartender.

"You think they think we're gone?"

"Long gone."

"Good."

We wait for what seems like hours. I don't move. I barely even breathe. We're safe in our hiding place, but our location could be revealed at any moment, so I stay exactly where I am. His hand's still on me, steadying me. My breathing's ragged and unsteady.

I blink in surprise when I see the bartender. I hiss to Cain, "I saw him. He went in just now through the back door to the stock room. Plan of attack?"

He grunts. "I'll go in first. I'll—"

"Let me go in first. I'm smaller and it will be easier for me to find him."

"Absolutely not, and do not interrupt me again."

I stifle a whine. *Of course not. Yes, sir! ::inward eye roll::*

His voice rings with authority. "I'll find him. I'll question him. You'll do what I tell you."

I grumble at him, "Take notes on my notepad and maybe make you a sandwich?"

The grip on my waist, which I *almost* forgot about, tightens. "Careful, Miss Price. Don't push it."

Now why would I do a thing like that? *Grrr!*

I see a glimmer of red hair through a window.

"He's definitely there."

"Where?"

"Ten o'clock, behind the door, but close enough to a window if you need that entrance as well." Ha, who am I kidding? The only one of us who'd fit through a window is me. He'd be lucky to get a leg through.

I hear the unmistakable sound of a gun being cocked. "Let's go."

Seconds later, we move as one, crouched but running to the back entrance of the restaurant. I test the handle and find it locked. Silently, Cain jerks his head for me to get out of the way and pulls a small, slender device out of his pocket. He slides it expertly in place. The lock clicks, and the door swings open.

Cain goes in first. Prepared for an ambush, I don't look. This is not going to end well. The ginger bartender looks at us, turns, and tries to run away. In one swift move, I take my knife out of the ankle harness, aim, and fling it through the air. It lands like an arrow, the blade sunk deep into the wood of the doorframe half an inch from his head.

"Stay right there."

CHAPTER SEVEN

Cain

I KNEW she was skilled with a knife, but the way she stopped him mid-stride was fucking beautiful. So graceful, it fucking made me hard. Her skill goes way beyond beginner.

I don't waste time. In three firms strides across the room I've got the bartender by the neck.

"Name."

"Jeremy Guard."

"Why the fuck did you try to get rid of me?"

His eyes water and his voice squeaks, like a cornered mouse.

"Because they'll kill me."

"Who will?"

"I don't know names."

"Are they the people that took my sister?"

"I—I think so."

I grip his shirt and shake him.

"Yes!"

"Where are they?"

"I don't know. Said something about heading to Canada, but I can't tell you anything beyond that."

Fucking Canada?

"Why will they kill you?"

"Because they don't want to get caught. Because they'd go to jail for life. Because it would end their little shopping spree." He's crying freely now.

How fucking dare he. I give him another shake, furious he had the nerve to call it a *shopping spree.*

"That's my sister we're talking about."

Jeremy nods.

"Give me one fucking reason why *I* shouldn't kill you."

"Because I'm your ticket to finding them."

Wily son of a bitch.

"Yeah? You have no names. You've got no connections. How do I know what you've said is true?"

"Because they come all the time. They'll be back."

"And what's your role in this?"

He closes his eyes and winces. I shake him again, but Violet is so over this. She gives him a swift kick to the calf. "He asked you a question!"

He flinches and cries out. She glares at him, beautiful and feisty but ferocious as hell. Christ, even I'd answer her question. I did the right thing hiring her.

"They paid me! And I need the money."

A deadly calm comes over me. My gun burns on my hip, ready to dance in my grip and make him pay. "Why?"

"I owe a bookie," he sobs. "I didn't want to do it."

"Do *what?*"

He doesn't answer but closes his eyes and cries harder, like he knows his honest answer will sign his death warrant.

"You tell me, or I'll hold you down and give her permission to beat you. Is that what you want? To be beaten by a woman?"

He winces. Violet assumes a fighting stance, fucking ready.

Gorgeous.

He shakes his head. "He paid me to... slip them roofies."

Motherfucker. The date rape drug.

The hand holding him in my grip shakes with fury. "Then what?"

"Then he'd... pick them up. Take them home. And I don't know what from there. I try to respect people who—"

"Oh, fuck *off.*"

He stares at the gun in my hand.

I don't give him a chance to explain further. He starts to cry. "I never meant to hurt anyone."

I grab him by the hair and shove him to his knees. If I had time, I'd torture the motherfucker. I want to see the same pain in his eyes the women he fed to the goddamn wolves felt. I want to hear him cry harder and beg for his life until he's hoarse.

"You fucking piece of shit." My voice shakes and the room blurs. "If my sister's with a rapist right now... if he hurts her... it's your fucking fault."

I knee him, and when he doubles over, I hammer my fist to his jaw. Bone snaps, blood spurts. Violet watches in approval and cracks her knuckles like she wants to help me.

"You're a worthless, spineless bastard. Any man that helps another take advantage of innocent women deserves punishment worse than death." I grab him by the hair and yank his head back. I want to slit his throat. I want to feel his warm blood spill on my own hands as his life seeps out of him. I want to watch his eyes grow lifeless.

I have to get to Skylar. And Violet's watching.

I hit him again, and again, until he's whimpering and bloodied, his eyes swollen shut.

"Cain," Violet whispers. "We have to go. He deserves this. He deserves to be tortured and raped just like those girls he helped hurt. But we have to get Skylar."

"This asshole slipped roofies to unsuspecting women. He

helped a known rapist who now might have my fucking sister."

I don't think about the choices. Out of time, I pull my gun and slide the silencer on. I ignore his pleas, the way he cries like a baby and begs for mercy. I put the gun to his temple.

"You'll never hurt another innocent woman."

"No! God, no, please," he says through blood and spittle. The hand holding my gun shakes.

"You can look away, Miss Price."

"No."

I pull the trigger.

Violet watches with a slight frown as his body hits the floor, blood splashing on the floor beside her. She kneels and takes his pulse.

"You're right. He won't."

I call Joe.

"429 Might Street. Team alpha."

"Five minutes out, sir."

I hang up the phone and look at Violet. She doesn't look upset, as I expected her to. She doesn't even look disturbed. Her lips are a thin line, and something like triumph lights her beautiful, vivid eyes so they sparkle like amethyst.

That should warn me. Sane people don't watch someone being executed and rejoice in their death. But I don't feel anything but a sort of camaraderie.

"I'm sorry you had to see that."

She gives one short shake of her head. "Don't be. I'm sorry his death was so quick." She stands in silent acceptance that I just killed a man. We both know it's only a prelude to what I'll do when I find who he was helping.

We don't talk. We barely look at each other.

There was a time when I could still remember the names and faces of the people I'd killed.

That was a long time ago.

In exactly three minutes, our team has arrived to take care of the details.

I jerk my chin at her. "Let's go."

This time, she walks with me of her own accord and there's no need to threaten her.

"You didn't hesitate."

"Hesitate?"

"To kill him." Her voice is a bit strained, but she looks otherwise normal.

"No. Why would I?"

She shrugs. "You just... you didn't second-guess."

"No."

"You shot him because he deserved it, and you have no regrets."

I don't even think about my answer before I speak. "Yes."

"If I ask you an honest question…"

"You'll get an honest answer."

A beat passes before she tips her head to the side and asks, "Do these pants make me look fat?"

I stifle a snort. "How can you make jokes at a time like this?" I can't help the corners of my lips from turning upward.

"You'll see I'm surprisingly skilled at comic relief during the absolute *worst* times. It's one of my skills I should've mentioned during our interview."

The door to the room shuts fast behind us, hiding our team and the body they'll dispose of.

Our boots stomp heavily on the concrete toward my truck.

"I'll look forward to it."

She releases a shuddering breath. I look at her sharply. Good God, she's not going to start… *crying*. Is she?

But no. When she catches me looking at her, her eyes are dry and her lips are in a thin, firm line. "I pulled up everything I could on our little friend."

"The one we left with our other friends?"

"The very same."

"Tell me in the truck. Someone helped him, and I'm not sure who, but we aren't safe here."

She steps up the pace, and I move closer to her. When we reach the truck, I don't wait for her to fight her way up and bang the hell out of her shins again. She thinks I didn't see that. I remember the feel of her against me when I pinned her to the ground, and the feel of her body pressed to mine while we crouched in wait. I want to feel her again.

Before she has a chance to react, I reach for her and lift her up as easily as if she were a child. Her feet scissor and she gives a little squeak, but I don't wait around for the inevitable lecture or eye roll. I plop her down safely and walk to my side.

As soon as I open my door, she starts in.

"Excuse me," she says sternly, before I get the door to the truck closed shut.

"I know, don't touch you, don't help you, let you bruise the shit out of your shins. No." I crank the engine and look through my rearview mirrors, not an easy feat considering they fucked my mirrors up.

"Why? How? Seriously, how do you justify being such a control freak?"

"Me? Control freak?" I laugh quietly to myself, and mutter, "You have no idea." I would enjoy the ever-living hell out of having some modicum of control over her.

Dusk has settled on the city, the bluish haze of late summer making everything look mysterious and ethereal. I drive toward the road that takes me home, glancing in the rearview mirror so many times I'm barely watching where I'm going on the main road.

She's typing away on her phone, muttering to herself, taking notes, when she looks out the window and stares.

"Thinking?"

She doesn't reply for long minutes, just picks at a cuticle on one hand. "What do they do with the body?"

This would be a shitty time for her to start crying about all this.

"Better if you don't know, but it won't be a problem." A beat passes.

"Take me home now, please. I've never needed a shower more in my life."

I don't want to take her home. I want to keep her with me until we find Skylar. But I know we have research to do, and my team is on it. We have to find the person who hit us today and follow up on the contacts on Skylar's phone, along with whoever else at the bar's connected to the disappearances. And I'll be worth shit if I don't get some sleep.

"I'll take you home, and you do all the research you can. Tomorrow, we meet with my team to compare what we've found and hopefully make moves. Remember what I said about packing a bag."

"Right."

Tugging down her top, she moves her bra to the side and pulls out the sprig of delicate white flowers. I swivel my eyes back to the road so I don't confirm how the little sprig of flowers left an imprint on her bare breasts. I shift uncomfortably in the driver's seat, trying to rein in my focus. She has small, perfect breasts that would fit—

Christ.

"We need to keep this in mind. Whoever's taking them leaves flowers for them before he goes. One of those signature moves? There were flowers on the walkway to your sister's house, and your sister was looking for the meaning of them. I found it in the search history of her phone."

Shit.

"We don't really have the luxury of assuming anything's a coincidence right now."

We don't.

She's quiet, looking out the window. Holding something back from me.

"What is it?"

"It's just... well, there were flowers at work. I teach kickboxing classes to little kids, and before I left the other night, I saw some. It's probably not related, though."

"Is your studio near a florist or a delivery shop or a supermarket that might sell flowers?"

"No."

"Fuck going home," I tell her, as I turn to take the entrance to the highway. "You'll come back to my place." To my home, the goddamn fortress, where I've got my own army of trained soldiers who aren't afraid of combat.

She draws in a breath then releases it slowly, but she doesn't respond at first.

"I'm not giving you a choice in this. I'm—"

"Giving me a choice or I walk." I feel my brows snap together, but before I can respond, she continues. "I appreciate your concern. But I'm fully capable of taking care of myself."

"I thought we already had this discussion this morning, and that conversation ended with me on top of you."

Her hands clench into fists, but I don't fucking care. My sister's with God-knows-who, I've got no leads whatsoever on whatever the fuck is going on, I just put a bullet through a man's skull, and now she thinks she has a choice in this.

"You may have noticed, Miss Price, that my entire staff resides at my house."

"I have." She frowns in a way that looks almost like a pout. "It's odd and borderline cultish."

I won't let her get a rise out of me.

"I have my reasons. Scattering my employees and the contractors that work for me would be a terrible decision, as my necessary resources would be dispersed and weakened. I provide ample accommodations and security."

"Right. But what you may not have noticed is that the only female in your residence is an elderly, likely married woman."

"And the doctor."

"Oh wow. You hired a female doctor? How modern of you."

There's a low rumble in the truck I don't realize is my own damn growl at first.

"I'm not offering for you to live with me, Miss Price." I huff out a humorless laugh. "Don't flatter yourself."

She mutters something under her breath.

"What's that?"

She doesn't respond.

Her stomach growls, loud and clear. Now that I understand. "You're hungry. At least come and get something to eat before you go home."

"I'm good, thanks. I've got plenty of food at my house."

"Are you hungry or not?"

"Starving, but legitimate hunger's good for the soul. I'll somehow make it this time."

Stubborn. So goddamn stubborn. I don't miss the way she sits as far away from me as she can, as if somehow forming a physical distance will keep her safe.

I try another tactic. "I prefer the people that work for me to be safe. You don't have reliable transportation or a way to get anywhere if I need you right away. You were the one that picked up on details today we need to pursue, and I want you to report to my team directly so we can pool our resources. If anyone or anything hurts you, our entire operation is at risk."

She nods, slowly. "I see. But still, no."

Maddening woman! I clench my teeth and force myself to speak calmly. "And what will you do if someone attacks you?"

She's quiet for a minute, then finally shrugs. "You're not the only one with weapons, Mr. Master."

This woman's full of surprises.

"Fine. I'll take you home. Pack a bag so you're ready for the next time we work together. I'll send one of the company cars to your house for your use."

"Thank you." Finally, something she doesn't argue with.

She gives me her address, and we drive the rest of the way to her home in silence.

"You're brooding."

"I'm not brooding." Jesus, I haven't met anyone in years who's so goddamn free with me. Does she have zero sense of self-preservation? We don't speak again for long minutes, as the houses and cars pass by our windows, dimly lit in the moonlight. Streetlamps cast shadows on the street and sidewalks.

When we're a block away, she turns to me.

"I'm sorry about your sister. Tonight, I'm going to look up anything and everything I can. I'll make a list of notes and leads, and come over tomorrow to help you continue the investigation. And if anything happens while I'm gone, please let me know."

"I will. Look up everything you can about the flowers and the cases they suspect are linked."

"I will."

"You should get some sleep, though."

"So should you."

We both know neither one of us will sleep tonight.

I hate that my sister's out there. I hate that we have so little to go on.

It's easier to handle cases that don't involve the people you love.

And I hate that Violet's going home.

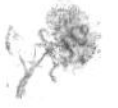

CHAPTER EIGHT

Violet

IT SEEMS like I've lived a dozen lives this week, and I'm weary. So tired, my bones feel like they creak, and my eyelids feel paper thin. I want to crawl in my bed, face first, right on top of the blankets and not get up again for a good, long while.

I left here this morning wanting to get hired by Cain Master.

I got a lot more than I bargained for.

His huge, ambling truck pulls out in front of my place. My landlord Troy's smoking a butt on the top stoop, and he doesn't even bother to try to hide the fact that he's scoping out Cain and his truck. I watch him take a drag, then let the smoke out slowly. He tosses it to the next step down and grinds it under his heel before he starts to come our way.

Seriously?

"Who's this?" Cain murmurs, his voice deceptively casual.

"Landlord. Usually just keeps to himself. This is weird."

"He got a thing for you?"

I can't help but snort at that. "Uh, no." No one's got a "thing" for me, but I don't think Cain believes me. Troy anchors his hands on his hips and glares at us.

"Come at me, bro," Cain says quietly.

"Okay, relax," I say with an eye roll. "He is *not* worth your time. Trust me. I can handle him."

"That was never in question," he mutters, releasing the wheel and cracking his neck, like he's limbering up for a fight. Maybe he wants someone to pick a fight with him, to help burn off the intensity of the aggression that rolls off him. Maybe he wants to kick some ass.

Shiver.

"Alright, fine. I'll have a car brought here within the hour, and I want you at my place at eight a.m. sharp tomorrow morning."

Well then. Someone likes to gain back control. Well played, Mr. Master.

I'll play along right back.

"Of course. And thank you."

"Don't forget to pack your clothes."

I bite down some snarky remarks and turn away from him so he doesn't see my eye roll.

"Yessiree," I mutter, as I swing my legs around toward my side of the truck. The clouds shift, and a stream of moonlight hits the ground beside it. I look up at the full, brilliant white moon, and a pang hits my heart. *Skylar*. Where is she? What's happening to her? Is she okay?

And she isn't even my sister. I can't begin to imagine what he's going through. He's learned how to school his features, how to hide his feelings. Years of service and what he's been through would do that to a person.

We'll find her.

I push open the truck door. Cain opens his mouth to say something, but I don't give him a chance.

"Thank you for everything," I say loudly, infusing a lilt of flirtation in my voice, as if he just brought me home after homecoming, for Troy's benefit. *Cringe.* "I'll see you in the morning."

He gives me a little finger wave but doesn't reply. He's focused instead on watching Troy.

"If this fucker gives you any trouble..." he begins in a low rumble.

"Kick him where the sun don't shine. On it." To be more accurate, I'd curse him out and call Candi, since I typically try not to get into any altercations with my landlord. I did that once, and things got a bit... messy. It's hard to find a new apartment mid-month.

I step down from the truck, and Cain yells from behind me, "Call me before you go to bed, baby!"

God. He's doing that fake boyfriend thing again. I shoot him a glare over my shoulder, but that only makes him do this deep, manly, sexy chuckle I feel straight between my legs. *Grrr!*

Troy stares. What the hell is his problem? "Tell your boyfriend he can't park there," he says, but once he catches sight of Cain, he starts to take a step backward. Smart move, asshole.

It's on the tip of my tongue to tell him he's not my boyfriend, but I think better of it. It might be good for word to get around I've got a boyfriend the size of Paul Bunyan, who drives a truck the size of Paul's big blue ox. I amuse myself with the memory of the fabled Paul Bunyan rolling over in his sleep and causing an earthquake, and digging out the Great Lakes by hand.

I fantasized about being friends with Paul Bunyan when I was a little girl, bullied by my foster parents and bullied at school. No one would bully a girl with a friend who was bigger than life.

I guess I never outgrew that.

As Cain's truck drives away, I square my shoulders and head inside.

I walk up the steps and grab my mail, and for once in my life my landlord doesn't give me shit or follow me. Thank you, Mr. Master. I did tell him I don't need help, and I don't, but I might as well take advantage when opportunity knocks.

Now that the sun has set, it's cooler, and even the humidity's lessened. My phone beeps. I look down to see a text from Candi.

Just checking to see if you're still alive.

I will be more alive after I get some food in my belly.

I'm so starving, my vision's blurred. I walk up the flight of stairs, open my apartment door, then shut it and deadbolt it behind me. I breathe a sigh of relief that I've somehow made it this far. We do breathing exercises when we train, and it comes naturally to me when I feel the tension along my neck and back.

Deep breath in. Release.

After everything that's happened the past few days, I feel like I need to scope my place out before I relax.

The kitchen looks untouched. Nothing out of place. I left everything locked up tighter than a drum, the windows shut and locked, the air conditioner on low. The kitchen's clear.

The bathroom's got a small, standing shower with a clear glass door, and it's easy to see it's vacant as well. Not a towel or tissue out of place.

I turn to leave the bathroom when a loud crash sounds behind me in my bedroom. I scream, swivel on my heel, and my knife's in my hand before I've stopped screaming. I stand in place, my hand trembling.

"Who's there? Come out! I swear to God, if you don't, I'll kill you!"

I walk into my bedroom. A light breeze flutters through an open window, a curtain dancing in the wind. No one's there.

That's odd. I never leave my window open. Why the hell would I forget this one?

I swing around and look at my closet, but it's wide open and so tiny, no one could fit in there if they tried. There's nowhere else to hide in my rinky-dink apartment.

Why the hell did I think this was a good idea again? *Why?*

Independence is so overrated.

There's a fucking serial rapist on the loose, and the guy I'm working for not only has an enormous kitchen stocked with food I saw with my very own eyes, he has things like security guards and guns. Big ones.

Not the only big thing he's got, I think to myself like a horny teen, but someone's got to break the tension, and I'm the only one here.

"Good one, Vi. Keep 'em rolling," I mutter to myself just to break the silence.

I walk around my room, suddenly angry that anyone's done anything at all to make me afraid, to think they can come into my goddamn house and hurt me. Blood pulses through my veins, boiling.

Come at me. Fight me. If even Cain Master himself took me on now, it would be a battle to the death.

"Who's there? Come out! Come show yourself to me!"

Nothing. Not a sound. I look on the floor as something catches my eye. A picture frame's fallen from my desk. The wind knocked it over, and here I am thinking I have a damn intruder.

I roll my eyes and pick it up. My doorbell buzzes.

Interesting. I go to the living room and push the intercom button, curious. "Yes?"

"Delivery for a Miss Price."

Delivery?

"What is it?"

"Sake and Sushi."

Sake and Sushi's the name of one of my favorite places to eat. "I didn't order Sake and Sushi," I say, even as my stomach growls and my mouth waters. I swallow hard. I *wish* that was my order.

"Delivery ordered from a Master Enterprises, ma'am."

No. He didn't!

"Come up."

I hit the buzzer, and a moment later, look through the peephole to find a delivery guy standing with an enormous takeout bag of food.

I open the door, and he hands me the bag. "Let me tip you—"

"Already been taken care of. Good night."

And off he goes.

The smell wafts through the air, and my knees wobble. I'm weak with hunger.

My phone buzzes with a text.

Cain.

I tap it, and a picture fills my screen. It's a stunning, hefty black SUV with chrome rims that gleam under the street-lights. Oh my God.

This is your company vehicle. It's been dropped off by your front door and I'm sending you an attachment with a digital key. Once you open it, you'll find the physical key in the glovebox, entry code your birthday. You'll have a gas card as well and unlimited mileage.

Okay, Mr. Master, what's the catch?

No response at first.

Most people say thank you, Miss Price.

I'm not most people. What goes up must come down and all that.

The catch is, I still want your ass at my place in the morning for target practice.

And?

And nothing. I'm assuming you'll do the work I asked you to do tonight, and that's all. Enjoy your dinner.

Thank you.

My hand hovers over the little smiley face emoji, but on second thought I don't send it. I have to stay strong. I can't let him wine and dine me.

Mouth watering, I open the takeout bag to find a small pile of white cardboard boxes. I swallow. Oh my God, there's enough food here for an army. Vegetable tempura, lightly breaded and fried until golden brown, skewers of savory beef and chicken teriyaki, steamed rice with their signature veggies fresh from their rooftop garden, shrimp and rice, delicate rows of spring rolls, and a variety of fresh, decadent sushi, neatly nestled in pretty silver trays.

Candi's got a night shift, and I don't know anyone else close enough to share this with. Ah, well. Breakfast, lunch, and dinner for the next week, and I am *not* complaining.

I eat standing up right at the counter, savoring every decadent morsel.

"My God, food this good should not even be legal," I mutter to myself around a mouthful of shrimp tempura as I open up the laptop and fire it up.

I've got work to do.

I start with the notes on my phone.

When I'm good and stuffed, I package up the leftover food and slide it into my fridge, my mind teeming with the knowledge I've gleaned.

Precisely thirteen victims since June.

God. It's worse than I thought.

Several eyewitnesses insist they saw the same man with a string of victims before they went missing, but things aren't adding up.

"I know it was him," one father said about his daughter's kidnapper. "He fits this exact profile."

Who? The profile fits a man by the name of Derrick Dossier, a former police officer, retired from the force at the age of forty-nine. Some sources even found his DNA at the crime scene and on victims, which normally is strong evidence to convict. But every single time, there was undeniable evidence that Dossier had an ironclad alibi, most with video and photographic evidence. And since humans are unable to bi-locate, he was let off despite overwhelming evidence against him.

I look at my notes, wishing I hadn't eaten that last piece of shrimp. My stomach's in knots.

ANITA CHARLES

Age: 18

Taken August 1, found dead August 4th.

Clear victim of repeated rape. Bruises found along inner thighs and anus, lesions throughout the body.

Note: Sources say she received bouquets left at her door several days before she was taken.

MARGARET *Sellier*

Age: 19

Taken August 5th, found dead August 7th

Raped multiple times. Bruised and subjected to beatings. Broken bones and teeth.

Note: Sources say there were fresh flowers at her residence when she was taken.

· · ·

CLAIR BOYD

Age: 18

Taken August 8th. Survivor.

Has no memory of abuse but shows signs of repeated rape and abuse. Trauma amnesia.

Note: No flowers on record

I SPEND the next two hours scrolling through every bit of social media involving the girls that I can, as well as every report I can get my hands on.

Anita left home at the age of sixteen and was estranged from her parents as well as her siblings. She came from a religious home and had nine brothers and sisters. "She left us for the occult," her mother's on record as saying. "I knew things would end like this. I knew she'd be taken by the Devil for her sins."

A lump rises in my throat, reminding me of the minister's wife who rejected me. I don't know how some people live with themselves in the name of something that should be good.

Anita has a mere twelve followers online, and the news said no one came to her funeral.

Strange.

I flip through her pictures, not surprised to see she classifies herself as Wiccan, but has very few friends. There are patterns like the pieces to a puzzle scattered on a table, beginning to take form but still just a jumble of cardboard. I need to fit more pieces into place before I can see the whole picture.

Margaret Sellier has a similar story. Left home at eighteen, got a double associates degree from a local community college. But reports say she was "strange" and "odd." Further investigation shows she was known for resisting mainstream culture, publicly and vocally.

I pace my apartment. Thinking.

If I were someone looking to take advantage of women... I would want to take someone no one would miss. It would cover my tracks if I took someone who might be involved with things their family didn't approve of, so said family might blame their social groups or behavior on their disappearance...

It's after midnight when I close my laptop and go to shower. I strip my clothes off halfway down the hall and toss them into the hamper just before I get to the bathroom. I wish I could cleanse what I've read from my mind, but I'm determined now. I will find the person responsible for these crimes.

A pang of guilt hits me.

I haven't thought about finding my parents' murderers in hours. I haven't gone that long without thinking about them in... God, years.

I tell myself this is only a means to an end. Help him, and he'll help me. I'm only working with him for this one reason, so I can leverage his power and connections.

I put the water on to scalding and glance down at myself. God, I'm a mess. Between the stupid accident and bruising my shins all to hell today on Cain's car, I'm covered in bruises and lacerations and smudges of dirt. How could that guy hit on me?

Did he hit on me?

I stare at myself in the mirror, just before the steam fogs it up entirely. My body may be damaged, but my eyes are the same vivid shade of violet as ever.

I should maybe get those color-changing contacts. If I'm on the hunt for someone, they'll remember a girl with eyes like mine.

I text Cain. I bet he'll be able to get them quicker than I will.

> Hey, I know it's late, hopefully you do the 'do not disturb' after a certain hour thing

The response is immediate.

> Everything okay?

Guess he doesn't.

My heart thumps. I probably woke the guy up, and his first question is, am I okay? This is *after* he bought me dinner and *a car*.

And after he tried to boss you around and showed absolutely no respect for your self-respect or autonomy. NO THANK YOU.

> I'm fine, but I wondered if you

I pause mid-text, trying to figure out how to word my question just right. My finger is hovering over the phone when my eyes graze the windowsill in my bedroom. I'm on the second floor near the fire escape. The breeze still flutters the curtains at the window, only now the windowsill isn't empty.

A sprig of purple irises sits on the ledge.

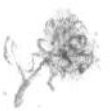

CHAPTER NINE

____

Cain

I WATCH the little dots on the screen dance, then stop, dance, then stop. I asked her if she's okay and expected a quick response, probably something snarky like,

> Fine, just polishing my guns. You?
>
> All good, haven't found any strange men lying in wait or abductees behind my shower curtain, how bout you?
>
> I'm fine, you can call off the babysitters now.

I sent her a car, but I sent a small team to watch her, too. If she's right about the asshole being after her, I don't want to take any chances.

A minute passes. Two. Three.

No response.

I'm in my bedroom in shorts and a tank after a shower, prepared to do whatever work I can through the night. I've got a team ready to be briefed in the morning and people working around the clock already.

I go to text her, then stop. Then again. Finally, I decide the hell with it, and shoot her another text.

> Hey. You were typing and now nothing. Everything alright?

No response.

I pick up my phone and call Henri, the head of the team I sent to her apartment. His phone rings and goes to voicemail.

No response.

I pull on shoes and grab a jacket, slipping it on as I leave my room.

"Everything alright?" Joe asks me when I hit the foyer at a jog. I fill him in.

"You think she's in danger?"

"After today? Not something I wanna risk."

I should've duct taped her to her seat and made her come home with me.

"I'll join you. You taking the Audi?" His eyes gleam, hoping I am.

"Hell yes."

The truck is good for an ambush, for safety, for a potential shoot-out. But when I have to get somewhere *fast*? I take the

Audi. It goes from zero to sixty in 2.8 seconds and drives up to two hundred seventeen miles per hour. It's swift, takes corners with agility, but is small and sleek enough not to cause too much attention if I'm careful.

Her apartment is twenty-five minutes away according to GPS. We'll get there in ten.

"What are you packing?" Joe asks. We step into the room we affectionately call the armory, where our weapons are securely and discreetly stored.

"Ruger and a blade. You?"

The Ruger EC9 functions as one of the best compact concealed pistols money can buy, small and sleek but lethal.

"EC9. Which blade?"

"MK3." I take it from its sheath and give it a quick look-over. "Are there any others?" The Ontario MK3's a standard Navy SEAL weapon, six inches of hardened steel perfection finished with a solid, ergonomic handle that doesn't slip. It hides as easily as a shadow but cuts hard and deep and fast.

I won't be throwing my blade like Violet.

Goddammit, I never should've let her stay at her own place.

I should've insisted. I should've reasoned better with her. Instead, I let her have her way, and now what?

I call security again but get nothing.

"Swear to God," I mutter under my breath. "If they don't have a good reason not to pick up this phone..."

I don't finish the sentence. Joe blanches and looks out the window as I drive so damn fast, rocks fly behind us, the ground whizzing past in a blur. I call Violet and Henri one at a time, over and over.

My phone buzzes with a text. I look quickly at the screen, but it isn't any of the people I want to hear from.

> Armand: Boss, I think I found something of importance.

I don't respond. I don't have time for his bullshit right now. I would've fired him if I hadn't gotten distracted by Skylar's abduction.

"Tomorrow, you fire Armand's ass," I tell Joe.

He freezes but doesn't respond at first. I look over at him, and he seems to snap out of his stupor. "Armand?"

"Yes."

"Yes, sir. Will do."

I fill him in on everything, even why I'm here to check on her.

"Just so we're clear, sir. She was texting you, you asked if she was okay, and she didn't respond."

"Correct."

He seems to be mulling this over.

"Could she... have fallen asleep?"

I curse under my breath and push the gas pedal deeper. The roads whiz by us like they're on speed.

"If she did," I say with measured patience, "we'll leave well enough alone."

Again, he doesn't say anything but the silently raised eyebrows say it for him. He thinks I've lost my fucking mind.

He can think that, as long as he does what I tell him.

We're two minutes out when my phone buzzes again. I growl, glancing at the screen to see another text from Armand.

It's important, I think you should know

Jesus.

"Text Armand, tell him I'm driving, and ask him what the hell is going on that's so urgent."

Joe scowls and mutters a "yessir," already texting. No response at first. I pull up to Violet's house and park at the corner.

"You see anything?"

"No. You?"

I shake my head.

"But you don't know if it's one person or several we're looking for, what they look like..." his voice trails off.

"Correct."

A woman laughs on the other side of an open window, and a few teens sit on the stoop licking ice cream cones. A dog barks in the distance, and someone's lighting off fireworks a few blocks away. It looks just like any typical late summer night.

I walk up to her front door when the dumbass we saw earlier comes out. He's unsteady on his feet. Drunk.

"Ahh, Violet's lover," he says. Joe looks at me sharply.

"I'm her boss." She'd kill me for that, but she'd kill me faster for pretending to be her man. I'm not playing games right now.

"Right, like that matters," the asshole says with a snicker. "Why are you back?"

"I need to get into her apartment." There's no way on God's green earth he's going to make this easy on me. He'll need to be persuaded.

"And?"

"And I need you to let me upstairs."

He smirks at me and leans against the railing. "Can't do that without the pretty lady's say so. How do I know you didn't get into a fight and you're using me to get to her?"

Joe glances at me, ready to spring into action. I shake my head at him.

I want him all to myself.

Every second that passes places her in greater danger than before. The asshole that took those women moves fast, and I'm not fucking around.

In two seconds, I've got him by the collar, and I yank him inside the entryway where no one can see us. My MK3's pushed up to his neck, a bead of blood coloring the blade.

"Hey, man!" he says, panicking like a girl. "Hey!"

"Let me in and do it now. You do not call the cops unless you want a building inspector here by Monday. I've got connections in places you really, *really* don't want to go and will have this place condemned before you can wipe your ass."

I press the knife harder, drawing more blood.

"Jesus! Go!" he says in a strangled voice, stepping aside and handing me a set of keys. "Her key's the purple one, 208."

I toss him to Joe. "You escort him out of here and make sure he doesn't cause trouble."

Joe's grin is chilling, even to me. "My pleasure."

I take the stairs two at a time, listening. Something crashes inside her apartment. I double-time it.

She's got a deadbolt on the door, and I can't open it. It's reinforced steel, no goddamn way I can knock it down. I grab the key and shove it in the lock, then unfasten the deadbolt. The door falls open. I enter, Ruger in hand, and kick the door shut behind me.

My gaze slashes across her kitchen. Nothing.

Living room. Nothing.

Goddamn it, if I find her asleep in bed after all this—

I hear a scream and a growl, and I take off at a run down the hall. I try the door to her bedroom and find that locked, too. Too many keys on this goddamn key ring to find the right one, but this door's a basic wooden one.

I come at it full force, my shoulder slamming into it. Once. Twice. On the third hit, I knock it down, and it splinters like kindling. Violet turns to look at me, a pink handprint across her cheek and blood streaming down the side of her face. The hand holding her knife shakes. A curtain on her window flutters in the breeze.

"He got away!"

No.

I'll kill him.

Her voice quakes, her hand's trembling. I fight the need to hold her, to make sure she's okay, that she isn't hurt worse than it looks, but I can't let the fucker get away. I move past her and crane my neck out the window, just in time to see red brake lights on a small Mazda as it peels around the corner.

"*Motherfucker.* Did you see him?"

She nods, her eyes filling with tears, and she swipes them angrily away. "I did. It's the guy I found tonight in my search, the same goddamn guy they suspect for all those crimes but haven't been able to prove."

Okay, alright. She'll come back to my place, and we'll clean her up and find out what she knows. Who he is. We'll make sure she's okay.

"You're not safe here."

She winces. When she blinks, a tear rolls down her cheek, mingling with the blood. *Fuck.* "I had him. I fucking *had him*," she says.

"Are you hurt?"

"No," she says, vibrating with anger. "I'm *furious*."

It's anger, then, that makes her cry.

She could be in shock. She could be injured. We've got more evidence now so we can track him down and find him, but first I have to make sure she's okay.

"Sit down."

She looks from me to the window, then back again. With effort, I gentle my voice. "Sit. Please."

It kills me to see those eyes of hers filled with tears. She cries, letting the tears go unchecked, and finally sits down. I don't realize until I kneel in front of her that I'm shaking.

"Oh God, you've got... you came in with a knife and a gun?"

I look down to see my Ruger in one hand and my MK3 in the other. I lay them down.

"Yeah, I have a tendency to overdo shit," I say, just to calm her down. If the motherfucker was in front of me now, I would wish I had more than this on me. "You alright? Do you need immediate medical attention?"

She stretches for a tissue from her bedside table but doesn't quite reach it. I hand her one silently.

"No, I'm okay." She continues to swipe angrily at the tears.

I want to kiss her, blood and sweat and tears and all. I want to haul her up into my arms and carry her away from this shitty apartment, bring her to my place, and treat her to the lap of luxury. I want her body to soften underneath me, to yield to everything and anything I want to do to her. But I can't do that to her. I can't do that *for* her. She's the type of woman who'd feel belittled if I treated her that way.

We'll get there.

I need to make her feel safe. I need her to trust me.

"Alright, woman." I reach for the box of tissues and place it beside her. "Tell me everything."

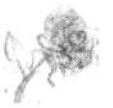

CHAPTER TEN

I'M SO angry with myself I could cry. Hell, I realize when I swipe my hand across my eyes and find my fingers covered in blood and tears... I *am* crying.

Arrggh. *I do not cry.*

The only time I *do* cry is when my anger doesn't have an outlet. I ball up the tissues he hands me, desperate for some sort of release.

He's gone off to the bathroom to fetch a first aid kit and returns with a frown and the tiny plastic generic kit I got at a discount store. "You call this a first aid kit?"

I roll my eyes at him. "I don't usually get into a knife fight with intruders, Mr. Master. I get bruises from training and things like *paper cuts*. Like normal people."

His eyes gentle as he kneels in front of me again, and I'm momentarily struck by the enormity of this. He's so huge, even when he kneels, his head nearly comes to my shoulders. But something tells me he isn't a guy that kneels very often.

"Normal? Violet, you're anything but normal."

I like my name on his lips, like spiced honey. I snort out loud to cover the way my heart speeds up. "As *if.*"

He quirks a brow at me and doesn't take the bait.

"So let's hear it."

"Okay, so I came home and I did inspect the place. Promise. Everywhere. And yes, Mr. Master, like a good girl I checked every room to make sure no one was here, and the coast was clear."

"Very good. And call me Cain."

I want to reach to his chin and run my finger along the stubble. Make him look at me. Instead, he's fumbling through the kit and pulling things out.

"Cain." I like the feel of his name in my mouth. "You're named after the world's first murderer."

A wry smile ghosts across his lips before he sobers again. "Something my mother never let me forget."

"It was intentional, then?"

"Yes." A flicker crosses his gaze before he shutters it again. "Now back to the story, Miss Price."

I want to hear him say my name, the word like a seductive caress.

"No more Miss Price either, please."

"Alright, Violet." Such a small thing, hearing my name from him, but the way he says it sounds like a poem. He lines up gauze, antibacterial wipes, and bandages. "Now. Everything."

I speak quickly. We need to move. I know more about who might have his sister, and I don't want to waste any more time.

"After I knew no one was here, I used the bathroom, when I heard a crash." Those eyes of his are fixed on me with an intensity that I feel straight to my belly. "I came in here to check, but there was no one here. The window was open, and a curtain was kinda blowing with the wind, but the room was empty."

"Did you open the window?"

"No. I looked out the window and saw no one. Nothing at all. I assumed I'd forgotten to close it and went out to the kitchen."

He makes a noise that sounds like a growl, but waits for me to continue. For a big, grumpy guy he can be patient when he wants to be.

I give him a curious look. "Wait, how did you know what I liked?"

"Stick with the story, please. You answer my questions first, then I'll answer yours." He tears open a gauze pad and gently swipes across my temple. He pulls it away stained in blood. I continue.

"I texted you, and then when I turned around there were irises on my windowsill."

"That weren't there before."

"No."

The savage cruelty I saw in his eyes when I first met him returns. I draw in a ragged breath. I look into his clear, sapphire eyes that glimmer like ice, the same frigid eyes that pulled the trigger next to a man's temple today without remorse. He watched that man crumple to the floor without blinking, then called for his team.

It was apparent to me from the moment I met him that fury and power war within him. He's only played nice for a little while.

Today I saw the real Cain Master.

With military precision, he slides a bandage open, then cradles the back of my head. The whole base of my skull fits easily in his cupped palm. With gentle pressure, he pulls me toward him as he puts the bandage on my cut. My breath catches at how gentle and careful he is, like he knows I'm injured and can't bear to cause me any more pain.

If only he knew.

I shiver.

His heavy brows draw over his eyes, and his mouth forms a thin, angry line.

"Go on."

He opens another antiseptic packet and lifts my hand in his. My hand looks so small engulfed in his much larger hands. Mine are bleeding. I don't remember why. The adrenaline and fear blinded me.

I draw in a shaky breath as he wipes the grit and blood from my hands. It stings, but I don't let myself flinch. "After I saw the flowers, I put my phone down. I considered calling you. I decided I was going to drive to your place after all, and when I came into my room, someone hit me."

He lets loose a string of curses.

I want to find the man who attacked me. I want to find him, and I want to kill him. I want him to pay for everything he's done. So I speed up my story.

"I felt the blow and blocked on instinct with a slip." It was drilled into me how to block a kick or punch, arms up to defend the face while squatting to block the gut.

He nods.

"When he was on the downswing, I turned and jabbed him straight in the gut."

"Did you get any names in your research?"

"Just Derrick Dossier, the man suspected but released on the rape and abduction charges."

Cain picks up his phone and makes a call. "I want you to get everything you can on Derrick Dossier. Report on my desk within the hour." He doesn't even wait for a response but hangs up his phone and shoves it back in his pocket.

"This motherfucker's playing us. He's after you and may have my sister. We can't fuck around anymore, Violet."

There's my name again.

"Yeah. I'm coming back with you. We need to put our heads together. Pool resources."

He narrows his eyes. "What a novel concept. Pack a fucking bag."

"Do you ever say please?"

He looks down, his eyes on my shins. I'm wearing a pair of shorts, my legs on full display. Angry purple bruises mark my shins from earlier.

"Did you get these from my truck?"

"Yeah, your truck can be pretty damn aggressive."

He lifts one of my legs in his hands, cradling it just like he did my head. My heart beats faster at the rough feel of his hands on my skin and the way his brows draw together angrily, his mouth pressed tightly in a harsh frown. That focused, steady gaze unwavering.

He bends. My breath freezes. In shock, I don't breathe when he places a tender kiss on my legs, his lips brushing across the black and blue so tenderly it's barely more than a whisper. When I start breathing again, I'm acutely aware of the sound.

We don't speak. Seconds tick by, the only sounds in the room are my heavier breathing and his gentle, fluttering kisses across my skin.

If he looks at me, there's no turning back. If his eyes meet mine, I can't tell him no.

He lets me go. I shiver at the loss of his warmth.

He stands and walks away from me.

I'm saved.

Then why do I feel so disappointed?

"I'm sorry. We have to get out of here. On second thought, you're not packing. I'll buy you whatever you need. We're leaving now, and you'll tell me the rest of what happened on the way back."

"I can pack in less than a minute." I'm already on my way to the closet. I need to walk away from him.

He grumbles but uses the time to toss the bandage wrappers away. I grab a quilted backpack Candi gave me from the back of my closet and quickly shove folded clothes, underwear, a pair of sneakers, and my phone in the bag. He's waiting for me, his arms crossed over his chest. "Can you find the little pink bottle of lotion on the bedside table, please?"

I need to distract him so he doesn't see what I grab next. *No one* sees that, not even Candi.

"I can get you as many little pink bottles of lotion as your heart desires, let's go."

"That's a special one, it was for Candi's bachelorette party."

I got it as a freebie in the mail. I hope he doesn't see through the lie.

Another grumble, but he fetches it just in time. I yank the zipper on my bag closed and get to my feet.

"You had a guard here, didn't you?"

"Yes."

"I didn't need—"

"You fucking did, and he better have a good excuse as to

why he didn't do his goddamn job." He slams the drawer closed and turns to stalk over to me.

I could never, *ever* be with a man like him. *Do this, do that.* He's about as supple as a steel rod, and I have to remember that.

They call him the executioner.

I can't let the gentle side of him mess with my mind. That's where women go wrong. They know in their heart a guy's no good for them. They *know* it. Yet something he does makes them forget all logic and they believe the stupid lie that they have a magical pussy that somehow cures all, that he won't ever drink/steal/lie again, or whatever the heck they tell themselves.

I won't let that happen.

When my mind wants to replay the feel of his full, hot lips on my aching skin, I shove it away. When my brain wants me to remember that he came to find me, that I didn't respond to his text and he knew I was in trouble and he *came for me,* I don't let myself dwell.

He's dangerous, ruthless, and arrogant, and so bad for me he's poison.

Poison.

When we exit the building, I try to hide my fear. Logically, I know there is no madman waiting for me outside, but it still feels like there could be.

I don't miss how he walks beside me. His razor-sharp gaze notes everything. If there's anyone here to try to take me now, they'd better have backup, a hand grenade, and a cannon, because no one's getting me without a declaration of war.

The ride back to his house hurts like *hell*.

"You've got ibuprofen back at that mansion, right?" I mutter, my head falling on the seat behind me. My eyes close.

"No sleeping," Cain snaps. My eyes fly back open.

"You really are a slave driver!"

That gets Joe's attention, but he doesn't say anything.

"You can't sleep now. You could have a concussion."

"Fine. But God, am I tired. How long do I have to stay awake?"

"Until the doctor gives you clearance."

"Oh God. I'm gonna need a coffee. Double shot of espresso, straight up."

"Need me to stop and get some?"

I sigh. "No. I don't drink coffee."

He shakes his head.

"What?"

He changes the subject. "Back to what happened."

"So I got him with a jab. I believe that's where we left off."

"You have a mean jab," Joe chimes in.

I stare at him. He's never seen me fight.

"How do you know?"

He shrugs and laughs. "I can just tell. You're a fighter. Little fireplug."

He's lying. I look at Cain, but his face is a mask of stone.

"I threw a jab and he fell back, and he would've gotten me but I aimed a very, *very* well-placed kick to his crotch that was *meant* to incapacitate him. And that was when everything began to go wrong."

Cain sighs and accelerates.

"This car is gorgeous, by the way. *Stunning,* with this all-leather interior. Are these heated seats?"

"Yes. Thank you. Get back to the story."

"There's not much more to tell. He rebounded, slapped me across the face so hard I bit my lip, and we literally brawled. I tried to pull my knife, but I was too slow, and by the time I got it out..." I sigh. I hate this part of the story. "He was out the window and onto the fire escape."

Cain frowns. "He slapped you?"

I nod. Of all those details I just told him, that's what he thinks about? "Yeah."

His back goes rigid.

"Remember I said you'll be at my place at eight a.m.? Now that order's null and void, since you're coming back with me."

Order? I think sometimes he forgets he's not my commander.

"Yesss...?"

Where's he going with this?

"Scratch that. Tomorrow morning at seven a.m., unless we have a breakthrough and find something we need to pursue, you'll get your first lesson in how to handle a gun."

I stifle a squeal. I've wanted to learn how to shoot a gun forever but haven't taken the time to do it.

"You have a trainer?"

He frowns, those glacial eyes glancing my way before he looks back to the road. "Yeah."

Joe chuckles softly. Is this an inside joke or something?

"Did you find anything before all this happened?" Cain asks, and his eyes meet mine in the rearview mirror. Something like camaraderie flashes between us, so quickly I wonder if it's my imagination.

He doesn't like that I was alone in the apartment and attacked. He wishes he was there.

Why does it excite me to imagine what would've happened if he was?

I should be appalled that he shot a man today. Without remorse. Without hesitation.

I'm not, though. In fact, quite the opposite.

It's the single most attractive thing he's done since I've met him. He's the man who could help me, and will.

What on earth does a guy like him find attractive about a girl like me? *What?*

Maybe I need to play into this. Maybe, if he were attracted to me...

No.

No, no, no. I've gotten this far without whoring myself out, and I won't start now.

Something tells me he'd make it worth my while...

"You mean, did I do any research? Damn right I did, and I have a list of leads we need to pursue as soon as possible. Has anyone contacted you about your sister?"

"No."

"Have you checked all your social media accounts and email and phone number?"

Again, the flash of stunning blue in the mirror. "Check my social media?"

"Do you... have social media?"

"No."

"Well, that makes things simpler."

I look out the window and Joe chuckles again, so softly I barely hear him, but the sound is unmistakable. What's so funny?

"When we get back, you'll see the doctor and we'll make sure you meet with my team. We'll combine what we've found so far." He glances in his rearview mirror again, but he doesn't look at me this time.

"Someone following us?"

A long gaze in the mirror again, and he finally shakes his head. "No."

The interior of the car is a soft, matte black leather, luxurious and decadent. The carpet's pristine, the windows and chrome details like new. More notable is the way it drives, though, so seamlessly you don't know it's accelerating until the world flies by you. So sleek, it cuts through the air with military precision.

"Is this your getaway car?"

"It is."

"The next time you rob a bank, I'll be your getaway driver."

"What's your going rate?"

"Oh, for you, I'd cut you a break and let it go for a cool mil."

He nods, as if thinking this over. "You're right. I *would* consider that a good deal."

"Take him for two," Joe chimes in over his shoulder. Cain almost smiles. His lips thin before the smile reaches his eyes.

Almost.

"So this is how you got to my place so quickly. You must've been driving like over a hundred miles an hour."

He doesn't reply, only gives me a slow, lazy shrug, like driving at the speed of light is seriously no big deal.

"So why so much slower now?"

He doesn't answer. Joe speaks up from the passenger seat. "We've got cargo now."

Cargo?

Oh.

Oh.

Me. I'm cargo.

Well then.

I think as a woman I should be offended by that, but some-how, I feel it's almost sweet.

And it's definitely something I could use to my advantage.

It's warm and comfortable here. I lean back against the seat, my senses overwhelmed with the rich scent of leather. I took ibuprofen from the first aid kit before we left to dull the pain, and it's kicked in, my bruises and scrapes no longer throbbing.

I've had bullshit luck with this kinda thing lately. Between the accident and this, I'm almost ready for a nice, boring day in the office—

Who'm I kidding? I'd stab myself in the eye with a pencil.

What I'm really ready for is some adventure that doesn't involve Violet Price, punching bag, as the main attraction.

I'm floating, and it's comfortable here, and for once in a very, very long time, I know that no one's going to hurt me.

"Do *not* fall asleep!"

I snap to attention, my eyes flying open. The next second, a surge of adrenaline powers through me and I glare at Cain in the rearview mirror.

"I'm not sleeping."

"You aren't *now*."

I can't believe I ever thought of seducing a guy like him. I would strangle him in his sleep.

We pull into the long driveway that leads to his garage. The house is alight. His team's awake.

I want to sleep. I was exhausted *before* all this, and now I'm at the point of no return. I'm so tired I could cry.

I open the door and shiver with a gust of night wind. I wrap my arms around myself and follow them both into the house.

It's different tonight than it was earlier today. Tonight, even though it's way past midnight, the place is teeming with people. Even Alma, his housekeeper, is in the kitchen in her robe, putting a kettle on the stove.

"Good evening," she says to me pleasantly. "Tea? Coffee?"

"Tea would be great, thank you."

In the kitchen, right up next to the counter, are large, padded, spindle chairs. They're so fun, they make me want to play music on a jukebox and wear a poodle skirt. But right now, every one of them is occupied by one of Cain's employees.

A bowl of popcorn, nothing left but kernels, sits on one side of the counter, and on the other, there's a large platter of cheese and a fruit tray pretty well picked over beside empty pizza boxes and energy drink empties. Laptops and note-books are scattered about, and in one corner of the room, a series of monitors are set up.

Cain grabs a mug. Strange he doesn't let his house help get it.

Something's changed between us. Something... shifted... from the very first moment his lips touched my skin back in my apartment.

Hell, it was before that.

From the very first time I stared into his eyes after he'd ended a man's life.

"How do you take your tea?"

"Dash of milk, please."

He places it in front of me while the milk still swirls, and I sip. It's so hot it scalds the roof of my mouth, but somehow it's exactly what I need right now. I wrap my hands around the ceramic mug, the heat of it warming me through. One small comfort on a day fraught with violence.

Cain clears his throat. The room stills.

"For those who haven't met her yet, this is Violet Price, a new contractor who will be working for Master Enterprises in the short-term. Violet's skilled in kickboxing and knife throwing, speaks multiple languages, and will be a valuable asset to our team."

I look around the small group. The man who hit my car last night isn't here.

A few of them murmur greetings and some nod to me.

"Violet and I are in pursuit of someone we believe kidnapped my sister. We have reason to believe the man's a serial rapist who intends on abusing, possibly even fatally hurting, Skylar and that the same person has hinted at coming after her next. Tonight, she had an intruder in her apartment. She'll be here indefinitely, while we search for Skylar."

I take another sip of tea, not quite as hot now as it was before.

"Violet, are you in a position where you are ready to talk?" Cain gives me a curious look. I don't know what he means. Why wouldn't I be in a position to talk?

I look at him in surprise, as I finish my mug of tea and place it on the counter. His housekeeper scoops it up with a smile and stashes it in the dishwasher before I've put my hand back in my lap.

Okay, I could totally see why having a housekeeper is a good thing.

"What do you mean?"

He crosses the room to me, all fluid grace and muscle despite his bulk, and leans across the counter on his arm, speaking in a low rumble. "You okay? Or do you need some time to yourself?"

"I'm fine," I lie, my voice distant while my heart beats a thunderous beat in my chest. I can handle his arrogance and anger, but concern... now that's another story.

He nods. "Then why don't you fill us in."

CHAPTER ELEVEN

Violet

AN HOUR LATER, we wrap up for the night. Cain calls it "taking a break," giving me a good idea of what it's like to work with him. I'm not surprised, though. With his background, he's used to working in godawful conditions at any hour he needs.

I saw the doctor, a rather short, stocky woman with wiry black hair graying at the temples and thick, round glasses. She was brief. She pronounced me banged up but otherwise unharmed, her examination taking place around me talking over her shoulder at the guys.

"Someone already bandaged you up pretty well," she said. When I told her it was Cain, she didn't respond.

His team has a list of details to investigate, and we're trying to get a read on Dossier. I want to stay up and help, but my eyes feel so heavy I can hardly keep them open.

We have work to do. I have to let his team handle it.

I gave them my information. I don't want to put this down right now, but I can hardly keep my damn eyes open.

The bartender told us they were going to Canada. A lie, maybe?

Derrick Dossier has no listed address, no job that we can find, and virtually nothing to lead us to where we might find him. Honestly, the rest of the details begin to meld into my brain. I'm so tired, I feel like I'm starting to short-circuit.

Cain's standing by Joe, his arms crossed on his chest. I'm behind him on one of the stools, trying to sit upright before I keel right over. He looks over his shoulder at me, then turns around and faces me.

"You need to get to bed."

I yawn widely and want to protest like a small, petulant child. *I'm not tired.* But I'm no good to anyone if I can't see straight.

"Yeah."

I go to pick up my bag, but he reaches for it and swings it over his shoulder. I'm in no mood to fight with him, so I let him. Without a word, he slides his hand over the small of my back.

A moment ago I felt like I could fall asleep and not wake up until Christmas. Now, I'm suddenly very, very awake.

We were pretending earlier that I meant something to him. Why's he doing this now? A part of me wants to pull away, and another part of me realizes that stumbling right now would only make me look foolish.

"This way," he says, like the only reason he's got his hand on my back is so he can show me where to go.

Very interesting, Mr. Master. Very interesting indeed.

He leads me to a staircase I've only seen from a distance. I stare at the steep, hardwood stairs and briefly consider asking if he'll let me sling myself up on his back, but that seems kinda desperate, and I don't even have the energy to do that.

When he takes his hand off my back, I wobble a little. I'm vaguely aware of him frowning at me. I push myself to move, to put one foot in front of the other, but every step feels like my feet are getting heavier.

Finally, we reach the top of the stairs. My vision blurs as he steps to the left. "This way."

In my mind's eye, his voice is the low rumble of volcanoes churning. I follow the rumble automatically.

"Why so far?" I ask, my words slurred. I'd sleep on the damn landing at this point. That carpet looks pretty inviting.

"Just about there," he says almost gently, in that tone he used earlier. "I want your room near mine."

Of course he does.

He stops short, and like an idiot, I don't stop in time. I crash into his back like I've just learned how to walk. He turns and catches me as I wobble on my feet.

"Sorry."

"Christ, woman," he says in a low rumble. Without a word, he does what I wanted him to do but had been too proud to ask. He bends, then effortlessly lifts me, my feet dangling and my head lolling to the side on his chest.

"Well, this is a nice office perk." I sound like I'm drunk.

That earns me another grumble.

The door to the room is open, but I hardly notice. My senses are on overload, and every damn detail is filled with *him*. The masculine scent of him, raw and primal. The broad stretch of his muscled shoulders exposed because he's wearing a tank, his stubble thicker now that it's so late in the day. The heavy sound of his breathing.

Can he hear how fast my heart beats? Can he feel the way my skin heats?

Can he see the flush that creeps over my body because we're touching?

I'm intoxicated from lack of sleep and adrenaline from all the events of the day.

I try to keep my body erect so my head doesn't snuggle up in that hollow of his neck like I want it to. "You're crossing a line here, you know."

"Doing what?"

Thump goes my heart. "Touching me."

A beat passes before he responds. "I know." It's dark in here save for the yellowed pool of a nightlight beside the bed, but even with the shades drawn and lights dimmed, I can tell this room's outfitted in luxury. I don't care.

He could have had one of his men show me the way. He could have pointed or gestured or even just walked beside me.

I need him. I need what his team can do for me. I have to make sure I don't say or do anything that jeopardizes what I need.

He's still holding me. I'm barely breathing, afraid if I move too quickly, I'll wake and find I was only dreaming.

Men don't touch women like me, and those that even think about it face the consequences.

I want him to know it's okay, or maybe I just want to assure myself.

So I reach my hand to his jaw and do what I wanted to from the first time I saw him. I lay my hand on his stubbled jaw, thrilled at the prickly feel.

"I'll help you find your sister," I whisper.

Heat flares in his eyes. "You will. And we'll find your parents' killers."

I swallow, not sure what else to say.

I have to get ahold of myself.

"You could put me down, now." My voice doesn't sound like my own, all breathy and whispery yet somehow husky. I feel... *sexy.*

How does he make me feel sexy?

"I could."

Still, he doesn't.

I want him to kiss me, but there's no telling what will happen if he does.

Just a kiss, I taunt myself. *What harm could come from a kiss?*

His eyes spark at me, like he's reading my mind. Maybe he can, I think in my sleepy state. He's already larger than life and fearless. It only makes sense that he has superhuman abilities too.

I feel as if I'm standing on the edge of a precipice. One gust of wind, and I'll plummet to my death.

But I've always been more afraid of complacency than taking chances.

Slowly, so slowly at first I think it's my woozy, exhausted imagination, he bends his head a bit closer to me. I stare at his full, gorgeous lips, and imagine what it would be like to lick and bite them. I wonder what he tastes like.

Fire licks through me.

My eyes rove over his stubble, then down to his neck. I watch him swallow. The cuts he sustained are no longer bleeding, but the skin's an angry red between his collarbone and neck.

"You're hurt," I say in a hushed tone. And before I know what I'm doing, my hands are at his neck to anchor myself and I'm pulling myself closer to him. My lips meet his skin, kissing it better. I feel like I could cry.

The energy between the two of us crackles and sizzles. I tremble at his nearness, at his scent. I want to *taste* him.

I close my eyes and go for broke. I lick where I just kissed.

The groan he utters lashes through me as his grip tightens. I suckle his skin. I want more. *I need* more. I swear I feel the *snap* as his resolve breaks.

His mouth is so close I can feel his breath. I'm on the bed. I don't even know how I got here. He kneels beside me, the bed sagging under his weight.

Strong fingers grasping my chin, he lifts my mouth from his neck, and for one heart-stopping moment, I don't know what terrifies me more—the thought of him kissing me or the thought of him turning away.

His fingers tangle in my hair as if to prove to himself that I'm real, that I can't get away from him. I watch his lips part. My heart slams against my rib cage... then his mouth meets mine and my thoughts come to a stuttering, screeching halt as my brain short-circuits and I fall fully into my body.

Like everything about Cain Master, his kiss is *too much.*

Too much everything.

My heart beats too fast, my breathing's too ragged, my body's on *fire* just from this one kiss. He tugs the lock of my hair wrapped around his fingers, pulling my head back, and when I gasp from the intensity of it, he takes advantage, moving to fully claim my mouth until there's no room for escape.

I want everything. *All* of him. His hands on my breasts, his naked body pressed to mine, his length inside me. *I want him in me.*

I want to live in this moment, revel in it. Every fiber of me's alive with excitement, need and desire rolling through me to the tips of my toes. I don't know if I'm awake or dreaming, but if it's a dream, I don't want to wake. If I'm awake, I don't want to fall asleep.

I squeeze my legs together as pressure builds between my thighs, a throbbing, burning need.

Something behind him blares like a foghorn. At first, he ignores it, but at the second raucous shriek, he pulls away. I stifle a whimper.

His goddamn phone.

"I have to take this." He slams his phone on and smacks it to his ear. All I have to say is, whoever's on the other end of that line better have something important to say or the both of us won't think twice about murder.

"What?"

I sit up, awake, but can't hear a thing.

He curses. "I'll be right there."

When he hangs up his phone and glares, I know his anger isn't meant for me. He doesn't like to be interrupted on a *good* day, never mind now.

"I have to go. We got a lead on another case we're working on." He runs a hand through his hair. I've never been so jealous of another person's fingers. "I need you to get some sleep. Tomorrow, we will investigate further, and you get your shooting lesson."

He turns to leave. I feel cold and hot all at once as I watch him. Before he goes, he looks over his shoulder at me.

"I'm sorry." I don't know if he's apologizing for leaving or for kissing me. Maybe both. "Shooting range is opposite the pool. Meet me there at seven."

The door shuts with finality.

I stare at it for a moment, wondering if everything that just happened was my imagination. My fingers roam to my lips, and my eyes flutter closed.

I did not imagine that.

He kissed me. He kissed me, and I want more.

Did I just sell my soul to the Devil?

CHAPTER TWELVE

Cain

IT'S two o'clock in the morning when I finally get to bed. I signed off on a job involving several of my men, because I want them back here as soon as possible. Every other job we're working on needs to be finished, and quickly, and thank fuck we're closing in on one deal so I can free up more of my men. Tomorrow—Jesus, *today*—we need to make headway on finding Skylar.

But my mind's on the woman across the hall from me. It's a damn good thing I got the call when I did, or who knows where we would've ended up.

I don't regret it, though. I want her to know that I want her.

I whip off my clothes and climb into bed, ignoring the raging hard-on I still have from kissing her earlier. I need sleep before tomorrow. I punch my pillow, frustrated that she isn't beside me.

I close my eyes shut tight, willing myself to sleep. My body's fatigued, but it's something I'm so used to, I've trained myself to stay awake. Once, when I was stationed outside of Paris before the fiasco with the gendarmerie, I stayed awake for thirty-six hours straight, waiting for news from the White House. When I finally heard what I needed to and dozed off, we were under attack an hour later.

I'm no stranger to lack of sleep. Still, I need some or I'll be useless tomorrow.

I go over the day in my mind. Her coming to me, asking for the job.

I asked Armand to make her think it was her idea to come here. And he did. How was I to know he planned on fucking *risking her life* to do it?

I interrogated the shit out of him but didn't let him go until today. I'll have to follow up with Joe. My mind's focused on all things Violet.

Violet.

I need her out of my mind. I have to find Skylar, but we have no fucking leads.

Tomorrow, I'll burn the city of Salem to the ground to find her.

I close my eyes and see vivid violet eyes.

I remember the way her mouth tasted like berries and cream, fresh, sweet, and decadent. I remember the way her skin felt in my hands, warm, silk-wrapped seduction that I wanted to worship. I remember the way she yielded when I touched her, the only softness she may ever succumb to.

I never have trouble falling asleep. I train hard, I work hard, and when my head hits the pillow, I'm asleep. But tonight, I'm distracted by the woman lying in a bed only paces from my room, and guilty that I'm even thinking of her when my sister's in danger.

Why Skylar?

Why Violet?

I can't shake the feeling that it's someone after me, someone seeking to get revenge. The list of my enemies is as long as my arm, and I can't even begin to decipher who it could be. I never heard the name Derrick Dossier before tonight.

She promised she'd help me. I know she will. Together, we'll find Skylar.

I fall into a deep and dreamless sleep and don't move or wake until my alarm clock sounds a few hours later.

I stifle a groan and smack the alarm off, get to my feet, and head to the bathroom. Use the facilities, wash my face, scrub a hand through my hair. I sleep bare-chested, the dog tags I wear glinting in the bright overhead lighting. They aren't mine, but I won't take them off. They remind me of the man who made me who I am today, for better or for worse. They remind me how I got here.

Where's Skylar?

Is she hurt?

Is Violet?

Did she sleep well?

I don't drink, but for once, I understand the appeal of a Bloody-fucking-Mary.

I tug on a tee, jeans, and a pair of socks and boots, then check my phone.

No messages, which shouldn't be surprising since I only slept a few hours. I glance at the clock. Six thirty. She's supposed to meet me at the target range at seven.

I've got just enough time for a cup of coffee. The door to her room is shut tight, no sound from the other side. She might be tired, but so am I, and if she's working with me, she'll learn to deal with sleep deprivation. She'd better not be late.

The house is either wide awake or most of my staff never went to bed last night. I pay them well to work hard for long hours and give them all six weeks of paid leave throughout the year. I guarantee them the best benefits of any other private firm on the East Coast. They're loyal to the core.

A door slams in the distance, and I pause on the landing. Someone shouts, then Joe's voice—deeper, calmer—replies.

Armand? Did Joe do what I told him to?

I find Alma at the landing. She's already dressed for the day, her hair tucked into a solid blue bandana, a dustpan in hand. I tried to hire her just to do the cooking, but she insists on doing the cleaning as well. So, I hired a small staff to assist. This house is huge.

"Good morning, Mr. Master."

"Morning, Alma. What's all the noise?"

"I don't know, sir. I keep my business to myself, you know." She gives me a tight smile, swiping her rag along the side tables until they shine. She doesn't suffer dust or fingerprints. Someone could rob our place, and she'd have the prints wiped off before the cops could arrive.

Not that we'd need them.

"But I *think*," she says, turning so I can't see her face. I'm sure she's smiling, though, because she's always smiling. "Your little lady has already awoken."

My little lady?

She is little, I'll give her that.

"Has she?"

"Yessir. She came down earlier looking for a few things."

I'm walking down the stairs as Alma fills me in but have half an ear out for Armand and Joe.

"What was she looking for?"

"Cucumbers, filtered water, fresh mint, and some moisturizer." I'll have her make a list tonight of everything she needs.

"And?"

"I got her everything she requested, sir."

"Thank you."

The smell of coffee wafts past me, along with the low murmur of voices in the kitchen. I trot down the remaining steps and head to the kitchen. Violet's nowhere to be seen. Joe's sitting at the head of the table with a cup the size of a

Great Lake in front of him, along with a few others. They all look up when I enter.

"Morning. Anyone seen Miss Price?"

"Morning, sir," Joe says, his eyes twinkling at me. "I believe Miss Price is ready for her... instruction?" He leaves enough of a pause between his words to make the other men guffaw. I'll give him a fucking lesson.

"At the shooting range?" I don't want her there without me. We've got weapons that would blow the arm off a giant.

"Yessir."

"She has no shooting experience. I don't want her at the range without someone who knows how to shoot."

"No shooting experience?" Joe looks baffled. He's probably wondering why I hired someone with no shooting experience, but I don't owe him an explanation.

On paper, she's got skills. She's got many things she can offer my team. In real life, I want a hell of a lot more than her skill set.

"I'm sorry, I didn't know. It won't happen again."

I nod. "Did you do what I asked you to?"

"Yessir." He was supposed to fire Armand this morning.

"I'm guessing that didn't go over so well?"

"No, not at all, but it confirmed for me you made the right call."

The other men watch us. Alma comes into the kitchen and

grabs a broom, quickly sweeping up imaginary crumbs. "Did it?"

"Yessir."

I pour myself a steaming mug of coffee.

"And what was that?"

"That it was time for him to go." He frowns. "He had nothing but shit to say about all of us in his exit interview."

"Exit interview?"

"Yeah, my euphemism for the profanities he yelled on his way out the door."

Why am I not surprised? The clock on the kitchen wall chimes six forty-five. I need to meet her at the range.

"I'll arrange for his things to be boxed up and shipped. Your job's done. Thanks, Joe."

"Of course, sir."

"Do we have any more information on Skylar?" I'm standing by the door. I don't like that Armand left angry with us. He could compromise our operation with the right motives.

Joe shakes his head sadly. "No. I checked in with Lottie, and she still hasn't come home, but there's no evidence that whoever took her reached out to anyone."

My hand is on the door to go out.

"How about Derrick Dossier, anyone find any more information on him?"

"I found something encrypted on a server, and we're working on it. One thing to note is that it does appear he's former military, dishonorably discharged."

Dishonorably discharged. Just like me.

Christ.

We have a history together; I just don't know what the fuck it is yet. There's more to his name than appears.

"Call me the second you find anything."

"We have a list of the survivors, Mr. Master, and their addresses."

I turn around to look at Joe. The room's grown quiet, all eyes on me. "I want a printout when we get back from the shooting range."

Joe nods. "Yessir."

Today, we hunt for sources that lead us to Skylar.

Alma pulls a huge pan of steaming hot muffins out of the oven, and several of the men grab them before she can put them on a serving platter.

"*Dios mio!* You'll burn your fingers off. Leave some for your boss!"

I've told her a hundred times I don't eat breakfast, and still, she keeps trying.

Violet and I have an hour to practice before we go over the names and locations of the survivors. If we can interview them... we might find what we need after all.

I start to turn the doorknob but pause as Joe's phone rings, and he answers it. He frowns, his eyes coming straight at me. "You gave her a gun? And now the door to the target range is locked?"

Jesus.

The kitchen door slams behind me with a bang.

CHAPTER THIRTEEN

Violet

OH GOD, he's going to absolutely fucking *murder* me for this, but it will be worth it. You only live once, so you might as well make that one time so worth it.

I tried to sleep last night and did end up finally catching some zzz's, but it was nowhere near enough. My mind was teeming with everything that had happened... and that kiss. So when I woke, I knew where I had to go.

I knew he was meeting me here. I asked in the kitchen about who the shooting instructor was, and by the way they all looked at each other knowingly and laughed, I knew it was Cain.

I wanted to get here ahead of him. I didn't want to give him even that little bit of control over me.

So I came here first, even though I don't know what I'm doing.

I guessed he doesn't just leave guns sitting around, but I found Joe in the kitchen, and I may have told a bit of a white lie embellished with what I knew Joe heard last night about our practice. Joe allowed me to come down here, but there was another guy, some big dude with a shaved head, training outside. He was the one that let me in.

The floor beneath my feet's sparkling clean, made of concrete. Each practice area, sectioned off like cubicles, has a place to stand, a small table covered in velvet where I'm presuming you lay your guns, a hook with headphone things, and in front, targets at a distance. Half a dozen people could safely practice in here at once.

 He's coming here, coming soon, and my body heats with this knowledge. I want him so badly I can taste it. *I want so much more than a kiss.*

Even his attention's nice, and I know I'm going to get more than I can handle if he catches me in here. I'm early though, at least fifteen minutes. I'll put this all away before he comes.

I may have never shot a gun, but I'm no fool. I got a few hours of sleep, then pulled up a YouTube video on my phone and watched a series of "intro to shooting" videos. I didn't want to be a complete newb.

I just want to touch the guns. I just want to feel them in my hand, see how heavy they are.

I have to admit, I didn't know guns were so *gorgeous*.

I lift each gun, feeling the substantial weight of them in my palm. I don't know why I ever bothered with throwing knives when guns were an option. I caress the heavy barrels, finger the finely crafted details. I can't believe I've gone this long in my life without ever holding a gun. I've been missing out.

I doubt these are all the weapons he has on his property, but I'm pretty happy with what I can play around with for now.

There's a compact pistol that feels like I'm holding a stick of dynamite in my hands. I place it back in the box, gingerly. Whoa. That thing's deadly.

Next up, a revolver. Don't know the name but it's exquisite. I feel energy pulse through me, and for one brief moment, imagine electricity lighting up my veins like live wires. I'm not tired anymore when I hold the revolver.

There are handguns and shotguns, some that make me think of private investigators wearing suits and trench coats, others that look like they should be strapped to the backs of a military brigade.

I'm not dumb enough to load any of them. I put down the revolver and pick up another gun, imagine pointing it at the target. How hard is it to pull the trigger?

"Come at me," I whisper, remembering what Cain muttered at Troy last night, his words laden with a deadly threat. "*Come at me, bro.*"

I pull the trigger just to see what it feels like.

Fire erupts from the gun.

I fall to the floor, too stunned at first to feel the pain in my shoulder. My ears ring from the deafening roar of the shot, and the instinctive fight or flight part of me feels like I should run for cover.

The door to the firing range bursts open, and I know before I even look to see who it is, Cain Master has entered the arena.

Great.

I am in so much damn trouble it isn't even funny.

I place the gun gingerly down on the ground—too little, too late?—and leap to my feet. "I had no idea it was loaded!" I say in my defense. I flail my arms defensively, so he doesn't actually murder me with his bare hands, but I suspect if he really wants to, my waving arms aren't going to hold him back.

I knew the first time I saw Cain that he was capable of anger. I knew it from the moment our eyes first met, when I saw a world of hurt and rage simmering in his eyes. I knew it when we began hunting for his sister, and I saw him control and harness that anger when he killed the bartender last night.

But this... this isn't controlled anger. It's nothing but unadulterated, boiling hot rage, and he's coming straight at me.

He has to stop at some point, I reason. He has to... stop walking and... *halt.*

But he doesn't.

When he reaches me, he grabs me by the upper arms and shakes me, hard enough to make my teeth rattle, before he shoves me up against the wall with a growl I feel deep in my belly. Cold concrete hits my back as his fingers grasp my chin. I've never wanted to look away from someone so badly in my life, but his grip on my chin makes that impossible.

He says something to me, but my ears are ringing from the sound of the shot and the blood pounding in my head. I shake my head to signal to him that I can't hear him.

He raises his voice so loudly, my stomach clenches.

"You think you can shoot a gun? With no training, no experience, nothing to keep you safe? Do you?" he snarls. A vein throbs in his temple, his nostrils flare. I cringe. What else am I supposed to do? I'm wilting under the heat of his glare, and I totally deserve this. Shooting a loaded gun is *really* fucking stupid. I wouldn't blame him if he made me leave or fired me or made me go peel potatoes in the kitchen, or whatever it is a military guy does to someone who's royally fucked up.

My voice shakes. "I didn't mean to. I didn't know it was loaded."

My ears still ring. I want to cover them to still the aching reverberation.

His eyes are sharp as ice, blue rivulets of churning fury, as he holds my gaze.

"Who gave you the gun?"

"I—I don't know his name. A guy with a shaved head? He was outside."

"Claude."

Still holding my gaze, he reaches for his cell phone and

makes a call. I'm trembling, scared of what he'll do next, scared to say a thing. He puts it on speakerphone.

"Yes, sir?"

His voice cuts like a scalpel. "Did I give you permission to give Miss Price a weapon?"

A pause, then, "No sir."

"She did not have permission to touch a weapon, and I'll punish her for that. But if you ever again give anyone a weapon without my express consent, I will fire you. Consider this your one and only warning. Do you understand me?"

Punish?

"Yes, sir. Of course, sir. I'm so sorry."

"Miss Price, I believe you have something to say as well."

I'm shaking in his grip, and my voice sounds distant and muffled. "I'm sorry I asked you for a weapon. I'm sorry I got you in trouble."

I'm sorry I got myself in trouble?

Why did I think it was okay to work with him again?

I'm shaking as he hangs up the phone and shoves it back into his pocket, which, unfortunately, brings his furious gaze back to focus fully on *me*.

Gah-reat.

I open my mouth to speak, but I don't know what I'm going to say. I have to say... something. But when I go to speak, he shakes his head at me.

"No."

I don't know exactly what he's saying "no" to, but I clamp my mouth shut. It's convenient, since I don't know what I would say anyway.

I look down at his hands on my wrists and realize he's shackled me in his grip. With the cold concrete wall at my back, there isn't a single move I know that could get me out of this position. He dwarfs me, my whole body shadowed by his.

When he speaks, his voice vibrates with anger.

"Are you familiar with the Four-Step Approach to Progressive Discipline, Miss Price?"

Ouch. We've gone from the hottest kiss of my life to "Miss Price."

I shake my head, still not sure if I'm allowed to speak.

"Step one." His words travel down my neck to my collarbone and warm my skin. I swallow hard. "Verbal warning. The supervisor tells the employee of their concerns and listens to the employee's side of the story, then issues a verbal warning of disciplinary actions." His fingers flex on my wrists.

I nod dumbly. Yes. Mhm. Got it.

"Step two," he growls. Oooh, boy. "Written warning. Self-explanatory, yes?"

"Yes, sir," I whisper. I don't have a submissive bone in my body but showing some respect right now might help my plight.

His eyes soften for a fraction of a second at my response. I feel about two feet tall and would feel about ten years old if my body didn't react the way it did to his intimidation tactics. My pulse races, and my mouth goes dry, remembering the last time we were this close to one another, what he'd done next.

I can't look away from his eyes and wish I could.

"Step three involves suspension. Paid or unpaid leave for a defined length of time, presumably during which the employee considers their behavior and decides how they will proceed."

A pause where neither of us speaks, before he finishes, "Step four is termination."

Silence can be loud sometimes. Right now, it's deafening.

He releases my wrists, but I still can't move, because he leans in on one forearm, his other caging me in. I'm just as secured as I was before.

This *may* not be the time to once again remind him that I'm not his employee, but an independent contractor.

"Do you know how many men I've let go, Miss Price?"

I shake my head.

"One. This morning. And do you know why?"

I shake my head again. I feel as if I'm going to cry.

"Because he could've killed you with his stupidity."

I can't breathe. I try but my lungs don't seem to want to work.

The man I affectionately called Douche... Armand, I think his name is... Fired. Because... he could've killed me?

I don't know why I mean anything at all to Cain. But there's no point in denying the fact that I do. Probably more than I deserve.

"I'm sorry," I repeat. "I really didn't know it was loaded."

His shoulders rise as he draws in a deep breath before he releases it. "The guns down here usually aren't loaded, because I want my men to bring their own ammo with them. We do have loaded guns on the premises, because the only people who ever set foot here are trained in weaponry and shooting, and because having loaded weapons on hand helps in matters of self-defense."

I nod. I don't know how else to respond.

"Lesson one. Always, *always* assume that a weapon in your hand is loaded."

I want to smack my own forehead with a resounding *duh,* because that sounds like something that should be obvious.

"How are your ears?"

"They're... okay."

"Lesson two." He's still holding his body pressed to mine, still pinning me to the wall. His breath skates across my skin, a reminder of what happened last night. My lips tingle. "You can permanently damage your hearing from *one* gunshot if you don't have proper protection. Always wear electronic earmuffs or ear plugs."

I nod.

His gaze travels down to my shoulder. "Did you hurt yourself on the kickback?"

I forgot about the pain until he mentioned it just now. *Ouch.* Tears sting my eyes, and not just from physical pain.

"Yes."

With a scowl that would freeze hell, he reaches for my collar and gently tries to tug down my T-shirt so he can inspect my shoulder. The collar's unyielding, though, and he can't see anything.

Frowning, he steps back and folds his arms across his chest like he's surveying me. "Off with the shirt."

I try to play this off. Lighten the mood, you could say, to take his focus away from my trembling hands and the way I'm flushing like I'm sunburnt.

"My, my, Mr. Master, so early in the morning and you're—"

"Not. Playing."

The flirtation dies on my lips as I reach for the bottom of my shirt. I try to tug it up so he can only see my shoulder, a really futile attempt at holding onto some semblance of control through this, but it's no use. With a sigh, I take it off. My shoulder *burns*.

"Of all the guns you could've shot, you chose the one with the quietest sound but meanest kickback."

"Right. Good one, Vi." I swallow my need to cry and wince when his fingers graze my shoulder.

I remember the way he kissed my bruised shins when he bandaged me yesterday. I remember the way he cradled my head and comforted me. While still obviously angry, he's no less gentle this time than he was the day before.

Sliding one hand along the small of my back, he braces me as he inspects my shoulder. "You shouldn't be bruised," he whispers. "These all happened on my watch. Never again."

Not all, I want to remind him. The car accident wasn't his fault. Hell, none of it is. Why does he blame himself?

"You don't need to see a doctor for this, but we should wait on any more practice for today."

I shake my head. "No. No, please, Cain. I'm fine." I move my arm around just to show him I'm okay, but I can't hide the wince when pain explodes along my arm and shoulder.

"The hell you are."

I watch his gaze rove hungrily over my barely clad breasts and flat belly before I yank my shirt back on.

"I need to learn how to shoot! I need you to teach me."

"You do not make demands around here, Miss Price."

Fuck him with the Miss Price bullshit.

"I'm not Miss Price!" I yell in a fit of frustration. "My name is *Violet!*"

Something snaps in him. I see it in his eyes. One minute, he's staring at me angrily, prepared to argue with me. The next, there's cold decision in his gaze.

"You want me to teach you?" he asks, his voice an alarming purr. "Fine. I'll teach you."

His words ring in my memory.

I'll punish her for that.

"The gun on your left is the perfect gun for beginner's practice. Lift it with two hands and point it *away* from you and repeat the first rule I told you."

I nod. "Always assume a gun is loaded."

"*Always.* Do what I said and place it on the table in front of you." Ahead of us are the targets, a few bullseyes, but most covered in thick paper in the shape of a human body.

My hand shakes a little, but I will the trembling to stop. I pick up the gun, point it away from me, and lay it on the velvet table in my cubicle. My hands hang by my sides awkwardly.

"Good. Now lean over the table on your forearms."

I blink. "Lean over the table?" What the hell does that have to do with holding a gun?

His icy blue stare pins me in place. "Lean. Over. The. Table."

I turn away from him, shaking, as I do what he tells me. I hear him walk up to me right before I feel his heat at my back. I still when he leans over me, pushing me against the table while he reaches for something I didn't see before—small leather loops on the table, no doubt meant to secure weapons when they're not in use. Only it isn't the gun he's securing.

"Cain! What are you doing?" I hate that my voice shakes. Hate that he's scaring me.

Without a word, he slips my wrist in the first leather harness, then the next.

Click. I can't move my arms. I'm bent over the velvet table, my wrists secured in front of me.

"The target range is soundproof, Violet. No one will hear you if you scream. So go ahead. Scream to your little heart's content. I'll enjoy this more if you do."

If he didn't have his hand on my lower back just now, I'd be terrified. As it is, I wouldn't say I'm exactly at ease…

I hear the click of metal, a swish. Is he… unfastening his jeans? What?

My hands shake, and my belly quivers. I…what will he…

"Repeat rule number one, Violet."

I love the way he says my name.

I swallow, my voice still distant even as the ringing fades. "Always assume a gun is loaded."

"Maybe this will help burn it into your memory." There's the sound of a swish, then a line of fire lights up my ass. I gasp, too shocked to do more than that. I whip my head around to see him standing behind me, his belt folded over in his grip.

Heat fans my core while indignation rises.

I could tell him off. I could tell him to go fuck himself and keep his big hands to himself. But then I'm fucked. Then I'm back to square one, where I've been for so long the very thought of going back there makes me feel desperate. No.

No, I can't walk away from him, not now. Not when I've come so close to what I need.

I catch his gaze for one heart-stopping moment. I'm the utter focus of his attention. A bomb could go off beside him right now and his attention wouldn't waver.

His icy voice shatters the silence. "Did I give you permission to turn around?"

I hold his gaze. Is he... into this?

Am I?

I shake my head wordlessly. He makes a twirly motion with his finger and points. "Then turn back around and stay bent over that table." I didn't even realize I'd stood up, hunched over as my wrists are still secured.

Shaking, I do what he says.

"Tell me rule number two."

I cringe, knowing he's going to punish me now, somehow craving and dreading it at the same time. "Always wear ear protection."

Again, the whir of leather and another searing strike. I cry out this time, but before I can recover there's an additional lash of leather.

Rule number two. Two strikes.

I bite my lip. Even though it hurts, I know a man as strong as he is could tear the skin off my back if he whipped me at full strength. He's moderating his strength, by a lot.

"Earmuffs on." He's right up next to me when he slides

them over my ears. The ringing stops, but all other sounds are muffled.

His voice sounds as if it's far, far off in the distance.

He's still standing behind me. I can feel his eyes burning through me as vividly as his belt.

"Rule number three."

Oh, God, will that be three strikes?

"*Always* keep your finger on the outside of the trigger guard, nowhere near the trigger, until you're ready to shoot."

Leaning across my body, he slides the gun between my secured wrists. "Show me."

I make sure my fingers are nowhere near the trigger.

He nods. "Good. Just like that." He takes the gun away. "Bend over the table."

"Oh my God! Again?"

"You didn't really think we were done, did you?"

I ignore the way excitement builds in my belly, because I don't have any fucking idea why the knowledge that he's going to continue to punish me thrills me.

I shake my head numbly. I bend over the table again. This time, I squeeze my eyes shut tight.

No warning at all, but his belt lands with rapid precision, each line of fire building on the one before it until my body screams in pain.

One.

Two.

Three.

Then he's in my space, his body over mine and his pelvis pressed up against my aching, heated ass. I look down at his large hands placed on either side of me and shiver. I feel his prickly stubble along my cheek as his mouth comes to my ear. "Did you learn your lesson, Violet?" His teeth clench on my earlobe, and I hiss in a breath.

Heat races through me. I close my eyes. I'm drowning in him, in his nearness and dominance, his voice and clean, masculine scent. My heart beats along with his as he's pressed up against my back.

"Yes, sir."

"Tell me something, then."

"Yes?" I whisper.

"If I slid my fingers into your panties, would I find you wet?"

My mouth falls open. "What?"

"I spanked you."

That felt like more than a spanking. My voice trembles. "You call that a spanking? A spanking is over your lap with your palm."

"I can arrange that, too."

Gah! I think I swallowed my tongue.

"Cain!"

"*Violet.* Did your punishment turn you on?"

In my trademark nonsensical way, I answer a question with a question. "If that was punishment, would I be in trouble for being turned on?"

"Of course. You'd have to wait until I got you alone later to do anything about that." I slam my lips together so I don't do something stupid like beg.

I feel his hands anchored on my hips and he draws me closer to him. His erection presses up against my ass.

I'm not the only one turned on.

He unfastens the cuffs, turns me around to face him, then slides his hand along my jaw, his anger dialed back to a low simmer.

"Today's lesson's over, but we're nowhere near done here. We have unfinished business, you and I. Understood?"

I nod. "Yes."

"Tomorrow morning, you'll meet me here at seven a.m. You do not enter until I am here. You do not pick up a weapon until you have permission. You do not shoot a gun without my permission. And I'll be sure to help you remember each rule."

I nod again. Does that mean he'll... turn this into what I think he will?

How will I focus when he's doing *that?*

I wish our lesson wasn't over for the day, but I'm not sure how much more I can take. I'm already turned on beyond reason, so much I'm shaking.

People always say I'm intense. Some can't handle my brand of intensity. They want me to play nice, to follow the rules. They like things like polite conversation and social norms. Not me, though. That's never been who I am.

I once dated a guy who got angry with me when I wouldn't let him pull out my chair or order dinner for me. I told him I take care of myself, and I'm not giving that up for a guy I hardly know. "You're too intense," he said when he dropped me back off at my apartment.

Too intense.

I held those words within me. I remembered them. And when I found myself alone, or wishing for some kind of companionship, I'd pull them up again.

Too intense.

I was too intense for anyone to ever love.

"Where'd you go just now?" Cain asks, his sapphire eyes boring into mine. "You sometimes go somewhere in your mind, like you're dredging up memories. Where'd you go this time?"

There's no need to hide the truth.

"I was just thinking that... until I met you, I'd never met anyone more intense than I am."

A glimmer of a smile that doesn't reach his eyes. They're almost... sad. No, not almost. "You think I'm intense?"

"So intense you make me forget to breathe."

The flutter of breath on my forehead warns me he's drawing

closer. I close my eyes as his lips brush my skin. I look at him when he responds.

"You're so intense, you make every cell in my body aware of your presence," he whispers, and his anger lowers even more. "You shine so bright, it almost hurts to look at you, like I'm staring directly at a beam of light." My throat tightens. He has to stop. He's going to make me cry, and I do not cry. "You're so beautiful, I feel as if I stare too long, I'll turn to stone."

"Stop."

We stare at each other in silence for two full beats before he speaks again. "Why?"

I don't know why. Words seem ludicrous when the feelings in your heart boil over. "I... Because we just met." Because I'm uncomfortable with praise, it's so foreign to me.

He shakes his head, and I don't know why.

Slowly, so slowly I don't realize what he's doing at first, he threads his fingers through my hair. The feeling's exquisite, sexy, relaxing, and comforting all at once. "When you touched the guns earlier, did you know right away which one fit in your palm? Did awareness strike you?"

The question surprises me almost as much as my answer. "Yes."

"There was a certain comfort in the touch, wasn't there? As if the others held power, but that one was designed just for you? Like someone waved a magic wand and crafted it to fit your palm?"

"Exactly. Yes, that's it."

He nods. My skin feels all prickly and hot. "That's how I felt when I saw you for the first time."

I brush off the compliment, because I'm squirming under his praise. "Cain, the first time you saw me, you looked as if you were bored by me."

His response is to lower his mouth and brush his lips across mine. I get the distinct feeling he's rejecting my comment, but I can't understand why, and then I forget what the comment or question even was. Because he's kissing me, our lips joined in a heated moment, and when Cain Master kisses me, the world fades to dust.

CHAPTER FOURTEEN

Cain

I DIDN'T MEAN for this to happen.

We've got an hour before my men will have their report ready for me.

I wasn't supposed to let her drive me to distraction, and I most definitely wasn't supposed to punish her.

Not now. Not here.

I love the way her eyelids flutter closed, and her hands wrap around my neck for support. I love the way she lets me hold her.

But we have a job to do, and I'm a shit teacher if I don't teach her how to use this gun.

I change my mind about waiting until tomorrow morning. "We need to practice."

"Right," she repeats. "Practice."

We pull away reluctantly.

She's a natural.

I want to wrap her up in my arms, carry her back to my room, and tie her to my bed.

No one would ever touch my Violet. She's mine.

What I'd do to her when I had her there...

But we have a job to do, and we don't have any more time to waste.

"You're really fucking good at this."

I love the way she flushes under my praise. "I have a good teacher."

"There are some things you can't teach. Some things that only come naturally."

I don't know if it's because she has years of training, because she's incredibly skilled at knife throwing, or because there's just something inside her that innately knows its way around weapons, but when she holds a gun and shoots, she does it as if she's had years of practice.

She doesn't trust me at first when she turns back around to shoot.

"Stop looking over your shoulder at me."

"I'm afraid you'll—do something to me again." She gives me a look halfway between a glare and a pout.

"Like spank you?" I love watching her squirm.

"Or—something."

I release a labored breath. "I will never, ever do anything to distract you when you're holding a gun." I shake my head. "Goddammit, woman, you think I wanna lose my balls?"

"Ah," she says, standing the way I showed her with her legs spread apart and knees slightly bent. "So I'm safe from being dominated when I hold a gun?"

I huff out a breath. "Yeah."

"I'll have to bring a gun with me to bed, then."

"Try it," I say dryly. "See how that works out for you."

She turns back to her target with a coy little smile. The first shot hits in the yellow ring, a shoulder strike for the human-shaped paper. "I meant that," she mutters. "I don't really want to kill anyone."

"If they're pulling a gun on you, yes, you do."

She doesn't reply, but her next shot strikes straight between the eyes.

"Good shot." I glance at my watch. Eight o'clock. "We have to go now. You'll join me here every morning at seven sharp."

I note the regret on her face when she lays her weapon down. "And lemme guess, no coming here without you even if I follow the rules?"

"If you come here without me, you're *not* following the rules."

"I'm not going to get any better if I don't practice."

"Trust me. We'll practice."

She draws in a breath and squares her shoulders. "I want to see you shoot."

"You want to see me shoot?"

Her pupils are dilated, and I realize... she's aroused.

No. She's on *fire*.

"It turns you on, doesn't it?"

"What?"

I feel a slow, lazy smile spread across my face. "All of it. Your spanking. The gun. Me, dominating you. Watching me hold a gun."

She swallows but doesn't look away. "Yes, Mr. Master. You could say that."

"Give me your knife, Violet."

Trembling, she bends and slips her knife out of its sheath.

"What about knives?" I hold the knife to the light. The blade glints like crystal.

"What... about them?" Her chest rises with a sharp intake of breath. I watch as her fingers come to rest on her hips, but her body's tense. Waiting.

"Have you ever played with knives?"

"Of course. All the time. The only way you learn to throw like I have is to—" Eyes wide, she swallows before she continues. "That's not the kind of knife play you have in mind, is it?"

"Not at all, sweet girl."

I brush the handle of the knife across her temple. Her eyes flutter closed, her lips parted. "Knife play can be intensely erotic. You would never want to play with a novice, but with the right person...if you have full trust..." My heartbeat races. "Stay still, Violet." I drag the edge of the knife along her jaw, a thin scraping that makes her skin white. She stands absolutely still. If she moved too quickly, she'd break skin. "Edge play takes you right to the very brink of danger and foreplay." I gently drag the knife from her jaw to her neck, the tiniest scrape of metal to skin. I lean in, my mouth against her ear. "But it intensifies *everything*."

Her eyes flutter open, and she licks her lips.

"You're good at that," she whispers.

"Good at what?"

"Intensifying everything."

I gently take the knife off her skin and hand it to her.

Brilliant violet eyes meet mine, unblinking. "I want to see you shoot. Please."

I step past her, my shoulder brushing hers, and my own need to claim this woman flares. I reach for my baby, the Ruger EC9. A striker-fired pistol with an easy trigger and immovable sights, it's my favorite for fast, meticulous shooting.

"Tell me where."

"Left shoulder."

Boom. Hit it.

"Midsection."

Boom. A hole tears straight through the abdominal region.

"Left ear."

Boom. Blast the ear straight fucking off.

"Right wrist."

Boom. Bingo.

"*Shit.* You're a perfect shot."

I shrug. "Some guys play video games. I relax at the target range."

"Why does this not surprise me?" I can't miss the unmistakable pride in her voice. It does strange things to me I don't know how to unpack. But we have to go.

I show her how to lock everything up. "Back at the house, you'll find clothes in your room. Wear something professional, so we get some answers."

I turn away before she can reply. I don't want to listen to any of her bullshit about not wanting the clothes I gave her. She'll wear the clothes.

My phone rings. Joe.

"Yeah?"

"Lottie called. No change. No word from Skylar, nothing at all."

I've never been a patient guy, and I sure as fuck am not one now. I hate that we're in a holding pattern until we can get more information.

"Thanks. You have that list of victims for us?"

"Yes, sir. Waiting for you in your office."

I head to my office to get the papers, then do a quick change myself so I look professional. Khakis, dress shoes, polo shirt. Someone knocks on the door.

"Come in."

The door creaks open, and I don't look up at first, fully consumed by the details I'm reading about the people we'll see today. When I get my hands on this motherfucker...

"Ahem."

I look up. I blink. I sit back in my chair and admire the stunning woman before me.

Violet's dressed in a white top and dress pants that show off her trim figure and gorgeous thighs. Her top fits her snugly, but drapes about her, somehow pulling off both professional and stunning all at once. Her hair is pulled back in a stylish braid, and she's wearing makeup that makes her cheeks brighter, her lips fuller, and her eyes... *God,* her eyes.

"Lock that door behind you and get over here."

A pleased smile tugs at her lips. "Is that an order, Mr. Master?"

Christ, I love it when she calls me that.

"It is."

She captures her lower lip between her teeth and casts her eyes down, but dutifully turns and locks the door behind her. When she turns back to me, her vivid eyes are even brighter.

"I literally have no idea how to fix this hair and makeup, so you can't muss it up." She thinks those hands on her hips somehow give her authority.

So cute.

I crook a finger at her. Her cheeks flush brighter.

"We have work to do."

"We do."

I tap the papers together on my desktop and push them to the side, shove away from my desk and walk around to the front. I meet her at the same time she reaches my desk, lift her, and place her on the edge.

I love the way she gasps and her hands fly to my shoulders to steady herself. I reach for her, embrace her, and tuck her against my chest.

"This is risky. You know that."

"I do."

I bend and kiss her, and for one brief moment in time, the world stops spinning.

"I could've worn the skirt," she says, as if to distract me from her stunning beauty. "But you can't run in a skirt, and you just never know..."

"You don't. Smart girl, we should be prepared."

"And I've been thinking."

"Yeah, baby?"

I love the way her eyes go soft when I call her *baby*.

"I don't think we should start with the victims. The only survivors don't remember what happened to them. We know that he went to Bubbles and Broomsticks, and we know that he has witnesses for every place he's gone."

"Exactly."

"But something occurred to me when I was getting changed just now."

I step back to look at her, so I can take her seriously.

"What's that?"

"The alibis for the times Derrick Dossier supposedly abducted his victims? They're detailed, but almost... *too* detailed. Here, look."

She takes out her phone and pulls up the notes app.

"August first. Flowers show up at Anita Charles' door. She goes on a date with a mysterious stranger and doesn't return. Her body's found two days later, but he has video evidence that he was shooting pool at the bar when she was supposedly abducted, then he was working the other hours. Like, he didn't even go home to get changed?"

"Odd."

"There's more."

I nod.

"Next up, Margaret Sellier. Flowers show up at her door. Like the others, same thing, goes on a date with a stranger and doesn't return. That time, he was with three buddies fishing in Panama, and couldn't possibly have kidnapped anyone, yet..."

Her voice trails off. I wait for her to finish.

"Yet there's actual DNA evidence to prove it was him."

I shake my head. "That doesn't make sense."

"We don't know who struck us yesterday in the car, but we do know that whoever this person or persons are, they're specifically targeting people who..." She flushes pink. "Who mean something to *you*. But... you didn't know me until yesterday."

I can't tell her that isn't true. She'd run.

No one knew she mattered to me.

"I say we go back to the bar. I say we bait him. He has bartenders there that slip roofies in drinks for him so he can do his thing, right? At least the one we already took care of."

"Right."

"Then use me as bait."

"No *fucking* way."

My hands have risen to her shoulders, and she gently pushes them down to rest on her thighs.

"Yes. I can go in and pretend I'm asking more questions, searching for more answers. I'll be a sitting duck drawing him out, and the entire time, we'll have your team keep looking to see what they can find. He's already tried to get me anyway; we'll just make it that much easier for us to find him."

"*No.* And if you try to do it on your own, I swear to God, Violet—"

"I know, I know, you'll tie me up, right?"

I curse under my breath, and she waves me off.

"He's watching us. You know he is. You know he was at my place and he knows I'm here now, he has to, if his motive is to get the people that matter to you."

I shake my head. I hate that my sister's missing. I hate that she's in danger. But there has to be another way.

Holding my gaze, her voice softens. She takes one of my hands from her thigh and turns it around so she cups it in two of her own. "We have to do something."

My throat feels tight. I nod. "Yeah."

"We have to find out who he is. Let's sit with your team and piece together what we have. But I really think our time's better spent at the bar than here or questioning those poor survivors who were traumatized anyway."

I cringe. "Right."

Her eyes harden. "I looked at the pictures of the victims. I've made connections. And I saw some things I never, ever want to see again." She cringes. "I won't tell you details because of Skylar, but believe me, we need to stop this guy."

"Agreed." I pull away from her with reluctance. "Let's go."

We're ten minutes out. I love the way she's hyper-focused and aware, her back ramrod straight as she sits next to me in the truck.

"Some people like pretty cars," she says softly, fingering the leather details on the interior of my truck. "Some like race cars or convertibles or expensive, luxury cars. I mean, your Audi's nice," she says with a shrug, in the same tone of voice one might say, *I mean, it'll do.*

I feel the corners of my lips quirk up. *It'll do.* "But you?"

She sighs contentedly and runs her hands palms down over the leather-clad dash. "If I could, I would spread my legs for this truck and fuck it good and hard, cowgirl style."

I nearly hit the curb and catch myself just in time. "My God, woman. There's a visual I won't forget. What do you love about trucks?"

With a contented sigh, still running her hands over the leather, she grows meditative. "I like dangerous, powerful things. Your pit bulls, for instance. Some see nothing but a vicious, lethal dog. I see strength and loyalty, and they're so beautiful to me I could cry. I love how when you sit in a truck like this, you're above everyone else."

"On top of the world," I say softly. Violet gets it.

She moves closer to me, our bodies flush against each other in the cab. "I've always loved powerful, dangerous things." Her fingers trail down my bicep, tracing the edges of muscles and veins. "Makes me feel... protected, I guess, but at the same time... not safe at all." With what I know about her background, I understand. She sighs. "That doesn't make sense."

"It makes perfect sense."

I accelerate when we get on the on ramp. Her grip on my arm tightens.

We're five minutes out.

My phone rings. Joe. I hit the button on the steering wheel so we can both hear.

"Yeah?"

"I've got Derrick Dossier on the line for you."

CHAPTER FIFTEEN

Violet

IF LOOKS COULD KILL, his phone would be incinerated right about now. I cringe at the latent threat in his voice.

"I want everyone in surveillance on this call."

"On it, sir."

I watch as he releases a breath. "Connect the call." There's a series of clicks. "Cain Master speaking."

"Ahhh, Mr. Master. We meet again." I shiver at the unpleasant sound of Dossier's voice. Some voices are musical, almost lyrical. Others are neutral. Dossier's makes the hairs on the back of my neck stand up. "You don't remember me, do you?"

Cain glances at me. Someone he does know, or should know, as we suspected.

"No. Where's my sister?"

"Settle down, Mr. Master. I have your sister right here."

Cain's shaking with anger, but I can tell he's relieved as well.

Skylar's alive. I exhale and reach my fingers to his knee. I give him a reassuring squeeze.

"Why don't you put her on the phone." His tone is deceptively calm. He's a raging inferno, ready to annihilate. I'm not even the one he's angry at, and his roiling fury has me trembling.

"Now, now, Mr. Master, no need to be hasty. Relax. Skylar and I are having a brilliant time, aren't we?"

Do I detect an accent? If there is one, it's faint.

"Cain!" A young female voice sounds frantic on the other line. "It's a setup. Don't come!" Like that would stop him. An armed squad paired with a bomb threat wouldn't stop him.

There's a scuffling noise then the sound of a thump and a muffled cry.

"If you hurt her, I'll kill you." I feel as if actual fire shoots from Cain's eyes.

"That's what you like to do, isn't it? You kill people just for the hell of it, don't you? You don't care who you kill. You don't care if people have family. The ends always justify the means with you, don't they?"

Cain doesn't respond but goes deadly calm.

His eyes flick to mine and I can't quite read him.

"What do you want?"

"You can't give me what I want, Master." Oh, the irony of him calling Cain Master. "So I'll do what you do oh so well. I'll take what's mine."

"If you—"

The line goes dead. He grabs the phone, curses, and it looks like he's going to whip it right out the window. I grab his arm. "Stop! You'll need that if he calls you again. I know, I want to break things, too."

The truck comes to a rumbling stop at the side of the road. He tosses it into park and buries his head in his hands. Shoulders heaving, I wonder at first if he's crying. The thought terrifies me.

Gently, I reach a hand to his shoulder. He's breathing heavily, his body tense like a bowstring pulled too tightly. He's going to snap.

"We'll find her," I tell him, determined. "I don't care what it takes. We'll find him."

When he lifts his head, his eyes are too bright, but he hasn't cried. Still, it breaks my heart to see him so tortured.

"He's right, Violet. I did kill, and I have no regrets. I did it for my country. For my soldiers at arms."

I read his files. I know what he did, what he's capable of. But I don't see a bad man. No. Only a good man would feel the weight of his actions the way Cain does. Only a good man would lay down life and limb for the people he loves. He's loyal to his very core.

I gentle my voice. "One thing at a time. Let's go over what he said. Did your team get anything at all?"

"The call was too brief, all ability to track expertly blocked."

"Okay, alright, so let's put our heads together. He says you know him. How would you know him?"

"Must've been when I served in the military."

"In France?"

He gives me a short nod. "Yeah."

"Tell me what happened there. Would anyone have reason to want to kill you?"

"*Lots* of people want to kill me. Fucking dozens. I was in charge of protecting the U.S. Embassy. It came to my knowledge there was going to be an attack, so I acted." He blows out a breath. "If I had it to do over again, I would behave differently, but honest to God..." His voice trails off, and he shakes his head. "I did what I thought was best at the time." He glances at the clock on the dash. "I don't have time to go into detail."

"Summary, please. I need to know."

"Fine. The short version. We were subject to a hostile militia attack at our embassy access points. They began at night and went into the day. The attacks were unprovoked and considered an act of war and had to be stopped or many, many more would've died. The attacks focused on the arrival of American diplomats who'd come to the Embassy to sign an agreement with the U.N., but the agreement had a direct impact on weapons sales across the Mediterranean."

I nod. Following.

"It was one attack after another. Since we were attacked, we sent an airstrike, which killed dozens. So when I got word the militia was preparing for a counterattack, I sent our men to ward that off." His lips thin. "Their initial attacks cost us twenty million in fire damage, and we lost two dozen of our soldiers, not to mention dozens of innocents. I couldn't let more devastation happen."

"Of course not," I say, squeezing his knee. I hate that he bears this burden, to this day.

"So we attacked them before their counter strike, and we killed the entire militia. It's the worst memory I have, and one I wish I could erase forever."

"I understand. I have a few like that myself."

We're only a few blocks away from the bar now.

"There are ways of erasing bad memories," I say gently.

He reaches for my fingers and gives my hand a little squeeze. "Yeah? How?"

"You replace them with new ones."

We drive by the business section of town, where the office parks are lined up near restaurants and retail shops. Something flashes by my window, and suddenly, a spark fuses in my brain and I have the answer, with lightning clarity.

I *know*.

"Stop!"

The truck comes to a screeching halt as he yanks the steering wheel to the right and pulls to the side of the road. "What is it?"

"The flowers. Oh, God, Cain, the flowers. You said you think this guy has history in France, right?"

"Yes."

"The flowers he's been sending. The beautiful purplish-blue flowers, those are irises, right? He puts them next to the baby's breath."

He's staring at me now with so much intensity, I feel hot under the glare. "Yes?"

"The iris is the national flower of France. Baby's breath represents innocence, doesn't it?"

He nods.

"Criminals who leave clues think they're clever, that they can outsmart the police. Most of them are narcissists. He did this out of pride, to taunt us."

"Did *what*?" He's clearly running out of patience.

I talk faster. "The fleur-de-lis emblem, the one with the flower and leaves? French symbol. *Fleur-de-lis.* He's taken every single woman right here in Salem, the *very same* city with the Fleur-de-lis Memorial."

His phone rings again as he pulls back out into the intersection. *Joe.*

"Boss, we found something we think you need to know."

"Don't keep me waiting."

"You ordered us to find the names of the people killed in the counterattack of the Embassy to see if anyone was connected to Dossier. We found none by the name of Dossier, sir. We did, however, find a *Dozier*. Actually, two.

Twins. One was killed, the survivor moved to America. We found him, and he fits the profile of the man they've suspected of being behind these attacks."

I suddenly feel cold. "Could... someone from another country become a police officer here in the States?"

"Depends on the state but yes, many departments will allow it."

"So the former police officer that's suspected in the abductions and rape cases... could've been the same man you fought overseas... especially if he fudged his age here in the U.S."

"Yes."

I think this over. "Cain. Dozier's French for willow... it's the surname for someone who lived near a plantation of willows... if you killed his twin..." I smack my forehead. "Skip the bar, we can't go there. We have to go to the Salem Willows, it's where the Fleur-de-lis Memorial is!" My heart races with excitement. We've had a breakthrough. "It's a hunch, but my hunches are very, very good."

"Don't get too excited. He likely laid this out precisely so we'd find him. Remember, Skylar said it was a setup."

The Salem Willows Park is thirty-five acres along the ocean, named because of the white willow trees planted along the walkways to offer shade. The long, graceful branches nearly graze the ground they've grown so long, and on warm summer days like today, it's not unusual to find families strolling along the paths, ice cream cones in hand, or cyclists whizzing past on two wheels. The rocky beach borders large, grassy fields, where people often picnic or play frisbee.

Around the Willows, though, are several residential houses, apartment complexes and rentals, video arcades and vendors selling carnival food and treats.

The Fleur-de-lis Memorial stands in the center of Salem Willows Park, only steps away from the main attractions.

When we arrive, the park is teeming with people, dogs, and bicyclists. We park the truck at the edge and move quickly to the Fleur-de-lis.

My skin prickles.

Here. He's here.

They're here. I know they are.

Cain whips his head around, scouring the passersby, but it's hard to tell even where to begin.

"Too many people here," he mutters. "Too many goddamn civilians. We'll have to find them and isolate them."

A shiver skates down my spine. I've read what he does to them when he has them alone. "But first we have to find them."

When we draw near to the Fleur-de-lis, I don't see anything that can lead us to where Dossier's got Skylar.

We walk up and down the paths, intent on finding details or something that would give us a clue.

Near the arcade, something purple catches my eye.

"Cain." I point wordlessly, as my stomach churns with acid. Bordering the entrance to the arcade are gorgeous purple irises in full bloom.

"They usually bloom earlier in the year," I say to Cain, shaking my head. "But spring was late with the cold weather, and they've bloomed later than usual." He exhales as I continue, "He used those flowers because he wants you to find him."

His hand takes mine as we walk side by side. "You ready for this?" Cain asks.

"The man tried to attack me. He used intimidation tactics and hurt me. He came after your sister and other innocent women and did the very worst things he could have. Am I ready for this?" I huff out a mirthless laugh. "I may fight you off so I can kill him myself."

My breathing hitches when he tugs me a little closer to him and says in a low voice laced with approval, "That's my girl. We'll fight him. We'll rescue Skylar. And then we'll kill him."

"They do call you the executioner. I hope you live up to the name." I love the way his eyes light up, even as a mask of fury and resolve etches lines around his eyes.

"You do know how to flirt with a guy, don't you?"

"Not in the slightest. But with you, I'm learning."

We move gracefully. As one.

"We'll go into the arcade. See what we can find. I texted Joe and my surveillance team, they're getting back to me with specs on the arcade's layout."

It's dim and hot in the arcade. Skee ball flanks one wall, across from air hockey machines and foosball tables. Large, clunky machines spit out coins and tickets, and everywhere we turn, I see flashing lights. I can hardly hear myself think in here with the bells and whistles and loud, raucous music.

Cain says something to me, but I can hardly hear him. I shake my head to tell him I can't hear him. He lifts his phone. He's got the arcade blueprint.

Two floors. The first houses video games, skee ball, and the table games, but upstairs are the classic games, virtual real-ity, and funhouse. Behind the funhouse are storage rooms and a small studio apartment.

They could be anywhere.

According to this map, the stairs are to the left of the foos-ball tables. I reach for his hand so we don't get separated in the crush of people. I locate the dimly lit back stairs. He goes ahead of me but reaches his hand behind him so we don't let go.

The noise increases as we go upstairs. At first, my heart beats faster at the sound of a scream, but at the top of the stairs I see a macabre Halloween game with a screaming banshee. A few teens are laughing and playing, racking up points for every scream the banshee shouts. A few feet away, my body's tall and distorted in the funhouse mirror, and Cain's looks oddly frightening with a twisted clown's face staring at us.

"I hate arcades," I mutter to myself. "I fucking hate them."

I once got lost in an arcade as a child and never forgot it.

They're easy to get lost in. Cain doesn't know how much it means to me that he's holding my damn hand.

I jump when one of the teens hits the jackpot, the screaming banshee's wails pitching louder and louder. Cain frowns, his eyes narrowed. Here, right behind these walls, are the storage rooms and studio apartment, likely designed for the owners to live in or rent.

"Those fucking screams don't help," I mutter. His body goes rigid.

"Christ, Violet. That isn't the machine," he says. I look wildly back to see the teens have gone, the game is back to the "start" menu, but the screams haven't stopped. A chill runs down my spine.

"Through here," I say, pointing a finger at the break room door. "In here."

It's locked, but that doesn't stop him. It's an old wooden door that opens inward, and the locks look flimsy. A perfect setup. "Back up."

The guy's a human bulldozer, larger than any other human I've ever met, and he knows how to use his body. He lets loose with a roundhouse kick, followed by a shoulder ram. The door whines and cracks. Another kick, shoulder, kick, shoulder. The door splinters and breaks. I help him kick the broken wood aside, half expecting someone to attack, but no one comes at us at first.

He steps through, and I follow behind him. "Be careful, Violet." Like him, I expect someone to attack at any moment. No one comes. My spine straightens at another scream, louder this time, and it's not coming from behind us but in front of us.

In seconds, I've got a knife in each hand, and he's cocked his gun. I wish I was experienced enough to have one too, but I'll get there. The knives are only my backup. My body's my main weapon.

There's no movement ahead of us or around us. I don't look at Cain, both of us focused. It's a small room that leads into another, the curtains and shades drawn tight so the room's darkened. A yellowed, bare bulb hangs from the entryway, throwing off a weak glow. Broken arcade games surround both sides, some with wires hanging out, others with cracked screens, the machines tilted on their sides like discarded gaming carcasses. I shiver. There's something eerie about them.

Another scream. My heart beats so fast I feel nauseous. Cain breaks through the rubble and runs. For the huge guy he is, he runs *fast*. I run behind him, panting to keep up, and we come to another doorway, this one with no door. This room must've been part of a haunted house or something similar back in the day. Discarded party decorations litter the floor. We enter the room; it's lined with boxes, so dark it's hard to see a damn thing.

A wall of stench hits my nostrils, and I cover my mouth and nose. The unmistakable scent of body odor, sweat, and sex lingers in the air. My mouth waters with the need to vomit, and bile burns the back of my throat, but I have to keep my head on straight. I can't lose my shit now.

Cain's boots crunch on broken glass as another scream tears through the quiet.

Cain sees them before I do. I know this the second he whips out his gun and aims. "You motherfucker. Put the light on, Vi. I want to see the life leave his eyes when I kill him."

Him. One. There's only one? He stands directly in front of me so I can't see a damn thing.

I look around frantically for a light switch and finally see one behind a stack of boxes. I lean in and flick it on. The room lights up, revealing a bulky guy not much older than I am wearing an eye patch, his long black hair covering his face like a shroud. He grins like he's just won the lottery. Beside him tied to the bed lies a young woman in a tank top and nothing else, her body laced with lacerations and angry red welts.

"Cain," she says in a tearful voice. "I told you not to come, I don't want you to get hurt."

"Ahh, Mr. Master. I see you—"

"Get down and cover."

I take a split second to process the command he snaps out before I drop to my knees and cover my ears, the cold metal of my knives on either side framing my face. One gunshot, two, a third I feel straight in my belly, and Dossier's body falls to the floor heavily. He screams, grabbing his arm.

"Secure Skylar, Violet. Leave him to me."

"Cain!" I stare in surprise as a second man enters the room who looks remarkably like Dossier. He brandishes a gun in the doorway. I don't think, but fling my knife with perfect precision directly at him. It strikes his belly as gunshots erupt. He falls to the floor, his face a mask of fury as he lunges for me. I roll and duck as he strikes out, dodging every attempt to hit me.

I have a second knife I whip at his leg. It hits precisely above his knee. He grabs at the knife, howling with rage, just as a gunshot hits his shoulder. Another one hits him in his other shoulder. I look up to see Cain staring down at him, his gun still smoking.

I know he's a perfect shot. He didn't aim to kill. He's here to capture. The killing will be a different story.

Dossier's bleeding behind him, his hand on his head as blood drips down his fingers.

Cain pulls out his phone and makes a call.

"Upper room. They're both alive, but not for long so fucking *move*."

"You bastard! You think this is over?" Dossier spits blood and spittle on the ground in front of him.

"Oh, no," Cain says with that smile that chills me to the bone. "Nowhere close to over." He falls to one knee beside Dossier. "Violet, you secure the other asshole."

"Happily." I yank my knife from the guy's leg and hold it to his temple. "You hurt innocent women. If you move, I'll slice your throat." My hand shakes with the effort of holding myself back.

"You tried to kill my brother in Paris," Dossier shouts. "You left him for dead. You son of a bitch, so proud of yourself."

"I defended my country. You kidnapped and raped innocent women," Cain says. I turn to look as Cain reaches over and squeezes his shoulder. Blood pours out of the wound and Dossier screams like a dying animal. "We'll both burn in hell for what we've done, but not until I'm good and ready to let you go."

Twins. The one supposedly killed wasn't dead after all. It all makes sense.

Dossier and his brother worked in tandem, one with an obvious alibi while the other kidnapped their victims. I'd bet good money both raped them. DNA evidence proved Dossier was the perpetrator because he was. Twin DNA is often so close it's indistinguishable.

Now that it's clear, I don't know how we missed it before. Twins. Fucking *twins*.

I scream when something strikes my back, pain radiating from my spine to my neck. I grab at my back and feel something wet and sticky. I look in disbelief at my hand covered in blood.

He sliced me with my own damn knife, but not very well. It grazed my skin but didn't stick.

"You son of a bitch." Cain lands a vicious kick to the Dossier he's got, then another and another until he slumps onto the floor. He swivels and lands a vicious kick to the other's belly. Blood spurts to the floor, and before he can recover, Cain hammers an uppercut to his abdomen with his right hand, then a jab to his jaw with his left, a brutal combination that leaves the other Dossier wheezing as he collapses again.

"You took my sister." Cain strikes him again, his fist like an anvil. "You raped innocent women." Dossier number two yanks his arms up to cover his face and openly cries, his tears mingled with blood, but I feel no sympathy. I want to see him suffer. I want to see him cry. "You dared to hurt *my woman.*" The next punch breaks bone. Dossier number two is a human punching bag and Cain has hit his rhythm, punching until he's unconscious.

"Cain!" I damn near risk my life and grab at his arm as he rears back to deliver what will no doubt be the blow that kills Dossier. The latent power in his arm sizzles through me, and I almost release him, but make myself hold fast. "While this is highly entertaining, you have to stop." He's panting with the exertion, sweat dripping down his face. I gentle my voice. "You have to stop, Cain. You have to leave something for us to interrogate."

The other one lunges at me, and I step out of the way just in time.

"Right." Cain faces the other Dossier, baring his teeth. "You piece of shit. You'll get a taste of the same fucking medicine."

"Cain," I say pleadingly. "Let me?"

He reaches down with a sickening smile and grabs Dossier by the hair. "Have at it, baby."

I swivel and give him a roundhouse kick. I hit him as hard as I can. He doubles over, grabbing his stomach. I knee him in the back and he falls to the floor. "You hurt his sister. You hurt innocent women. You broke into my house, and you made my man *bleed.*" I puncture every word with another jab, strike, and kick until he's whimpering and begging for mercy. It hasn't even begun to satisfy my thirst for violence when Cain speaks.

"Alright, Violet," Cain says, with unmistakable pride in his voice that makes my chest swell.

"He deserves more than that."

"And I'll make sure he gets what he deserves."

I look into Cain's eyes and reach my hand up to cup his jaw. His icy blue gaze locks with mine. *"Promise* me."

Gently extracting my hand from his face, he kisses each bloodied fingertip, one by one. "I promise you, sweetheart. I'll make them pay. Both of them."

A thrill of arousal races through me.

I might love this monster of a man.

Satisfied, I look around the room and see wires hanging out of a broken video game. I slice them with one of my knives, then tie both men at their ankles and wrists so I can get to Skylar.

Cain and I unfasten her and lead her off the dirty bed, grabbing a sheet to wrap around her waist. She trembles but walks beside me.

"Are you alright?" I ask her.

She looks away and doesn't answer at first, then finally nods. "I am now."

I walk back to the bed while Cain drags both men to it. He hauls one up like he's a sack of potatoes and tosses him unceremoniously on the bed. The guy whimpers. He takes the second, hog-tied and immobile, and tosses him beside his brother. Even though they're beaten beyond recognition and tied fast, he has me hold both men at gunpoint while he makes the call.

 I don't even want to think about what he'll do to them when he brings them back to his place. I haven't even begun to explore the many rooms he has at his home, but something tells me the target range isn't the only soundproof room in the house. And I remember what I've read about his methods.

These men will wish we'd killed them here.

Skylar stares at me with large, frightened eyes.

"Who are you?" Her voice is wobbly, broken. My heart splinters. I don't even want to think about what she's been through.

I give her a gentle smile. "My name's Violet."

Skylar gives me a tentative smile back, through her obvious pain. "That's a beautiful name."

CHAPTER SIXTEEN

Violet

IT'S late into the night. Darkness settles over the house on the hill, as the sun set hours ago. Skylar's soundly sleeping in one of the guest rooms on the main floor, sedated by the doctor. She needs rest now more than anything.

Cain has her heavily guarded. I didn't think I liked Cain's straightlaced bodyguard the day I came here. Now I've never been so happy to see him.

Today, we brought down the men responsible for the abductions and rapes. Under Cain's... questioning, one might call it... we got full confessions. And I was right about them working in tandem. We have much to unpack, and will, but the greatest threat is over.

Cain takes on the task of telling his team all that happened, and instructs me to call Candi. "Then go to your room. Relax and get some rest. I'll come see you when I'm through down here." I know without him telling me that he'll be "through down there" when his men lay twin bodies in shallow graves. I'm not upset by this. I'd be disappointed with anything less.

I'm not surprised there are two armed men on either side of my door when I arrive at the guest room. We have to make sure neither Dossier was in league with anyone. We don't know for sure yet that this was the end of the attacks.

So when I'm finally settled in, I call Candi and alert her that we've found the men responsible for Cain's sister's abduction, but they were killed.

Candi's voice is weary when she asks, "Do I want to know the rest of this story, babe?"

"No, Candi. You don't."

"Are you safe?"

My answer's no more certain now than it was the last time she asked me. Once again, I lie to my best friend. "Yeah. I'm safe."

"Violet... be careful. Cain Master is a dangerous, *dangerous* man. I don't like that you're involved with him. I don't like it at *all*."

I don't know how to tell her the fact that he's a dangerous man might be what draws me to him the most.

She takes my statement and tells me she'll come for a full report in the morning. I look forward to it. Somehow, seeing my best friend here might make this all seem real. My two worlds will collide... but it's time.

I don't want to see anyone else right now and definitely don't feel like talking to anyone, so I settle into my room for the night. I've showered and put on pajamas. I played mindless games on my phone. I'm too wired to settle down.

I get up and go to the walk-in closet. I finger the clothes, stroke the fine fabrics, and marvel at the sheer volume of luxury. They're gorgeous, every single one of them, and he says they're all for me. I'm too tired to try anything on just now, but when I dressed earlier, everything I tried fit me perfectly.

And the *shoes*... good God, the shoes alone could buy me a townhouse right here by the ocean. Heels and flats, sandals and boots, an array of colors and fabrics that would be the envy of any shoe aficionado.

Why?

How long does he think I'll stay?

It's a little unsettling, if I'm honest.

What's the catch?

And does it matter? I'm here for a reason, and I won't leave until I've done what I came for.

But now I make myself face the truth I've been avoiding.

I want to see Cain. I want to touch him, feel him.

And I want much, much more than the kiss I got last night.

After what we've been through...

I hear heavy footsteps outside my door, and the low rumble of a voice that can only be him. I sit up in bed, my heart racing, as he knocks just before the door opens. He stands in the doorway, the light from the hall casting him in shadow, but I know it's him.

"No one fills a doorframe like *that*."

He turns his head as if just realizing there's a doorframe there.

I can hear the humor in his voice when he responds, "No one fills a bed like *that*."

I look around me at the cavernous bed. "I'm *hardly* filling it." I give him a little pout. "There's plenty of room still here."

The door shuts with an audible *bang*.

I jump. Liquid heat pools between my legs. I forget to breathe.

"Are the guards still there?" My whole being is filled with wanting.

He prowls closer to me, the shadows falling behind him. "Of course not. I told them to go because I'm here now."

I briefly close my eyes to quell the rise of emotion. He told the guards to go because *I'm safe with him*.

I open my eyes. As he draws nearer, he never takes his eyes from mine. The shadow's behind him now, and the pale yellow light from the bedside table illuminates his features.

His ruggedly masculine face, lined with weariness, is speckled with blood, his jaw covered in thick black stubble, but I've never seen anyone so beautiful in my life. His strong features hold inherent masculinity, underscored by the harsh slash of his mouth softened by full lips. When I first met him, I wondered if he could pull a sword out of a stone or bare his teeth and show me his fangs. I almost laughed at myself, at my imagination.

Now, I know he could do that and more. So much more.

He locks me in the power of his gaze. His eyes show the same raging fury and power they did when I first saw him. Only now, I see that the simmering anger only boils at the surface. It will take me years to unearth what lies beneath.

I can wait.

He sighs wearily when he reaches the bed. Bending to grasp the edge of his T-shirt, he lifts it up over his body, the fabric bunching and swaying before he tosses it to the side. I briefly wonder if his broad shoulders ever bow under the weight of what he carries.

I wonder if he'll ever share that burden.

I let my gaze rove lazily over his chest, the smattering of dark, coarse hair, defined abs, and a thin chain with dog tags. When he sees me looking at them, he lifts them off and places them gently on the bed. That's a story for another day then.

"You alright?" he asks, his voice a low rumble that sets my nerves on fire.

I shake my head. "No. You?"

"No." He gives me a slow, lazy smile. "I need a shower, baby. So fucking bad. Think you can help me?"

I love it when he calls me baby.

I'm on my feet before I realize what I'm doing. My hands shake when I reach for his belt. I unfasten the clasp and slide it through the loops, then lay it on the side of the bed. He watches me, his hands on his hips, as I reach for the button of his jeans and slide to my knees in front of him.

With slow precision, I remove his pants, my breath catching as I tug them down his legs. He steps first one foot out, then the other, and his pants join his tee on the floor.

I can see the outline of his erection through his boxers. Like everything about him, it's larger than life. I lick my lips and swallow. I imagine what it would be like to take him in my mouth, to please him. I've never done that for anyone before, but I want to for him.

I don't know why, but I'm overcome with emotion. Maybe it's because I've been through so much in such a short time. Maybe because I know now that we've found his sister and she's safe, it's time to move on to the job I know I have to do.

Or maybe it's because I know I want him and can't bear the thought he doesn't want me the way I do him. Does he? I close my eyes and lay my cheek against his thigh. The dark, prickly hair scratches my cheek, as his hand comes to the back of my head and holds me there.

We don't speak. I kneel between his legs, my arms wrapped around him. I need a moment, and somehow, he knows that. He gives it to me before he bends, then kneels in front of me. Holds me. Right there on the floor, nearly naked, he tugs me onto his lap so my legs wrap around him to straddle his waist.

My body kindles with my need for him, his length pressed up against my panties. He wraps his fingers around the back of my neck and tugs me closer to him. My eyes meet his, and I know he's going to kiss me.

He rises with me in his arms, my legs still tucked around him, then lays me on the bed. His hands tangle in my hair and he holds my mouth to his but I need no persuasion. His huge, muscular frame pins me to the bed. I release a breath he swallows and makes his own. My breasts heave, pressed tight against his unyielding chest, and liquid heat cascades between my legs. His tongue licks mine, drawing an inhuman moan from me.

"I want you, Violet. All of you."

I nod dumbly, ready to give him anything and everything he wants. Right now, I want his hands and mouth and cock and body joined with mine in every possible combination. I want to kiss and lick and worship his body.

I want to bring him pleasure and surrender to bliss.

I want *everything*.

His hand cups my breast, and I whimper with the sudden flare of need that makes me tremble. His thumb flicks over my nipple. I nearly come.

"Cain," I whisper on a choked breath, so desperate to be closer to him I can't speak.

Silently, he lowers his mouth to my breast and licks the hardened nipple. A spasm of pleasure ripples through me so hard my hips jerk upward. He suckles again. My clit throbs on the edge of release. "*Fuuuccck,* baby," he growls in my ear. "I need to taste you."

I'm a ragdoll to his touch, pliable and boneless, as he arranges me on the bed and drops to his knees. When he looks at me, my heart turns over in my chest. I hold my breath as he parts my knees like he's worshipping me, the sexiest damn thing I've ever seen. He kisses the inside of my thigh, as he slides his thumb along my panty-clad slit. My hips buck. My pulse races. He kisses my right thigh. I'm still gasping for breath when he tugs my panties down and releases a deep, masculine groan I feel straight between my legs.

Holding my thighs in his big, very capable hands, he spreads them further apart. Exposing me. His eyes meet mine with a burning insolence, as if daring me to turn away now. I couldn't if I tried. My choice was made when he stepped through that door.

No. My choice was made the day I came here.

His eyes burning into me, he slowly lowers his mouth. He lazily drags his tongue along my swollen, throbbing clit, again and again. I cry out, my hips jerk. A moan of ecstasy slips through my lips, my palms flat on the bed on either side of me to keep me from flying away. My body quivers on the edge of ecstasy, the first spasm of orgasm echoing through me. He pumps his fingers in me. I shatter.

 I can't breathe, I can't think, as my body bucks under the pressure of my climax. I come so hard, so many times, his heavy body atop mine, his length pressed between my legs. I scream his name until I'm hoarse.

Still riding the waves of ecstasy, I feel his breath in my ear before he says in a ragged voice, "I want to be in you when you come again. I want to feel you climax with me."

"Again? I'll die." I grab the back of his neck, pull him to me, and slam my mouth on his. "Bring it."

His low, masculine chuckle sends a spasm of pleasure straight through me. "I promise you, baby. I'll make it worth it. Over. And over. And over again." He kisses my cheek while he holds me, his length throbbing along with my pulse. A deep sense of peace invades my senses. I feel like I belong here. I know I can trust him.

Hypnotized by his touch, I surrender to him. I've never surrendered to anyone in my life.

This feels so right.

I study his face unhurriedly, each perfect, harsh, beautifully masculine detail. I love the way he looks at me hungrily, the way his muscles tighten, as if he's holding himself back.

"Make love to me, Cain."

His weight flush against me, he moves with determination, braces himself over me, and lines himself up between my legs. Then my wrists are trapped in his big, unyielding hands, as he puts his lips on mine.

He thrusts. I scream out loud. He stills.

"Don't," I pant. "Don't stop. *Please.*"

He skims a hand down my side as he thrusts again and again, gliding in and out of my slick heat in a perfect rhythm. Every thrust undoes me, every bolt of blissful pleasure makes me whole again. He swells inside me, but I take him. Each thrust sends sparks of pleasure rolling through me until I can't hold myself back any longer.

He releases a deep, masculine moan so ragged and raw, I lose myself to bliss and join him in ecstasy.

Seconds, moments, hours later, I'm still tangled in his taut limbs. He rolls over and tucks me to his chest. I can't move. I can't even open my eyes. It's a wonder to me he even has the strength to lace his fingers through my hair, and yet he does.

"I'm on birth control," I say on a sigh, half dead.

"Your timing's impeccable," he says with another one of those manly chuckles I wish I could record and play in an endless loop. I'd pay money to hear that again.

"I'm good like that. You still need to shower?"

"No, baby. I don't need anything now."

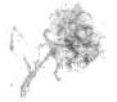

CHAPTER SEVENTEEN

Violet

"EYES ON THE TARGET. Do *not* take your eyes off the target."

"If I take my eyes off the target, do I get—"

"Don't try me, woman."

I grin as I pull the trigger.

Boom.

Boom.

Boom.

Three perfect shots right where I aimed.

Yes.

I feel his heat behind me before I see him, warm hands on my hips. I close my eyes when he kisses my cheek.

"I've never seen anyone learn how to hit a mark so quickly."

Oh yeah? I want to ask him. What do you call this?

I haven't returned to my apartment. I'm here for a reason, and I'm not leaving now until I've fulfilled my job. Until my mission's complete.

At least that's what I tell myself.

I feel the cool of his dog tags on my neck, and mentally imagine they kiss my scars. I'm feeling a bit sentimental today.

Skylar's home safe, and Cain has his answers.

Now it's my turn.

Unearthing who he is—who *I* am—is as much a mystery as finding Skylar's kidnapper.

"Eyes on the target, baby," he repeats. His much larger hands cover mine.

We stand as one.

We breathe as one.

Pull the trigger as one.

The blast of the gun reverberates through me, but we brace for the kickback together.

We shoot a perfect bullseye.

CHAPTER EIGHTEEN

Cain

THE END of the Dossier twins is the end of the terror inflicted on the innocent women of Salem.

Skylar needs time and some TLC, but I make sure she has it. She's bonded with Violet, and sometimes I don't know who appreciates that more. They become fast friends.

I'm glad.

It gives me a reason to keep her here.

I'd put a ring on her finger if it were up to me.

Not now. Not yet. My caged bird will fly if I try to hold her in captivity.

But now it's time...

I can help her find her parents' killers, and I will help her seek the vengeance she craves. I know I have what she wants.

What she doesn't know yet is how badly I want *her*. All of her. Completely, irrevocably... forever.

One day after target practice, I ask her to come up to my office. When she walks in the door, my heart does a somersault. I lean against the edge of my desk and beckon to her.

"Come here, baby."

I love that look she gets when I call her to me. Part daring, part hopeful, and all kinds of aroused.

When she reaches me, I run my hand up and down her back slowly, until she breathes a little freer and she lays her head on my shoulder. She fits right here, within my arms. She belongs here.

The office is so quiet, my words hang heavily between us.

"Candi says we've had nothing but quiet here in Salem. The biggest issue is keeping the teens from toilet papering the House of the Seven Gables on Halloween."

"I could stop them."

She snorts. "I bet you could, but you've got bigger fish to fry, don't you?"

I do. I run my hands along her shoulders, then down her slim waist to rest on her hips.

"You want to find your parents' killers, Violet?"

I watch her shoulders rise as she inhales, then fall as she lets her breath out. "I do, Cain. More than anything in the world."

Anything in the world.

I trace my fingers along her spine. "You helped me find my sister."

"Yes."

"And that, sweetheart, was your first task for me."

She nods, as I slowly turn us so she's now leaning against the desk and extend the trajectory of my touch. Past her back. Up her shoulders. Over her collarbone, then lower to where her ass meets the desk.

"But I want more than your work, Violet."

I place a gentle kiss on her neck, then open my mouth and suck in her damp, sweet flesh. I watch her knuckles whiten on the edge of the desk.

"What do you want from me?"

I place my hands on either side of her. My frame dwarfs hers. "I want *you*."

A slow blink as she absorbs my words.

"Me?"

"You. *All of you.* Carte blanche to do whatever I want to you, whenever I want to. Anytime, anywhere."

Her eyelids flutter closed, like a little bird's, her words a mere whisper. "I have the distinct feeling I'd... both hate and love every minute of what you'd do to me."

"Love and hate are so irrevocably entwined, aren't they?"

She places her hand in mine, and her eyes flutter open. "Yes."

I'm not sure if she means yes, she agrees with the sentiment, or yes, she agrees with what I want.

"Yes?"

When she smiles, her eyes light up, moon-kissed amethyst that enchants me to my soul. "Yes, Cain. I accept your terms. I'm yours."

CHAPTER NINETEEN

Violet

"KEEP YOUR EYES STRAIGHT AHEAD. Do not move away, even for a second."

Cain's deep rumble of a voice vibrates in my ear. Of *course* this is one of the very many ways he'd test me. Just hand me a gun that requires immense concentration to handle, give me an instruction to keep my eyes on the target ahead, then hover his magnificent, muscled body so close to mine I'm nearly trembling in anticipation.

"Bet no one else has target practice like *this*," I mutter, more than a little annoyed. I don't want to have target practice. I want to tear his clothes off and jump his bones, right now, right here, on the cold concrete floor of the target range. I'm annoyed I can't do that, and annoyed he's made me feel like a wanton slut.

"That's right, Violet," Cain says in my ear, as he ghosts his tongue over my earlobe. I stifle a whimper. "There's no one else here who uses target practice for the sole purpose of muffling their screams when they come."

"It's not the *sole* purpose," I mutter under my breath. I mean, I'm a damn good shot now.

I brace myself, grit my teeth, and pull the trigger. Fire explodes from the gun, the bullet tears into the paper target shaped like a human, and I watch with gleeful satisfaction as I tear a hole right between the eyes, the infamous "T-box" shot. Lethal, every time.

"Well done, little protégé," Cain says with approval. Warmth flares through my chest at his praise. It's rare that he doles out praise to anyone, and sometimes I feel he's toughest on me. The others know I mean something to him, and he doesn't want anyone to think I get preferential treatment.

I do, though.

I *so* do.

"Tell me the three types of gunshots," he says, nestling his hands on my hips. He's been training me now for nearly two months, and only a small portion of the training takes place with actual tactical work.

I try to stand up straighter, but his body's pressed up against mine. Not that I'm complaining. I reload my gun as I spout off details. "The three main types of gunshot wounds include non-penetrating, perforating, and penetrating. Non-penetrating wounds mean the bullet grazed skin without embedding, perforating wounds involve an entrance and exit site, and penetrating wounds have an entrance site with no exit."

"Very good. Which type of gunshot do we aim for, Violet?"

I answer like I'm under his command, because it tickles my fancy. "Whichever is the most expedient, sir."

Sometimes we shoot to warn. Sometimes we shoot to injure. Sometimes we shoot to kill.

I hold my position, vividly aware of his heartbeat against my back and his warmth that surrounds me like a heated blanket. He'd kick anyone's ass for engaging in target practice while so close to another, but I know it's partly how he likes to test me.

I aim for the target and pull the trigger again.

Bam. Hit the kidney, an excellent debilitating and potentially fatal shot. The perfect one to incapacitate and cause pain without immediate death, if we're feeling like we need to have a little chat.

"Good girl. Excellent."

I don't react. I don't want anyone to see how I bask in the little rays of his praise. It's kind of pathetic.

"Aim for the left shoulder."

I pull the trigger and stifle a grin when the paper target of a shoulder tears open.

"Heart."

Another on-point hit.

"Right shoulder."

Boom.

I don't wait for further instruction, but aim a few more shots, the last one landing straight in the groin area.

"Fuck, my balls clenched at that."

"Your balls clenched because it's fucking cold out here. Did you see what I made for you?"

I grin at him over my shoulder, and he quickly brushes his mouth against mine. I didn't expect that, but I don't stop him. I love the feel of his hot, sensual mouth on mine, the way my body melts against him and my heartbeat quickens.

"No, baby," he whispers with a smile. "What'd you make for me?"

"It's a heart, see?"

He looks over my shoulder. "Ah, so it is. You shot a heart shape in a human body. If that's not the most romantic fucking thing I've ever seen..."

I grin. "I knew you'd like it."

"Should I frame it?" he teases, as I clean up the little table at the range and carefully put the ammo and guns away.

"Of course. Put it away so I can regift it to you on Valentine's Day."

"You're so damn romantic."

"I try."

He takes the gun out of my hand, lays it down on the table, and reaches for me.

"This is why you love target practice."

I gasp when his fingers tangle in my hair, his grip firm but just exactly what I need. My mouth parts to release a whimper he quickly swallows. His tongue touches mine. My belly melts.

My hands find their way around his hard, muscled back, grasping for purchase as he takes the kiss deeper. Harder. I meet his tongue with mine, relishing the sound of his deep, male groan.

"Tell me again," he grates in my ear, a firm command that makes my nipples hard. "The three types of gunshot wounds, Violet. Nice and slow."

"Non-penetrating," I say on a groan, as his fingers find the hem of my shirt and gently lift it. I feel the warmth of his touch on my belly, then one finger grazes the curve of my breast. He flickers a thumb over my bra-clad nipple. My body's used to his touch. My hips jerk.

He nods. I think I know what he's doing.

"Perforating." Strong fingers slide past the elastic of my leggings, past the silk top of my panties, and dive between my legs to do their magic. I open my legs and moan, surprised at how wet I am already. I shouldn't be. He knows how to play my body, how to work it to climax in any way he knows how.

"Good girl. And the last one?"

I close my eyes. "Penetrating."

Thick fingers plunge into my core, jerk upward, and I cry out from the sudden stabbing thrills that explode through me.

He's done wicked, dirty things to me in here, and it seems he's nowhere near finished.

"I fucking love to see you come," he growls in my ear, his hand cupped possessively around my pussy, which is still spasming. I breathe hard, then softer, slumping against him. I'm barely aware of where we are or what we're doing when he slides into one of the straight-backed chairs at the back of the range which we keep for guests and tugs me onto his lap.

It's been precisely seven weeks and four days since we rescued his sister Skylar from a vindictive serial rapist. It feels much, much longer.

I've left my day job and moved into Cain's house in Salem, a large, rambling estate where many of his employees live. He treats them to the lap of luxury, as he should. They run a top secret, clandestine organization that charges top dollar. Their clients pay more for a job with Master Enterprises than most people ever earn in their lifetime. Tonight's security detail, for example, runs a cool million dollars.

"Got a present for you, baby," Cain whispers in my ear.

"Cain—"

"'You shouldn't buy me so many things'," he finishes in a high-pitched voice. "'Stop spoiling me. I don't need all these things'."

I mutter under my breath. But when he nestles a heavy, large, solid black box onto my lap, I close my mouth. My heart beats a little faster.

"What's that?" I whisper.

"Open it and see."

My hand shakes when I slide my finger along the edge of the box top and gently lift it. I lean against his large, sturdy frame to help still the trembling, but it doesn't work. I'm shaking. I don't handle expensive gifts well, and something tells me this one's not cheap.

I don't deserve it, I think to myself, *whatever it is.*

He wouldn't like it if he heard me saying that.

"It's way too big of a box for jewelry and way too small for a car."

His low, manly chuckle makes me smile.

"You don't want a car, baby. Even I know that. You want a truck."

Not just any truck, I want the gorgeous Toyota Tundra 4WD with the Rockstar Rims that sits in his driveway. The gorgeous force of nature with thirty-eight-inch mud terrain tires and black rawhide leather interior with blood-red inlay. *Swoon.*

I lift the lid, and my jaw drops open. I can't breathe for long seconds, my eyes water with tears, and my nose tingles. There's a lump lodged in my throat. I don't trust myself to speak.

"You deserve it, baby," he whispers in my ear. No. No one deserves a masterpiece like this, and most definitely not me.

"Is this the Wilson?" I whisper.

We were looking at high-end handguns the other day, and when my eyes fell on the Wilson Combat Tactical Super-grade, I almost lost my mind. It's absolutely *gorgeous*, hand-crafted from carbon steel, the premier in defensive handguns.

Gunmetal gray with silver details, it's solidly built yet somehow lightweight. The handle's decorated in a pattern that looks like sunbursts. Every detail is finely crafted perfection.

"I had this custom made for you, baby." Of course he did. Cain doesn't do cookie-cutter. "Takes eight rounds. Four-pound trigger pull, starburst grips, five-inch carbon steel slide." He goes on about the details, front sight something something, blah blah blah. I've got guns that I absolutely love. Some that have become like friends to me, comfortable in my palm and ready to shoot. But this... this was custom-made for me.

"It's lightweight, beautiful, and deadly," he says.

"You do say the most romantic things."

I feel his stubble across my cheek when he kisses me, and while a thrill shimmers through my body, I'm focused on the stunning weapon I hold in my hand.

"I can't take this, Cain." I shake my head. It cost *five thousand dollars*.

"You can. You're worth it."

I shake my head, but he gently pushes me off his lap. "Go show me, Violet. Show me what you've got. We've got the security detail tonight, and if you're comfortable with it, you'll take this with you."

He's got harnesses and holsters galore for me to choose from, so that shouldn't be a problem.

I stand, new energy coursing through me with my new toy in hand. I tremble in anticipation as I slide the ammo into place. I've used his guns. I've borrowed guns.

I've never owned one.

I take in a deep breath, get into position, and aim.

Boom.

Boom.

Boom.

My God, it shoots as if enhanced with magic. Each bullet hits its mark with perfect precision.

This is it. I'm holding the weapon I'll use when I kill my parents' murderer.

CHAPTER TWENTY

Cain

"BOSS."

I stare at the screen in front of me, half aware that I'm not alone but still too busy reading the latest report to really focus. Someone clears his throat. I look up to see Joe, my employee and friend, standing in the doorway with two steaming mugs of coffee. "You got a minute?"

I nod, shut my laptop, and gesture for him to take a seat. "Yeah, of course. Make it quick, though, Violet and I need to get ready for Monstraut tonight."

"Ah, Monstraut," he says with an air of dignity as if he's narrating a high-end travel show on the Home and Garden Network. "Mandy Fontaina's family residence, located in Manchester-by-the-Sea, the private, single-family home sits eighty feet above the impressive rocky shoreline so nothing but the Atlantic separates you from Europe. With elegant Italian travertine flooring, cathedral ceilings, and floor-to-ceiling windows, you'll enjoy a touch of privacy with a flair of elegance."

I roll my eyes at him as my phone chimes, and when I see it's from Violet, I quickly tap it. A picture pops up with her standing in the middle of our walk-in closet wearing nothing but a little robe. Her hair's in a towel. Joe's words fade and I quickly glance at the clock to see if I have time to pay her a quick visit.

Fuck. I don't.

What do I wear tonight?!

I smile and tap out a response.

Something gorgeous that doesn't let anyone see what's mine that's also versatile enough for you to run in if you need to.

Ah....

I put my phone down to see Joe looking at me with a knowing twinkle in his eyes. "Violet?"

I don't bother to respond but just grunt at him. "What do you need? And how did you know that was Violet?"

He leans back and laces his fingers behind his head, untroubled by my irritated tone. "You don't get a look like that on your face unless you're talking to her."

Whatever. So they've never seen me in love before.

"You come here to give me shit about being a human fucking male with a pair, or you got shit to say?"

At that, he sobers, leaning forward to rest his elbows on his knees. "We've got trouble. Armand's talking shit."

I blow out a breath. "I fucking knew it."

Armand has an ax to grind, and dealing with him won't be easy. I let him go for fucking up. He had clear instructions but decided to go about them by orchestrating a car accident with Violet. He could've fucking killed her. And I won't allow anyone on my team to do something so stupid.

Should've let him go years ago. Only reason I kept him around so long was because he saved my ass overseas, but I won't let the asshole put Violet in danger.

Problem is, Armand knows shit I'd like to keep between us, most notably when it concerns Violet.

"Have you told her yet?"

I clench my jaw and look away, confirmation enough for him that I haven't. I know exactly what he wants me to tell her. That I knew her long before she ever came here. That I looked into her background, had her fully searched, damn near stalked her before she ever knew I existed.

That I had her play directly into my hands so I'd have her all to myself.

"I need time," I tell him. "I want her to trust me fully, and I want to tell her on my terms."

He gives me a reluctant nod. We both know I don't have time.

"If I tell her now, she'll run. And I can't have that, Joe." I fucking hate that anyone else but Joe knows how this happened, that Armand's got this evidence against me to blackmail me with, affecting the woman I'd give my life for.

But I hate that there's something like a lie between us. I never lied to her, no. I couldn't do that. But I haven't told her the truth, which is as good as a lie.

He swallows.

"I'll take care of it." I will. "Tell me the details about tonight."

I rarely take on security detail cases but thought it would be a prime opportunity to continue Violet's training. She's learned a lot since she first came here and has quickly become the most accurate shooter in our company. That said, what she doesn't know about the jobs we do could fill a small volume, and she still has a lot to learn. Plus, tonight will give us a chance to be close to each other and pad our wallets.

He doesn't respond at first, only straightens his shoulders before giving me a nod.

"Mandy Fontaina's family residence, located in Manchester-by-the-Sea. Two hundred expected guests. Security detail's expected to cover both home and private beach. Our team's already obtained full background checks on the entirety of the guest list, and are on call to safeguard the premises and assets." He leans forward. "Rumor has it Mandy's mom recently obtained half a dozen rare pieces of art she intends to reveal at tonight's little gala, to the tune of a cool six mil." He leans back and shakes his head. "And either she's paranoid or has a real concern about safety, because she wants everything from the beach to the last goddamn bathroom secured."

Huh. Interesting. The teen idol turns twenty-one years old today, and her parents are known for showing off.

"Francine Fontaina wants her home swept for bugs before we go, too."

"Woman hiding something?"

Leaning back, he shrugs his shoulders. "It's a distinct possibility, boss, but I'm just relaying the information to you."

"Got it. They're paying high. You'll each get a bonus for this."

He grins. "Works for me."

My phone buzzes again, this time with Violet standing in front of her full-length mirror wearing nothing but a thong and a bra.

> This work? I can move pretty freely dressed like this.

> I'll be right there.

An hour later, she's dressed in a slinky navy gown, with a slit to high heaven that allows her to run if need be but paired with knee-high boots to hide her weapons.

I stand behind her in the full-length mirror and rest my hands on her hips, ignoring the way my cock strains the closer I get to her. I pull her closer to me, and when her ass presses up against me, she grins.

"My, my, Mr. Master. If I didn't know you had the gun in your *holster,* and not your pocket..."

I lean in and drag my lips across the shell of her ear. Inhale her. Close my eyes and relish this brief moment in time when everything's perfect. "Behave yourself, woman. You move one more inch and I'll have no choice but to fuck you right here, right now, against this wall, and then we'll be late." I shake my head with mock regret. "And I'll have to punish you for that."

Her eyes roll back and her head falls to the side, giving me full access to the creamy skin at her neck and her full cleavage. I smack her gorgeous ass, and she gives a little yelp, then a moan. "That's supposed to stop me?"

A knock sounds at the door. With a groan I pull away from her and adjust myself. "Yeah?"

"It's me, boss." Claude, tall, with a shaved head he's had since his time in the service, comes in with a matte black box in his hand. He's dressed like me in a charcoal-gray suit custom-made to hide our harnesses and weapons.

"Oh, you brought us pressies," Violet says, her brilliant amethyst eyes lighting up. She loves weapons like other women love jewelry.

I take the box from Claude. "Give it here. No other man gives my woman weapons."

He grins at me. I open the box. Nestled on the left are sleek black earpieces with mics, but on the right are new, custom-made thin Tantos. I take the slim one made for Violet and give it to her. The silver blade of the throwing knife sparkles like jewels in her slender hand.

I made her learn to shoot because a knife can only go so far, but Violet's real skill lies with a blade. "Show me, baby. Target, ten o'clock."

She wields the knife with the skill of a master, the silver blade flashing in the overhead lighting. She takes her position gracefully like a dancer, and with a flick of her wrist sends the knife soaring into a target we have on the wall for this purpose. It stabs like a dart, straight on the mark.

Claude whistles. "She could slice the hair off my balls and leave 'em intact," he says.

"You keep your fucking balls away from her or there will be no *intact*," I mutter.

Violet grins. "Aw, babe, I love when you get all territorial on me. Gonna piss on me before we hit Monstraut?"

I reach for her, drag her over to me, and stab my fingers in her hair. "Don't tempt me."

"And, that's my cue," Claude mutters. "I'll leave you two to suit up and see you tonight, then." The door clicks shut behind him.

"Aw, honey, you keep embarrassing the children." Her eyes twinkle at me. "Now, leave me alone so I can fix my hair. We'll never get there in time."

"Your hair's perfect as is."

Still slightly damp, it hangs about her shoulders in gentle waves.

"You like the beach wave look?"

"I like every look."

"You'd like me with cellulite and stretch marks after babies?" she asks, her head tilted. Though her tone's teasing, there's a hint of authenticity in her tone I don't miss.

Still, I heard the word *babies* and my mind's still there, not quite sure what to make of a concept like *that*. She laughs, a musical, addictive laugh I'd pay good money to hear over and over again.

I lace my hands about her hips and drag her closer. "Of course. Even then you'd be gorgeous."

"Oh? And what if I got into a car accident and they had to amputate my legs or something?"

"Even then, baby."

"What if I—"

I've had enough of this game. "Violet. I don't like this game. I like you the way you are right here, right now, and don't want to imagine you hurt or damaged."

"Alright, alright," she says. Getting up on her tiptoes, she kisses me. "Let's go. God, I'm starving, though."

"Good. We're getting dinner first."

Her eyes light up. "Are we?"

"Yep. I finally got you out of yoga pants and a tank top and I'm not missing my chance."

She gives me a lopsided grin. "I'd get out of those anytime you ask, Mr. Master."

I slide my hand along the small of her back. "I'm aware, Miss Price. An office perk I like to take full advantage of."

My phone buzzes with a text. I glance at the screen.

> Joe: They need us there early. Ready to
> leave in ten?

"Motherfucker."

"Uh oh. Nothing like thwarted plans to bring out the big gun curse words. What's up?"

"No time for dinner. We need to go."

Violet pouts for about three seconds before she shrugs, turns, and reaches for the dorm-sized fridge I keep in my room. She opens it and snags two protein shakes. I catch one mid-air when she tosses it to me.

"I'll take a rain check."

"Name the place, babe."

An hour later, we're stationed outside of Monstraut. Mrs. Fontaina's given us the full tour of the estate, and Violet intentionally kept her eyes off mine as she did so. Later, she'll give me the full rendition in Fontaina's high-pitched, nasally voice. *"The glass staircase accesses the primary suite with water views, marble bath with a soaking tub, and private, ocean-facing deck."*

I didn't know anyone hated pretense more than I do until I met Violet.

I recently tried to gift her a diamond tennis bracelet, and she told me that it was lovely, but could I please get her a gun instead?

I did.

That's my girl.

When we're alone on the deck, Claude stationed at the front of the house and Joe on the bottom floor overseeing a small group of my men, I nod my chin toward the office. "You'll be my lead in checking for bugs. Let's go."

"What makes her think her place is bugged?" she asks, her brow puckered with curiosity.

"No fucking idea," I mutter. "Could be she's delusional. Who knows?"

We go through the standard routine, sweep the closets, the corners of the room, under the desk.

"I remember I once thought I was being watched," Violet says with a self-deprecating snort. My heart stops for a full beat.

There was absolutely a time she was being watched. By *me*.

"Yeah?"

"Yeah. I swear I always felt eyes following me, but it was just in my head."

"Oh? When was this?"

"Few months before I came to see you." She's crouched on the floor beneath the desk, checking for bugs. She rises when she finds nothing, then sweeps across the desk for another quick go.

It's on the tip of my tongue to tell her the truth. I can imagine it, her sidled up close to me while I tell her everything. I have files and files of videos I took of her, photos I shot, reams of background history. Everything locked up tighter than a vault.

One day I'll tell her, but today is not that day.

"And what if you found someone was watching you?"

She looks over her shoulder at me and laughs as if the very thought's preposterous. "Why would anyone want to follow *me*?" She shakes her head. "Honest to God, that's the silliest thing. I'm nobody."

I cross the room to her. The look in her eyes tells me she's wary of me, that she knows she's pushed it by calling herself a nobody.

"Okay, so I'm not a *nobody*," she begins, in an effort to backtrack that I'm not buying. We've been together now for a few months, but I've known her longer than that.

"You are not *nobody*," I tell her when she's within my reach.

"Cain," she murmurs, her eyes focused over my shoulder at the door. She's afraid we'll get caught like this, but I couldn't give a shit. She shakes her head, flustered and frazzled, until I tug a little lock of her hair just at the base of her scalp. Her eyes widen, and her lips part as her gaze meets mine.

"Not here," she whispers, begging me not to dominate her where someone could see us. She gave me her word when we closed our first case together that she's mine. That she'd devote herself to me, give me carte blanche in exchange for my serving her vengeance on a platter.

"Violet," I warn. She promised me. She gave me a vow that she'd give herself to me, and giving herself to me means I take her wherever, whenever, and however I want. I use that to my full advantage. Never said I wasn't an asshole.

"You are not nobody," I whisper in her ear. "You are the most brilliant, the most mesmerizing, the most intriguing woman I've ever met." *And I love you,* I mentally tack on, but I can't say it aloud. If I do, she'll run. I've worked every day since the minute she stepped foot on my property to build her trust, but we're not there yet. She still occasionally flutters her wings like a caged bird, ready to flee when the door opens.

"Well," she murmurs, placing her hand on my shoulder in an attempt to calm me. It works. "That still isn't reason enough to *follow* me. So the very idea's preposterous, Mr. Master." She cocks her head and gives me a teasing smile. "Since the only person who finds me so enthralling... is *you.*"

My heart stops. For one raw moment I think she's actually hit on the truth. But no... she can't know.

The handle to the door behind me turns, and we quickly go back to work. I'm distracted, though, as we do our detail.

Does she suspect anything?

The night goes on without a hitch, other than one minor incident involving an intoxicated ex, but Claude escorted him off the property so effortlessly, the crowd at the beach never knew what happened.

I do my job with only one eye toward the party, though.

As always, my main focus is Violet.

"Has anyone ever told you you're smothering?" she asks, sliding her hand into my back pocket as the evening winds down. She rubs her chin against my chest so briefly she's like a cat scratching an itch, before she resumes her professional demeanor.

"You're the one grabbing my ass in public and painting me with your smell as if to warn off any potential predators."

She reaches for my collar, and I look into her mesmerizing eyes the color of amethyst.

"I've got claws, and I'm not afraid to use them."

"Mmm. Is that a promise?"

She grins, and her belly growls as Joe comes into the room. "House secured. That's a wrap."

"Perfect. How late's Sake and Sushi open?"

She grins. "Late enough." It's her favorite, and I'm kinda partial to the spring rolls myself.

I want to keep her happy. I want to keep her safe.

I want to keep her right here by my side.

CHAPTER TWENTY-ONE

Violet

CAIN'S TROUBLED TONIGHT, but it's not out of the ordinary for him. I know this is just the way he is sometimes.

I blame it on his past.

Sometimes he wakes in the middle of the night, unable to sleep. He paces the room we share and stares out at the ocean. He tries to be quiet so he doesn't wake me, but I know him too well, and I often wake when he does.

We haven't known each other for long, but it feels like it's been much, much longer. Sometimes there's a depth to our relationship... an understanding, one might say... that makes me feel like I've known him for years.

After dinner at Sake and Sushi, my belly is full and I'm tired from the night's events. Cain's got a frenetic sort of energy driving him, though, and he hasn't even stripped for bed.

I don't ask him what's on his mind. If he wants to tell me, he will.

I'm lying belly-down on the bed, the pillow tucked under my cheek, when I feel the bed sag beside me from his heft. He's the largest man I've ever known, pure muscle, yet he walks quietly and folds himself onto the bed with surprising grace.

"You move so quietly, I hardly know you're there," I say with a smile, my eyes still closed. I feel his hand come to rest on the base of my skull, his fingers gently stroking my hair.

"Comes with my line of work. It pays to move silently so no one ever knows you're coming."

That makes me wonder... is there more to his "line of work" than I know?

"Clothes that don't rustle and rubber soles on your shoes?"

"Exactly."

We sit in silence for a moment while he runs his fingers through my hair. Finally, he breaks the silence.

"I'm heading down to the target range."

"Aw, without me? No fair." I'm only teasing him, though, and he knows it. Other guys play video games or watch YouTube to relax. Cain hones his skills at the target range. It's no wonder he's such a good shot.

"We'll go back tomorrow. I've got a new toy for you to play with." Given how he uses the range, he could mean anything from a new handgun to a new riding crop.

I'm so tired I can barely keep my eyes open, though. "I'll look forward to it."

He leaves a gentle kiss on my forehead before he leaves, and after I hear the door close behind him, I fall into a deep sleep.

Hours later, I hear the door open, and roll over. The room's gotten cooler, and I shiver before I draw the blanket up over my shoulder. Cain quietly dismisses the guard he keeps at the door when he isn't with me—both his sister, who lives here with us, and I always have a guard with us—and closes the door behind him.

"How'd it go?"

His voice is raspy and low when he responds. He hasn't spoken for hours, and he's tired now, too. "You're supposed to be asleep."

I prop myself up on the pillows and open one eye. "I was, but you know this is my favorite part of the day."

Even in the dim light, I can see the smile that ghosts his lips.

"Snuggling in bed with me?" Cain doesn't "snuggle." He kisses, he caresses, he holds me tight, but "snuggling" is too gentle a term for a man made of steel and iron.

"Nah," I say with a wink. "Watching you strip."

I'm not lying.

He's already stripped down to a T-shirt but still wears his dress pants from earlier in the night. I watch in silence as he sits on the edge of the desk chair and unties his shoes. Next, the socks, and his belt. I swallow when he folds it before he lays it over the back of the chair. I have vivid memories of what he's done with that belt.

I watch as his clothes fall to the floor and pool by his feet, marveling at the harnessed strength evident even in the darkened room. A glint of moonlight illuminates the wide breadth of his shoulders, the corded muscles of his arms, the defined planes of his chest and abs. My eyes travel down to his thick, muscled legs, planted like two trees on the ground.

"We should go apple picking," I say absentmindedly.

"Apple picking?" He quirks an eyebrow, tilting his head to the side.

"Yeah, apple picking. Like, you go to the orchard and pick apples. They have things like hayrides and apple cider donuts and scarecrows."

"Babe, it's November. You have to do that in like... September."

I sigh. "Oh. Right."

He shakes his head and continues to undress. "What brought that up?"

"Just imagining climbing up on your back and using you like a ladder."

"Violet."

I swallow, my mouth dry. He says one word, and my body starts to heat.

I close my eyes against a rush of emotion and need. I love when he says my name. It's sweetness and seduction, like chocolate-dipped berries.

"Yes?"

"We don't need to go apple picking for you to climb me."

Aw, fuck. I was tired, and now I'm very wide awake. I swallow. "I know."

I continue to watch him in silence. By the time he's stripped off the tee and stands only in his boxers, I'm on fire.

"Come here," I whisper, gently stroking the side of the bed. He gives me a curious look, as if not sure he knows how to take a command from me. He's usually the one giving them, so I decide to play nice. "Please, Cain."

A little thrill ripples through me when I realize he's actually doing something I asked him to. He sits quietly on the edge of the bed just like he did before he left, but this time, I slide out of bed. I position myself between his knees and gently pry them apart. He's already hard, already eager, and when I stroke his erection through the thin fabric of the boxers, my mouth waters.

"Hands behind your back," he says in a low command, as he gathers my arms and places them at the small of my back like I'm stretching for a yoga class. "Keep them there, baby."

Baby. I melt.

I don't have a submissive bone in my body. Never have, never will. I write my own rules and fight my own battles. But when Cain Master gives me a command, my knees buckle and my legs turn to jelly.

He's the only man I'll ever submit to, and he knows it.

I eye his hard cock tented in his boxers, lean forward, and kiss the very top.

"Please," I say on a hoarse whisper.

"God, woman. You don't have to ask me twice."

I sigh when the satiny-feel of his cock touches my lips. I lick the very top and suckle, making him groan. He pumps into my mouth like he's fucking me, and I take every inch of him, every perfect fucking inch. I tease and taunt and suckle and moan, eager to please, to own this small part of him that he grants me.

"Jesus, baby. *Stop.*"

I shake my head from side to side. I don't want to stop. I want him to come. I want to swallow him down and own him like he does me.

He leans down and tweaks my nipple, hard, as he breathes into my ear, "I said stop, Violet. Stop now or I'll come in your mouth, and I want your pussy wrapped around my cock when I come."

I moan in protest.

"Violet," he says warningly, already eying the folded belt by his desk. With a sigh, I lay my head on his lap.

"Get up on this bed." He may be a jealous lover, but he's never a selfish one. I'm enjoying my place here, with my head in his lap, though, so I don't move right away. "Now," he orders, yanking me up and over his lap where he gives me a good hard slap.

In seconds, I'm facedown on the bed on my knees, and he's behind me, hands on my hips and my pussy spread for him. I hold my breath until he slides into me, and I release a pent-up sigh at the fullness of him. Frissons of ecstasy explode through me when he thrusts, and a feeling of utter completion washes over me. We climax in unison, like we were made for each other.

I'm lying next to him in blissful contentment. Skin to skin, all our clothing tumbled to the floor like leaves shed for winter. I'm up on his chest and his hands are folded, resting on my lower back.

"You make a terrible pillow," I murmur, cheek smooshed against the hardness of his body. He chuckles, but quiets when I reach for the cool metal of his dog tags. I wonder if tonight he'll tell me. I don't ask, just gently finger them.

"Thanks for that."

I snort. "Yeah, it was a real sacrifice."

He smiles, sobering. "Thanks for being patient with me."

I only nod, afraid if I speak too soon, I'll scare him off again. I can feel we're on the cusp of more truth between us. He may be fearless and strong, but when it comes to personal revelations, he scares as easily as a spooked deer sometimes.

When he speaks, his voice has gentled, his tone contemplative. "I wonder if you'd have stayed with me if you'd met me when I was younger."

"You wouldn't have," I say with a laugh. "I was headstrong and willful with a chip on my shoulder the size of a boulder."

"Oh, because you're oh-so-docile and obedient now?"

I smile. "You know what I mean. I wonder what you were like as a younger man. Smaller?"

"A bit. I've always been a big guy but didn't body build until I was older."

"More cocky?"

He chuckles. "Definitely."

I absentmindedly run my fingers along the little curly hairs on his chest. "Your eyes would be more boyish, I imagine, and not—"

I pause. I've said too much. But he doesn't let me get away with half sentences.

"Not what?"

I swallow and cringe before I go for broke. "Maybe not so... guarded."

It's a poor choice of a word. Guarded isn't really what I meant. The first time I looked into his eyes, I knew he was a man who'd experienced deep, abiding pain, the type that rocks you to your core and leaves scars that never heal. He's only hinted at things that have hurt him, but hasn't told me much of anything. Yet.

"Maybe not," he admits. "Would you like to know where I got these dog tags?"

My heart soars.

"Of course," I say with forced patience, because the little girl in me's jumping for joy and fist pumping all at the same time. I love when he lets me in, when he trusts me a little bit more. I draw in a breath, then release it slowly. "I want to know everything about you, Cain."

He pauses a beat before he says, "And I'll tell you everything. In time."

I close my eyes against the sudden rush of emotion. Other women might swoon at a profession of love, and when the day comes for that between us, it will mean more than anything to me. But this... this right here, his granting of trust that so few have, is the next best thing.

"When I was stationed in France, I was trained by a guy named Court Fallow."

"That's quite a unique name."

"He was a unique guy. Born and bred in the Deep South, his family lived on a rambling farm that harvests corn."

I nod, giving him space to tell the story.

"Not sure you've had much to do with Henri. He keeps to himself." Henri's a quiet, unassuming employee of Cain's. He was the man that opened the door for me the day I first came here. I knew I detected a Southern accent.

"I've seen him, but we've never really even talked beyond work at all."

"He keeps to himself. Henri was Court's youngest brother."

"Oh wow."

"Court was the father I never had, Violet."

I didn't see that coming.

I gently stroke his shoulder. Keeping him with me. "Oh? How so?"

His voice takes on a huskier edge, reminiscing. "He took me under his wing. Showed me how to shoot, showed me how to protect the people under my care. He was the oldest of seven, raised to be a man of honor, and he taught me everything he knew."

"Well, that explains a lot."

He huffs out a laugh as he runs his fingers through my hair in a rhythmic motion, up and down, up and down, as if it soothes him. Maybe it does.

"Court was killed by friendly fire." My heart aches. Accidental death like that is so tragic, I can't imagine how it feels for the people who knew him or the people responsible for his death. "I was the one who found him. He bled out while I held him, waiting for emergency crews to respond."

"Oh, Cain." I've been through brutally painful times, but something like this makes me hurt for him.

"And before the rescue crews could find us, I was taken hostage. I took his dog tags just before they took his body and me, alive."

I put two and two together.

"And that's how you got the scars on your back." I knew it was some kind of torture or punishment he'd endured.

"Yeah."

"Let me see them."

He stills for a moment, before he lets me slide off of him. The bed's huge, a king-sized monstrosity as big as the old apartment I rented, so he rolls over with ease. He places his arms above his head, spreading his muscled, scarred back for me. My eyes have adjusted to the dim lighting in the room, moonlight lighting up the silvery-white scars that crisscross his back.

"Brutal," I whisper, my own body clenching at the scars that mimic mine. I bend, close my eyes, and kiss each scar that lines his back.

He lets me. My throat tightens.

"Don't tell me where your scars came from. Not tonight, Violet."

I still. Why doesn't he want to know? A part of me's relieved, because I'm not in the mood to relive any of those events.

"I won't. I don't want to talk about it myself yet. But can I ask you why?"

He rolls back over, reaches for me, then drags me to his chest again. His eyes are fire, giving me a glimpse of the inferno that rages inside him. Sometimes, he tames the fire. Sometimes, he hides it. But it's never fully quenched.

"Because when I find out who gave you those scars, I will hunt them down. I will make them pay. I want to be fully prepared, and tonight's not the night for that."

I'd smile, but he isn't joking.

I'm falling in love with the man they call The Executioner. I didn't come here by accident.

"Alright, then," I whisper.

I lay back down beside him and roll over. We both know it's

time for sleep, and the time to divulge secrets to one another is over.

For now.

He lays his heavy arm over my body, and I sigh. Nothing gives me comfort like the weight of his arm.

I want to ask him how we're coming along on the next job we have to do—finding my parents' murderer. I want to remind him that he promised me that he wouldn't leave me hanging. But I'm tired, and so is he. Tomorrow, then.

I yawn widely, my eyes closing.

"Thank you for that," I whisper, as slumber beckons.

"For what?"

"For trusting me with the truth."

I need to ask him about my parents. Have we made headway with anything at all? I'm feeling frustrated and impatient, so ready to move on this. But not tonight.

I fall into a deep sleep.

I dream of hunting, and weapons, and throwing the new knives he bought me, but every time I throw them, I miss the target.

CHAPTER TWENTY-TWO

Cain

"CAIN!"

I look up from my laptop, my eyes blurry from staring too long, and blink. Someone just called my name.

"Cain, come here!" It's Skylar.

I jump up from my seat and stalk to my office door, my pulse accelerating. Why the hell is she yelling for me? I yank it open, ready to grab the weapon I keep on me at all times. I check the heft of it in my holster, just in case.

It's been too calm around here for too damn long, and my head's been so buried in research I'm still mentally in the dark and dirty trenches of my research.

"Cain!"

My boots hit hard on the top landing as I jog toward the top of the stairs.

"What?" My heart's beating hard, and I don't hear Violet. Where's Violet?

I come around the corner at the top of the stairs, staring down the banister at the living room below. Skylar stands with her hands on her hips and Violet's in her shadow, shaking her head.

"Told her you were busy," Violet mutters, rolling her eyes. She's got a string of pinecones in her hand. "But she insisted." Violet looks up at me and her eyes go a little wider. "See? I told you not to yell his name. You scared the hell out of him. Lucky he didn't blow your damn head off."

"*I'm* not the one who shoots without reason," I remind her.

She rolls her eyes heavenward. "You shoot a weapon you didn't know was loaded *one time* and you never live it down."

"Never."

Joe snorts from the doorway, walking in with a steaming mug of coffee in one hand and a napkin in the other. "Boss, we got a call from a Miss Robbins? She says she has some urgent news."

Violet looks at me. "First time I ever heard of that one." There's a chill in her gaze I haven't seen often, and I look at her curiously.

"Yeah, because the case is as cut and dried as they come." I groan. "And seriously, this Robbins woman's intense."

Violet narrows her gaze so slightly it's barely noticeable, but I notice it. "I'm intense, too."

Really? She's playing this game with me now? I look at Joe when he opens up the napkin he holds and pulls out a cookie.

"For Christ's sake, don't walk in there getting crumbs all over the place," I tell him.

"I won't." He pops the whole thing in his mouth and grins.

"The garland," Skylar says, interrupting whatever's going on between me and Violet. "Violet says it's too much, but I love it, so you're the tiebreaker."

Violet grimaces.

They're arguing over... room decor? I knew I should've taken on the last two cases that came to me, but I wanted to free us up to focus on Violet's parents' case. I'm on the cusp of a breakthrough.

"Oh no you don't," I say to them. "No goddamn way I'm getting in the middle of you two about *that*."

Skylar rolls her eyes.

When they first met, Skylar wore nothing but black and often hid her gaze beneath thick, long bangs. She'd found her people among the Wiccans of Salem, and Violet knows and respects that. But much of the way she dressed reflected her dark inner world. Things are a bit different now. Skylar's... changed since she's moved in here.

She still meets with her Wiccan friends, and it's still a large part of who she is. But she doesn't hide the way she used to. Violet's brought her out of her shell, you could say.

Violet has that effect on people. She doesn't have what I'd call a cheery personality—no, she's really nothing like that.

She's honest, though, sometimes brutally. She hides nothing, so she values bold truth and unencumbered sincerity.

I love that about her. It's partly why I hate that I've hidden anything from her at all.

But Violet has secrets, too.

"I don't want to *decorate,*" Violet says, cringing. She throws up her garland-covered hands and gives it to Skylar. "Go ahead. Put 'em up. Get some... scarecrows for the front yard, or Christmas lights, or whatever the fuck. Peace out." She hands Skylar the pinecones and leaves the room. I hear the kitchen door shut behind her, then the whines and barks of greeting from Romulus and Remus, our pit bulls. They love Violet.

Joe stares at me, his cheeks still stuffed with cookie. Skylar gives me an apologetic look.

"I'm sorry," she says, shaking her head. "I don't... really know what set her off. Like, is she hormonal or something?"

Joe holds up his hands and leaves as quickly as he came, likely wanting nothing at all to do with a discussion about Violet's hormones.

I blow out a breath and shake my head. I suspect I know what's bothering her.

"It's not you," I tell Skylar. "Let me handle her."

Skylar turns back to the mantle and arranges the pinecones with a flair of victory. She got her way. "Oh believe you me, I am happy to stand back and let you handle her, as long as you handling her is done behind closed doors."

This, from the girl who once had a chair particularly suited for tantric sex maneuvers in her bedroom.

"Are those scented?" The smell of cinnamon and cloves lingers in the air.

"Mhm," she says triumphantly. "I wanted to get pumpkin spice, but Violet had an opinion on that." She sniffs the air in mock dismay.

It's sunny but chilly when I go out the back door to find Violet. I know I need to. I know I'm the only one that knows what's bothering her, and I don't want anything to fester between us.

I glance to the left where we often train. I've given Violet free rein to teach martial arts classes, and she's enjoying it. But the training field, the outside ring, and the semi-enclosed area near the pool are all vacant. Romulus and Remus are still by the back door, standing guard. I pat their heads.

"Where'd she go, boys? Target range?" They only lick my hands but don't betray Violet's whereabouts. Figures.

I look to the target range, but it looks undisturbed. I open the door just to be safe, but it's cold and dark when I enter. Vacant.

"Violet!" I call her name, hoping she'll answer, but the wind picks up and swallows my voice. Clouds part, brilliant light bathing the ground in front of me. Down by the private beach that flanks my home, I look for footprints, but find nothing.

I know where she is.

I walk down a hidden walkway built from rocks, so discreet and functional, it's as if the side of the mountain where my home's built was designed primarily for this function. I walk down to the beach, hang a left, and head for the large, private open field where I've set up her training station.

My men use it, too, but we all know it's Violet's.

It took a solid week of construction, and the equipment needed would buy me a new truck, but it was worth every penny. The waterproof, outdoor-proof training station is suitable for stretching and boxing. Featuring cables, a dual stack functional trainer for combat and rebounding, two pull-up stations, and monkey bars, it's state-of-the-art.

Violet calls it "going out to play," but the intensity of the equipment and how she uses it is anything but. To the left of what looks like a souped-up playground, we set up a secure shed to house heavy sandbags, strength bands, medicine balls and kettlebells. We have a fully equipped indoor exercise room, but Violet prefers working outside. She thrives in the outdoors with nothing but the sky above her.

I can see her tiny, petite frame, dangling from a pull-up bar, suspended in the air like she's weightless. I stand against the rocky wall that leads to her workout area. Watching.

I cross my arms on my chest and lean back so she doesn't see me. I love to watch the way she curls her body upward, then down again, her slim figure taut as she stretches and elongates her muscles. She pulls up then lowers down once, twice, three times, then swings from the bar, preparing to vault herself toward the parkour station I've set up behind it.

I watch as she gracefully leaps over and under the bars, vaulting herself forward before she swings herself with ease to a platform at the very top. I've set up a ropes training course here as well which she navigates with ease, keeping her instincts primed, her body strengthened, and her reflexes sharp.

She lands barefoot on the springy landing platform at the foot of the highest bar, crouches, and looks my way. Her right side drops lower, her knuckles grazing the ground, a primal look if ever I saw one.

She scowls. "Stop lurking in the shadows and tell me why you followed me. Hiding's so unlike you," she says with disdain.

"I'm not hiding." I step into the light, arms still crossed. "And you're getting mouthy as fuck."

"Getting?" she says with a sneer. "You knew when you kissed this mouth what you were getting into."

It doesn't really bother me that she's impossible to break, impossible to understand, and headstrong as they come. I fucking love that about her.

She turns away from me as if to dismiss me, and heads to the singlesticks, otherwise known as cudgels. She lifts one and weighs it in her hands. A slender, round stick nearly three feet long, it's thinner at one end and thicker at the other, a suitable weapon for someone of her slim stature.

"You're better than this, Violet," I say, heading toward her. I grab a cudgel myself and kick my shoes off.

I face her, stick in hand. I want to bend her over and smack her ass with the damn thing.

"Better than what?" she says, eyes narrowed. Behind us, the waves crash on the shore. Violet shivers with a sudden gust of wind, then shrugs it off with impatience, like she doesn't have time for that bullshit.

"Running," I tell her, just before I swish my stick through the air. She easily deflects the blow, then throws her weight into sending another one my way.

"I'm not *running*."

"The hell you aren't." *Thwack.* My stick hits hers with a thud. "You lost your shit in there, then stormed off like a pouty teen."

"You go to the target range, I come here. So shoot me." She rolls her eyes, swivels, and strikes again. I deflect the cudgel.

"I just want to know why you ran." I swing back at her.

She scowls at me, swings the bar, and nearly knocks me on my ass. "I. Did. *Not!*"

I deflect the blow, then toss her one of my own. She curses under her breath, stumbling with the effort of deflecting. "Oh for fuck's sake," she growls when she falls to one knee. She's down long enough for me to set her off balance with another whack of my stick on hers. She ducks, and seconds later I've got her pinned beneath me, the cudgels forgotten. Her wrists are in my grip, and her furious gaze is pinned on me.

"My, my, my," I tease her. "You're in an interesting situation, now, aren't you? In fact... I do believe this is almost familiar. Do you feel déjà vu or is it just me?"

"Get fucking *off* me," she says uselessly, still pinned in my grip. I'm so much heavier than she is, it's almost unfair how easily I pin her.

"You promised, Violet."

She wilts a little, the smallest flicker of fire dying down in her eyes. "I made several promises to you, Mr. Master," she says through gritted teeth. "But *you* made promises as well."

Ahh. So now we're getting somewhere.

"So this is about promises."

She holds my gaze, her jaw clenched. "Yes."

"Tell me, Violet. Tell me the promises we've made each other."

My heart feels like it's been stabbed when her eyes water. Violet only cries when she's angry, and now she's fucking furious. I hate that it's come to this. A part of me wants to hold her to me, kiss the tears away, and promise I'll make it better. And another part of me wants to toss her over my lap and spank her until she cries *real* tears, for being so goddamned infuriating and stubborn.

"I... I promised I'd never try to fight you again," she says, somewhat abashed. One could easily argue she was trying right now.

"Right. We work together. As a *team*," I say pointedly. "What promise did *I* make you when we found Skylar together?"

Her eyes flit away from mine, but I grab her chin and force her gaze back to me.

She blinks, a steely note coming back to her voice. "You promised me you'd find my parents' murderer."

I knew it was only a matter of time before we had this discussion.

"I did."

She pushes my wrists, but she can't move me. I double down and hold her more firmly. "And what, Cain? Here we are, and it's almost Christmastime, and what have we done along those lines?"

Ah. It makes sense to me now.

"Did we talk about a timeframe, Violet?"

She narrows her eyes at me. "Stop being an asshole and get the fuck off of me."

"Answer me."

I hold her harder until she growls and reluctantly admits, "No."

"And you forgot something else, sweetheart. Didn't you?"

She tries to look away again, but my fingers on her chin yank her eyes back to mine. "*Didn't* you?"

She inhales, then pushes her breath out and juts her chin. "I did."

"Tell me, Violet."

She clenches her jaw and doesn't speak.

I lean in closer, my grip tighter. "You fucking tell me or I'll make you, and you know exactly how."

She shivers. She won't admit it, but even angry she's aroused when I threaten to dominate her.

"Fine. *Fine.* I... I promised you that..." she blinks, and her voice is a little choked. "I promised you that I was yours."

I lean down closer and kiss her cheek. Her eyes flutter closed, and a cool breeze stirs over us.

"We made a deal, Miss Price. And I won't let you forget it."

She opens her eyes. The look she gives me stabs my heart. "You won't let me forget my promise to you, but what about your promise to *me?* Cain, I can't stand it anymore."

"Can't stand what?"

Her eyes plead with me. "Let me up, and I'll explain. You're heavy."

I let her go and sit on the ground beside her. She pouts, rubbing her wrists. "I've had it. Every fucking job we do that has nothing to do with why I came here. Fucking check the identity of a new hire. Done. Follow the cheating ex of your millionaire playboy's bestie. Done. Vet the legitimacy of a potential business partner for some god-awful billionaire and his harem. Done. Find the arsonist responsible for a crime. *Done.* I half expected Fontaina to ask you to babysit her daughter on her next goddamn tour, and the worst of it? I would've expected you to accept!"

When I cringe at that, she nods. "Exactly."

"My bad, then."

She drags her knees to her chest and buries her head on them. "I remind you why I'm here, and all you've got is 'my bad?' No apology?"

"I don't owe you an apology."

She leaps to her feet, and I half expect her to smack me upside the head with the cudgel, but I'm quicker than she is. In one quick movement, I've swept her off her feet and I'm carrying her back up to the house.

"Put me down! Put me fucking *down!*"

"No. I have to show you something."

"You can't show me while I'm on my own two damn feet?"

I don't say anything for long minutes while I carry her back to the house.

"Violet."

Sometimes the sound of my voice when I call her name is enough for her to settle down. She sighs, a little of the fight draining out of her. "What?"

"I asked you if you trusted me."

She nods, again trying to look away. Her face turns away from mine. "Yes."

"And do you remember what you said to me?"

We'd sat in bed, her curled up on my lap after target practice, a week after we found Skylar. "Do you trust me?" I'd asked her.

She blows out a breath. "I said there's no one in the world I trust more. But that was before."

"Before what?" We've almost reached the top of the hill. The bright beam of yellow light from the kitchen casts a welcoming glow on the path before me.

"Before I... knew you would take so long."

I almost laugh at that. I would, if she wasn't so damn serious.

"Do you trust me now?"

She thinks before she speaks, but it doesn't disappoint me. I like that she only speaks the truth. It gives strength and merit to her words.

"I do."

I wasn't ready to show her anything. I wanted more information before I let her in, because I don't want to give her false hope. But it's time.

We reach the back door. I settle her to the ground and take her by the hand.

"Then follow me."

CHAPTER TWENTY-THREE

Violet

DAMN right he should've talked to me.

He's got to go and play the damn *trust* card on me.

No fair.

Of course I trust him. There's no one in the world I trust more than him, but I'm not a patient girl. I've never even pretended to be any different than I am.

I don't trust people easily, but when you've been through what Cain and I have together... things are different.

I knew it the first time I looked into his eyes after he'd killed a man. There was a stark honesty and fearlessness I'd never seen in another human.

Ever.

And yes... I trust him.

But down in the living room, with the cinnamon-scented pinecones decorating the mantle, and pumpkin spice everything being cooked up in the kitchen... it reminds me that Christmas is coming.

My parents were killed at Christmas.

I feel as if the days are passing like sand through an hourglass, and I'm not sure where we'll be when the last grain of sand falls.

After we secured Skylar, I made a promise to Cain, and I always keep my promises.

I remember the conversation well. He was sitting in his office when he beckoned to me. He explained how he would help me find my parents and what he'd ask from me in return.

"WHAT DO YOU WANT FROM ME?"

"*I want you.*"

"*Me?*"

"*You. All of you. Carte blanche to do whatever I want to you, whenever I want to. Anytime, anywhere.*"

"*I have the distinct feeling I'd... both hate and love every minute of what you'd do to me... yes.*"

"*Yes?*"

"*Yes, Cain. I accept your terms. I'm yours.*"

· · ·

AND I'VE GIVEN HIM... me. All of me. Over, and over, and over again, and no, it hasn't been painful. Ours is a unique relationship, unlike anything I've ever experienced before, and it honestly goes far beyond mere sex.

There's an intensity to Cain I crave. A fearlessness. One might label him an "alpha male," but that only scrapes the very surface of who he really is.

What he really does.

Cain Master is a man in a camp of his own.

And I prided myself on understanding that. On understanding *him*.

At what cost?

Has he used me? Has he kept me here with him for companionship, never fully intending on helping me find my parents' killer?

Or... has he found that there's nothing but dead ends?

I don't know what to expect. I don't know what to hope for.

I don't even know if I'm ready to face my parents' murderer, but I know it was what brought me here, right to his doorstep, ready to barter.

I didn't have the money he charged for a job like this. All I had to offer him was me.

My skills. My talents.

My body.

I never planned on whoring myself out, but now that I'm here...

No. No, I won't let my mind go there.

Cain's huge, rambling mansion of a house overlooks the Salem waterfront north of Boston. This time of year, the leaves have mostly fallen, leaving stark branches that warn of cold winter days and impending snow and ice, but a few brilliant orange maple leaves still cling with tenacity to low-hanging limbs. Cain brushes past them, and a few more flutter to the ground.

He yanks open the back door, and the smell of roasting chicken, potatoes, and Alma's homemade bread wafts through the door toward us.

I hate the thought of leaving here. I hate the thought of starting afresh when I had the promise of everything I wanted right here. I hate the thought of leaving *Cain*.

But I'm too independent to wait on a man. Even the huge, hulking, alpha of a man plowing his way to his office right now.

"Dinner will be ready in thirty minutes, Mr. Master," Alma calls from the stove, where she's stirring a large skillet of greens.

"Might not be down tonight, Alma."

Interesting. How much does he have to show me?

She looks over her shoulder at me, and I shrug at her. "Would you like me to keep the food warm for you?"

He shakes his head. "No, thank you. I'm not sure when we'll be down."

"I'll send it up then."

"Perfect."

Well that's promising. Maybe he's got more to tell me than I expected he did.

We walk through the house, him a few paces ahead of me. My senses are assaulted by everything Skylar's done to decorate. Scented pinecones on the mantle, rustic wooden orange pumpkins on the bookshelves, and a smattering of scented candles in yellows and browns on a little side table.

I should be happy she's enjoying herself. The weeks following her abduction and assault were dark for Skylar. At first, she wouldn't get out of bed or talk to anyone for days on end. I pushed through. I made her talk to me. I would bring her breakfast in her room and chatter away, even though she sometimes didn't respond at all. It was days until she began to talk to me, and once she did, it seemed she had quite a bit to say.

Cain likes that we've befriended each other. He's told me we're the two women who mean more to him than anything in the world, and he likes that we're here, under his roof. Can't be that way forever, though, and we both know it.

Eventually, Skylar will have to be independent again. She'll find a love interest, or a job that requires her to travel, or... something.

And me? I don't belong here and never have.

I'm here to fulfill a mission. I'm here to fulfill my end of the bargain. And when that's over... my heart hurts at the thought.

Henri's in the living room, on his laptop, when we enter. Older than I am but a bit younger than Cain, Henri is pale, with a receding hairline, but wiry and strong. He lost eyesight in one eye during a fight overseas, and now swears off any formal office arrangement.

He nods in greeting to us, but never takes his eyes off the screen. He says he's allergic to a desk. I think it has something to do with his poor eyesight and the bright lighting in here by the large picture windows.

Henri opens his mouth but, seeing that Cain's on a mission, he slams it shut.

Joe's gathering a few men in the hall for a training of some sort. They're wearing camouflaged gear and boots, and standing at attention like soldiers in boot camp. When Cain passes, they all watch him with wide-eyed wonder and admiration.

He inspires that type of response no matter where we go. It's got something to do with the way he carries himself, I think.

"Cain," Skylar yells from her room on the third floor. "When can we get a Christmas tree?"

"Christ," he mutters and rolls his eyes. I'm guessing that won't be an after-Thanksgiving special for him then.

His phone beeps with a text, then again with a call. He glances at the screen with a scowl, then powers it off.

Oh. Oh, wow. I've never seen him shut his phone completely off.

He really is giving me his undivided attention.

I wonder if I've read him wrong all this time...

When we reach his office door, he drops all semblance of being Mr. Nice. I watch, with more than a little trepidation, as he yanks open his door, then gestures for me to go in. "Please," he says with a frown. "You first."

I walk ahead of him tentatively, as if waiting for him to pounce on me at any minute or at the very least smack my ass.

I have no idea why. I can't really put my finger on it. I don't know if it's the predatory look in his eyes, or his take-no-prisoners tone of voice. I don't know if it's because he's basically told everyone who works for him to leave us alone, or because I threw down the gauntlet by the training field. But he has plans for me, and I have no idea what those plans are.

The door shuts behind us, and I let out an audible gasp.

"Why so scared, Violet?" Cain asks, in a tone that tells me he's fucking pleased with himself.

"You just have that look in your eyes."

"What look?"

He stalks to his desktop like he's about to wrestle it to the floor, and when I don't respond at first, his narrowed gaze cuts to me. I open my mouth, and I'm about to respond, when there's a sharp knock at the door.

"Who is it?" Cain practically fumes.

"Joe."

"Come in." He points to a chair for me to sit in, and I glare right back at him. No, you do not, Mr. Master. He shakes his head at me, his frown promising that we're going to have a serious talk when Joe's gone.

The tension in the air must be palpable because Joe freezes mid-step and looks from me to Cain. "Bad timing?"

"No. What is it?" Cain asks. He fires up the laptop.

"Got another call from Robbins."

"Fucking hell," Cain mutters to himself. "What now?"

"Wants an update?"

"I'll give her a fucking update," I volunteer, but Cain slices a hand in my direction as if telling me to knock it off. The goddamn *nerve* of him...

"She says it's been three days, and she wants to know when you'll have the information."

"You can tell her, per our *contract*, that I need a week or more before I respond, but that I always try to respond within a week. It's been three days."

He grimaces, then nods. "She's impatient."

Cain's eyes narrow. "So am I."

He's got that right.

The door finally shuts with a bang when Joe leaves. Cain stands, storms over to the door, then throws the deadbolt.

My heart beats faster.

I let my eyes rove over him for a few seconds, and I don't breathe while I do. He's wearing one of those long-sleeved faded tees in a dark gray that brings out the blue-gray storms in his eyes he gets from time to time. It's tight across his chest and arms, like most clothes designed for normal humans typically are. He's wearing faded jeans, frayed at the bottom. One might think they're stylish, but if I know Cain, it's because it's one of only a handful of pairs he owns, and he's owned them for decades.

His heavy, thick boots are planted on the floor, and his hands are on his hips. I sit in his huge, leather desk chair, absolutely dwarfed by it, and nonchalantly plop my feet up on his desk.

I like poking the bear.

He growls low.

"What?"

"Strip."

I stare at him in surprise, not expecting that command. "Strip?"

"You heard me." He doesn't move.

Oh, great. He's pissed, and now he's either going to fuck me to remind me who's boss or use my body in some way to punish me.

"Okay, so let's get this straight. You made me a promise. I made you one. I kept my end up, and now you're... getting mad at me or something?"

"Do I look mad?"

I nod. "You look fucking *pissed*."

He frowns slightly, then nods. "I am."

I throw up my hands in exasperation. "You're maddening, you know that?"

"Takes two, babe."

"What? You think I'm maddening?"

"I do." No reaction. He glances at the clock on his desk. "You have two minutes, starting right now."

"Or what?" I throw back at him, even as my hands fly to unfasten my shoes.

"Or I'll strip you myself, and I'll strip more than your fucking clothes."

Oh *God*.

My hands tremble as I remove my shoes, then stand up and quickly disrobe. The rest of my clothing falls to the floor in a crumpled heap until all I'm doing is standing in front of him wearing nothing but my birthday suit.

"You're beautiful."

I look away. I can't handle praise like that. It makes me uncomfortable.

"Thank you," I murmur. I shiver, though I'm warm in here. He pulls out his phone and talks into the speaker. "Tell everyone I don't want to be disturbed until further notice."

He slides his phone into his pocket.

"Come here, baby," Cain says. He walks to me, sits at his desk, then pulls me onto his lap. Once again, I'm struck by the contrast of him fully clothed and clothed well, and me stark naked, straddling him.

He lives for an imbalance in power.

Thrives on it.

I'm not so sure how I feel about this.

"Are we... talking about avenging my parents while I'm... naked?"

"We'll be talking about a lot of things with you naked on my lap like this."

A glimmer of excitement rushes through me before I can stop it, and it aggravates the hell out of me because this puts him at a decided advantage. After only days with Cain mastering my body, I began to be conditioned to crave more.

And I like it. I like all of it. I love the way he is with me. But I wonder if this isn't to his full advantage to "discuss" things when I'm not wearing any clothes.

"It sounds to me like you'll be getting the long end of the stick on that one?"

He shrugs. "I don't know. You might be getting the long end of the stick, too."

Oh *God. Men.*

There's a smile in his voice though.

He wants me naked and at his mercy, begging for him to touch me or allow me to come... because that's when I'm at my most submissive with him, and he knows it.

I sit up straighter on his lap, as if to remind both him and me that I'm not going to cave so easily.

"I know there doesn't seem to be a pattern about the cases I've been taking, but there is. You think I've been wasting time or taking random cases, but I haven't. Every single one of these cases were related."

"Were they?"

He nods, gently kneading my shoulders, and my rigid spine begins to soften. It doesn't take long before I nestle up against his chest, and he weaves his fingers in my hair. "They were."

"How so?"

"I'd like to see if you can put it together like I did."

"Checking on my intellect and ability?"

"Violet."

His tone is a warning he underscores with a sharp tug of a lock of my hair, but I don't back off. I want to know.

"I'm serious. Are you checking to see if I'm as astute as you thought I was when you hired me?"

He leans in close, gathering my hair between his fingers, and pulls me to him so that his eyes bore into mine. "No. You've blown every fucking employee I have here out of the water. I want to go over the facts, because I want to be sure *I* didn't miss anything."

"Alright, then," I say, very, *very* aware that I'm naked, and he's not, and I'm at his mercy.

When he's got me good and secured on his lap, he wraps his hands around my waist like a seat belt. The concept amuses me, even as my body thrums with need. His thick fingers graze the very edge of my sides. As he talks, he strokes the pad of his thumb down my side.

"You assumed I'd forgotten about your parents."

"Well... no, I wouldn't go that far."

He stills the gentle massaging. "Why the tantrum then?"

I sputter. "I didn't have a *tantrum*."

"Babe, you stormed out of the house. You went to the training field. You grabbed a fucking cudgel."

"I love working out with a cudgel."

He holds still, his fingers still wrapped around my body before he continues. "You like working out with a cudgel when you're angry."

I don't deny this.

"And you're angry because something set you off today, reminding you that we've made no headway with your parents."

I'm glad his back's to me since I don't really want to look in his eyes right now. He has a way of peeling back every defense mechanism I have with his eyes alone. If he had a superhero talent, I'd hazard a guess it would be x-ray vision.

I stare at the painting on the wall that hides his safe. When I speak to him, my voice is low, tremulous. "I know how to move that painting, Cain. The one that hides your weapons. I know the numbers to push to unlock the safe. I know when the safe door opens, the exact pile of weapons that will wait for me, the heft of the knife or the barrel of the gun when it slips into my palm. To others, the closed safe looks like a work of art. I, however, know it's only a doorway."

His arms tighten an infinitesimal amount. He doesn't speak.

"Anyone else would think it's only something pretty to decorate your wall. I know better, though." I draw in a deep breath. "Do you know that you're the only one in the world who's ever found me out? The only one who knows how to manipulate me so that I open up, revealing my inner truth."

My eyes flutter closed when he kisses my bare shoulder before he grazes the sharp edges of his teeth along my bare skin. A pulse of arousal thrums between my legs when he licks the place he bit.

"Don't I fucking know it," he says in a low whisper. "And feel honored that you'd trust me with that."

I close my eyes, trying my best to hold onto the truth, to really push him to reveal everything he knows to me. I decide to let him in a little more.

"Today, when Skylar began pulling out the decorations, it reminded me that Christmas is coming. Every time the door opens, and the freezing cold air rushes in, it reminds me that Christmas is coming." I draw in a breath, before I release it slowly. "My parents were killed at Christmas."

I can still see the bloodstained carpet in front of the tree, the flash of brilliant red that told me they were gone. I had been only four years old and remember hardly anything else about that time, but I can't forget those few details.

He nods slowly. "I know."

He knows. What else does he know? My voice is quiet, but I'm slightly on edge when I respond. "You have done research, then."

"Every damn night, Violet. I haven't said anything to you because I didn't want to give you false hope."

My heart soars, then sinks, that quickly. Elated that he's done this, that he's given himself over to doing exactly what he promised—then deflated again when he admits he may not have much to go on. False hope?

I square my shoulders. "What have you found?"

Nestling me square in the center of his lap, he pulls me slightly to the left so he can get a better view of the computer screen. "First, public records."

He double taps an innocuous icon on the bottom right corner of the screen, and several police reports come up. They're poorly written in scratchy handwriting and the details are hard to read with the darkened page, but they are neatly organized. My throat feels tight when I see my parents' names alongside mine... or the name I used to go by, anyway.

RUSSELL AND ANYA BATES, *murdered on Tuesday. Found dead. Buried in a funeral mass celebrated by Pastor Descamps at the First Church of Christ, Salem*

"WHY DID you change your name, Violet?"

I don't know why it surprises me that he knows I changed my name. Security and investigation are his bread and butter.

"How did you know that?"

He doesn't answer at first, then scrolls further down. "When I began investigating, I found no local deaths for anyone by the name of Price. And there aren't that many Violets in the world, you know."

He hasn't really answered the question.

"I know." It's why I changed my last name. I couldn't bring myself to change the name that my mother gave me. I have this strange feeling that it's the only part of me that's unique, the only part of me that no one else can ever replicate.

"Once I found out my parents were killed, I felt it best to hide who I was."

It feels awkward that he knows my history, this small part of me that no one has ever really truly seen, but in order for us to find the real truth, he has to.

He nods. "Now it's time to tell me everything. I can't help you piece together what you need to find if you don't."

I knew this was coming. I'm prepared.

I nod.

"Violet, you told me when you came here, your father was an assassin. How did you find that out?

"I was only four when I first went into foster care, so I don't remember much about the first few couples that had me. I was thrown around like so much baggage, really, but it wasn't until I was much older that I realized someone fabricated a story around me. By the time I was ten, it was well accepted that my parents were killed in a car accident during a rainstorm. I didn't argue with what people thought they knew. By then, I knew there was a reason for the lies and discrepancies."

"Understood. I'm not surprised you were clever even as a child."

I shrug. "I tried. Sometimes I succeeded and other times I didn't. I was terrible in school..."

"Let me guess. Not because you weren't academically gifted, but you had a hard time doing as you were told."

I smile at the sardonic lilt in his voice. "How'd you know?"

He pinches my bare ass. "Doesn't take a genius to figure that one out, baby."

I smile. "So anyway... I was finally taken in by a minister and his wife." I can't keep the bitterness out of my tone. "They made no pretense about liking me but had no qualms about taking me into their home. Their kids were sheltered and judgmental, and the years I spent with them were the most miserable of my life."

Cain's quiet while I tell him this. I stare at his screen, at the old police reports, and imagine I can see the police station, the officer who's likely retired by now, filling out all the details and leaving so many blanks. "Tell me what they did to you."

I can't stop the shudder that runs through me, that runs through him, at the memories he pulls from me with those few little words. The memories I've tried so hard to keep hidden.

"No."

Again, his arm tightens around me. No one says "no" to Cain, so when I do, it always seems to throw him for a loop.

"Violet." Another warning tone, but the gentle caress of his thumbs across my thighs softens the rebuke. "I want to know."

And just like that, I'm ten years old again, locked in the dark closet where they punished me. I didn't have to do anything wrong to make them put me there. It was who I was they were trying to cleanse from me. It was the wife who beat me, when her husband wasn't home. I wasn't the only one—she beat all her children, quoting scripture as she did. None dared to cross her, and even the littlest one would flinch when her mother turned her way. But I bore the worst of it.

"Look at my back and tell me what you want to know," I say. "That bitch told me she'd scourge the devil out of me and God, did she try." I flinch at the memory.

I feel Cain's fingers along my back. I don't see them, but I never forget they're there.

"Their names."

"Cain, *no*."

I know him. I know what he'll do. He'll make it his mission in life to punish them for the harm they did me, over a decade before he ever met me. His justice is swift and merciless. I've stared into his eyes after he's killed, and I know when he feels it's justified, there's no remorse. My grim reaper in the flesh.

"I'll find them, Violet. You know I will. I just wanted your buy-in before I do."

I blow out a breath. Now that he knows, I can't stop him.

He strokes my back until I relax, until I'm slumped against him.

"Now, baby. Tell me the rest, and we'll get started."

CHAPTER TWENTY-FOUR

Violet

IT'S late into the night when we've compiled everything we know between the two of us.

It's admittedly not much to go on.

I've known since childhood that my father was an assassin because I overheard the minister's wife talking to her husband. They knew, somehow, and used the knowledge as justification for the way they treated me.

We scoured everything we could together; he'd made some progress before we even talked.

We have the names of the people who fostered me, all of them, including the ones who had me for the longest time.

As an orphan in the system, someone could've adopted me, and it was a question I struggled with for most of my childhood.

Why not? Why not me? Why were other kids in foster care adopted into homes, but never me?

I didn't want to be part of the families that took care of me, not until I was a much older teen and found myself in the care of a family that treated me like a human being. But by then I was independent and headstrong and wanted nothing to do with ties to anyone.

I'm still on Cain's lap, snuggled in like I belong here. He lazily strokes his hand across my shoulder. Behind me lies the tray with the dinner we ate a while ago, the remains of chicken and potatoes that filled our bellies.

"It's time to come up with a summary. You've filled in more blanks than I have. Took me four fucking weeks just to compile the list of foster parents."

"Why?" I shake my head. "That doesn't make any sense. And for God's sake, if you'd only asked me…"

"You'd remember the name of the family that took you in when you were six?"

"Well, no, but I could remember *some* things."

"You did, baby, but not the details from when you were a child. Hell, Violet, I think you blocked half of them from your fucking memory."

Maybe I did.

He pulls up a screen and begins to read the notes we've compiled.

"Your dad was killed when you were four. Your name at the time was Violet, should've been Violet Bates, but nowhere in any record do you exist."

According to public record, my parents had no children. "That's odd, isn't it? How was someone who didn't exist put into the foster care system?"

He nods. "But you needed something to graduate high school, to get a job. What did you have for paperwork?"

I shrug. "My social worker gave me everything. But if there's no record of my birth, where did she get it from?"

He makes another note to find her, then taps something onto his phone to Joe before he continues summarizing everything we've found.

"You believe your father was an assassin, because your foster parents at one point mentioned to each other they had you in their care because they were trying to right a wrong, and we can assume that wrong was your father's history."

"Well, yes. They said my parents."

He pauses. "Is there a chance your mother was an assassin, too?"

I sit with this for a moment. "I... remember her being gentle. I remember she liked to sew. She didn't eat meat, but she'd make me chicken tenders." I shake my head. "How could a seamstress vegetarian be an assassin?"

Cain spins me around to look at him. "Never, ever assume." He bends down and kisses me, a gentle brush of his lips to mine, before he looks away. "I can be gentle, too, Violet."

I shiver. I know Cain's called The Executioner, and he's told me a bit about his past, but I never really put the words *assassin* and *executioner* side-by-side.

"Do you consider yourself an assassin, Cain?"

He doesn't blink or look away. "I do."

I'm falling in love with a murderer. Someone who takes the lives of others without regret, and I don't know how to stop.

He holds my chin so I can't look away. "You knew when you came here who I was, Violet. You knew when you offered to work for me what I do."

"I know *some* of what you do, yes, but not all of it."

"You knew that I killed for hire, and that I'll do it again."

My voice is hoarse with emotion. "I do."

"But this isn't about me. Soon, I'll tell you everything I learned about how to be a *good* assassin, since this knowledge will help us find more about your parents."

I straddle him, reach for his face, and frame it in my hands. My fingers graze his stubble. "Tell me now."

He lays his hands over mine. "We go through the rest of what we know, and then I'll tell you." He bends and kisses the very top of my left breast, then the right. Shivers skate down my spine. "I want you in bed when I tell you."

Ah. So we'll have one of *those* conversations. His specialty.

My sex clenches, eager to be filled by him, manipulated by him, eager for what I know he could give me and will.

With reluctance, I turn back to the computer screen.

"These are the names of some of the people who fostered you. Most seem innocent enough. They fostered several dozen kids spanning several decades, and still have solid relationships with some of them. Joe researched them for me. This family, though... the one you were with when you were ten. They're problematic."

I can still see her glaring at me over the top of her glasses before she hauled me to the closet. *Bitch.* "Yeah. I know."

"I can't find them on record anywhere. No names. No history. It's why I asked if you knew if they were alive, because there is no record of where they are now."

"How strange."

"But there's one single thread that unites *all* of the families that took you into their homes."

I look over my shoulder at him. "Really?"

"Yeah. They were all married at the same church, by the same minister."

Okay, so he really did do his research. "Yeah?"

He nods. "Guy by the name of Gray Descamps. Still stationed in the First Church of Christ, North Shore."

"Huh. Well, that's weird. Anything odd about him?"

Cain frowns, scrolling down the document he's saved with names and dates and details. "I don't know... there is, but I can't quite put my finger on it."

"Are there any other details?"

He shakes his head. "I think we need to pay the minister a visit."

Oh, dear.

"He's got to be ancient by now, doesn't he?"

"Suppose. Doesn't matter."

"Cain, you can't go in and threaten an old guy with torture or death."

He straightens. "Why not?"

"You just... can't. It isn't right."

He spins me around to face him, gets this wicked gleam in his eyes, then bends and licks one of my breasts. My nipple peaks, and he gathers it into his mouth to suckle before he releases it. I stifle a moan. "According to whom?"

"Oh no you don't," I say, but I'm already panting when he leans me over the desk. My head nestles against the padded top. I thrust my fingers in his hair as he makes his way down my front. I'm still straddling him, so my legs are on either side of his torso, my body laid out like an offering to him.

He licks my nipples and weighs my breasts in each hand, fingering one hardened bud while he laps the other, until my body's slick with arousal and need.

"Come upstairs with me, baby," he whispers against my ear. "I'll tell you everything else I know, but I want to be in you when I do."

He doesn't have to ask me twice. I throw on my discarded clothing but leave the bra off. He scouts the halls, and in less than a minute, we're back in his room.

"Grab the fucking headboard," he orders, in that tone that means he wants in me, and he wants in me *now*. He follows up on his orders with a solid whack to the ass.

"Ah, so we're in *that* sort of mood," I say, as I grasp the sturdy headboard. I gasp when his palm slaps against my ass again, hard. Who am I kidding? Playful Cain is the exception to the rule. Boss Cain's the norm.

"Yeah, baby."

I'm already undressed, losing my clothing the minute I stepped over the threshold, and he's making quick work of undressing behind me. I hear the rustle of fabric, the swoosh of his belt, then he taps it against my thigh. "Behave yourself."

I make a choked sort of sound and get on my knees. My fingers grasp the headboard, my legs splayed for him. I hear the sound of a match being struck, then the scent of warmed cinnamon. His favorite candle, one bought expressly for the purpose of torturing me.

I love it.

"The rules of an assassin," Cain begins, when he kneels behind me. "Repeat them after me so I know you're being a good girl that listens well. If you're going to get the revenge you need, you'll learn these rules."

My heartbeat spikes.

I nod. "Yes, sir. Of course."

He loves it when I submit to him. This is the only time he gets it. Cain has a rules kink—when he gives me rules to repeat, he loves to dominate me. My first taste of this particular kink was on the target range when he punished me for shooting a gun without permission. He's done it several times since, so it doesn't take me by surprise now.

"Assassins have plans to succeed, Violet. They never take on a job they think they can't handle, for failing at their job has dire consequences. They take on what they can do, and don't commit to anything they can't."

I nod. "Got it. Assassins plan to succeed."

I gasp when he snaps a towel out on the bed for me to kneel on. He has plans for me tonight. Dirty, naughty plans, and I'm here for it.

When the towel's secured to catch anything messy, warmed oil licks down my back. The cinnamon candle. Heated through, it melts into a massage oil that can be used anywhere on the body, and I do mean anywhere. I close my eyes at the glow the heat creates across my skin, then moan when I feel him rub it into me.

"Assassins get paid up front. No credit. No payment plans. Cold, hard cash."

The oil seeps into my skin, and I'm enveloped in the scent of warmed spice. My grip loosens on the headboard from my palms slick with sweat. His palm cracks across my ass.

"Hold onto that headboard like I told you."

I quickly obey and repeat the rule. "Assassins get paid up front."

"Good girl. Next rule, and this one is vital. Are you paying attention?"

"Mhm," I say absentmindedly, just to get him riled up.

"*Violet.*" He tweaks my nipples.

I gasp. "I'm listening!"

When he's satisfied he has my attention, he continues,

speaking deliberately so his words hold weight. "Assassins kill with their heads, not their hands."

That's so hot. Oh, God, why is that so hot?

He strokes between my legs, then pumps two fingers into my core.

"Oh, God," I moan. "But you do know what to do with those hands don't you?"

"I do," he says with a low chuckle. "Now repeat the rule before I take my hands away."

"No," I moan, rocking my hips against his hand. "Don't go." I'm panting. "Assassins... kill... with their heads... not their hands."

"Good job. We don't need brute force, though proficiency with a weapon works well. We need to be astute and on point, prepared to pull the trigger when the time is right. Taking a human life isn't as easy as it sounds, because we've muted our responses to such things with video games and movies. It's a hairline fracture we walk, and we always, *always* have to be alert, ready, and mentally prepared."

I nod. "Understood."

"Any numbskull with a knife can kill someone. To be a professional, you have to know your shit."

He stops stroking, and my temper flares.

"Is that a rule, or are you just elaborating?" I say tightly, earning me another slap to the ass.

"Watch your tone of voice. You wouldn't want to be

punished by going to bed without your dessert, now, would you?"

Goddamn.

"No," I say, as repentant as could be. He continues his perfect, brilliant stroking, until I'm panting and nearly begging him for more.

"Assassins trust no one."

What an odd rule, considering he's asked me to trust him over, and over, and over. Could it be that he's gone so long without trusting anyone that he needs to know there's still someone who can?

I moan at the feel of the head of his cock at my entrance. He swirls the hot tip through my swollen, slick folds, releasing a moan of his own.

"Assassins don't get fancy," he says. "This isn't the movies. This is real life. We don't use car bombs or poison fucking appetizers at a ball when a simple bullet or slit throat will do."

"Got it."

He shoves in me, a thrust that takes my breath away and makes ecstasy erupt in every damn cell. I moan, pushing back against him just to feel his thick, hot cock pulsing in me again.

"Fuck, baby," he groans.

My fingers tighten on the headboard as he pumps his hips and makes little sparks of electricity dance across my skin.

"You're so tight," he whispers in my ear, as I near release.

"Is that another rule?" I lower my voice but have a hard time concentrating. "*Be tight.*"

His dark chuckle washes over me as my eyes flutter closed against the rush of emotion. "Don't you let go," he orders as he comes inside me, filling me with his hot release. I come when he does, giving in to the pressure and release that fills me as I shatter into ecstasy. "Don't you ever fucking let go."

We collapse on the bed, tangled in each other. His words echo in my ear.

They should make me feel special. Wanted.

Instead, I hear them as a threat.

What happens if I do?

CHAPTER TWENTY-FIVE

Cain

"BOSS."

Joe's pounding on the door to my bedroom. Violet's wound in the sheets, her head on my chest and hair all around me. I extricate myself with a groan. The door's locked, and it's likely urgent.

Cursing, I tug on a pair of boxers and walk to the door. I yank it open. Joe stands on the other side with an apologetic look on his face.

"I'm sorry."

"Have you ever tried texting? Fucking calling me?"

"Don't kill him, Cain, your phone's been off for hours," Violet mumbles behind me.

"She's right," Joe says with a grimace. "I got a call from the Salem P.D. They've got a warrant for the arrest of that

Robbins woman. Seems she's been dabbling in counterfeit money."

"Fucking hell."

"Yeah."

"Get Henri down there with Claude. Find out what you can. I can't close this case today; Violet and I have a job to do."

He nods, takes down some further instructions, then shuts the door. I turn to find Violet sitting up in bed, frowning at my phone.

"He is a persistent motherfucker, isn't he?" she says teasingly.

"I only hire persistent motherfuckers." I toss her a pair of jeans and tee. "Get dressed, woman. We've got work to do."

She tosses off the blanket, stretches, and yawns. "Coffee on the road?"

"I'll take you to Java Witch."

In Salem, various restaurants and locales are named after witches, our signature mascot, one could say. Known for the infamous Salem Witch Trials, we now wear what should be shame like a badge of honor. Violet does love the Java Witch brew, though.

"Can I get one of those twisty cinnamon things, too?"

"Babe, get whatever the fuck you want." She knows I don't give a shit what she gets, but she still likes to ask me. For a ballsy woman, she's fucking cute.

I sling my holster on and pack my favorite Ruger.

"Jesus," Violet moans behind me. I look over my shoulder at her.

"What?"

"There's nothing that makes me want to fall to my knees and suck your cock more than seeing you suiting up for a job." She feigns swooning before she sits on the edge of the bed to tug her boots on.

"Wish I could say the same for you," I say, as she slides her new knife into her ankle sheath before she reaches for her new Wilson.

"I know, I know," she says with an eye roll. "Watching me get *my* weapons makes you want to... I dunno, handcuff me to your bed or something."

"Don't need the threat of a weapon to bring out the handcuffs."

She smiles and gives me a coy look.

"Alright, where to first?" she asks, as she heads to the bathroom and quickly fixes her hair and makeup. "Pastor What's-his-name?"

"Yep. See what he has to tell us."

Suddenly, she pops her head out of the bathroom, her toothbrush shoved into the side of her mouth. "Way a mim," she mumbles.

"Huh?"

She takes her brush out of her mouth. "Wait a minute. Now *wait a minute.* Cain, what's the typical payout for a hit?"

I shrug, testing the safety on my Ruger. "Hugely varied. Could be ten thousand, could be ten mil. Why?"

"Your rules went through my mind while I slept."

I nod, pleased. It's partly why I went over the rules before we went to bed. She's fucking brilliant, and her mind works even when she's at rest. I knew she'd wake and have them memorized.

"Yeah?"

"Assassins get paid up front. Right?"

"Yes."

"Like there's no assassin layaway plan or credit or anything. Cash only."

"Right."

"And... they get paid *lots*. Last I checked, the average annual salary of a typical assassin was about eighty million dollars a year."

I nod. "Right."

She throws her hands up in the air. "Then... where's my parents' money? If my father was an assassin... he was worth money. *Big* money. Right?"

I nod. "And if you weren't supposed to exist, and no one knew they had a child..." my voice trails off.

"Right?"

"I'll call Joe. Put him on it."

If she has money owed to her and someone fucking took it...

She nods, heading back to the bathroom, and soon we head out. She takes a minute before we go to get to her knees and pat Romulus and Remus, kissing each of their furry heads.

"You are crazy about those dogs."

"You know I love them."

I watch as the two dogs moon over her when she leaves. Hell, *everyone* moons over her.

We all love Violet.

I hate the thought of her leaving. When she's found what she needs to... when she's completed the job she was supposed to... what then?

My phone rings, and I go to silence it, when I see it's the Salem police.

"Hello?" I answer the phone as I open Violet's door.

A loud, high-pitched voice comes over the speaker.

"Mr. Master. It's me. I've been trying to reach you for three days."

For fuck's sake, I forgot the PD puts calls from the jail through their secure line, no doubt so they can tap them.

"Have you?" I don't miss the way Violet's eyes narrow as she snaps her seat belt shut and mouths *who's that?* I shake my head and head to the driver's seat.

"I told you I couldn't help you immediately and would need some time." I hear something in the background, and a series of clicks.

"I paid you all my inheritance for your help!"

I blow out a breath and try to speak patiently, though I want to hang the fucking phone up. "And I'll help you as best I can, but allow me to remind you, you've been taken into custody, have you not?"

"I have! And I need you to get me out of here. You're the only one with enough clout that you could do it."

"I'm sorry. That's way beyond my pay grade. My team will be in touch."

"Mr.—"

I hang up the phone.

Violet stares out the window for a moment in silence while I type in the minister's number on my phone.

"Desperate much?"

"Tell me about it. Jesus."

"Something's off about her, Cain."

I roll my eyes. "You're just jealous."

"I am not just jealous. And holy *shit*. What is *that?*"

I look in my rearview mirror and groan. Doesn't anyone listen to me?

"You... weren't supposed to see that yet," I say, shaking my head. "Jesus."

Her jaw drops. "You are holding out on me! Oh my *God*. You bought another truck and didn't tell me?"

She doesn't know because the goddamn truck's for her.

"They weren't supposed to bring it yet," I say, backing up so we can leave.

"Oh my God, I want to touch it. Plllleeeease. Pretty, pretty please, can I touch it?" She runs her hand along the dashboard of my truck, as if to appease herself.

"When we get back," I promise, then add in a teasing voice, "if you behave yourself. Now tell me where to go."

"I'll tell you where to go," she pouts. I pinch her thigh, and she squeals. "Okay, alright. So we're heading south of the historical district."

"Perfect."

"So back to what I was saying earlier. Where on earth is that money?"

"That's a very good question, and I think it would be worth our while asking Gray Descamps that very question."

"Agreed. If I'm no one, and my parents made all that money... their income has to be hidden somewhere. It can't just be like... under the mattress."

"It's pretty hard to hide millions under a mattress."

"But it could be done."

I snort. "Have you actually *seen* what a hundred million dollars looks like in cash?"

She raises a brow to me. "So we've gone up to a hundred million. I have not. Have you?"

"I have. I was once contracted to assist with a drug bust that ended up revealing the largest amount of cash ever confiscated in the history of the East Coast. We apprehended the drug dealers who'd kept two hundred and fifty million in cash in a bedroom."

"So *that's* why your bed's the size of a small island?"

I laugh out loud. "I knew you'd find out eventually."

"Two hundred and fifty million is a *lot* of fucking money. And if your father was as successful as you thought he was... well, that money's definitely somewhere, isn't it?"

She looks out the window. I wonder if she's imagining herself wealthy, what she could do with that money. What she doesn't know is that everything I have is hers for the taking, and there's a reason she couldn't afford my services.

Violet's mine. I won't ever let her go. And everything I own is hers.

"I know what you're thinking," she says.

"You're a mind reader now?"

"You could say it's one of my talents."

"And?"

"You don't like the thought of me being wealthy." There's a pained sound to her voice I don't miss.

She couldn't be further from the truth.

"Why wouldn't I want you to be wealthy? Of course I do. Things are easier when you have money. I don't like the thought of you going without at all."

"No, Cain," she says in a softer voice. "You don't like the idea of me not *needing* you."

I scoff. "I'm not that insecure, babe."

She doesn't reply. We'll battle her goddamn insecurities until she knows exactly who she is and how much she's worth.

"We're only five minutes out now. What's our plan?"

"He might suspect who you are as soon as he sees your eyes. Maybe we should've put your contacts in."

She has color-changing contacts for times like these, when I don't want anyone to remember her or identify her in a line-up.

"Nope. I want him to know *exactly* who I am when I interrogate him."

"Wait, just last night you were saying that you didn't want to hurt an elderly man."

"Perhaps I've changed my mind," she says decidedly.

"Oh? And what did that for you?"

"I want answers, Cain. I didn't come to you for the good food and better sex."

I reach for her hand but can't help but smile when I give her a squeeze. "I know, baby."

Violet blows out a whistle as we near the address on the map. The tight houses around us spread out to orchards, sprawling mansions atop massive cliffs that overlook the water.

"I thought ministers were poor?" she says curiously. "This guy lives in the lap of luxury." Her brows knit together. "That doesn't bode well, does it?"

"Not all ministers live in poverty, and not all rich ones are corrupt, but..."

I have my suspicions about him. I tap my phone. "Call Henri."

"Hello? What can I do for you, Mr. Master?"

Henri's like a brother to me but has never lost his Southern charm and formality.

"Henri, we need what you've found on Gray Descamps, the shortened version." I've had him working on it since last night.

"I see you're almost there."

"I am." I have my team track my whereabouts and Violet's at all times.

"I'll make it quick, sir. Gray Descamps has been married four times, has seven children with various women, and is the second wealthiest minister in New England." Violet curses under her breath.

"Court cases?"

"None, sir, though there are a few allegations of sexual misconduct in the workforce that were settled out of court."

Violet cringes. "Could this guy get any more predictable?" She sighs. "What does he drive?" Violet asks.

"What does he drive?" I repeat and give her a curious look.

She shrugs. "We'll need to find out what he values. What matters to him. If he's wealthy, it's likely his possessions." She looks out the window with a scowl. "If he has that many children with that many women, it will be hard in this short timeframe to find out which we could use to threaten him with."

"God, I love how your brain works."

Henri clears his throat. "Sir, you're three minutes out."

I wink at her, and she sticks her tongue out at me. She'll pay for that. "Go on."

"Four years ago, he had a paid television show that was very popular. He's known for his fire-and-brimstone sermons on repentance and good works, but his show was shut down during the allegations of sexual abuse."

"Does he have any known phobias?" I ask.

Violet tips her head to the side. I'm not going to walk in and bloody the old man up, but I'll have to get answers, and something tells me he won't make it easy.

"None obvious, but perhaps... water, sir. He had a pool in his backyard he had filled in a few years back, and all his vacations are on land."

It's not much, but it's something to go on.

"Does he have any ties with any known criminals?"

"No, sir, he—no. Wait just a minute." He's silent for a moment. "Four years ago... just around the same time his television show was cancelled, there was a threat to his life. Rumors of 'organized crime' made the press, but no names and no details."

"Of course," Violet says. "No news press is going to name a mafia group, would they." She curses under her breath again and pulls her knife out. I watch as she runs her finger along the sharp edge of the blade. Thinking.

"We're here." At least, we're in the neighborhood. GPS puts us at the foot of a hill. At the top of the hill stands a wrought iron gate and an intercom.

"Stand by, Henri. May need you to work a lock remotely."

"Yessir."

"Cain, is it wise to just go in the front gate like this? Won't he be waiting for us?"

"I want him waiting."

She shifts on her seat and squeezes my hand in silent approval. I lift her fingers to my mouth and kiss them.

I press the button on the intercom, and a man's voice answers immediately. "May I help you?"

"We're here to see Gray Descamps, please."

"Do you have an appointment?"

Violet rolls her eyes and chimes in. "It's about the salvation of my soul. Are such appointments necessary?"

The intercom is quiet for a moment, and I shake my head at her. The woman's fucking unpredictable.

"I'm sorry, you'll have to make an appointment. Mr. Descamps is unavailable for the next four weeks. You can find his assistant's email listed on his website."

Apparently, saving someone's soul can wait a month when you're sitting on property worth millions. I want at this motherfucker.

"Please tell him it's urgent," Violet says from the passenger seat. Her tone is also urgent , with an edge I know all too well. Violet's about to lose her temper.

I reach my hand to her thigh and give her a gentle squeeze, a reminder that keeping our tempers will work better than coming in guns blazing. She narrows her eyes at me. She doesn't like those reminders.

"I'm sorry, you'll have to make an appointment on the website. Have a good day."

There's the sound of a click, the lock securing. Pretty much what I expected. There's a long, curving driveway. Uniformed guards make their presence known.

"Count them," I say in a low whisper to Violet.

She nods as I back out of the driveway.

We drive along the main road, but we aren't leaving this property until we get what we came for.

"Take a right," she says quietly. Out of the corner of my eye, I see her pull out her gun and shine the handle on her shirt.

"Not sure we'll need that."

"Shame."

Violet's a fucking good shot, and I know she wants an opportunity to use her skills and her new toy.

"An elderly minister has to be approached a certain way."

She sighs. "I know. So I don't get to see you beat anyone up today."

I can't help but smile, because I know she's only half-joking. Every goddamn time I train with one of my men, she's practically dragging me to bed afterward. It's part of how she's wired, and I love her for it.

"Nope. The way to get to someone like him is to really, truly determine what he's afraid of. We need to know what he fears most so we can make him tell us the truth."

"Perhaps he's afraid of heights," she says in a bored tone before she makes a sound of disgust. "So plebeian."

"Or spiders."

She rolls her eyes. "Cliché."

"Or maybe...." her voice trails off as she taps her chin thoughtfully. "Let's think about this. What would a wealthy man who preaches from the Bible fear above all else?"

"Slander to his reputation. Losing all his money."

"Precisely. Oh, Cain! There!" She points to a rusty gate that leads to the back of Descamps's property. I pull the truck over to the side of the road, leaves crunching beneath the heavy tires.

"Perfect. Good eye, baby."

In minutes, she's disassembled the lock. She faces me with a look of triumph. "Ready?"

Before we go, I reach down and loop my fingers along the nape of her neck, pull her head back, and capture her mouth with mine. "I'm ready, baby. Let's do it."

For all his riches, Descamps has gotten lax when it comes to security. My property's heavily guarded, with video surveillance. We don't have so much as a squirrel that crosses the perimeter of my home without our knowledge. Descamps, however, is either lazy or stupid.

The gate leads to the back of his property, everything so overgrown here there's not a chance security would see anything even if they had cameras positioned here. No guard dogs, no armed men. Nothing.

"Wow," Violet says. "Bet you're about to burst a blood vessel imagining how shitty his security is."

I snort. "I'd burst a blood vessel if it were *my* home so easily compromised. With him, I'm more than happy to make myself at home."

"Agreed."

It's difficult to walk quietly through a wooded area in the fall, as crunchy leaves and branches snap with every step we take. But the wind rustles the leaves, masking the noise we make, and by the time we get to a clearing, thunder rolls overhead.

"What do you see?" I ask her. I'm your man for brute force, but when it comes to hawk-eye vision and strategy, Violet's unparalleled.

"He's got a barn to the right that looks neglected. Roof's seen better days, hay bales sloppy and unkempt. That's where the pool used to be, and a... hot tub? There's a pool house, too."

"Any entrances from the back?"

"Lots. Looks like there's a door by the pool house which

leads to a back entrance, as well as a bulkhead, and there's an actual open door on the property as well."

"Let's try the pool house." It's chilly enough this time of year, that part of the house likely doesn't get much use.

"Let's do it."

We move as one, silently and quickly, as several yards of bare ground before us leaves us uncovered and more likely to be seen. In less than a minute, we've made it past the pool house and to the door that leads us into his home.

"Locked?"

Violet frowns at the digital lock on the door while I ring Henri.

"Boss?"

I quickly whisper what I need and send him a picture of the lock. He has data on how to unlock everything from a padlock to a jammed door, and quickly finds not only the year, make, and model of this lock, but succinct directions on how to disable it.

"Let me do it?" Violet asks.

I nod and step back. She's small and lithe, so she easily maneuvers her way into situations just like this.

"Told you it'd come in handy having someone small like me on your staff."

"You did."

"And was I right?"

I hold her slender hips with my hands. "You were. I could pick you right up and tuck you into my pocket."

"*Cain.* Your timing sucks." Then she quickly nods her head. "I know, I know, I agreed. Now please, let me focus before I lose my concentration here. You and I could take the six security men he's got that I counted, but I'd rather not break a sweat while we're here." She frowns. "I don't want to have to wash my hair again." It's adorable what crosses her mind sometimes.

"Alright, alright," I concede, as the lock clicks open. "But I go in first." I'm happy to let her work her magic with a damn lock, but there's no telling what waits for us on the other side.

CHAPTER TWENTY-SIX

Violet

GOD how I love working with Cain. I love the way his brilliant mind works. I love the way his eyes narrow, sharp and determined, when we need to do something that requires concentration. He unravels mysteries with a fearless resolve that makes me goddamn wet.

It's dangerous, sometimes, how deeply he affects me.

"Go on," he says in a low voice, his hand on my lower back. It took me a while to get used to his protective nature around me, but I'm getting there. I'm so used to taking care of myself, I had to remind myself at first that it's okay to let a guy touch you, it's okay to let a guy want to lift heavy things for you, it's okay to let someone... take care of me for once.

Not sure I'd let anyone but Cain do such things, though.

"Jesus," he mutters. "Not a single person in sight."

I shouldn't be surprised there's no one here. Nothing but an empty hall and the dank smell of an abandoned basement.

"It's almost as if he wants someone to break in," I say, shaking my head. "Why hire all that security only to have it be so easy to get in?" I lower my voice and retrieve my knife. It's quieter at times like these. "Unless..."

"It's *intentionally* too easy."

"Right."

It's likely Descamps' security's absolute shit.

And it's just as likely we've been set up, and they're only biding their time before an ambush.

We walk, weapons ready, to the doorway that leads to the basement hallway. Old houses like this on the North Shore were solidly built, some at the turn of the century, with large, roomy basements for both storage and safety in the event of a hurricane or storm. The ceilings are low, but the walls tight, not a draft or wisp of cold air escapes even on the coldest of days.

We walk silently, waiting for a sign that we're seen, that someone's nearby. I hear nothing but the distant dripping of water and wonder idly where it's coming from. A clock chimes.

It smells like an old library down here, slightly musty but familiar. The basement's finished, with a thin Berber carpet, and tidy, even the wooden beams on the low ceiling gleaming. It's dark, though, with only a few small windows letting any light in.

We both freeze at the sound of voices and footsteps overhead.

Then a thin, reedy voice travels to us from above. "Then find them. I don't want anyone coming here unannounced. You know that." The voice quickly dissolves into a hacking cough that morphs to a coughing fit.

"I think we've found our man," Cain whispers. I nod. They've taken our bait.

To the left is a staircase that leads upstairs, but to the right, there's a door. Cain opens the door, and his eyebrows raise. If we weren't avoiding being found, he'd probably whistle. I peek around him to see what he does, surprised to find what looks like a mini spa, complete with a jacuzzi and sauna and fluffy white towels. It smells vaguely of lemon and mint, and tiny white fairy lights dance around a table with a tea kettle and teacups. It's a perfect paradise of relaxation, right here in the minister's rambling home.

"Someone enjoys himself here," I mutter to Cain.

He nods but doesn't reply. His lips are set in a grim, thin line, his brows knitted together. I know before he tells me exactly what's on his mind—this is the room he'll use to get our answers.

"We draw them out," he says in a whisper. "Get security locked down, then bring our little friend down here for some answers."

"Perfect. I always wanted to do an interrogation wearing a fluffy white robe. If only there were a pair of slippers nearby..."

Cain gives me a lopsided smile, takes my hand, and gives me a firm squeeze.

"Make some noise, baby."

"Shouldn't we secure the security exits first?"

"Already done."

I glance quickly at the door where we came in to see the deadbolt's been thrown from the inside, then quickly look to the windows. They're so tiny even I couldn't climb through, and I'm used to getting through tight spaces. These windows are no bigger than a shoe box.

Cain's made sure no one's getting in from this entrance.

"We need to get the stairs situated. Can you do that, baby?" he whispers. I know why he wants me to handle that part of the job. I'm half his size, so it's much easier for me to climb the stairs without making them creak like aching bones. I nod.

I tiptoe up the stairs as quietly as possible, and when I get to the top, I check all the locks. There's one that bolts from this side, as well as another lock. We need to lure Descamps down here, then lock the door. Once we do, no one will get to us.

"Now, Violet," Cain says in a whisper, his gun in hand and ready to shoot. "Go."

I grab a metal can filled with screws from a nearby shelf, yank open the door, and whip it as hard as I can toward the stainless-steel dishwasher. It explodes on impact, making a deafening noise. In seconds, we can hear shouts and yells, but I'm already down the stairs behind the staircase with Cain when they finally come.

It takes him three shots of the gun to take them down. One on the left, bullet to the leg. One on the right, wound to the left shoulder. Last one he shoots is the third target, and he's prepared. He ducks, then lunges for me, acting on instinct. The son of a bitch must know Cain would lose his shit over me being hurt before he would himself.

Doesn't matter. I'm glad to have the chance to get at one of them. With a quick duck and jab, I nail him straight in the solar plexus. He doubles over, and I waste no time, my knife to his throat before he can even blink.

"Stay right fucking there and I might let you live when all this is over," I whisper in his ear. He freezes, not even breathing. I have him on his knees while Cain secures the others, and in one minute flat, we've got all three tied to chairs, secured with duct tape. Not the most original tool, but damn does it get the job done.

Three. Only three. Cain nods to me, eyes on the stairs, then jerks his chin at the guy I secured. I hold my knife to his neck.

"Any more security on today?"

He shakes his head.

"He's lying," Cain says. I trust Cain implicitly. I don't question or give it a second thought, but press my knife to the guy's neck until he bleeds. He pants, sweat dripping off his forehead.

When I first began working for Cain, interrogation intimidated the hell out of me. I still don't like it, but I've come to see its merits. I don't fucking like it when someone lies to me.

I lean in and give him one more chance. I'm shaking with anger. I want answers. "If I find you're lying to me, I'll find whatever it is that matters to you, and you'll wish you'd told me the truth."

"One more," he gasps out. "Didn't count the personal bodyguard."

Cain nods, both accepting this and giving me permission to let this guy go. I secure his mouth like the others and walk quietly to the stairs. Listening. I don't have to wait long.

"Who's down there?" Cain's eyes cut to me. The voice is the high-pitched, nasally one we heard before.

Cain and I stand as quietly as we can, side by side under the stairway. From the stairs, no one can see the guards we've secured far to the right.

A foot hits the top stair. A worn, ancient leather moccasin. I wish this guy wasn't an asshole. I usually sort of like old people.

Cain squeezes my hand. He knows how I feel about inter-rogation.

"I get him secured, and you'll go upstairs and look for the other guard." His lips press in a thin line, and I know exactly why. He'd much rather have me babysit while he runs interference, but in this case, it isn't the wisest decision, because I'm smaller and faster.

"Got it, boss," I say with a teasing wink. I'm the only one of his staff that doesn't usually call him "boss." He gives me a wry smile back, making my heart thump a little faster even now.

I wait, crouched, while Descamps makes his way further down the stairs. In seconds, Cain's got him fully restrained in his arms. Descamps shouts and kicks, but Cain easily secures him.

"Go, babe. Meet me by the sauna."

I knew that's what he was thinking.

Taking the stairs two at a time I race to the top, my Wilson tucked securely in my palm. I don't have to wait long. I turn the corner, gun at the ready, when I hear someone move behind me. I duck and swivel just in time, missing the meaty punch of Descamps' personal guard. I step back, giving myself room to maneuver, and quickly let loose a roundhouse kick to the gut. I've trained with both knife and gun and use them well, but when push comes to shove, I'll always prefer to use my own body as a weapon.

He's bigger than I am, though, so my body won't be enough. He's winded and on his knees from the kick I gave him, but I have to make sure he doesn't hurt me. I slice at his thigh with my knife, ignoring the fresh, hot blood that cascades onto the tiled floor. He screams like a little girl, whimpering, but not before he gets a good solid punch to my cheek. I see stars, my head spinning, but don't lose my concentration. I slash again, striking his arm, then again, until he recoils in pain.

A minute later, he's secured with duct tape as well. I'm not sure I'd have been able to hold off a man as large as he is if I hadn't had the element of surprise on my side.

"You'll stay right here," I say with a patronizing pat on the head. Any son of a bitch who defends that guy we're about to interrogate deserves absolutely no mercy. "Anything we need to know about your boss before we begin?" I ask pleasantly, in the same tone as one might ask, 'Do you want fries with that?'

He shakes his head vehemently from side to side, glaring at me like I just killed his puppy. Likely embarrassed he was taken down by a girl.

I, on the other hand, am pleased as punch and can't wait to haul this asshole down to Cain.

I leave him secured at the top of the stairs where I can see him and go down to Cain.

What I see when I enter the room would've chilled me to the bone a year ago.

Gray Descamps, with a generous belly and meaty jowl, sits, secured in a chair beside the jacuzzi. He eyes the tub with terror. Score for Henri.

"Gray," I say pleasantly, taking the folding chair Cain hands me. I sit across from him. "I'm sure I'm not familiar to you."

He stares at me, unblinking, and at first doesn't respond. He opens his mouth to speak, then clamps it shut. I don't tell him not to. I let him look into my eyes. He won't be able to hide his recognition of me if there is any.

His eyes hone in on mine, narrowed with suspicion and anger, but when I lift my chin so the overhead light shows the color of my eyes, he freezes.

"I know you. I—I knew your parents, too, I think. Is that why you're here?"

I look to Cain. He nods. Sometimes he has an agenda. Today, we just need answers.

"It's one of the reasons. Why don't you tell me about my parents and how you know who I am."

"You're the girl with the violet eyes. Name's Violet, isn't it?"

I nod. "It is."

"Your mother had the same color eyes." His voice is high-pitched with fear. "I remember her. That was a long, long time ago. A lifetime ago."

A cold shiver runs down my spine. No one in my entire life has ever told me that. "Did she? What else can you tell me about her, Gray?"

My voice is not my own, sounding distant and disembodied like I'm a ghost speaking to someone on Earth.

"I—I didn't know her."

Cain shakes his head like a disappointed father. "Now, now, Gray," he says, while he pushes himself to standing from his seated position. "We won't allow lying. We've gone to a lot of trouble to come here today, and we want answers."

His phone buzzes. He glances at the screen and scowls. Cain's voice drops to a menacing octave. "And the intel my men just sent me makes it a *lot* easier for me to put the screws to you if necessary."

"Tell me."

His eyes quickly dart to mine, then back to Gray. "Those accusations? Some were true. We have court-verified intel and eyewitnesses. And some of the women were minors at the time."

Fucking hell. My hands clench into fists when I see the wide-eyed terror Cain's words bring out in Gray.

He's guilty as fuck.

"Now tell us, please, before we have to get a lot more unpleasant. Did you really not know my parents?"

Gray clamps his jaw shut and looks away. Cain moves as if by instinct. He walks to the jacuzzi, flicks the chrome handle, and water begins to pour into the tub. "Something tells me you don't like water, Gray. Is that true?"

His face is red, his eyes beady as he shakes his head from side to side.

"He's lying," I tell Cain.

The water in the jacuzzi's already a third of the way to the top. Cain shuts off the taps and steps toward Gray, who shakes his head from side to side. "I didn't know them! I swear, I didn't—"

Cain ignores him, picks him up bodily, chair and all, and drags him over to the jacuzzi.

"No! No, don't, please!"

"Tell me, Gray," Cain says, his lips a thin line of fury. "Is that what the girls you molested said to you when you took them into your home?"

Without another word, he dunks the minister's face in the pool of water. I want to look away, but I don't. What Cain does and who Cain is are inexorably intertwined. If I love him—and I do—I love all of him, even the cruel, vindictive parts that lurk in the shadows. Those are the parts that make all of him whole.

I watch Descamps struggle, thrashing in the chair he's secured to until I know he can't breathe. My own air's constricted in my lungs until Cain brings him up. He hasn't even broken a sweat.

"Anything more to tell us, minister?"

A pause. He's breaking. When he doesn't say anything, Cain submerges him in the water a second time.

The first time I saw Cain torture someone, I had to look away. I hated that I did. I wanted to face the cruelty he inflicted, because it was always, *always* justified. With ruthless determination, he gets what he wants when he wants it, but he always has good reason. He doesn't torture for sport and never without a damn good reason.

This is why I hired Cain. This is what we came for. I need these fucking answers.

Bubbles emerge from the water. He's got Descamps right on the edge.

Cain looks in my eyes as the minister faces his own mortality, and I feel that stark, honest truth to my very soul. We don't speak. We don't blink. We stare in solidarity of a shared purpose, and I love him for it.

He lifts Descamps out of the water. A rivulet of water floods his eyes and face, his hair dripping onto the cold concrete floor below. The light blue dress shirt he wears is soaked from the collar to the first three buttons, his pants still untouched. Cain slams him back on the floor.

"Answer."

"Fine! Fine," he says, crying softly to himself. He glares at Cain, and his words feel like venom. "I had an affair with her mother when I was newly ordained."

Now that, I didn't expect.

Ew.

"And?" Cain stands with his arms crossed on his chest. "If you think we have all day, minister, I can speed things along—"

"No! No," Descamps whimpers. "I... I knew her well. We ended what was between us and went our separate ways. I began my ministry and she... she married Violet's father. They had her less than a year after they married, but I always kept in touch with Anya."

Anya. I've never heard anyone use my mother's name.

Cain nods. "Go on. I know you've got more to tell us, Gray."

"You were the one that married them," I said.

Gray nods.

"And you were the one that knows why they were killed."

Gray looks away, not answering, but when Cain lifts the chair, Descamps screams. "I'll tell you more!"

Cain thumps the chair back on the floor. "Go on."

Gray shivers and looks out to where his team sits, but every one of them's restrained. Still, just to be sure, I walk over to the door with my Wilson in hand, half hoping someone will give me a reason to shoot. Cain continues the interrogation.

"Her parents did some work for them. For... for me."

He hangs his head and looks at the floor.

He didn't say my father... he said... my parents?

I turn back to him just as something crashes behind me. My gun's raised and pointed in seconds. A huge, muscled guy with a gun comes straight at me. My finger hovers over the trigger. I've shot the target at the range so many times I could do it in my sleep, but I've never shot a human. In a split-second, I imagine the torn flesh and blood, the pain in his eyes. My hesitation costs me. He tackles me to the floor before I can shoot, as a gunshot blasts.

He screams, grabbing at his shoulder, and as crimson blood spurts to the floor, he rolls, and Cain's deadly voice echoes in the small room.

"Move again, and I shoot you between the eyes."

I want to kick myself. Goddammit, I couldn't pull the trigger and Cain had to come and clean up my mess. I want to cry.

Instead, I make up for my hesitation in the only way I know how. I swivel, propel myself forward, and grab his wrists to secure him in place. Cain comes up beside me and ties him down.

"That's my girl there, buddy," he warns in a tone that's anything but friendly. "You fucking try to hurt her and you're dead." The guy stares at Cain like he just saw the devil himself. Cain has that effect on people.

"You were saying, Gray?"

Gray shakes his head, crying, but when Cain reaches for his chair, he screams like someone's bitten him. Cain drops the chair to the floor. Blood spurts from Gray's temple.

He's shot. Someone shot him.

Adrenaline courses through me while I look for who could've possibly killed him. Cain looks to me, then immediately dismisses me. I stare at my own gun as if it shot him without my permission.

It makes no logical sense and takes half a minute to really register with me.

Someone shot Gray.

That someone was not me, and it was not Cain, nor was it any of the bodyguards we have restrained here.

Someone shot him because he was about to reveal a truth they didn't want known.

Cain curses and pulls out his phone.

"Get down for cover, Violet," he grates, as tires squeal. Whoever killed Gray just took off. I fall to the floor and lay flat as Cain makes a phone call.

"Team Alpha," he says with resignation. His clean-up crew will have to come and clean this shit up.

CHAPTER TWENTY-SEVEN

Cain

I PRIDE myself on knowing what's happening and when, of being one step ahead of any of my enemies. But today... today, someone pulled a fucking fast one on me.

I thought everyone was secured. Never fucking dawned on me a sniper would off the one witness I need. I'd interrogate the rest of his staff, but I need to get Violet the hell out of here before she's hurt.

Team Alpha shadows me only minutes away during a detail, and today is no exception. They sweep in with the ease and practice of a well-oiled machine, while I secure Violet.

"Do exactly what I tell you. Keep your head down. Follow me. Don't respond to any bait, and if I tell you to shoot, you fucking shoot."

Could be one sniper, could be a goddamn team, there's no telling, but I don't want her here for another second longer.

We got some information, but not enough. We'll have to keep digging, but I'll have my team get cracking on that.

Violet's my priority. And I know she's here to find the people that killed her parents, but none of that matters if she's dead.

I leave my team with strict instructions to find whatever they can from who's left. Henri, Claude, and Joe are the ones I trust with my life. Today will be no exception.

We walk straight to the front door, my reasoning being that no one who's actually going to attack us would be so bold as to attack us here, though I've honestly been wrong before and don't take any chances. I cautiously open the door and tuck her against me, using my body as a human shield.

"I can cover myself, Cain," she says, glaring at me, but I know she's really mad we have to cut this shorter than we hoped.

"I know you can but do not try me now, woman." She'd better not fight me on this.

Violet's a force to be reckoned with, but so am I.

We walk out the front door where a ride's waiting for us, brought here by my team. Someone watches in the distance. This whole operation's gone to shit. I peer over the hood of the car to see who it is, but only see a flash of green before that's gone. Jesus.

We get into the car and head back to my place, but it isn't safe anymore.

"Dammit," I swear under my breath. "We need to get you somewhere safe."

"Your house is Fort goddamn Knox," she says, scowling.

"Not if we're followed by a sniper."

She shrugs. "Then lose them."

"That easy? Just lose them?"

She nods. "Yeah. We won't be any safer anywhere else."

I know she's right, I just hate taking chances. Just the same, I nod. She has a point.

"Fine. We'll go home. You're right, I've got more resources there than anywhere else, but first I need to make sure we aren't followed."

"Naturally. I'll make sure, too. Let me drive, and you can do surveillance."

If I could drive and do surveillance at the same time, I would. I curse under my breath, making her grin. She knows I don't give up the driver's seat lightly.

"You just saw me torture a man, and now you're damn near grinning? God, you need a spanking so fucking bad." I slam the door as I reluctantly take the passenger seat.

That only makes her grin widen.

"You're just so cute when you go all alpha."

"You're out of your fucking mind."

"I know, it's what you love best about me."

"Wouldn't say *best,* but it's up there."

She giggles like a little girl, a rarity for my Violet. I take one second, just one second, and yank her over to me so I can plant a kiss on her forehead, before I shove her back in the driver's seat.

"If we get into a car chase, I will never forgive you for making me do this," I say with a growl.

She shakes her head. "Aw, baby, you do say the sweetest things."

"Buckle up," I grumble.

She's already snapping her belt.

I see no signs of anyone following us at all. Whoever it was took off in the green car. Fucking wimp. Pussy. Who takes off like that?

We're heading back as I watch the road.

"No one's tailing us, Cain, I'd have seen them."

I nod, while I run my hand under the seats and visors of the car. "I don't see anyone either. However..." my fingers clasp around something secured to one of the visors. I yank it down and lay it in my hand.

She looks over out of the corner of her eye and whistles. "So even this is tracked, eh? Did you have the car we drove in checked?"

"With what time, babe? We literally just left."

"Bet my left boob that thing's got a tracker then."

"Your left *boob*? Jesus."

"Guys say left nut, what's a girl supposed to say?"

"Nothing. You say nothing."

She glances out the window, and the smile fades from her face. "Something bothered me about what he said during your questioning, Cain." I don't know why the tone of her voice sends alarm bells clanging in my mind. It's like a warning bell, like the wailing of a siren before a storm. I shake my head, willing myself to stop acting like a pussy.

"What?"

She frowns, and hits the gas, her speed creeping up as she heads onto the highway.

"Babe, watch the speed."

"We have to get back to the house."

I stare at the mirror to see if we're being tailed. Still, nothing. "Doesn't do us any good if we arrive in body bags."

She rolls her eyes. "You're being dramatic."

"Slow down, or I'll make you pull this car over."

She glares at me and punches the gas again. Oh, this woman is in so much goddamn trouble. Before I can respond, something catches my attention in the rearview mirror. A flash of green.

"Keep it steady, Vi. Someone's behind us."

I flip the switch on the side of the seat so it reclines, fold the headrest back, and kneel, gun in hand. I don't care if anyone sees us. I don't care about fucking anything but making sure we get home safe and sound.

Hardly any cars are with us on the road, but Violet zooms past every one of them. I'm not telling her to slow down now.

I kneel on the folded-down seat, gun in hand, my eyes on the target. If this is anyone of importance…

The green is gone. I wonder for a second if it was only my imagination, when a flash of green appears a second time.

"Come at me, bro," I whisper. Violet's peal of laughter makes me smile. God, I love this woman. She just watched me interrogate an old man, almost kill another, and now I've got a gun trained on someone following us, ready to pull the trigger. And she makes jokes about her left boob and *laughs.*

"You're either perfect or psychotic," I mutter.

"Aw, you do say the most romantic things. Do you need me to maneuver in a way that gives you better vision?"

"No, babe. What you're doing is perfect."

The flash of green is only a speck, so far behind us I can't see much. I don't want her to slow down because that could put us in a compromising situation, but I want to see the motherfucker up close.

"Can you see anything at all?" she asks.

"Looks like a sunroof… but I can't see much else."

Violet frowns. "That sounds familiar, but I can't place it."

"Me neither."

"Fuck, they took an exit."

I watch as the green car slows and gets off the highway behind us.

"Maybe they weren't following us?"

I shake my head. Doesn't make sense they weren't. Doesn't make sense at all.

My phone rings, and I quickly answer it. "Yeah?"

"Boss." Henri. "I've got some information for you that may prove useful."

Violet takes the exit that brings us home.

"I want to hear it but first, I want you to notify the team at the house that Violet and I are almost there, and we are pretty certain we were followed by a green car."

"Green, sir?"

"Yeah. Ring a bell for you?"

"I don't want to point fingers or raise unnecessary suspicion, sir. Is that all you have to go on?"

"Yeah. Henri." My voice is tight. "Spill."

"Armand had a green car, sir. Would he be so foolish as to follow you without bothering to get another car?"

"I don't know."

Foolish, maybe. Lazy, definitely.

"What did you find, Henri?"

"I've found a record of Violet's mother, sir. And it's... let's just say it's interesting. I have to investigate further though."

That tells me nothing. "You have nothing else to tell me?"

"Not yet, sir."

We'll have to double down our efforts. But we're making

progress. We're getting somewhere. I hang up with Henri, and Violet looks my way.

"What?"

"Armand drove a green car."

"Well that doesn't mean anything. Lots of people have green cars."

I nod. "Yeah, but I've heard it on good authority that he doesn't let shit go."

She blows out a breath. "Of course not. That would be far too simple, wouldn't it?"

Oh yeah. It truly would.

Her stomach growls when we pull into the drive at the house. I check on security, and all confirm—no one followed us here. Surveillance has been doubled. We're safe here.

"Inside."

"Cain, you're acting like a sniper's just going to jump out at us at any moment."

"They did at Descamps' house."

She snorts. "They weren't at *Cain Master's private house*, were they? Cain, when I hired my first ride here, the driver wouldn't even come this far."

"No?"

"No. He found out who lived here and he was done. Dropped me off a mile away and made me walk."

"Now that's a form of bullying. I want his name."

"You can't beat up everyone that isn't nice to me."

"Watch me. And how did you know that's what I wanted to do?"

She rolls her eyes. "Because you're super fucking predictable."

Oh she is in *so much trouble.*

I practically kick open the door to the house and usher her in. "Get in there."

"Yes, sir," she says in that sickly sweet tone reserved for nothing but sarcasm. I slap her ass.

"Cain," she says, abashed.

"Violet," I mimic. I take out my phone and dial Henri. "You find anything else out?'

"Was just about to call you."

"Yeah? Why?"

"We found out some more information. It wasn't Violet's father who killed anyone. He was their I.T. guy, not an assassin."

I blow out a breath as I meet Violet's eyes. This intel challenges something she's held as truth for years.

"Any more intel?"

"We're working on it, sir. I'll let you know as soon as we have anything. Joe's got one of the security guys to talk."

"Excellent." I don't ask how. I don't need to know anything at all.

When we enter the house, the rest of my security detail swarms around me. Violet's swept out of my arms and inspected; someone swabs antibacterial ointment onto a cut I didn't even know I had. I grunt my way through updates and get another call from Team Alpha. The investigation is under full swing, and Henri's trying to get camera footage from the chase we had.

"Okay, kids," Violet says, shooing away anyone else who tries to come anywhere near her. "Leave mama be."

I shrug off Skylar, who's holding gauze in one hand and glaring at me. "Sky, babe, leave him be," Violet says over my shoulder, but we both know what Skylar's been through and sometimes we don't know what will trigger a response.

Skylar's eyes fill with tears. "You guys scared the shit out of me," she sniffs, angrily wiping her eyes. "I saw that car come after you, and I—"

"Wait, what?" Violet says.

Skylar's eyes widen. "What? Did I do something wrong?" She's not normally this skittish, but something's got her worried.

"Skylar, how did you see us? What footage?"

"There's that camera in your car, Cain." She flushes. "You told me I could play around with the surveillance footage, get familiar with it, so I did. That one wasn't turned on, but..." her voice trails off as a cold trickle of sweat falls down my neck. The surveillance footage. Skylar's been able to access it because I gave her permission and the password. I thought it was the easiest job to give her, one that wouldn't trigger any response...

But there's more than our standard footage on those recordings. Goddammit, I've got every video I ever took of Violet on those. If she saw them...

"Cain!" Violet turns to me. "We have to go see what she found. If there's anything on there that gives us a better view of the person following us, we need that intel, and now."

"I'll get it." I give Skylar a sympathetic look, as she's staring at me as if I have two heads. "When Henri's done with what he's doing right now, I'll have him contact you. Thanks, Sky." I tug a lock of her hair and give what I hope is a reassuring grin. "I need to talk to Violet alone."

"Why?" Now Violet's giving me the confused look.

"Vi. Upstairs," I say, and I feel like a total douche when I actually feign limping. "I have to get off my feet for a bit."

Douche.

DOUCHE.

Violet nods and takes my hand. "Alright. Sky, I'll be in touch. And thank you."

"You guys need something to eat?"

"Yes, God, *please,*" Violet says with a smile. I grunt in agreement. "Send up sandwiches or something?"

We head upstairs. I quickly shoot Henri a text.

> Sky found our archives. Delete. You know what.

I slide my phone in my pocket.

"You know... some days, I feel like we just met. Other days feel like we're an old, married couple."

My mind is focused on the footage, what's on there, what Skylar could've easily found if I wasn't careful.

Did she already find it?

"Yeah?" I'm distracted.

"Yeah." On the landing, she spins to look at me, her voice wary. "Okay, Mr. Master."

My heart does a little leap.

"Yeah? Violet, move."

"*Move?* Now I'm your employee?"

Her voice takes on an edge.

"I am not letting you bait me."

"Oh, don't I know it," she says, her violet eyes snapping at me. "You'd just as soon haul me over your knee, wouldn't you? Hmm?"

"What the actual hell has gotten into you?"

"The better question is, what the hell got into *you?*"

Oh no, she does not turn this back around on me. "I'm warning you. Knock it off, or you do *not* like where this is gonna go, babe."

She stands her ground, hands on her hips. "And now you're threatening me? Oh, no sirree."

I've had it. I bend, yank her over my shoulder, and finish

walking up the stairs. She predictably scissors her legs and slaps my back.

"Don't you dare use your big, huge body to overpower me!" A door opens, and our housekeeper Alma holds it wide. "Oh, my, my, my," she says, then goes right back in and closes her door again.

I slap Violet's ass perched over my shoulder, hard.

"Don't you dare!"

"Just did. Or what?" I spank her again.

"Or I'll *scream!*"

"Then what? Scream to be rescued?"

She howls and smacks my back. I walk past my bedroom to the library, slam the door behind me, and lock it.

"What are you doing?" she asks, her tone laden with panic. "Caiinnn..."

I'm driving her to distraction while Henri does what I asked him to. I don't want to fucking fight with her anyway.

"Cain, are you doing what I think you're doing?"

The wind howls outside the window, raging with the threat of freezing rain. But here, in front of the fire, the wood crackles and burns with the ferocity of a dragon.

"What if I don't want to?" she says, even as an edge in her tone begs me to take her, dares me to make her.

"You promised me." I'm already unfastening her jeans and shoving them halfway down her thighs. "Hands over your head."

With a whimper, she wriggles but obeys. My jeans tighten when she makes me hard, that angry but obedient side to her the hottest thing I've ever seen. She wars with herself. She fights it. There isn't a submissive bone in Violet's body, but she wants this.

Needs this.

Craves this.

And she doesn't like to flat-out defy me. She's done it a few times, but most of the time, Violet does what she's promised … to give herself to me fully.

I reach for the top she wears, fitted to her body like a glove, and yank it up and over her head. She wears nothing but a little red bra with cotton cups and tiny satin laces. In one flick of the wrist, the bra is open and her breasts fall free. I take a moment to lick and nibble, kiss and worship each of them, until her back arches and she releases a low moan.

"Yes. Mmm. God, yes, I love it when you torture my nipples."

I take that as an invitation, and sink my teeth into one hardened, throbbing bud, while I stroke between her legs. I flick my tongue over the very tip, making her moan and gyrate her hips. The fire flickers in the hearth, as I lay her on a soft rug.

"You put… this rug… here just for this, didn't you?" she pants, bracing herself on her palms before the fire.

"No, I put it here for show." I bite her other nipple. "Of course I bought it for this. Who else ever comes in here?"

The library is at the end of the hall past my bedroom, and Violet's really the only one who frequents this area of the house, which is why it's the perfect spot to keep her occupied while Henri does his work.

God, I hate myself for this. All this time, I told myself I was trying to build trust with her, but am I doing the one thing that might cause her *not* to trust me?

What will she do if I tell her?

I watch as her lips part, and lose myself to pleasuring her. I've never been one who was eager to please, but with Violet... God, with Violet, I'll give her anything she wants. *Anything.*

I immerse myself in her, in the way she tastes, her intoxicating smell, the way her body moves when I touch her. I inhale her fragrance and lick her breasts, I smell the salty-musky scent of her seduction wrapped around me like a cloak, and I'm lost.

I tear the rest of her clothing off and ignore the vicious *rip* sound when I tear her panties. Her clothes are in the way, and I want them off *now*.

"Me, too, Cain, let me," she whispers, her fingers clasping my belt buckle and quaking. I nod, while I yank the hem of my tee and tug it over my head. Violet's eyes go half-lidded, and she runs her tongue along her lips.

I shove every other thought out of my mind. I won't dwell on fear. I've got Violet, and that's all that matters to me right now.

CHAPTER TWENTY-EIGHT

Violet

I WAKE in the middle of the night with something so clear to me, I can't stay in slumber. I sit up in bed and blink my eyes.

My mother was the assassin.

It wasn't my father.

I close my eyes, but I'm wide awake, going over every detail.

I thought everything added up to their being assassins. Weapons had lain hidden in armored boxes under their bed. I was forbidden to touch them, but knew that's what they held when years later one of my foster parents had a hushed conversation about the "evil weapons" my parents held. I overheard enough hushed conversations to know that someone—I assumed my father—was responsible for the death of so many.

But now...

I need to read the cryptic notes in her diary again. When Cain rescued me from my apartment months ago, I made sure he wasn't looking, then snuck into my closet and brought her diary with me. I'd read it over and over again, and there were entries that never made sense to me.

I wonder if they will now.

Before I get the diary, however, my mind is playing tricks on me. A sinking feeling takes root in my belly.

If my mother was an assassin... what does that make me?

I quietly pull back the covers and walk over to my phone. It's sitting on the charger; I stare at it before touching it.

Somehow... I already know what I'll find when I look into the details of my mother. For reasons I don't quite understand, I often work things out in my sleep. I'm not sure why. Some might say it's a hidden talent of mine. When I was in school, I'd sometimes go to bed with a math problem on my mind and wake up with the detailed answer.

So when I'd gone to sleep, I'd known full well that the answer to this riddle would be my mother's true identity. I sort of expected something would reveal itself.

I just didn't know it would happen like this.

I pick my phone up from the charger, then clench my fist when I realize I never plugged it in last night. Ugh, it's almost dead. I gently put it back on the base and plug it in for real this time, then reach for Cain's phone instead.

He never cares if I use his phone. He's given me his bank credentials and passwords, and even got me a charge card on one of his accounts to use. He insisted I use it, so I finally did. He laughed when I told him I bought something for Romulus and Remus so it was easier to justify the expense.

So I don't think twice about taking it. I take his off the charger—totally charged *of course*—and silently fire it up. I don't want to wake him.

I look over at him. He's still dead asleep with his arm slung over his head.

God, did he give it to me good tonight. It's rare that he knocks himself out this hard. Poor guy. I turn with my back to him and walk to the little sitting area in the living room attached to his bedroom.

I nestle into the corner of the couch and pull a tattered blanket from the back. He says this was the blanket he used when he bought his first office, so he'll never get rid of it. I like using it. It makes me think of a younger Cain and feel an imagined connection we didn't have when we were younger.

I flick on Cain's phone and enter his password.

Wrong password.

I frown, and enter it again, slower this time so it's more deliberate.

Wrong password.

I stare unblinking at the phone.

Did he change his password? I'm not going to wake up the poor guy to ask him *that*. I frown and try one more time.

Phone locked for fifteen minutes.

I didn't think twice about using his phone before, but now... an odd sense of guilt consumes me.

Is he deliberately trying to get me not to use his phone? I try to think when the last time was that I used his phone and can't remember. I wasn't paying attention.

Sometimes people change passwords and just forget about it, I reason. But not Cain... Cain's a creature of habit, and has very, very deliberate passwords that he never changes.

I go to the closet where I keep my personal things. It's filled to the max with clothes, shoes, bags, and jackets Cain's bought me. He loves to spoil me, and in recent months has realized that what I like above all is guns and trucks, so the clothing purchases have tapered off. I smile to myself sadly, running my hands over soft, silky tops and luxurious leather shoes and boots.

I don't want to look at my mother's diary. I don't know if I'll like what I find if I finally figure out those mysterious entries.

Cain doesn't know it's in here. I tell him everything else. It feels odd hiding this one thing from him.

I take down a heavy, sturdy shoe box and pull out a slim book—my mother's diary, nestled into paper wrappings I'd repurposed from a pair of leather boots and wrapped around the diary to protect it. It's been a few weeks since I've read it. I sit on the closet floor cross-legged and open it up.

The front of the book is just a normal diary. She talks about my father, but mostly about me. *Violet had her first steps today. Violet called me mama.* She was an infrequent writer, so the entries are spaced widely apart, the last one just before my fourth birthday. *I can't believe my baby is four.*

Though those are the pages I've looked at more than anything, that's not where I look now. Hands trembling, I turn to the very back of the book where there are tally marks and initials. They fill two pages.

ST. 10/3 *150k.*

JL. *1/3 500k.*

MO. 3/8 *1 mil.*

HENRI SAID he didn't think my father was the assassin, yet everything I unearthed when I was younger pointed to my father being the murderer.

My father wasn't the killer. My mother was.

A cold chill washes over me as I look at the log in her perfect handwriting, slightly slanted right. I'm looking at the log of her murders and the payouts.

I let the feeling consume me for about one full minute. I close my eyes and feel the tingle in my nose, the tightness in my throat, the constricted weighty feeling in my chest, and wrestle with the question that plagued me before, that I can't eradicate from my mind.

If my mother was an assassin, what does that make me?

There is no question in my mind that I was called to find the person that murdered my parents. I've always loved weapons and strength, more than anything really.

And Cain says I'm the best fucking natural he's ever trained.

Why? *Why?*

Is it in my blood?

I take the diary with me and put it on the bedside table.

I return Cain's phone to his charger and go back to bed.

When the bed creaks, he says, "Morning, beautiful," in that sleepy-sexy drawl that usually makes my heart thump faster. Today, though, I'm in a different world.

"Morning." My voice sounds distant.

Why would he change his password? Last night, he seemed distracted, but I thought it was only because he often retreats after an intense day at work.

He hasn't even opened his eyes yet, but lifts his arm to beckon me to come to him. I slide under his arm and nestle my cheek against his chest. He wears a clean, crisp white T-shirt. I close my eyes, the fabric warm under my cheek, as his arm settles heavily on top of me.

"Cain." I'm not one to let things fester and simmer. I want shit out in the open where I can deal with things.

"Yeah, baby?"

I don't want to have a hard conversation. I don't want to sound like I'm accusing him of anything.

I love this man.

It's on the tip of my tongue to tell him that. To profess my love and tell him I want to be his not just now... but forever.

But I can't distract myself from the truth. I can't ignore the feelings that settle around me like murky water, hiding what lies in the depths.

"I went to use your phone just now."

Is it my imagination, or did his body stiffen? He doesn't stop the slow, gentle brushing of his hand down my back.

"Yeah?"

"Yeah. I wanted to look something up. And the password was changed. You remember what it was?"

"Of course. Sorry 'bout that, babe. Henri told me it was safer change passwords every once in a while, but I forgot to tell you."

"Oh, okay." Something feels off, though. It's unlike Cain to hide anything from me.

Isn't it?

I haven't known him *that* long, the logical side of my brain reasons. He could be hiding... a lot more than I suspected.

"So... what's the password?"

He opens one eye and gives me his crooked smile. "Violet 1."

My heart warms. My name and his lucky number.

"Tell me again why number one's your lucky number," I say, smiling against his chest. I like this story. His hand comes to nestle at the nape of my neck.

"Number one is the alpha. Alpha as a Greek number repre-sents the number one, so as both a symbol and a phrase, it refers to the first, the head."

I don't know anyone else whose favorite number is one. For Cain, it makes sense, though.

"Got it. May I use your phone, please?"

"Of course."

I don't move.

"Aren't you going to go get it?"

"Actually, I'm quite comfortable." It's warm and cozy here by his side, his huge body enveloping me like a weighted blanket.

"Careful, baby," he says with a groan, as he reaches for me and yanks me over his chest. My legs straddle either side of his, my body pressed to his.

"Yeah?"

"Morning wood," he says, only one eye open. I bend down to him, frame his face with my hands, and kiss him. His lips are full and warm, and his hands come to rest on my hips while we kiss. My heart beats faster, my pulse racing, when he licks my tongue and rolls over. In seconds, I'm pinned beneath him and he's very, *very* awake.

Without a word, he releases my mouth and drags his lips along my chin, then my neck, and as he kisses his way down my body, my legs part of their own accord. I groan when he glides his hard cock, silk-wrapped steel, against my throbbing clit.

"In me," I beg. "I want to feel you in me. But you're half-asleep," I whisper.

"Doesn't matter. Dreamt of this when I slept."

I lose myself to our lovemaking. I push aside all thoughts of my mother… his passwords… *us*… and just enjoy what we have right here, right now.

We're in the shower together, and I'm lathering up his back —one of my favorite parts of his body—reveling in the way his muscles turn me on, when his phone rings.

He leans out of the shower and hits a speaker that connects his phone to Bluetooth.

"Sir?" Henri.

"Yeah. I'm here with Violet."

I freeze, my hand still covered in lather, staring at his back. Since when does he tell anyone he's with me? They know who I am and why I'm here. I listen in on every conversation, especially as the details to our current investigation involve my parents.

"Sir, we found the owner of the car that followed you yesterday. You were correct, sir."

"Armand?"

"Yessir."

Cain curses, turns around, and I lather his chest and arms, half-distracted. The man's an exquisite masterpiece of male perfection, and that's hard not to notice when you've just made love and he's covered in steam and lather. I kiss one perfect bicep.

"What else?"

"He hasn't moved. Still living in an apartment in downtown

Salem. Looks like he's out of work, but that can't be true because his bank account says otherwise."

I don't always like that Cain has such easy access to private details, but I've come to expect nothing short of a full investigation.

"Why was he following us?"

Henri doesn't answer at first. Cain's jaw is clenched, his eyes not meeting mine as he glares at the wall behind me.

"I'm not sure, sir."

"Find out."

"Yessir."

I lather up his legs, enjoying the feel of the soap and water on our skin. He takes a fresh washcloth and squirts my light green body wash on it, then makes the swivel motion with his finger. His glare cuts like a laser. I know he's not angry with me, but at whatever's on his mind.

I spin around and let the water caress me as he washes my body.

"I want a full report by lunch. Going to debrief everyone in about ten minutes."

"Yessir."

Cain reaches out and hangs up the call.

"You just give them orders and they all 'yessir' you."

"Mhm." He brings the showerhead down and rinses my body.

"I always think that's so hot."

He smiles. Is it my imagination, or is the smile a bit sad?

"You're fucking gorgeous," is all he says. He still sounds angry.

"Thank you?"

"Why the question?"

"You sound really angry. Furious. It's just distracting me."

He shuts the water off and reaches for a towel, hands it to me, then grabs one of his own. I wrap myself in the fluffy terrycloth and step onto the thick bathmat. Like everything about Cain, the shower's huge, with plenty enough room for both of us.

I weirdly feel we need that distance right now.

I can't put my finger on why things are off or what's going on here at all, but I know that something isn't right.

We dress in silence, and I watch him suit up with his weapons, again, in silence. I tug on a pair of jeans and a fitted tee, then my boots, but don't feel fully dressed until the knife's in my sheath and my Wilson's secured in a harness.

"We're gonna find shit out today, Violet."

I nod. We'd better. We have to move forward on our investigation. Descamps was involved, he knew things, and the people he was involved with knew more.

"Cain..."

His eyes shoot to mine. "Yeah?"

Why does he look panicked?

I stare at him a moment, not sure how to respond. "What the hell is wrong?" I finally ask. That's not what I intended at all.

He doesn't deny there's anything wrong but doesn't speak for long minutes. I watch him tug on his boots and secure his holster. When he doesn't speak, I do.

"That's not what I was going to say. I know you get distracted sometimes."

"I don't want to lose you, Violet."

I freeze. I didn't expect his response to hit me so hard. I turn and give him a curious look. My heart beats rapidly, and my palms are sweaty. A sudden feeling of nausea fills my belly.

"Why would you lose me?" My voice sounds distant, as if it isn't my own.

"Shit's about to hit the fan. We're going to find the people responsible for your parents' death. And after that…"

The same thought's occurred to me. What happens when the purpose of my being here's resolved?

"You've never killed anyone, Violet."

I look at him in shock, cold fear trickling down my spine. "You don't know that."

I watch him slide his hands on his hips and fix me with a curious stare. "Have you?"

"I… haven't killed a *human*."

A small smile spreads across his face. "You've killed… what, aliens? Sea creatures? Ghosts?"

"Well, no. I killed... I killed a rabid dog once."

He looks a bit stunned. "Did you? A rabid dog?"

"It was harder than it looks, and it was only for safety reasons. I was fifteen."

"Why did you kill it?"

"It was... I was staying at Candi's house." Candi, my best friend, is a local Salem police officer who can hold her own with a gun these days. Back then, though, she was terrified. "Her dad had guns, but he was traveling, and her mom was out. They lived kinda far from the city. We were babysitting her younger brothers. There was this crazy dog, foaming at the mouth. And I just... shot him."

Cain's brows rise, but he doesn't respond. Finally, he nods.

"So when it comes to protecting the people you care about, you can pull the trigger."

I swallow. "Yes."

I think?

"I'm ready. I'll handle this just fine."

He faces me, his gaze so intense I can't look away. My mouth goes dry, and I lick my lips. He's got something to say.

"Come here."

Of course he gives me an order. I refrain from rolling my eyes.

"Yeah?" I walk to within a pace of him. He reaches one

large hand around my lower back and drags me closer to him, then tips one finger under my chin.

"Violet, I..." his voice trails off. Is that fear in his eyes? I'd have sworn a few weeks ago there was nothing Cain feared, but I know now that's untrue. He fears the people he loves getting hurt. He fears letting people down. He fears my being in trouble and not having the ability to help me.

And now... he's afraid I'll leave him.

"Cain, I—" I'm not even sure what I'm going to say. "Can you..." His mouth slams on mine, and I moan into it. The frissons of awareness that light my body ignite, and I respond without thinking. My hands on his neck, his hands on my ass, I reach for his belt to anchor myself.

Too soon, we break our kiss. His forehead meets mine, and his voice drops. "I love you, Violet." He breathes a sigh as if relieved when he finally says it. "God, woman, I love you. And I don't want anything to come between us. Not now, not ever."

He loves me. *He loves me.*

My throat gets tight and my nose tingles. I feel hot and cold and light and heavy all at once. I want to cry, long and loud and ugly, and I don't know why.

"You love me?" I ask, and he smiles that crooked smile. "I know, I know, that's not what a girl should say after a profession of love."

"You're not just any girl."

And that's why I love *him*.

"I love you, Cain." I've never told anyone I loved them before. No one, not anyone in my entire life. I wish it felt better than it does, but for some reason, it makes me ache inside.

Loving someone makes you vulnerable. So fucking vulnerable. And I don't like that.

He holds me to him, his fingers tangled in my hair as if to keep me here.

"Why are you shaking?"

"I don't like the way it makes me feel and I wish I did. If I'm honest... and I always want to be honest with you... it scares me."

"I know, baby. Me, too."

He holds me in silence for a moment, and I can't help but give thanks that he gets that this is hard for me. I love that he doesn't question me, or act defensive, or make me feel like shit for admitting that loving him scares the living shit out of me. Cain has too much integrity to act like a pussy when we face hard things. It's one thing I love about him.

"Violet... what does that mean for you?"

I never expected a question like this.

"To love someone?"

"Yes. Tell me, Violet. Tell me what it means to you."

"It means... accepting someone no matter what. It means loving them for who they are. It means... it means working through everything that's difficult and threatens to tear you apart, because if you love someone, you make it fucking work. It means helping the other person become the person they were meant to be."

"Yes, baby." He kisses my cheek. "All of that."

He releases me with reluctance, concern in his eyes. "Violet, I—" He pauses.

"Yeah?"

His phone rings. Henri.

"We've got intel, sir. Serious. You on your way?"

"On our way."

He hangs up the phone and nods.

"Cain," I say in a little voice. "We need to bring something with us." I reach for my mother's diary. He holds my hand and at first doesn't respond. Then he takes it in his free hand. My heart pounds harder knowing that my two worlds have somehow strangely collided.

"No matter what, Violet. No matter what happens, trust me. And remember what you just said."

I can't help the feeling of foreboding that builds in my belly.

"Of course," I tell him, but my words feel hollow.

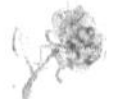

CHAPTER TWENTY-NINE

Cain

I WOKE UP WITH A PLAN.

Violet needs to know everything.

I've put this off long enough, and now there's a threat to her finding out in a way *I do not want her to.* She has to know, because I'm not letting her go. She has to know I've wanted her from the first time I ever saw her. She has to know I knew she was the one for me.

But Jesus, the timing on this...

I told her I love her because I do. And when the truth comes out, I need to believe that it's enough, even if I have to fucking grovel on my knees for her.

We walk hand-in-hand to my office. The house is oddly quiet today, and it isn't until we get to my office that I see why: all hands are on deck.

Claude, Henri, and Joe, as well as all of my new hires and trainees, and even our damn doctor, wait for me in my office.

Violet whistles. "Whoa. Now *this* is quite a greeting, you guys."

I meet Joe's eyes. He looks grim, goddammit. I run my fingers through my hair and grit my teeth.

Claude stands and gestures for Violet to take a seat, but I shake my head. "She'll sit with me." I want her to be as close to me as possible when we hear whatever it is they tell us.

I sit at my desk chair and she perches on my knee, alert and focused, but her hand rests on my thigh. My fingers wrap around hers.

"Not gonna waste time, boss," Joe begins. Everyone quiets and looks at him. "We found Armand tracking you last night. Seems he hasn't gotten over being let go, and he's got an ax to grind."

I nod. Figured as much. All of my men, like me, were former military. We all have a history together, too. But when Armand threatened Violet's life last year, I'd had enough. I wanted her brought here, but safely and on her terms. He got her in a car accident and could've killed her.

He was the first one I'd ever fired.

"Understood."

"Armand was the one who got into an accident with me," Violet says. She frowns. "Kinda thought he was a douche."

"I seem to recall you calling him that, didn't you?" Joe asks, his eyes twinkling.

She shrugs. No regrets.

I love this woman.

Claude speaks up. "Armand wanted to be number one with Cain. Never really stepped up enough to get there, so he wasn't happy when we let him go."

"Got it." Violet nods. "Does this have anything to do with what happened at Descamps' house last night?"

"I'm getting there," Joe says.

"We don't have all day, Joe." Violet's eyes snap at him, her anger evident.

She needs to be patient. I keep my voice low. "Violet."

She frowns but nods.

"We interrogated Descamps' team. They've been taken care of. They were all ready to talk once he was out of the picture."

I nod.

"He's in with the Rossis."

I blow out a low whistle.

"They're organized crime, right?" Violet asks.

"Yeah. They're the biggest mafia group in New England. Practically run Boston, oversee all imports in the Northeast. They practically *own* every harbor from here to Newport. Got a family home just north of Boston, too."

Violet blinks. "Wow."

"Yeah," Joe continues. "It seems your parents did some work for them." He clears his throat and looks to me.

"She knows they were assassins, Joe."

I wince. Here it comes.

Henri looks to me before he speaks, and I give him a nod. "Her father wasn't. He was a bookkeeper for them but not a made man. Neither of them were actually in with the Rossi family. Both were contractors that worked for them."

"She contracted hits," Violet says in a low voice. She winces. "Didn't she?"

"Your mother did, Violet," Joe says gently. She nods. She's already figured this out.

"So she was an assassin for the Rossis. Then why were she and my dad killed?"

"The Rossis were not responsible for their deaths. They did a hit for the Rossis, but the hit was on one of their rivals. We suspect the Rossi target brought vengeance back to them."

"You suspect?" Violet's voice holds a note of anger. "I want more than suspect."

"We're working on that, Violet. Descamps's men gave us everything they knew."

She nods. "So we go to the Rossis."

A murmur goes up in the group, and Violet gives a questioning look.

"You don't just... go to the Rossis, Violet."

She tips her head to me. "No? And why not?"

"They're the most notorious crime ring on the East Coast, that's why. They'll blow your head off and bury your body, then pour a glass of wine and call it a day before we've gotten anywhere."

"Well that's rather drastic," she mutters. "I can play nice."

"I'll go with you." My men all look my way. Claude shakes his head slowly from side to side, and Henri's mouth drops open.

"Sir," Henri says. "They can't be trusted."

"I'm not trusting them. We have questions, and they have answers."

"They do. And we'll go together." I turn to Joe. "Bring Armand in."

He holds my gaze but doesn't respond at first. I know he's worried about what Armand will say to Violet, but I can't hold back the truth any longer. I need her to know exactly where we stand.

There's a knock on the door. "Yes?" I answer.

The door opens, and Skylar comes in. She stares at me with accusation in her eyes, her arms crossed over her chest. "Excuse me. There's an all-hands-on-deck staff meeting, and no one invited me?"

"Come in, Sky." One of the guys stands to let her sit, and she waves him off.

"I'm one of the team now, since I looked through all that footage." Her gaze swivels to mine, and she clears her throat. "And I do mean *all* the footage, Cain. That wasn't my initial plan, but it's how things worked out. And it seems there's lots that needs to happen and be brought to light, no?"

Shit.

"There is, Skylar, but in time. Right now, we have to move on the Rossis. They were likely the ones that sent someone to silence Descamps. They're onto us, and we need to be proactive."

"Right. Is Violet going with you?"

I nod. "We'll go together."

She blows out a breath. "Take me with you."

The room goes so quiet, I can hear the slow ticking of a clock on the wall.

"Excuse me?"

"Take me with you." There's a note of steel in her voice that's unlike Skylar.

Is my baby sister quietly blackmailing me?

"Sky, you haven't trained with him," Violet says gently. "We've worked for months on my knife and gun skills."

"No, but I've trained with *you,*" Sky says, holding her own. The first time I ever saw Violet, she was training young kids in martial arts. Skylar's been working with her for months, but is still very much a novice.

"It'll be a dangerous situation, though," Violet says, her voice tighter now.

"Listen, I have reasons for wanting to go, okay?" Skylar says. "Plus, I know them."

"You know the Rossis?" I ask.

Skylar shrugs. "I used to read Tarot cards with the youngest Rossi girl. And I *maybe* had a little fling with... one of her brothers," she says in a rush.

I swear under my breath. "You had an affair with one of the Rossi brothers?"

"Cain, honey, take a deep breath," Violet says, running her hand along my arm. "That vein's pulsing in your temple again..."

"My sister slept with one of the Rossi brothers, read Tarot fucking cards with the sister, and you want me to calm down?"

"Now wait," Skylar says, her brows coming together. "I didn't tell you I slept with any of them."

Violet rolls her eyes. "Kids, kids, settle down." She gives Skylar a pointed look. "Sweetie, you hang your laundry on a *sex chair*. There's no shame."

Skylar shakes her head. "It's a *tantric chaise*. Fine. Are you going to take me with you or what?"

Violet looks to me. The room's gone silent, as if everyone's holding their breath waiting for me. "Could be really helpful having someone with us that knows them, even if her history is a bit... dubious."

"Did you cheat on any of them?" I ask sternly.

"Cain!"

I need to know. "Did you?"

"Of course not," she huffs out, offended.

"Did any of them cheat on *you*?"

"No. The only reason we didn't see each other anymore was that he went to college internationally and we just sort of lost touch. In fact, he was quite the gentleman in bed." Oh, God, I do not need to hear this.

"And his sister's lovely. We still keep in touch."

"Boss, might be a good idea," Joe says. "They're a lot less likely to attack if there's a friend between you."

"Honest to God, Skylar, you cannot ever do something so stupid again. Seriously."

"Cain, I've grown up now. You know that. I can handle myself just fine, and with the skills Violet's teaching me, I'll be even more prepared than ever."

"Fine. *Fine.* But don't do anything without my permission, is that clear?"

She nods eagerly, while Violet takes out the diary. She hops off my lap and speaks in hushed tones to Henri, who takes the diary with a nod and jots down notes. I know it will all come clear in the end.

I hate that the two women that mean more to me than anything in the world are in a dangerous situation like this. I hate that I can't trust the people we're going to see.

And I hate that I haven't told Violet the truth. Skylar knows, I know she does.

I can't hold this back anymore.

"Sky, I need to talk to Violet alone before you come with us." I don't look at Violet. I can't. Not yet.

"You do," she says with a nod. "I understand. I'll wait for you in the truck."

I shake my head. "I'm not sure how long this will take. I'll call you when we're ready to go."

I feel like I'm going to be sick. I don't like the way Violet's face has paled, or the way she gently tugs her hand out of mine and wraps her arms around her body.

"Okay," Skylar says with a nod. "Violet, just remember you love him, okay?"

Violet looks sharply at Skylar, and I groan. Seriously, Skylar? *Seriously?*

"Skylar, go read a book or something, and stop interfering," Violet scolds. Skylar shrugs and heads to the truck. Maybe I should send her to the house. Who knows how long this will take.

When the door shuts behind her, Violet turns to me. Her amethyst eyes glow with fire, and she stands up straighter. My girl may be a tiny thing, but she's powerful and potent, and I feel that straight in my gut right now. She raises one brow at me. "Spill, Mr. Master."

"Target range."

She slow-blinks, then nods. "Do you plan on seducing me after you tell me whatever the hell it is you need to tell me?"

"No, babe. I'm not planning on seducing you." I can't keep the melancholy out of my tone.

Jesus. I've waited months and months to get Violet to myself. I've worked my ass off building trust, establishing what's between us. I want Violet, and I don't want to share her... not now, not ever.

But I'll have to give her a chance to walk away.

I've never felt so helpless in my life.

We get to the target range, and the world seems eerily silent. It's as if the entire planet is waiting on the conversation I'm about to have with her.

A part of me hopes there will be a distraction of some sort, that a meteor will fall to Earth, or a bomb will explode, or... something. Anything, to keep me away from having the conversation I have to have with her.

She shuts the door with finality, then turns to me. "Cain, I feel like I'm going to be sick waiting for this."

"Me, too."

Her voice is pained when she pleads with me. She places her hands on my shoulders, nearly standing on her tiptoes. "Then tell me, babe. Please."

I bend down and brush my lips to hers. It might be the last time I ever do. I want one more chance with her, one more taste of her, before I lay out what could destroy us.

When I pull away, her eyes are filled with tears. "That felt like a goodbye. Why did that feel like a goodbye?"

I'd flay the very skin off my back to keep her happy. To keep those eyes from filling with tears like that.

There's no more time. I have to man the fuck up and tell her.

I have to tell her everything.

"Violet, when you first came here, that day you came and asked me to help you find your parents' killer?"

She nods slowly. Waiting. There's no easy way to say this.

"I already knew who you were." I watch her eyes grow troubled, but she doesn't speak.

"It was my intent from the very beginning to bring you here. I... had been obsessed with you for months."

A look of confusion crosses her features. I'm sure she's replaying everything in her mind, trying to figure this all out, trying to decipher my meaning. "What do you mean?"

I sit heavily on a chair by the door and tug her down to my lap, but she gently extricates herself from me and sits beside me instead.

Jesus.

"I was doing surveillance with Armand and Joe. There was an asshole cheating on his wife, and we were monitoring people at the mall. We had cameras set up, and we recorded everything to get evidence. And...well, there you were."

"At the mall?" She looks perplexed. She needs a full view of things before she can make any judgment call. It's her way. "Oh. Oh, wait." She pales. "Cain, that was... back in the spring. I did a demonstration at the mall. That was... months and months before I met you." Even her lips look paler.

Jesus.

"I know." I clear my throat. "I saw you there, and I had to have you. You looked at the camera. You didn't even know that you did, and I... saw your eyes. They mesmerized me. I remember thinking they looked like amethyst caught in moonlight."

She looks at me sadly. "You had me followed."

"I followed you myself. I watched you. I looked into you."

"You stalked me, Cain." Her voice sounds distant and hollow. I reach for her hand, but she pulls back. I feel stung. She hasn't yelled or gotten angry or hurt me in any way.

A part of me wishes she would.

I'm not going to sugarcoat this. "I did, baby."

Her voice is a whisper. "Don't call me that."

My gut clenches. "I was obsessed with you, Violet. No. I *am* obsessed with you."

"You never told me. If you'd only told me…"

"You would've run from me."

"You don't *know* that!" Now, I see the anger. Now, I feel it. She stands, but I quickly tug her back down so she doesn't run. We have to talk this out.

"I don't, but I know you well enough to know that vulnerability scares the living hell out of you. I knew I had to show you that you could trust me."

"By lying to me?" She laughs mirthlessly. "Tell me how that works?"

"God, babe, no. By showing you I was a man who had your best interest in mind."

"And in your mind, stalking me, luring me here, and acting

like I was a perfect stranger the first day we met was somehow the right thing to do?"

My phone rings, but I silence it.

"Go ahead. Take it," she says, looking away. "I need a minute."

"No."

She looks at me and purses her lips. "Suit yourself."

"Listen to me, Violet."

"That's all I've done is listen." Her arms are wound across her chest as if to wall herself off from me. As if she wants to ensure I don't touch her.

"So when Armand got into that accident with me… it wasn't an accident at all? You put him up to it? How, Cain?"

I blow out a breath and go for broke. "You're the kind of woman who values independence. You need to know that things are on your terms."

"So you thought it best, in that omniscient mind of yours, to make those decisions *for* me? Oh, I get it now. Lovely."

She blinks, and a tear rolls down her cheek. Fuck.

Fuck.

"I knew I could help you. I knew you'd want me to. But I had to make sure you were doing things on your terms."

"Cain, how could I ever trust you again after this?" She stands and shakes her head. I reach for her, but she bats my hand away.

"I deserve this," I tell her honestly. Jesus, I deserve this and so much fucking more. I wish she'd yell at me, or hit me, or throw something at me for fuck's sake. I wish she'd slap me or even come at me and fight, which she absolutely could do. She hasn't really, other than the little spat with the cudgels, since that first day she attacked me and I warned her never to try to fight me again. I wouldn't defend myself, though. I'd let her hurt me and know I deserved more than whatever the fuck she gave me. "Sorry seems so futile, babe."

"Don't call me that," she says, and when her voice wobbles a little, my heart breaks. I've done her wrong, and I'm paying the price. I'd give up my goddamn kingdom to erase the hurt in her eyes. I'd give up damn near anything.

"Violet—" I reach for her, but she throws her hand up, palm facing me.

"No, Mr. Master. I'm Miss Price to you. I came here for your help in finding my parents' murderer, and now we're on the cusp of a breakthrough. We'll finish this job." Her voice is cold and distant, as hollow as an empty shell. "And then we're over. I can't be with a man I can't trust." Her voice breaks, and fresh tears spill down her cheeks. "You were the only one I thought I could."

I expected her anger. I even half-expected her to react like this, hurt and distant and angry. But a part of me hoped we could talk it through. That she'd forgive me. That we had enough trust between us that we could work through *anything*.

My phone rings again, the only sound in the soundproof target range. I look at this place that holds so many memories for us. It's become the place of our trysts, the place that belongs to just the two of us. The others rarely even come here anymore, since they know it's sacred to us. In seconds, I take in everything that has meaning in here, unsure of what to say or how to respond.

"You should answer that, Mr. Master," she says in that same cold, distant voice I don't ever want to hear again. "It could be important."

I yank the phone out of my pocket and see Joe's name. "Yeah?" It isn't his fault everything's gone to shit, but I'm pissed that anyone's got the nerve to interrupt me right now. My sun has disappeared, leaving me in bleak, cold darkness.

I put the phone on speaker so Violet hears.

"Boss, you gotta move. The Rossis leave this afternoon for their home in Tuscany and won't be back for another month."

I curse, gripping my phone so hard my fingers hurt. "When do they leave?"

"Two hours. Skylar's waiting by the truck. She's rigged up, and we've got you on surveillance. Anything they say or do will be recorded. Go now, and Henri will fill you in on what you need to know on the way."

Violet nods. "Thanks, Joe. We're on our way."

The furious energy in me boils and simmers to a dangerous heat. Someone's left a velvet-lined box of throwing knives, Violet's weapon of choice, on a nearby table. I grab the nearest one, pull my arm back, and whip it at the target at the end of the range. Violet flinches when it sinks straight into the heart. She grabs a second one from the box and I half-expect her to throw it, too, but she slides it into to her ankle sheath. My girl loves her throwing knives.

My girl.

My woman.

My everything.

I don't even remember the last time I cried but fuck if it doesn't tempt me. Throwing the knife hasn't helped at all.

A brisk wind kicks up when we step outside, flecks of snow and ice raining down. This time of year in Salem it's rare for snow, but the occasional freezing rain isn't out of the question. My instinct is to drape my arm around Violet to protect her from the cold, but the way she holds herself tells me that wouldn't be welcome right now. She doesn't want me anywhere near her, and I don't fucking blame her at all.

Skylar waits for us.

We have a job to do. I gave her my word, and even if everything's over between us—even if she wants to leave forever—I made her a promise, and I intend on keeping it.

CHAPTER THIRTY

Violet

I HATE that I'm in this truck with Cain and Skylar, knowing that I have to leave. I hate that he's told me all this now, right when we're on the cusp of doing what I came here for. A part of me reasons that he didn't tell me before now because he didn't want to jeopardize this operation, but... I know better.

It kills me to know that everything I had here—the friendship, the family, the love of a man a woman could only dream of—is now gone.

I look out the window and see Romulus and Remus staring at me, their eyes hopeful that I'll come home. They wait for me in the window when I leave and wag their little butts when I return. But this time... I'm not returning.

How could I? How could I trust anything at all after what Cain told me?

I'd had sneaking suspicions, but all this time figured it was only in my head. Someone was following me. Someone was trailing me. Back when we hunted for the man who abducted Skylar, he was after me, too, and I assumed that those feelings of being followed were only because of *him*, because I didn't feel that way anymore after we apprehended him and the brother he worked with.

But I know the truth now. I didn't feel like anyone was following me anymore because I was *with Cain*, and he had no reason to track me when I was *in his fucking house.*

All people react differently when they're angry. Some scream and throw things, and I have vivid recollections of a foster mother who'd done just that. After being on the receiving end of one of those adult tantrums, I'd made up my mind that would *never* be me. Ever.

Some people cry. Some drown themselves in cookie dough and ice cream, and others in alcohol or drugs.

Me? I shut off my emotions. I can't feel anymore when I'm angry. I retreat to a place of practicality, a pragmatic approach, I suppose. I think of what I can control, what I can do, and I throw myself wholeheartedly into that. Sometimes that means cleaning the hell out of my bedroom, my car, or a closet. Sometimes that means running until my feet feel like they're on fire and sweat drenches my body. Sometimes that means a boxing workout, no gloves, that tears the skin off my hands because for some reason, that feels damn good.

And I can't do any of those things right now. I breathe in through my nose and out through my mouth, willing myself to stay calm.

Cain takes the driver's seat, and I don't argue. This truck's hard to maneuver, and I don't trust myself not to wreck it in the state of mind I'm in.

Skylar looks at me, then Cain, then blows out a breath. "So, I'm guessing you all had that conversation that I suggested?"

"You knew?" I ask, my eyes flashing.

"Not on purpose," Skylar says. "Recently stumbled on some incriminating evidence, but I wanted Cain to be the one to talk to you."

"Oh yeah. Well he did, and I don't want to talk about it, Sky."

"Violet..." her voice trails off.

I grunt in reply.

"I mean it was a shitty thing to do, but I—"

"I literally just said I don't want to talk about it," I snap.

"But Violet, seriously."

Cain makes a growling sound. "Skylar, *enough*. Knock it off," he says in that big brother tone that means business.

"Don't yell at her."

He looks at me in disbelief. "I was defending you."

"No, you weren't *defending* me, you were getting all bossy and telling her what to do, which, I might add, is like your favorite thing to do anyway, so I shouldn't be surprised."

"Oh for the love of fucking God," he grumbles.

"Ew," Skylar says, pinching the bridge of her nose. "Watching you two fight is like when someone throws *one* bone to Romulus and Remus."

"Did you seriously just make that analogy?"

"It is! They growl at each other and act like they're going to snap each other's damn heads off and gouge their eyes out, but you know they're inseparable and will end up sprawled all over each other come bedtime."

I grimace at the mental image of me sprawling all over Cain. I don't want to even look at him, much less touch him.

I've got something to say. "Okay, so I'm here for a reason, and I shit you not, it has literally nothing to do with getting relationship advice or even discussing anything that doesn't have to do with our meeting with the Rossis. Got it?"

Skylar nods and Cain sighs. "What she said."

Cain's phone rings. Henri.

"Answer it on speaker."

Normally, I love Cain's commanding attitude. Hell, I crave it and even find it hot. Right now? He is pissing me *off*.

"Anything you say, Mr. Master," I mutter in a singsong voice. Apparently when I'm angry I get petulant, too. Skylar shakes her head slowly from side to side, and I finally just flip her off to shut her up. I hit the speakerphone on Cain's phone.

"Henri here. I need to fill you in on the Rossis."

"On it," Cain mutters.

"Family home north of Boston, not far from here. Oldest brother's Romeo, youngest Mario. Grandfather's Giorgio Rossi, nicknamed The Iron Fist, do with that what you will."

Excellent.

"Mother's Tosca Rossi, seems she's tight with her kids and her husband, but she has a reputation as a flirt. Those should be the only ones you see today, if my intel can be trusted."

"Got it. Thanks for that, Henri."

"Sir, you know I don't like to give you advice."

"Right."

"But this time, just one quick word of warning, sir. I think you should have Skylar reach out to her connections. I've only researched the Rossis briefly and updated our files on them, but they are not what one might call approachable by any stretch of the imagination."

"Excellent," Cain mutters, his voice dripping with sarcasm. "Anything else we should know?"

"They have guard dogs by the front gate. Bring the treats Violet keeps in the truck for our boys."

Cain looks at me. "You keep dog treats in my truck?"

"'Course I do." I pull the dog bones out of the glove compartment.

Cain exhales audibly. "Thanks, Henri. We're not far out, so text me with any updates."

Skylar taps her foot on the floor, her fingers flying over her phone. She mutters under her breath.

"Any luck?"

"Marialena just woke up, she isn't going away with her family. She says it's fortuitous for me to reach out to her, she read her cards last night and found she would be approached by an old friend." Skylar smiles. "D'aw. Isn't that sweet?"

Cain rolls his eyes. He has no use for anything outside of the physical realm, placing all things spiritual and otherwise in the same category as the Loch Ness Monster or the Boogeyman.

"Very sweet," I say, placating Sky. "Can she get us in?"

Sky frowns. "Unfortunately, she's finishing up her classes and won't be home until later. She isn't going with the family to Tuscany because she needs to finish a few finals."

"Got it. So that leaves Loverboy?"

Cain makes a choking sound I dutifully ignore.

"On it," Skylar says in a singsong voice, apparently very excited that she has been brought into this. She taps happily away on her cell phone, and at least I'm relieved that she isn't trying to interfere in our fight.

We drive in silence for long minutes, as Skylar waits to hear back, and Cain and I have nothing to say.

So this is it. We've come this far with one purpose in mind, and if everything goes well with the Rossis, we'll close in on finding the people I've come for. The answers we need.

Skylar's phone chimes. "Score!" she says with a grin, making Cain flinch. Apparently, he doesn't like the idea of his sister scoring anything. If I wasn't so fucking furious with him, I'd reassure him. Right now, I am more than happy to let him handle this on his own.

We're over. We are *through*.

I want to sob and break things into little pieces. I want to run to the cliffs that overlook the ocean and scream until the wind carries my anger and hurt away.

And that's it. There's the rub. I'm more hurt than I am angry. I trust hardly anyone in my life. I can count those I do on one hand, and Cain was one of them.

But now... now after everything, I can't trust him anymore. And what's a relationship at all if it isn't built on trust?

"He says come on over. Meet him at the back gate, and he'll get us in."

"Excellent." I nod. We're one step closer.

We pull up to an actual, bonafide *castle*, the biggest estate I've ever seen, bigger even than Descamps. This one strangely doesn't have a security gate, though.

"Um, why did no one tell me this family lives in an actual *castle*?"

Skylar grins. "It's amazing, isn't it?"

I shake my head in disbelief. "And yet, no security gate? Or...moat?" I ask, curious about this one detail.

"They have dogs and snipers," Cain explains. "And they

trust their reputation. They've got a security team that rivals any on the East Coast."

I whistle. "Damn."

"Yeah."

"So where's your guy, Skylar?"

We drive slowly, our tires gliding over the black paved driveway with ease. She points to a large mansion up on a hill. "There."

A tall, good-looking guy with short black hair stands, wearing nothing but a T-shirt and jeans against the bitter cold wind. He looks like he could be a throwback to the James Dean era, his dark hair falling over his forehead giving him a bad boy vibe. He scowls when he sees me and Cain, his eyes narrowing.

"You did tell him we were coming, right?"

"Welllll," Sky says with an apologetic shrug. "I mean, I told him *I* was."

"Sky," I groan.

Cain parks the truck and exhales. "Violet, you stay here. I'll go with Sky and tell you when to come."

"Fuck. Off." I slide over and get out of the truck behind Skylar. She giggles softly to herself, and Cain slams the truck door so hard I'm surprised the windshield doesn't break. But I don't work for him. I don't take orders from him. I did for a time because we liked it that way. Because I told him I was his. But now... now he's lost that privilege.

"Mario Rossi," Sky says under her breath, "is loyal to the core. Keep that in mind. Say nice things about his family."

I see the dark eyes of his dogs lurking behind him and pat my pocket reassuringly. These treats are going to come in handy.

"Skylar." His voice hasn't ripened with age, and I'd guess he's probably a junior or so in college. Early twenties, though men in organized crime like this likely age a lot quicker than your run-of-the-mill boy. "You didn't tell me you were bringing company."

"Missed you, too, Mario," she says with a charming grin. "This is my brother Cain and..." she pauses, unsure of what to call me. "His co-worker Violet."

Ouch.

Mario doesn't respond.

"They need to talk with your dad or brother." Violet says unassumingly. "Please?"

"They're packing, heading to Tuscany. They don't want company right now."

Skylar sidles up to him and kisses his cheek. He rests his hand on her hip, and Cain's whole body tightens.

I don't care I don't care I don't care.

Mario grunts, whispers something in Skylar's ear, and she giggles like a little girl. God.

She whispers back to him. "Alright," he says with a nod. "Five minutes. I'll bring you in, make sure you don't get shot, then you're out of here, but all I'm giving you is five minutes."

"That's all we'll need," I assure him.

Storm clouds roll in overhead, as the large front door opens. A pretty woman, probably old enough to be my mother, stands on the front step. Her figure's impeccable, and her clothes are high-end. She wears torn jeans, a black fitted top, and boots to her knees, but it's the calculating look of charm she gives me I notice most of all.

"Skylar! How lovely to see you, my sweet. Come, come in, Skylar."

Skylar trots up the steps and kisses the woman on each cheek.

"Mama, this is Skylar's brother Cain and his associate, Violet. This is my mother, Tosca. They need to talk to Dad or Romeo."

The woman escorts us in. "Ah, of course. Come in," she says warmly. "My husband's busy preparing for our trip this afternoon, but my son should be here. Please, make yourself at home."

Four armed guards in suits stand nearby, their faces stoic and unmoving. One steps to the front.

"Weapons, please."

Cain and I don't balk, but hand him our guns without question. I don't move, hoping they don't notice the knife sheath. I give Cain a quick look and he shakes his head so casually, one might not notice. I don't take out my knives.

"Is that all?" he asks pleasantly, though his posture tells me this man knows how to shoot a gun and he isn't afraid to use it.

I nod. Probably not a good idea to lie, but it's a worse idea to go into the Rossi family home unarmed.

Though they seem friendly and their house is gorgeous, there's something I can't quite put my finger on in the air.

Skylar and Mario are gone. "Where'd Sky go?" I ask Cain.

His lips thin, but Tosca Rossi's all charm. "Ah, they went off a bit by themselves. Come, have a seat. Can I get you a drink, Mr. Master?"

I catch Cain's eye. She knows exactly who he is.

"Hot tea would be fantastic, thank you."

She smiles. "Of course. And you, Violet?"

"The same." Neither of us will drink the tea, but I know why he's asked for it. I'm surprised Tosca's fallen for it. A hot beverage makes an excellent makeshift weapon if push comes to shove.

She busies herself with preparing our tea, and even serves it on a gorgeous platter nestled by a plate of homemade cookies.

"Please," she says. "Help yourself."

I take a cookie, only to be polite, and thank her. We sit and stir our tea while she asks us about our travels, if we've been to Italy, and tells us all about how she loves their home in Tuscany but prefers the modern conveniences of living in Salem.

A few minutes into our conversation, the tea's grown cool when the door to the study opens and a tall man, older but resembling Mario, enters.

Tosca stands and plucks our cups out of our hands and puts them on the platter sitting on the table. "Now, now, Mr. Master, you didn't think I was so naïve, did you really?"

She places a hand on his leg, and I want to slap her away. How dare she flirt with my—no. No, he isn't mine. She can fuck him for all I care.

I ignore the way my belly churns with a fiery, volcanic heat.

Cain stands and extends his hand. "Cain Master. This is my associate, Violet."

Romeo Rossi shakes both our hands with a grave nod. "Welcome. Please, have a seat and tell me why you're here, though I'll thank you to keep our conversation brief. You've arrived just before we leave for a trip overseas."

"I apologize, Mr. Rossi," I say, as politely as I can. "Our matter's rather urgent, and thank you in advance for anything you can tell us that would help us."

He sits, crosses one leg over the other, and nods. Though he's attractive—one might even say hot, with his large physique and presence that fills the damn room—he's no Cain. There's a ruthlessness in his eyes I haven't seen in recent years, something that tells me he'd kill me just as soon as look at me. I imagine he inspires fears in his enemies and respect in his friends. I wonder idly if he has a lover. I glance at his hand and see no ring. Married to his work, then. I mentally roll my eyes. Aren't they all?

"Go on."

Cain sits beside me, his back ramrod straight. Tosca sits right beside him, so close her leg touches his. I focus on Romeo.

"My name is Violet Price, though that's a new name. I was born Violet Bates." No recognition in his eyes. "When I was four years old, my parents were murdered. For years, I labored under the assumption that my father was killed because he was an assassin, but recently I found further evidence that it was actually my mother who was."

He nods patiently, not a glimmer of emotion on his stoic features. "You understand my time is valuable, Miss Price. I'm happy to do a favor for a friend, but for you, we'd need more than an act of good will."

"If you give us the answers we need, we'll pay you."

He smiles at Cain. "From what I know about you, Mr. Master, you could well afford my services. But I don't need your money."

Oh, to have the luxury of not needing money. What privilege. I don't even want to think about what he's done to reach that position.

"What can I give you, then?"

He eyes me with a wicked smile I feel down to my toes, a predatory look in his eyes I've seen before.

Seems the Rossi family currency is sex.

Cain's voice is a deadly growl. "Violet herself is off the table."

I stand, prepared to tell him to fuck off. I open my mouth to speak, and I swear I might just offer to bed this man to get what I want and screw with Cain. "That isn't for you to say," I snap.

Cain's on his feet. Romeo draws his gun.

"Does he have you here against your will?" he asks me, gun cocked.

Oh my God.

I look at him in surprise. He thinks Cain has me here against my will? Would he shoot him?

I shake my head. I'm angry at Cain, but not so much that I wouldn't fight for him, even now. We might be over, but we have a history together I won't ever, *ever* forget.

"No. We're associates and no more," I say, my words laden with ice. "Mr. Master assumes a level of familiarity he no longer can. Now," I say in a pleasant voice. "Let's sit down and stop with the pissing match. Deal?"

I feel my words cut through the tension in the room.

We all sit down. Tosca never even stood. She glances at her nails and picks at an invisible cuticle, like this type of conversation is just par for the course.

"Perhaps we can barter services. Master Enterprises has the most reputable name you'll find in the Northeast."

He nods. "While I'm disappointed I can't have *you*, Violet, I thank you." He gets to his feet with a bored yawn. "And thank you for your offer to barter. I will tell you only this. Yes, I knew your mother. Her eyes were unforgettable. She worked for us for a time until her demise several decades ago. We suspect we know who was responsible for her death, but unfortunately, I can't give you that name since you're an outsider. I do wish you the best with your endeavors."

"But I—" It isn't enough. We need more.

He inclines his head. The door to the room opens and Skylar, looking a bit disheveled but wearing a shit-eating grin, comes in with Mario. The men nod at each other, and Romeo leaves.

"So sorry you couldn't get what you came for," Tosca says. She places a well-manicured hand on Cain's shoulder. I want to slap her so badly my fingers tingle. How dare she touch him?

Doesn't matter. Doesn't matter!

"Do come again?"

Cain bends and kisses her cheek. "Thank you for your hospitality. And we will."

I clamp my jaw when I realize it's unhinged. I'm staring at him as if he's sprouted a second head. *How could he kiss her cheek like that? With me standing right here?*

I look to Cain. Is that it, then? We just leave without getting what we came for?

"Thank you," he says, turning his back to me and heading for the door. "Please tell your husband I said hello."

She freezes. "I will, thank you."

We make it to the truck before I lose my shit. "How could you... just... *leave?*" I nearly scream at him. "We came here for a reason. And you *promised* me!"

"Hush, Violet," Cain says in that stern voice I *normally* heed. "Get in the truck."

"Fucking *no*," I hiss. "I need answers. I'm not leaving here until I get them. I didn't come here for a cup of fucking tea and a trip to what feels like a damn escape room or obstacle course. I swear we just left a goddamn insane asylum."

"Get in the *truck*, Violet, or I will pick you up and strap you in myself," he says through gritted teeth.

"Babe," Skylar says pleadingly, her eyes wide. "Please. Do what he says, okay? Just this one time then you can ignore him for eternity."

It's then that I realize every one of the Rossi guards stands in a semi-circle, their hands on their weapons, waiting for us to go.

I get in the truck and close my eyes. It's all gone to shit. Everything. *Everything.*

CHAPTER THIRTY-ONE

I HATE the way Violet looks at me, somewhere between fury and hurt; it makes me sick to my stomach. I hate the attitude she's giving me, though I freely admit I deserve it. Hell, earned it even.

We have a job to do, and I can't think about us right now.

"Violet, we left because the Rossis asked us to, and when Romeo Rossi asks you to do something, you'd better have a goddamn good reason if you don't. We also left because I'm confident that Skylar has exactly what we need."

"So, folks," Skylar says. She props her feet up on the dash with a wicked grin. I know she's got intel for us. "I do indeedy."

Violet blinks. "Go on, then."

"Your mother was hired by the Rossis for a variety of hits over the course of a decade." Violet nods. I wish I could read her expression, but her face is a mask. "It was before Mario's time, but the family has secret records, and he was able to access all of them. For a price," she says with a nod. "But it was *not* a hard price to pay, believe you me. He has this thing where he—"

"*Skylar.*" Violet and I both say in unison. She looks at me briefly, then flips her head away so she doesn't have to look me in the eyes.

"Okay, right. You guys don't like to think about sex even though you've probably christened every single place in that entire mansion of yours but *whatever*. So anyway, he says that there was a priest or minister or something by the name of Descamps who got into big trouble with a rival mafia group, the Castellanos. As a favor to Descamps, Rossi hired your mother to do this hit. Rival mafia group found out, paid back the Rossi family with a hit of their own, but then tortured one of the cousins until he gave them your mom's name..." her voice trails off until she finishes in a voice that hints at a whisper. "And the rest is history."

"Castellano," I mutter to myself. "*Castellano.*" I know I've heard it before, I just don't know where. "Where have I heard that before? I know I've seen it. Read it, even... and something tells me we need to know more about this."

"Babe," Cain says, then shakes his head. "Violet. How did you discover that your mother was an assassin?"

"She had this book.... That I keep. The one I gave Henri just now. It's partially a diary, but she also had all sorts of things scribbled and scrawled into it. She liked to draw and color little doodles and things like that. I took it with me that day you took me from my place and brought me to yours."

Ah, right. She distracted me and asked me to take something she never used out of the drawer in her bedside table and didn't think I saw her take a book out of the closet and tuck it into her bag. My job is to not miss details. I rarely do.

"Right."

"And in the book... well, she has a few strange things. Like she has pictures she drew of me as a baby, sitting by a crib, sitting in a highchair, eating baby food. But then there's one with my eyes colored violet, and next to it she's written in cursive, *Violet Price.* It's why I took that name..." her voice trails off.

"I gave it to Henri and gave him my theory on the names and payouts. She's mentioned Greenlief, Whittier, and Whitman."

Skylar frowns. "You know Greenlief Whittier's a private bank in Salem?"

Violet blinks. "No, I didn't know that."

Skylar whips out her phone and starts typing away. "Whoa. Babe. We need to go there next."

"Why?"

"The CEO of the bank's name is Whitman. He knows something, Vi. He knows something big."

"Hit the GPS, Sky."

"Are they following us?" Violet looks out the rearview mirror, and I follow her gaze. About thirty yards back, a sleek black Town Car's behind us. I frown and take a quick left then a right, and half a minute later, the Town Car's behind us again.

"Oh yeah."

"From the Rossis?"

"No... I don't think so. But let's keep an eye on them."

"God, I hope someone attacks us. I would *kill* to beat the shit out of someone right about now. All this pent-up energy."

"Same," I mutter. She frowns.

"We're five minutes out, but I don't trust this guy following us," Sky says. "Anyone got a weapon for me just in case?"

"Yeah, you can borrow this." Violet reaches into her bra and pulls out her tiniest throwing blade. "Remember how I taught you to throw it at the jugular to kill, side of the neck to injure and incapacitate."

Skylar squeals like Violet just gave her a box of her favorite chocolates. "Oooh, you didn't have to. Thank you! Can you teach me—"

Violet shakes her head. "No, Sky. Not now. I'll be moving out once this is finished."

My gut clenches.

Skylar nods, her face downcast like a girl who just lost her dog.

The bank sits on the corner of Oak Street and Institution Drive, a stately-looking building complete with red brick walls. The cold of autumn's struck the tree branches bare, but a few brown and orange leaves have fluttered to the ground around us as we enter the bank.

Violet looks at the names on the walls. "Ah, there he is. And look, the little indicator says he's here today." I look to where she points, to a red and green lighted workstation indicating who's in today and their hours. He's in.

"You two go outside," Violet says. "I need to do this alone."

"Like hell you'll—"

"I mean it," she says in that voice that means business. "Don't you *dare* try to patronize me or help me. It's important that I do this."

I nod. I understand. Skylar's jaw drops, and she starts shaking her head. "Skylar," I say warningly. Skylar sighs. "Alright, alright."

Violet continues in as we step back outside. We watch as Violet approaches an elderly man sitting at a desk, tapping away on his keyboard. She stands in his doorway and says something, and he looks up at her.

"Wish I could hear them from here," I mutter. "Can't hear a damn thing."

Skylar groans. "Same. I wanna know what the hell is going on in there."

"You're just as nosy as I am."

She snorts. "Hardly. Okay, so listen. While she's in there, you have to listen to me."

I nod.

Skylar continues, "I saw the videos. You know I did. I didn't want to be the one to tell her so I let you do that dirty work. You spied on her, huh?"

I nod, still watching Violet. The man at the desk pushes himself to standing and reaches for something. I feel myself tensing. I want to go in there and protect her so badly, my body aches from the tension.

I release a breath when he reaches for an envelope and pushes a button, then gestures for her to come with him.

"Stand down, Cain," Skylar warns. "Stand. Down." She squints and looks over my shoulder.

"What's wrong?"

"Nothing," she says, shaking her head. "Thought I saw something just now. Huh. Okay, so listen. You fucked up, dude. Big time. You watched her on video and I'm gonna guess you didn't tell her about those."

"You'd guess correctly." Like I want to stand here and listen to my younger sister lecture me about relationships? Hell no. The thought of Violet leaving... and she always does what she says she will... I can't.

I watch the door close behind Violet.

Looks like he recognized her. He didn't send her back out here. Therefore... something's going on in there.

"Aw, man, Cain. The most important thing in the world to Violet is trust. You know that."

"I do, it's why I feel like an ass and really don't need reminding of this." I don't want to talk to my sister about relationships. Instead, I'm watching everything in the bank, my mind roving over the name again. *Castellano. Castellano...*

"So how'd you get her to come here, then, if she didn't know you were tracking her?"

With a grimace, I tell her everything that matters. By the time I get to the end, her head's buried in her hands. "Nooooo," she moans. "You didn't."

"Gee, thanks."

Ugh. Where the fuck are they?

"Alright, then. There's nothing left for it but to grovel, brother."

"Grovel?"

"Ohhh, yeah. You have to pull out all the stops. Like *all* of them. She doesn't want you to buy her things, but that monster truck she's been eying might be nice, and perhaps a wee mini pit bull puppy would also be great. Maybe some of those killer high-heeled boots she's wanted..."

She'll have all of them by the time we're back. I'm texting Joe now. I'm not sure it'll make a damn difference.

"Noted."

"Now, none of those things will actually get her to forgive you, though, you know that right? It's just like an act of goodwill."

"Right. So how do I get her to forgive me?"

She frowns. "This might be harder than I thought." She taps her chin thoughtfully.

"I believe in you," I mutter.

"Well... Violet really needs to know she can trust you, so I think the single best way for you to establish that trust?"

"Yeah?"

"Back off and let her handle this. You don't need to swoop in and save her, no matter *how* tempting that is. Okay?"

I groan. "Okay."

My phone rings. Joe. "Yeah?"

"Boss, my tracking says Violet's in the GWW bank."

"She is. I'm outside."

"I see that as well."

"Something I need to know, Joe, or you just miss me?"

"That bank's owned by the Castellanos."

There they are again. *Motherfucker.*

"Tell me again why that name means something."

"Castellano—Armand's mother's maiden name, sir."

I look sharply at the bank, willing Violet to emerge. "Fuck. You guys find him?"

"No, sir."

"I'm going in. Spot me."

"On it."

Skylar's opening the door, her eyes sparking. She hasn't trained to my satisfaction but damn it if I don't need a second pair of eyes and hands right about now. As we enter, a mother with two little kids sucking on lollipops exits, and Skylar nearly loses her balance. The bank's crowded, people milling about in line and at various windows. It's hard to get a read on where Violet is.

"Where is she?" I ask Sky on a whisper. "Do you see his room at all?"

She shakes her head, frowning. Nothing. I feel the tension in the air, and I know we're being watched. Armand... fucking Armand. He's behind this, but to what extent? For how long? And what does his mother's family have to do with this?

"I see her," Skylar hisses, jerking her chin to the far-right corner of the room. Violet has emerged from an opening door, her chin held high and a glimmer of a smile on her lips. I half-expect someone to come up with a pistol, an alarm to go off... but everything's remarkably calm. Eerily calm, even. I see one teller look at another, then look my way. In the corner, a security guard talks on a walkie-talkie. Classical music plays in the background.

Skylar frowns, as Violet walks toward us.

"You look down. Why?"

"I wanted a shoot-out," she says. "In on the action."

A few people look our way. I roll my eyes and take her hand to tug her toward the exit where we meet Violet. "It's over-rated," I mutter.

"You look as happy as a lark," I say to Violet. "Good news?"

"Wait and seeeee," she sings happily, and for one brief moment it looks like the old Violet's back. The fierce, independent, indefatigable woman I fell in love with. I'm still in love with.

I have to let her go.

The door to the bank shuts behind me, and I follow the girls to our truck. Still, no one comes riding in with a semi, no one follows us with a gun. Someone's watching us, though. I know it.

On the street behind the bank, another sleek black car slowly drives by. I catch Skylar's eye. She saw them, too.

We climb back into our ride.

"Spill," Skylar orders Violet.

"Got the money," Violet says with a triumphant grin. "He knew who I was when I went in and showed him my I.D. I told him that I was the daughter of Russell and Anya Bates, and that I had reason to believe they'd stored their money here, at this bank. And voilà." She shows me a small gold key with a flourish, and a bank statement.

I blow out a whistle. "Wow, baby. That's a shit ton of money." Violet will literally never need for a thing. I can't feel elated, though.

"Why do you look worried?" she asks curiously. "Why isn't this something to celebrate?"

"Didn't say that it wasn't."

"Ah, right," she says with that gleam in her eyes that tells me she's pissed. If we were down by the training field, she'd grab a cudgel right about now. "You're not pissed, yet you're not happy, and it doesn't take a brainiac to figure that one out."

My own anger simmers. "Oh yeah? You figured me out before I figured myself out, did you?"

"Yeah. You want to be wanted. You need to be needed. And the idea of me being independent and not needing your money makes you insecure."

"Jesus, no," I say, shaking my head. "It's not that at all."

Why would my mind even go there, knowing that she's leaving me?

"Then what is it?" she asks, arms crossed on her chest.

"It was too easy. Too damn easy." I shake my head.

"What was?"

"Going in. Claiming the money. You have to jump through hoops to get any amount of money that is rightfully yours, never mind money you have to prove belongs to you."

She sputters. "Are you implying that it *doesn't* belong to me?"

"God, no. That's not what I'm saying."

I've never wanted to turn her over my knee so badly.

"You two *stop!*" Skylar puts her hands up like she's a ref at a football game. If she had a whistle around her neck, I'd be deaf right now.

"For God's sake, you're so fucked up over arguing with each other and this whole breakup thing you don't see the forest for the trees, do you?"

I turn down the road that takes us home.

"Spit it out, Skylar."

"The bank's owned by the Castellanos. They made a note on that account to alert them when the daughter of their enemies came to collect their money. Why? I dunno. But we know that Armand was following you, he's got an ax to grind, and there's a good possibility he worked for them. Yes?"

"Yes." We both nod in unison, then glare at each other when we realize we're agreeing.

"Go on," I tell her.

"So you have to draw Armand out. The guys haven't found him yet, but you *know* that he's lying in wait, just biding his time for a chance to come and ruin everything. Right?"

"Right," Violet says, warily. "Hard to do when everything's already ruined," she mutters under her breath.

I grip the steering wheel even tighter.

"Listen to me. Armand's a coward, right? That's like his trademark, isn't it?"

"It is."

"So what will make this easier for him? What would a coward do? Cain, what does he have that he can use against you?"

I swallow hard. I don't want to say it out loud. "Cain," Skylar prods. "C'mon."

"The bullshit I did to Violet," I confess. Makes me feel like I want to throw up.

"So, easy solution, then, isn't it?" Skylar says triumphantly. "Easy peasy."

Violet scowls. "Let's hear it."

"You go out alone. He doesn't know that she already knows the bullshit you pulled, does he?"

I shake my head.

"You act like you're still in love. Kiss or… whatever," she says with a wrinkled nose. "And then, separate. Like, Violet goes her way and Cain goes his. And if my suspicion's right, Armand will come for you to tell you the awful truth, Violet. You pretend to be shocked and outraged and to leave, and *boom*."

"Boom what?"

"That's where *you* come in, and *you* get the answers you need. Got it?"

Pretend to be into each other. Pretend to be in love.

It sounds so much easier than it is.

I grit my teeth. "Got it."

CHAPTER THIRTY-TWO

THE ROLLERCOASTER RIDE of emotion I'm on today is killing me.

He loves me, he loves me not. He loves me, he loves me not.

It's hard to reconcile the man I've fallen in love with... the man who knows me, who sees me, really truly *sees* me for who I am, with the same man who confessed to me today.

I can't get past what he told me. I can't reconcile my need for him, for *us*...with the need for truth and trust. How could I ever trust a man who would lie to me like that?

But at the same time... how could I walk away from everything? From Skylar and the boys, the house on the hill and my training ground... from Cain, who's become my best friend?

My throat aches. I swallow hard and try to stay focused.

And then finding out I'm worth so much money... I can hardly wrap my brain around it. I'm a merry-go-round of emotions.

I have enough to live on for the rest of my life.

But I have a mission to fulfill, and I won't rest until I've done so. I can't. *I won't.*

My parents died because someone thought it best to seek vengeance. I grew up parentless because of someone driven to retaliation. That can't go unpunished.

We arrive at the house, operating under the assumption that Armand... or whoever he's working for or with... is watching us.

Pretend to be in love, Skylar says.

How can I do that? How can I let him touch me again, knowing I have to leave? Knowing the truth?

"Cain," I say, holding myself aloof and hopefully being professional, because I can't get personal with him right now, I just *can't.* Cain's made damn sure neither of us is being bugged, but there's no telling who's following us right now, so I keep my voice low.

"Yeah?"

"He won't come to your house. He knows that this place is a fortress and he'd never make it out alive. We have to go to a place to bait him."

"Right," he says through gritted teeth. "We could go to the beach..."

"No," I say, shaking my head. "He wouldn't have the balls. He followed us on the highway, though, didn't he?"

"Yes," he says, stroking his chin. I want to be those fingers, grazing over the hard stubble on his jaw. Touching him. Stroking him. I swallow the lump in my throat.

I could get a two-bedroom apartment, far, far away from here. I'll get a job teaching martial arts, and maybe a dog...

"...and he'll have easy access to the highway or more, won't he?"

I blink, realizing I just missed half of what he said. "I'm sorry, I wasn't paying attention. Say that again?"

Normally, when I lose focus, I get that stern look he likes to give me or anyone on his staff, or some kind of reproach. I'm used to it. I don't like when people space out when I'm talking to them either, and I know he's the kind of guy who values respect. But this time, he doesn't look upset with me. He doesn't look angry. Instead, his jaw slackens, and his voice softens when he talks to me.

"Baby, where'd you go just now?"

No. *No, no, no, NO.*

"You can't..." My voice is thick and strained. I swallow, clear my throat, then push through. "Don't call me that. I told you. I'm Miss Price now."

Skylar flinches as if someone struck her, then turns away and hangs her head.

Cain doesn't react at all for long moments, just looking at me. When he finally speaks again, his tone is resigned. "You're right. He won't come here. So I'm proposing we go somewhere together where he'll see us. You can go on your walk, pretend you're training or something, alone. If we're right... he'll come to you."

I nod. We go through the motions in silence. Cain assembles his team in his office and fills them in, while I mentally tally where I'll live, where I'll go. He dismisses them fifteen minutes later, and we have a full team that will follow us. We'll make it look like it's just me and Cain, but the entire time, we'll have everyone with us.

"Violet—Miss Price," Cain says. "Before we go, there are a few things I've... acquired for you."

His formal way of speaking makes me want to cry.

"Yeah?"

"Yeah."

"It's because I told him he had to grovel," Sklyar says, glaring at him. I look at her in astonishment.

"What?"

I clamp my mouth shut.

"Because he was an asshole, he has a few things to give you to show you he's sorry."

"*What?* Do you two think I can be bought with gifts? Seriously?"

I hear a scratching at the door, and I blink in surprise. What the hell is going on here?

The door opens, and Joe comes in with a sheepish grin, holding a leash with the most adorable little pit bull puppy at the end of it. He's tan with large ears and wide eyes, as big as Cain's hands.

"Oh my God," I whisper, and fall to one knee. I open my arms, and he runs to me, like he knows he's mine. "Cain..."

The puppy leaps on my knee and laps at my face. My heart melts.

I don't forgive him. I *don't*. I will not be bought with pretty things, not now, not ever.

"I can't take him. I won't be bought," I tell Cain. But I don't put him down. I rise, cuddling the puppy to my chest. The sweet little boy sighs and nestles in, and my heart explodes.

"I'm not buying you. I'm giving you what you deserve. I'm apologizing for what I did. Take what I bought for you, they're yours. You can take them now or take them when you go, but I'm not taking them back."

Them?

He sighs. "You'll see later. We have to stay focused for now, but I'll show you everything else in time. For now... we have to go, ba—Violet."

"I'll call him Cudgel," I whisper, handing the sweet boy to Skylar. "Take good care of him until I get back."

"Oh, we will have the *best wittle time,* won't we? Auntie Skylar will spoil you with all the best little things she can, sweet thing. You come with me and we will be good and busy until mama comes back."

She leaves the office with Cudgel in tow, and when the door shuts, I'm alone with Cain.

Again.

God.

I don't like being alone with him anymore.

"Okay, so I know I need to go but what other things did you get me? If you don't tell me, I'll be distracted the entire time. I have to know."

He sighs.

"Bribery is a really low move. You're better than that," I say, crossing my arms over my chest so I don't hug him. I can't.

"This isn't bribery. Skylar read me the riot act. She was right. I was wrong, and I should've been honest with you. She said to grovel. This, Violet, is me groveling. You'll find those high-heeled boots in the closet when you pack to go."

"Which ones?" I ask him hesitantly.

"All of them."

All of them?

He doesn't sound as if he's trying to manipulate me, but I can't help but wonder... is he?

And this is why we can't work together anymore. I'll always wonder if he's trying to manipulate me, trying to get me back into his good graces. I can't *trust* the man.

"The team's assembled at the Willows," he says in a tight voice, his eyes trained over my shoulder. It's highly populated during the summer, but in the cooler months, there are far fewer pedestrians and civilians nearby.

"It's so crowded there, though," I say thoughtfully.

He nods. "It won't be. Joe's making sure there will be very few people there when we arrive."

I nod. I don't even want to know how Joe's planning this.

"Okay."

"Let's go. I'll explain on the way."

We're halfway to the Willows when his phone rings. Henri.

"Yeah. What is it?" Cain has zero patience.

"I looked through the diary Violet's mom left behind. All the initials correspond to the names of people who were killed on those dates, and I believe the number next to them corresponds with the payout she received. There were not one but two Castellano deaths attributed to unnamed snipers that year, sir. Not on public record, but I have some resources I pulled together."

"Good to know. Have we found Armand's location?"

Silence for a full minute.

"Henri?"

"We did, sir, but you're not going to like it."

"Why not?" Cain's voice is tight. "Why the hell not?"

"Because he's... he's been here the whole time, sir. We found a camp in the basement that we thought was vacant, but now know he's been using for his hiding spot. Not often by the looks of it, but he's come here more than once."

I curse under my breath.

"We fingerprinted the place and found for sure he was

there. As for his current location, I suspect your plan to bait him at the Willows is sound, sir."

They disconnect.

"He suspects," Cain mutters. "Well, I suspect my staff's in deep shit for not finding out Armand was sneaking around our property."

I nod. "I understand."

He looks at me sharply, then turns away again.

We pull up to the Willows, and he parks his truck. He blows out a breath when he faces me. "So..."

"So," I respond, wrapping my arms on my chest.

"We're supposed to pretend we're in love."

"Right, if he knows that you and I... aren't..."

I don't even know how to say it. It's utter bullshit that because of *his* mistake, I feel wounded and hurt. Abandoned like I did when I was a child, because the one person I thought I could trust is a liar.

I am pretending, though. Do I have to pretend to care about the man who knows me inside and out? Who's taken such good care of me these past four months? Who drew me out of the shell I lived in?

Who made me *whole*?

"How does one..." my voice is a little wobbly. "Pretend to love someone?"

His jaw clenches. "We could... kiss," he says with a frown. "That's a dead giveaway... I guess."

How could I kiss him? How could I do anything with him right now? Is he frowning because he doesn't *want* to kiss me? Knowing that I'm leaving, does he feel... repulsed by me?

I'm mentally warring with myself, my pulse racing.

He was the one who chose this.

He was the one that put me in this position to begin with.

Argh!

"Or," he says thoughtfully, "we could... maybe—"

He thinks he won't kiss me? He thinks I'm not worthy of his attention or something? Oh no. Oh *hell* no.

I reach for him. I frame his face with my hands and yank him down to me. He freezes for long seconds as our lips connect. My own body stills. Everything but my heartbeat.

The sun feels cold compared to the heat in his kiss. My heart flutters, sending little bolts of awareness to my fingertips. I melt when his tongue finds mine. His own deep, male groan echoes through my core, and when he releases my face long enough for his fingers to stab into my hair, I fade into heat and warmth and light.

My pulse races with the memory of our bodies joined as lovers. Memories surface, one at a time, like a photo montage. Cain, standing against the background of the ocean the first day we met. That stark beauty in his eyes only I understand, the steady anchoring of hands on hips displaying the courage he sometimes feigns. For wounded people like me and Cain sometimes cower. We sometimes hide. We don't tell the truth because we fear being left behind.

And isn't that the crux of it.

As he kisses me, a soft cry escapes my lips, and he makes it his with a deep inhale. That's what he does—absorbs my pain, my emotions, my deepest longings, into his very being. Unites himself with me.

I crave the push of his fingers on my scalp, and the sharp but brief flare of pain when he tugs my hair. Another tug makes me moan, then I'm on my back and he's on top of me, and my body melts beneath him like it knows what to do.

I'm spreading my legs, already so ready for him a few well-timed thrusts would break me apart, when I freeze.

I pull my head away. "Cain," I say. Why is my voice choked? Why are my cheeks wet?

He doesn't answer at first, but kisses my temple, my damp cheeks, then my lips again before he grates, "What, baby? Let me in you, Violet. We're alone here. The doors are locked, and if we want fucking Armand to believe we're really together..."

I shake my head. "No. We can't fuck this up. We have to stay focused, because this is crucial." My voice breaks. "It's why I came here."

With reluctance I feel deep, deep in my belly, he pulls himself off of me, but not before he brushes his lips against my cheek, then lifts my fingers and kisses them, too. "Here, Violet. Press your fingers to your lips when you want to remember me kissing you."

I watch him go. It feels heavy and dark when he turns away from me.

He flicks on his phone and taps the screen. "We're going to separate now," he says in that deep voice of his I love so much. "Team ready?"

"Ready," Joe says.

Cain curses and hangs up the phone. "Fine. Now it's time. Mother*fucker*." He stabs his fingers through his hair and yanks the car door open. "No matter what, Violet. No matter if you leave me or I get shot or whatever the fuck happens next... I love you. Keep the boots, and the puppy, and anything you fucking want, and know I love you."

I open my mouth to respond just as the truck door slams.

I know what I have to do. I have my whole plan carefully choreographed, and now I only have to make it work. But my legs don't want to work, and my heart... my heart's still joined with his.

He loves me. And he didn't have to say it out loud to make it so.

He loves me.

I turn to exit the truck. I will my body to move, to cooperate with the plan. To make this happen.

I didn't come this far to fail in the face of victory, knowing I'm so close to the Holy Grail. I tap the barrel of my gun for reassurance. My Wilson. It's the tool I need most right now.

I open my door. Cain smiles at me. It's all part of our act. "See you at dinner, baby." He takes a few steps toward me, gathers me to his chest, then kisses my cheek.

"Bye, honey," I say, part of my act again, a role I need to play. "I love you."

That didn't... feel like an act, though. It didn't.

He turns from me and stalks away.

It feels final. It feels real, and I hate that it does.

I lift my chin, remembering the first time here with him, when we rescued his sister. I shiver when a cold, brisk wind stirs around me, biting straight through the thin fabric of my top, and briefly wonder why the seasons change. Perhaps to remind us that the passing of seasons is like the passing of time, so gradual it's hardly noticeable until you look up one day and realize everything's changed.

I walk with my head down, my gun tucked safely beneath the long coat I wear. I won't use it, not now, but I'm ready for if I do. If we were followed, Cain believes that Armand will approach me any minute now. I turn to an ice cream shop, closed now that we're getting closer to winter, and finally find a hot coffee and cider stand at the very end of the boulevard.

That ought to do it. Order a cup of coffee, pretend all is good... and he'll come out of hiding. And if not... plan B.

I go up to the coffee counter and wait behind several customers, my hands shoved into my pockets. "I'll take a tall dark espresso, black, no sugar," I order, when I feel someone step up behind me. Out of my peripheral vision, I see a familiar face. I turn with a half-smile as my coffee's placed in my hand.

"Hello, Armand."

CHAPTER THIRTY-THREE

Cain

I DIDN'T IMAGINE that kiss had meaning. I didn't imagine there was power behind her profession of *I love you*. She loves me still, even if she's hurt right now, and that is the one thing that will help me get through this right now. And I'll do anything, *anything* to make this better.

I take my position watching her, even though it kills me to stay so far away from her. I know that the Castellanos have been warned, that Armand is nearby, and that we still have hurdles to jump before we find what we came for.

I feign going down a walkway that takes me to some residential housing, then quickly slip into the car with tinted windows that Joe's got waiting for me.

We watch.

The door to a green car opens, and Armand steps out. I'm surprised he had the balls to drive that car, knowing we have it on file, though he doesn't know we're on to him yet.

He looks older and tired, his cheeks gaunt and his eyes sunken and sallow.

"Jesus," Joe mutters, mimicking my own thoughts. "He looks about twenty years older. What the fuck is up with that?"

I shake my head. I don't fucking care. Violet's at the window of the coffee stand, ordering, when Armand steps her way. He looks obviously around her, over his shoulder, as if afraid that someone will jump out at him at any moment. I can't believe I ever hired such a fucking coward.

"No, Armand," Joe mutters. "We're not going to attack you... *yet.*"

I know that Joe's fucking dying to.

"Can't shoot from here, boss, and it wouldn't be wise," Joe says, raising his eyebrows at the gun in my hand.

"Just sort of jumped in there," I mutter, then slide it back into my holster.

"He's approaching your woman, you know he's armed, and you know he fucking tried to hurt her. Of course you want to attack."

"Right. I'll kill him. But I'll take my time."

Violet turns when Armand puts his hand on her shoulder. My hand clenches into a fist.

I swallow when she smiles at him, even takes a step toward him. If I didn't know any better, I'd think she was... flirting with him.

No.

God, no... would she?

"Good move, Vi," Joe mutters, then zooms in with the camera we've secured to Violet's lapel. "She's smart, your woman."

"Fucking stop calling her my woman."

His brows shoot up infinitesimally, but he quickly trains his features. "Alrighty. Noted."

"She's smart, yeah." I want to change this subject, now. "She'll know exactly how to play this."

"Shit." Armand's taken another step toward Violet. Violet retreats.

He pushes closer, physically intimidating her. My hand's on the door.

"Boss, don't. If you fuck this up, she'll never forgive you, and she's damn near there already. You do this, and you're a fucking *goner*. There's no coming back from fucking this up. Trust her."

Trust her.

It's the very same thing that I told her. *Trust me.*

Do I trust Violet? Do I have to trust that she'll do what's right and what's best, no matter how deeply it hurts me?

I have no choice.

I can't swoop in and save her.

I can't fix this for her.

I have to let her go.

Do I love her enough to let her go? Do I respect her enough to let her do what's right for her, even if it feels like this decision will kill me?

Can I?

"What are they fucking doing?"

"Looks like they're just talking. Friendly, even," Joe says, but he's scowling, as if he's seen something that makes him suspicious.

Armand says something to her. Violet stills, then draws her hand back and tucks it against her chest. Her face is drawn, and her eyes are wide. This could be it, when he tells her everything to destroy me, yet the power of the revelation's lost its punch.

Violet shakes her head from side to side.

"Fucking audio," I grate.

Joe smacks a button, and the sound of Violet's beautiful voice fills the car.

"I can't believe it," she says, shaking her head from side to side. "This whole time, I've had no idea that Cain was following me."

"I'm so sorry to be the bearer of bad news," Armand says, the fucking liar. "But I think you deserve to know the truth."

He's been waiting for this, we all knew it. We knew he was holding onto this last card to play to get back at me and regain some sense of power. But he's only a player, a pawn in this game of roulette where no one's the victor.

"Thank you," Violet says, her voice hollow. Either she's a good actress, or she's channeling the real hurt this revelation gave her. In either circumstance, it makes me feel like utter shit.

"Anytime." Armand starts to walk away, but opens his mouth to say something. Then he closes it, as if thinking better of it. He turns away. She turns her back to him, her head down. This is where he'll call the Castellanos, I know it.

Armand picks up his phone, taps a button, and the car I'm in with Joe explodes.

CHAPTER THIRTY-FOUR

Violet

I'M STILL REELING from processing all of this, but my senses are on alert, waiting for the attack from Armand's family. If Skylar, Cain, and I are right, then he's planned to manipulate me with this knowledge.

Or did he just come here to tattle on Cain? He did it like he's feigning guilt...

I walk away, imagining I'm walking away from... everything. Everyone.

For months, he had me watch you. Stalk you. He has days and weeks' worth of footage just watching you sleep. I had to monitor where you were, every time, and he never planned on telling you. Armand had a look of triumph in his eyes when he told me this, like he'd been holding the trump card and now is throwing it down on the table with a flourish. *Ta-da!*

Cain didn't plan on telling me? No. No, that isn't true, because Cain told me himself. Just because it wasn't *when* I wanted him to...

He didn't lie to me. He hid the truth from me, and one could argue that is the same as lying, but when I ask for the truth, he's given me nothing but truth.

I had to learn to trust.

Would I have run if he'd told me the truth sooner? Hell yes.

Then as soon as I start mentally going there, I force myself to remember my anger, my frustration and outrage at him.

No. I can't just forgive him for this.

What he did was wrong, so fucking wrong.

But isn't that what it means to forgive someone?

I shake my head because I can't think about this right now. I have to stay focused right here and now on what I'm doing and where I am. I look around me but pretend to be distraught. I go to wipe fake tears from my eyes when I realize they aren't fake at all.

It takes courage to tell the truth when you fear the outcome.

It takes courage to forgive someone and stay despite wanting to leave.

Cain is courageous.

And so am I.

I take one more step toward the tall willows that line the walkways when I hear a *boom* that rattles my teeth. I turn around sharply to see what caused the noise.

Cain's car.

People around us scream, running past the fire that erupts like the fire of a dragon. I push through the people swarming past me and run straight toward the fire.

"Cain!" I scream, my voice drowning in the sounds of screams around us and the blast of fire and broken glass. "Cain!"

I see him, slumped over in the passenger seat, Joe sprawled out on the pavement.

It would take two of me to drag a man the size of Cain away from anything. It looks like Joe is semi-awake, as he stumbles away from the billowing flames. I tug uselessly on one of Cain's arms, but I can't move him an inch.

"Wake up," I sob, yanking on him with all my might. "I can't carry you, Cain. Wake *up!*"

Even with the thrill of fear and adrenaline consuming me, I can't move him at all. I sob freely, yanking at him. It's then that I realize he isn't going to wake up.

I have to get him out, or he doesn't survive.

A huge, hulking, beast of a man watches in the shadow of the video arcade, screaming into his cell phone. "Salem Willows! Come quick, it's gonna fucking blow!"

"Get over here and help me!" I scream. The guy stares at me, petrified. Why the fuck do people freeze in emergencies? Instinctively, I grab my gun from its holster and cock it and I am *fully* prepared to shoot. "Get the fuck over here and help or I'll shoot you!" I scream.

He runs to me and grabs Cain by the arm, just as Skylar reaches us. I'm shoving my gun back in the holster when strong arms grab me from behind. I half-expect police to apprehend me and react by instinct when I see it's someone I've never seen before. I deck his jaw, and his head snaps back.

The second he releases me, I grab my gun again. I have to help Cain, but this guy's fucking attacking me. He lunges for me. I duck and slide my fingers in place around my gun, satisfied by the heft of it in my palm. "Get anywhere near me again, and I'll fucking shoot you."

"Not if I kill you first," he growls. He spits on the ground beside me, his face contorted with fury, then throws himself bodily at me. I pull the trigger.

I never miss.

He falls to the ground with a thud. I don't take time to check him. I don't bother.

The shot I took is deadly...just like every. other. damn. time.

His body lays still in my peripheral vision as I turn back to Cain. He's been pulled to the curb. I sag in relief.

Someone at the arcade's shown up with a fire extinguisher. Sirens wail nearby.

The world spins around me, and my ears begin to ring. I slump to the ground.

CHAPTER THIRTY-FIVE

Cain

"TELL ME AGAIN."

I'm sitting propped up in my bed, and Violet's laying with me, her head on my chest. She doesn't know it yet, but the door's locked up here. I kept my guards here just in case, and I've commanded the deadbolts be drawn downstairs.

Everyone thinks I'm taking extra precautionary measures now because we've been attacked by the Castellanos. I'm not. I don't fucking fear the Castellanos.

I want Violet to stay here, with me.

Right now, she's lying on me as if she's exhausted and I'm her pillow, and I'm not ready for this to end. I'm not ready for the inevitable that happens next.

"Armand came around the corner, pulled out his phone, and I swear he was calling the Castellanos when they blew up our car."

"I heard it, and didn't know what it was at first. What a terrible sound."

I nod. "That's all I remember. Joe doesn't remember much more than that, but Henri's footage is pretty clear. A Castellano blew up the car, likely as a distraction. They saw me get in with Joe. When you came to rescue me, that was their chance. They came to get you."

She nods. "And dude, that was the *wrong* time to try to kidnap me. He'd have been better off trying when I was asleep or something."

I growl low, making her laugh. "I love it when you go all alpha on me."

"I know, baby."

This time, she doesn't tell me not to call her baby.

There's scratching and a whimper at the door. Violet grins.

"Let him in!" she shouts to the security guard. Seconds later, a freshly cleaned little Cudgel vaults himself onto the bed, sporting a bright red ribbon. He laps furiously at Violet's face until she pulls him up to her and rolls him over so she can rub his belly.

"You little rascal," she says with affection. "You missed mama, huh?"

She gets him busy with a chew toy on the floor. I marvel at her grace, the simple lines of her body like the expert sweep of an artist's brush. She tucks her hair off her forehead and behind one ear, and when she catches my eye, she gives me a gentle smile.

She sits on the edge of the bed, bends, and kisses my bandaged arm.

"You've kissed my owies like ten times today," I say, but I'm hardly giving her shit for it. I love that she does this.

"And I'll keep doing it."

Suddenly, something outside the window catches her eye, and she leaps to her feet. "Cain!"

"What?"

"Who... how... *it's my truck!*"

"Motherfucker." Again, they screwed up the timing. "I gave specific instructions for them to wait to give this to you until I told them. Until after everything had blown over. I didn't want you to think..." I stop myself before I say too much.

She tips her head to the side. "Didn't want me to think what?"

"That I... was trying to buy your affection."

She smiles sadly. "I wouldn't ever think that."

"Why not?"

Her eyes meet mine, and for the thousandth time, I'm struck by the brilliant beauty of the violet hue. "Because that's not the man you are. You don't demand affection. You don't coerce love out of someone. You love them, fiercely, just as they are." She blows out a breath. "Just as *you* are."

My throat feels tight. I nod.

"So, I need to hear everything," she says, returning to the story. I don't miss how she skirts away from the discussion of love. "Henri's footage shows that the man that tried to grab me was a Castellano."

"Yes. And my sources say that he was the very same man who killed your parents."

My sources being my men who captured and interrogated Armand until he begged us for mercy, but I'd rather spare her those details. She's likely figured it out anyway.

She sits on the chair, dressed in nothing but my T-shirt, and it puts me in mind of the first day we met. A storm had been coming in, and she'd ripped her dress as she was trying to convince me to work with her. I gave her my own shirt, right off my back, and being the ballsy, fucking amazing woman she is, she slipped it right on like it was a dress.

I wish I could go back... no. No, I can't. A part of me wishes I could go back and tell her everything, but I still fear, even now, that she'd have run from me if I had.

She pushes herself off the chair and walks over to me. I hold my breath, uncertain of what she'll do next, when she sits herself on my lap and drapes her arms around my neck. She rests her head on my shoulder.

I hesitate for a second, before my own arms encircle her, holding her close to me. If only I could keep her here, just like this.

"Tell me like this," she whispers.

"With you on my lap?" My voice is thick with emotion. I clear it.

"Yes, Cain. Just like this."

No more "Mr. Master."

I nod. "You killed him, Violet. Team Alpha's disposed of the body. He won't kill another soul."

She's quiet for long moments.

"Will they... his group. Will they come looking for him? For retribution?"

"I've seen to it that they won't."

"Do I want to know how?"

"I'll tell you if you want me to, but no. You don't need to know." It involved two point four million dollars, an oddly specific number from the superstitious Castellanos, a convincing argument made by Joe, Claude demonstrating that Violet acted in self-defense, and the second-in-command in the Castellano family admitting that their man had gone rogue.

It might have helped that I made it fucking clear that they don't want to take me and my team on and that a mutually beneficial relationship would be more fortuitous for both of us. They agreed, and promised we'd never see Armand's face again.

"Alright, then," she says in that calm, graceful way of hers I've come to love. "Don't tell me."

The room's grown dark, with only a sliver of light before the sun's rays fully set, but I make no move to put a light on. I feel if I move too fast or breathe too heavily, I'll break the charm that binds us together. Maybe the Castellanos aren't the only ones with superstitions.

She sighs.

"Are you sad, Violet?"

"I... I don't know," she says honestly. "I was more angry than anything for a while, as I'm sure you know. I was furious with you, Cain. I hated when I felt like everything between us was a lie."

I have so many things to say I have to clamp my lips together to let her say what she needs. It's the least I can do. I owe this to her.

"And after all this time, I wanted to kill him. I wanted to know when I pulled the trigger that he was the one that murdered my parents and that he earned the bullet that killed him. That he was getting his just rewards and my parents were avenged for what happened to them."

Her voice trembles. "And I... didn't know if I'd be able to do it when the time came. If I could intentionally *choose* to take a human life, even if I was justified and had good reason." She sighs. "And now I'll never know. Now I'll spend the rest of my life never knowing if I had what it takes."

"Oh no you don't. Uh uh. *Nope.*"

I spin her around so she's facing me, her legs straddling either side of me. It feels so intimate with her here like this, which is precisely why she's here and not sitting over there apart from me, where I can't touch her, hold her, keep her.

"What?" she says, lifting her chin defiantly. But I don't miss the way her pupils dilate. I don't miss the way she swallows, or the way her breathing accelerates. She's turned on.

But we have something to discuss.

"You don't get to blame yourself for what you did. I won't allow it." She opens her mouth and is likely planning on reminding me that I don't allow or disallow a blessed thing, but she finally just shakes her head and clamps her lips together. Good, because I'm not done yet.

"Violet." I hold her chin. God, I missed the way her soft skin feels against my rougher fingers. The way her eyes widen when I make her hold my gaze. "Just because you reacted by instinct doesn't mean it wasn't intentional. It wasn't pre-meditated, no. It wasn't in cold blood, no. But listen to me when I tell you that if it was, you might never forgive yourself."

A pained look lights her eyes. "What do you mean?"

"You don't get used to it," I say gruffly. I make myself hold her gaze. "You don't. Taking someone's life, no matter how justified, never feels right. You go to bed at night wondering who you left mourning their loss. You wonder if you had all the facts straight, if they changed who they are and really did deserve to be killed." My voice lowers as my own emotions threaten to choke me. "You start to wonder if you've mistakenly given yourself more privilege than you're allowed, and you wonder if the universe will demand more of you now that you've demanded more yourself."

She says one word, one syllable, that brings the smallest measure of comfort to me. "Cain."

I swallow again and keep going. "You talk about forgiveness, Violet. What you don't understand is that once you take a human life on purpose, it becomes almost impossible to ever forgive yourself for becoming the person you have."

She bends closer to me and kisses me. Silencing me. Hearing me. Maybe even forgiving me.

I gather her to my chest, and we stay like that for long moments.

I finally break the silence. "So... are you still leaving?" I ask in a teasing tone.

She exhales. "Leaving?" she says, as if the very idea's preposterous. "And leave that sweet puppy and truck behind?"

"They're yours, though. Take them with you."

She laughs. "Surely not. I'm not taking anything with me that reminds me of you."

She lifts her head and braces herself with a hand on each of my shoulders. "Every day, I'd remember you. Every day, I'd want to be with you. Every day, I'd fight the urge to come back." She shrugs with forced nonchalance. "So, I decided it's best to not even leave to begin with."

It feels as if I can breathe again. As if I can see again. I feel as if she's given me new life.

"Cain," she whispers. "You say that it's hard to forgive yourself. Maybe if I'm here with you... and *I've* forgiven you... then we can teach each other how it's done?"

"Now that is a deal I can handle." I hold her face in my hands and take my time brushing my lips across hers. I groan at the taste of her, the feel of her so close to me like this. "I'm sorry, baby. I love you."

"And I love you," she says. "No more apologizing. This is all behind us. Everything. Now we're just two people who can't stand to be apart from each other. Deal?"

I grin. "Deal. I thought you'd leave when this was all said and done. I thought maybe once you'd gotten what you needed and had no reason to be here anymore, you'd maybe leave. You're too strong and independent to be held in any one place for too long."

"Oh, you give me plenty of reasons for staying, and it has nothing to do with your dogs, your amazing team, the location of this house, or the fact that I can train whenever I want to and go to bed at night properly fucked."

I groan. "Violet..."

"I worried that when this was all done, you'd have no more need for me anymore, too," she admits. "Wow, we make quite the couple, eh?"

"Oh, yeah. Trust me, babe. I need you. You're the one that makes everything clearer. And there's no fucking way I'm letting you go." I snort. "No need for you? Jesus. You're my world, Violet. Without you, I lose my center. I lose everything."

"I love you, Cain."

"And I love you."

She grins and gets that wicked gleam in her eye I know all too well. "Then show me, baby."

Violet

CAIN STANDS with his back to me, his hands shoved into his pockets, staring at the blue, blue sky over the ocean. I take a moment to admire him before I walk over. From here, the blue sky outlines his large, masculine frame. His shadow on the ground before him could be a giant. I remember thinking of him as the fabled Paul Bunyan. His thick, dark brown hair is tousled, and I know exactly how it got that way after this morning's romp. He never bothered to fix it. He knows I like it a little on the long side so I can tangle my fingers in it.

He looks to his left, but not at me, and I can see the ruggedly masculine face and square jaw, still darkened with a five o'clock shadow that never seems to go away. When he looks at me, I feel the power he holds, his intelligence and wit. But as I've gotten to know him... as I've grown to love him... a bit of the hurt he carries has seemed to dissipate. Maybe it's only my imagination. Or maybe he's found a way to heal.

Healing.

It's a wonder that two people so capable of love could hurt one another so easily. It's a wonder that the very same people are the ones that bring healing.

I marvel at his strength, his power, and all that makes him whole, before I come up behind him.

"Cain." He startles when I call his name. That's unlike him.

"I don't know if I've ever seen you jump when someone came up behind you. Are you losing your skills in your advanced age, sir?"

He smirks, his eyes twinkling. "No, babe. I think you're the only one who could do that to me."

"Oh?" I come up beside him and nuzzle my head on his shoulder. He drapes a heavy arm around my shoulders. "And why's that?"

"Because you're such a part of who I am, it's as natural as breathing to have you with me."

"Now, as romantic as that sounds, it's a lie, Mr. Master."

He chuckles, the sound rolling through me with a delicious heat.

"Oh?"

"It is. You know where I am, at all times. If you're not by my side, one of the guys *is*, and you make sure that I'm safe from the moment I wake up until the moment I go to bed, and even when I go to sleep."

A shadow darkens his eyes for such a brief moment, I almost miss it. "Do you feel smothered, Violet?"

I shake my head. I know the answer to this question. "No. I feel... loved."

For the first time in my life.

I know that if I decided to leave, he'd let me. He let me go once, even though I know it pained him to do so, and he'd do it again if he had to. It would wound him... scar him, even... but I'm certain that if I needed him to, he'd let me. The freedom that comes from being his, from really, truly, being his, is worth every smothering thing he does, because I know he loves me.

"Good, Vi," he says, kissing the top of my head, an easy target for him because of how tall he is in proportion to me. "I want you to feel that way."

A ferocious little bark sounds not far behind me. I turn to see Cudgel, nearly fully grown, bounding his way toward me with endless puppy energy. I bend to greet him, and he nearly tackles me over in his enthusiasm to greet me.

"He'll be a strong defender one day," I say to him. And to myself. *And soon we'll need that.*

I need to tell Cain. I will, I just... I want to hold my news to myself for a little while longer. I also want to take him to the target range for "practice," and I'm afraid he won't touch me if I tell him now.

"Got my new Wilson. You know, it's okay to actually make me *earn* these things every once in a while."

He grins. "You like it, baby?"

I grin back at him. "Ah, hello, I fucking *love* it. Is that even a question?"

"Then you've earned it. I've never seen anyone get as excited about a new gun as you."

I reach for his hand. "Not true. You lit up like a bonfire when your new Ruger showed up."

"Well, yeah, that baby was on back-order for fucking *ever*."

"Still, you can't deny you were excited."

He squeezes my hand. "Not denying anything. Want to test them both out?"

"Hell yes I do."

We head to the range. I've already set things up so we're ready. We shoot until our guns are hot to the touch and our stomachs are growling with hunger, but there's still plenty of time for a little more.

"I will never forget taking you here. I will never fucking forget that first day here. I teased you with the knife..."

"Mmm. Now that I haven't forgotten."

His eyes heat, and he reaches into his pocket. "You haven't?"

My mouth is dry, and my throat doesn't want to work. I shake my head from side to side.

"Good. Because I know an excellent way to establish more trust between us."

I blink before I nod. I want this. *I need this.*

"Hands over your head, baby, and bend over the table."

I obey by instinct, offering him my wrists. He quickly secures them in the straps above my head. My feet are planted on either side of me, supporting me, as I hear him draw the knife out of its sheath.

"There," he says, as if he's just revealed a perfect masterpiece. "I'll buy you a new one."

Panic slams into me. "A new what?"

"A new everything." *Rip.* The knife slashes through my leggings, and they fall to the floor like ribbons. Another tear, and my panties join them.

"Will I need to wear your T-shirt back to the house again?"

"I'll figure it out. Hush now, Violet."

I hush.

I close my eyes.

I draw in a sharp breath when the knife grazes my shoulder blade, then my neck. He draws a pattern across my back, then kisses the scars there, before he drags the knife between my ass cheeks.

"Cain," I gasp, trembling.

"Trust me, Violet."

I close my eyes and nod. I do. I trust him. I trust him implicitly. It's taken a while to get here, but he's proven himself so often, I know now that I can trust him fully.

The tip of the knife crosses lower still, to where my thighs meet my ass, and then he scrapes it along each of my thighs. The skin burns, then tingles, and I feel as if every sense has been magnified. I freeze completely when he places the handle of the knife between my legs.

"Open those legs up."

I trust him.

I do what he tells me. He glides the handle between my legs. It's cold and hard, but I'm so turned on, I'd come with one stroke of his fingers.

"Fucking gorgeous. Look at you," he murmurs to himself. "You really do trust me."

I nod. "I do. Of course I do."

"I love you."

"And I love you."

The knife makes its way down my legs to my ankles, then drags across the tip of each foot, until he's drawn a trail map across my entire body. He hasn't drawn blood, though, and that's where the trust comes in.

"I need to taste you, Violet," he whispers.

My mouth's so dry, I can only nod. My hips arch with the first feel of his tongue doing wicked, perfect things to me.

"Yes," I whisper. "Oh, please. Oh God, just like *that.*"

He laps and sucks and plunges his tongue in my core, until I'm nearly weeping with the need to come. I can't hold back any longer.

"Come, baby. I want to taste you. I want to feel you. Come on my mouth."

Light explodes behind my eyes, a sparkle of stars showering my vision when I'm enveloped in perfect ecstasy.

He groans, milking my orgasm, until I slump over the table.

He makes quick work of undressing, taking his position behind me, and when I feel his cock at my entrance, I moan and whimper a little. "Yes. Yes, please, just like that."

He plunges into me with one firm thrust, and my world shatters and rocks, ecstasy filling every cell as he works a perfect rhythm until we both scream our pleasure in the soundproof room.

I'm slumped over the table, riding the waves of bliss, his body pressed up against mine. I love this man so much.

"Oh, good. Now I can tell you."

He pulls out and cleans me off. He's got a little kit he keeps here for this very purpose, filled with all sorts of kinky accoutrements. Our little goody box.

"Tell me what."

"I was afraid if I told you before, you wouldn't fuck me, and I *really* needed to be fucked."

"Violet..."

There's my name in my favorite voice. I grin.

"The doctor would tell you it's perfectly fine, though."

"Violet, I swear to God if you don't tell me what the fuck—"

"I'm pregnant," I blurt out.

"You're... pregnant." He repeats it like I've just spoken in a foreign language, so to tease him, I do. *"Ich bin schwanger,"*

I say with a nod. I look over my shoulder at him. "And that doesn't mean we can't get kinky or have sex."

"You're... pregnant," he repeats again.

I nod.

"When?" he says. His voice is hoarse. It's so rare that he gets emotional on me, that my own eyes blur.

"In the fall. I'm due right around the end of September."

"A baby," he says, then he breaks out in a grin that reaches all the way to his eyes. "A baby! Holy shit. Oh my God. I'm gonna be a daddy!"

He looks almost boyish when he grins like that. I'm laughing and crying when he hugs me and calls Skylar. "We're having a baby! Did she tell you? We're having a baby, Sky."

Then he calls Joe, and Claude, and Alma, and before lunchtime, he's got a huge celebration planned for tonight with my favorite foods from Sushi and Sake.

When everyone's gone to bed, and the food's all put away, I lay on his chest and sigh.

"Today was perfect, Cain. There aren't that many things that are perfect, but today was."

"You're right. Nothing's perfect, Violet. But there are moments that are." He kisses my fingertips then places them on his heart. "Moments like this."

THE END

CHAPTER ONE

Aria

"Today, you are going *down.*" I shove my glasses up the bridge of my nose for the umpteenth time with a little smile, blinking at the screen in front of me. Although it's cramped in this small, makeshift home office which consists of a tiny desk I rescued curbside nestled in a corner of the room to give me the best access to my computer screens, here's where I do my magic. While I don't really mind teaching coding at the little community college outside of Coney Island, I don't like the red tape and long hours. I long to get back to my little haven, where my fingers fly over the keys and I truly come alive.

Today, in the most boring white conference room under harsh, fluorescent lights, tepid coffee in hand, I longed to get home to unwrap what I discovered last night: *the* motherlode of all encrypted goldmines. Way too complex for me to delve into before school, but now, when the night is young and the moon rises, I get to play.

Professor by Day, Hacking Goddess by Night.

At least that's what I like to think.

I glance at the time and stretch. I can out-code anyone in the world, bar none. One day, I'll no longer be known as Aria Cunningham, the nobody, barely scraping by at the local community college. I'll actually make a *difference* in this world.

I blink and stare at the screen.

Wait.

My heart beats faster. Is that...

No.

My mouth dry, I click the little icon indicating my download is complete. I scroll down, my hand covering my mouth as I'm seized with two conflicting emotions.

Elation — *I did it!* I successfully hacked into the most notorious database of criminal activity I've ever seen in my life.

And gripping, terrifying fear.

No one has ever done this before. And unearthing something this massive comes at a cost.

I stare, my mouth agape.

Names. Dates. Locations. Pictures.

Evidence.

Politicians and celebrities, CEOs and religious leaders, military icons and monarchs. I stare in both horror and glee as I realize...it *worked.*

I scroll past pages and pages of information that should be encrypted but reads clear as day now. Oh my *God.* This is worse than I thought. If this got out to the press...if anyone knew what these people have done. *No.*

And worse? If the owners of this information ever realize I've hacked into their database...

"Good thing you covered your tracks," I whisper to myself.

A blinding yellow light flashes. I stare for a second too long.

I leap to my feet. I smack the button on the surveillance camera that overlooks all entryways to my apartment. My blood runs cold at the sight of six armed men at the back door. I might be in an old, mostly unoccupied house that was nearly condemned, but there are still *three* access points, not including windows, and I don't take risks.

Shit.

Oh God.

My heart beats so fast I feel nauseous, bile rising in my throat as I quickly assess my options even as my mind whirs. *How?? How did they discover where I am so quickly?*

I'm so damn careful, sweeping *every* digital footprint as thoroughly as possible. I leave no trace behind and cover every possible angle. I don't have time to unravel this.

I kick my keys into the trash bin and grab my laptop. I have seconds as I scramble to my hideout in the tiny attic. The trap door glides into place at the same time my front door opens.

I slide into position, my heart beating so rapidly I feel like I'm going to be sick.

I listen. It's just as I imagined. I told myself I would never actually *need* a hideout. And yet here I am.

My mind races.

The type of information I discovered was under high profile lock and key. The people responsible for this set up an immediate alert in the event of a security breach and absolutely had the funds and resources for high security measures.

Oh God.

Footsteps sound on the floor below. How long will they look for me? How thoroughly will they search? With a pounding heart, I wait in the corner of the attic, well hidden. If whoever's here had the foresight to bring a search dog, I'll be fucked, but I'm mostly invisible to the human eye.

Glass shatters amid loud, commanding voices. Though I can't make out clear words, I know they're trying to get me out of hiding. I swipe at the tears that fall and clutch my laptop to me at the sounds of my meager possessions being destroyed.

I listen for words but can only hear muffled voices. From my perch in the attic, I crawl on my belly to look through the tiny, triangular-shaped window that overlooks the driveway. Three unmarked luxury SUVs.

Shit.

I hold my breath and pray the camouflaged trap door remains hidden.

The footsteps come closer. Someone bangs a heavy hand on the closet walls and ceiling. I slap my hand to my mouth to stifle a scream. The voices come nearer.

I hold my breath until I'm dizzy.

I wait until it sounds like every single one of my belongings has been obliterated and the cold, angry voices retreat. I stare out the small window and watch the SUVs reverse onto the street and leave.

I can't go back to any place that's familiar or home.

I have to run.

CHAPTER TWO

Aria

I clutch my laptop to my chest as I stand outside the towering door. The imposing estate alone almost makes me want to flee, but I didn't get where I am by running when I'm scared.

My finger hovers over the doorbell, my hand quaking. I will myself to push it. No turning back now. Loud chimes sound inside the elegant house.

What am I doing? Why am I here? I wish I didn't feel so out of place. I wish I had another option.

My heart's racing when the door opens and Tatiana, my old college roommate and former best friend, stands in front of me.

She blinks. She's barely aged the past few years and looks as beautiful as ever with her pale skin the color of cream, and her ice-blue eyes, a mass of thick dark curls framing her face. "Oh my God. *Aria?*"

"Tatiana," I say with a forced smile as I look over my shoulder. "Please. I need to come in."

The quick snap of her gaze tells me she understands. With a nod, she steps back and slams the door behind me.

"Come with me."

I follow her to a small room that looks like a study, complete with a sideboard and gleaming mahogany desk.

"Sit." She points to a chair. While I never bothered with small talk, Tatiana never bothered with formalities.

Without another word, she takes a glass from the shelf, opens a decanter with amber liquid, and pours. "Drink?"

I normally don't drink. It's too expensive and I like to stay in control of myself. But this is good stuff and God, has it ever been a week. I drink what she gives me until ice hits my teeth.

Tatiana gives me a half-smile. "How've you been?"

I swallow. "Been better. You?"

With a sigh, she nods. "Same. I knew you'd eventually come to claim your dues. So let's hear it."

Claim your dues. So that's what we're calling it now. Ah, well. She isn't wrong.

"I need to know that we're safe here. I cannot be overheard."

"We're alone."

My mind whirrs and clicks. I can't help it.

There were two cars in the driveway, four pairs of shoes in the entryway when I entered, and two sets of keys on hooks by the door. Either she likes duplicates, or she's lying.

I know her well, and I think it's the latter.

I give her a look with a pierced eyebrow. "Really?"

"It's recent," she says, clearing her throat, and looking away before she drags her eyes back to me. "I kicked him out. That's all you need to know, Aria. Spill."

At one point Tatiana and I were best friends. Eventually, as our college days passed, we had less and less in common. No one really liked me — I was too honest, too direct. I didn't play well with others. My clothes were never the right style, I didn't know how to drink, how to fit in, and my grades surpassed everyone else's. But we both know I'm the only reason Tatiana graduated from Suffolk Law.

She stares at me. "You've finally done it, haven't you?"

I wince and nod.

A slow grin spreads across her face. "I knew you'd do it someday. You're fucking amazing."

She would know. Whereas others might ask for help with homework or essays, I was the one people came to when they needed hacking skills. She was the one that came to me, tearfully begging me to hack into the school grading system when she was at risk for failing. I did, with the promise that one day she'd pay back the favor.

"Tell me everything you can."

"It's huge," I tell her in a whisper. "The more I tell you, the more danger you're in. You're in danger just being with me right now."

Her brow furrows, and her lips press together. She nods.

"Listen, Tatiana...The stuff that I found...if it ever got out to the press...it would destroy institutions across the world. You remember the Epstein scandal? Think bigger. Multiply it by a hundred, drag in every major institution you could think of, and you'll be getting closer."

"Holy *shit*."

I nod, my belly churning.

"World," she repeats, her eyes wide. I watch her swallow before she clarifies. "Not just the country?"

"World."

"My God," she mutters. "So if you're found..."

"I'm fucked." One of the people implicated could have me killed with a simple command, hiding all evidence laughably easily given the lack of contacts and influence I have. I lick my lips and nod. "Even the good guys can't help me this time." Because even the "good guys" are on that list.

"Are you in danger right this very minute? Do you have a place to stay?"

"Yes, I am and no, I don't."

I pull out my phone and tap the article I saved. Wordlessly, I hand it to her.

Mysterious Campus Attack Unleashes Panic as Authorities Hunt for Missing Professor

In a chilling turn of events, the tranquil campus of West End Community College is reeling after a brutal attack last night, sending shock and horror through the community. The assault, which authorities suspect was aimed at locating a missing professor entrenched in a high-profile investigation, has left students and faculty in a state of fear and confusion.

At approximately midnight students and campus security reported masked assailants arriving on campus. Some believe the assailants suspected Professor Aria Cunningham was hiding on site.

The attackers managed to evade capture, disappearing into the night as swiftly as they had arrived.

West End Community College has been placed on high alert, with classes suspended indefinitely, and students urged to stay safe. Officials are urging anyone with information on the whereabouts of Aria Cunningham or the attackers to come forward immediately.

Finally, she blows out a breath and nods. "My God. *Officials.* And you're telling me you found information on said officials that would destroy them."

I blow out a breath in relief. "That's exactly what I'm telling you."

She nods and smiles wanly. "I knew when you came to me it wouldn't be to set you up on a blind date or to borrow some gas money. How much do you need?"

I exhale. "I need more than money."

She stares at me as reality dawns. "You need protection," she says in a whisper. "Someone outside the law."

"Exactly," I whisper back.

She rises to her feet and paces the room.

"Holy shit, Aria. *Girl...*" Her voice trails off as she thinks over the implications of what I've told her. "This is too big for me. You'll need someone who can give you protection and money.

You need someone with power. I have money, but money will only go so far." She mindlessly tugs at the delicate gold necklace she wears. "You could — no, no, that's too much. Hmm. That won't work," she says, as she mentally sifts through ideas. "Could send you to — no. Not this time of year, it's too busy and they'll be looking for those records anyway." She blows out a breath. "You can't show me what you found?"

I shake my head. "I don't want to involve you. The more you know, the more dangerous it is."

And honestly? I don't know her. Not really. What if she decides she wants to turn me in herself? Suddenly, the thought of coming here in the first place was the worst thought I ever had.

My heart is beating so fast I'm dizzy. I can't wait any longer. I can't stay in one place.

I stand up.

"You know, I'm good. I think that I—"

"Aria! I've got it!" She reaches for my arm and grips it tightly, her eyes so wide she's scaring me. "There is someone who can help. I mean...he's...vicious. He's scary as fuck. But if you go to him, okay, *them*...and offer your skills...it just might work. I mean, you've got information that law enforcement doesn't want you to have. Your only choice is to go to someone who's *above* the law. Who doesn't care about niceties or following the rules. Who hates the Feds and would likely love fucking them over."

I eye her skeptically. She's right, but..."Okay?"

"The Romanovs," she says in a whisper.

The hair on the back of my neck stands up. "They rule The Cove and they despise local authority," she continues. "They're the only ones *above* local authority."

I lick my lips. "How?"

"Organized crime. You know? *Bratva.*"

Bratva. I do know. When you do what I do, sifting through the vast network of connections and people and places...you know exactly where the most powerful people live.

The Romanovs own The Cove, the large, sprawling "Little Russia" smack dab between Coney Island and Manhattan. That's all I know.

But I have no safe place to go. I could form another identity, uproot everything, and flee the country. I know enough that I could fabricate a new ID and start from scratch.

But I'd have nothing. No one.

"I've lost everything, Tatiana. I'm willing to pay the price of anything at this point."

She stares at me unblinking. "Anything?"

I swallow. "Anything." My small apartment is gone. My identity has been leaked. I don't have a job anymore and had no money to begin with. For the first time in my life, I'm thankful I have no loved ones I could lose.

"The Romanovs are in charge of everything in The Cove. I can tell you right now that whatever you ask of them, it will come at a price. A price you may not be willing to pay."

My mind goes over every possible price. Debt collection.

Forced involvement in crime. Unpaid labor, human trafficking...sexual favors.

What would they demand of me?

"I have what they may find to be a...marketable skill," I say, my voice trembling.

She blows out a breath, and relief floods me when she smiles. "Of course you do. What do you know about The Cove?"

I shake my head. "Honestly, not much." I want to hear what she has to say.

Tatiana's family is Russian, so she's a lot more familiar with it than I am.

"So it's this neighborhood known for having a lot of Russian influence. The shopkeepers speak Russian. There are restaurants, grocery stores, cultural centers. An Orthodox Church. There's like a beach, and a boardwalk. It's really popular in the summer, because people sunbathe and swim, and take walks. In the winter it's less crowded because of the drop in tourists. But that's when the Romanovs come. That's when they set up shop, or whatever the fuck they do. I don't know. They own everything. Literally everything. The restaurants, hotels, venues. But they also have apartment buildings and single-family homes, you know, residences. They own those, too."

"Wow. Okay."

I can do this. What do I have to lose? I've already lost almost everything. Almost.

She bites her lip thoughtfully. "This just might work."

CHAPTER THREE

Mikhail

"My condolences, Mikhail."

I stand a full foot taller than the old man in front of me, but despite Fyodor Volkov's smaller stature, no one ever mistook him for being weak.

Volkov reaches to pour me a shot of vodka, but I shake my head.

"So soon you forsake tradition, son?"

"Call me son again and I'll remind you who I am."

Volkov's bodyguards come to attention at the challenge in the air, but I don't fucking care. "Don't try me," I tell them. "This conversation is between your *pakhan* and *me*. If any of you dare to defile my father's memory, you'll wish you were buried with him."

Other than staff, a few of my guards and Volkov's men are the only ones present for this impromptu meeting in one of my restaurants. I chose this one for the security of its location – the beachfront at my back and only one access point. The secluded room is located deep within the walls of the building.

Though from the outside it appears to be an ordinary restaurant serving Russian cuisine, it's only a front. The atmosphere is thick with the rich aroma of Russian foods, the walls decorated with paintings of Russian landscapes and art, all underscored by the threat of unspoken violence. If these walls could talk…

A muscle twitches beneath the old man's eye, but before he can respond, I lean in closer. "Some men respect the elderly, cousin. Don't make the mistake of assuming I'm one of them."

"If you think—"

"I don't *think*," I snap.

One of his men starts. I know for a fact the last man that interrupted Fyodor Volkov lost his tongue. My fingers itch for his guards to come at me, but they don't.

Volkov holds a hand up, a silent gesture to hold them at bay. I'm done with the formalities.

"I know why you're here, old man. I'd like to remind you that by law we're in our days of mourning. If any of your number breaks that law, retribution will be swift and merciless. The only reason I've given you permission to be in my presence before now was out of respect for my father." I reach forward and adjust Volkov's lapel. "Is. That. *Clear?*"

We have ten days left and he knows it.

Muscles twitch in the old man's jaw, his watery eyes narrowed. He pulls away from my grip on his collar with effort. Though his men outnumber mine, the sheer strength of my cavalcade would overpower them, at least in this moment. My father trained us to be dynamite in human form, veritable panthers.

Volkov would be wise to hire more muscle.

"Ten days left," he says, before playing his final card. "But you know our traditions."

I need no reminder.

I wear the knowledge of my duty like a noose around my neck, tightening with each day that passes. The dissolution of my first arranged marriage agreement on the heels of my father's death was no accident. Volkov is notorious for hitting hard when a man is down, for striking the Achilles heel with no mercy.

My first fiancée went missing, and while we hunted for her, Aleks discovered their financial stability was fabricated. The second arrangement ended as swiftly as the first when my second fiancée was found dead. The third was much harder to secure after my history of arrangements, but we were finally able to. Money talks. And then my third fiancée was found dead this morning.

I nod my head to my cousin's men. "You've outstayed your welcome. You have three minutes to leave before I consider your presence trespassing on our territory and treat you accordingly." My guards practically vibrate with excitement, rabid dogs who smell blood in the air.

I take out my phone to send a red alert.

Krasnaya trevoga

Unlike Volkov's men, greater in number but languid under the leadership of their aging *pakhan,* my brothers obey on command. All are eager to show obedience and homage to their new *pakhan.*

Volkov stares around the room with those narrowed eyes of his for a few beats before he eyes me carefully and gets to his feet. Without another word to me, he gestures for his guards to escort him out. I've already dismissed him as I turn to my phone and send another text.

I tap the computer screen in front of me and wait, drumming my fingers on the mahogany table.

"Another drink, sir?"

I nod without looking at the waiter, scrolling through my notes in front of me. "A bottle of *Stolichnaya Elit* and a platter of appetizers. And send all staff out unless I signal you directly."

In my peripheral vision, I see him nod. "Right away, sir."

Quietly, he evacuates all staff from the room. I pay my employees well to be discreet and obedient, so they know the routine.

Aleksandr is the first to arrive. I wave a hand to greet him at the door, wordlessly point to the seat beside me, and turn back to the computer.

"Heard the news. Bad fucking luck."

I grunt in reply. "Luck has nothing to do with it. Sit."

Aleksandr takes a seat, leaning back and opening up his cell phone. While the rest of the world uses their phones to scroll social media and take selfies, Aleks runs an empire.

He scowls at his phone, his fingers dancing over the screen.

Aleks is younger than I am and in impeccable physical condition. Like all of us, he battles demons, but Aleks schools them under the weight of a barbell. The combination of brilliant techie and sheer brutal strength is useful in our line of work.

He looks nothing like me, which sometimes comes in useful. All of the Romanov men were adopted, a part of our father's intricate plan to build an empire.

It worked, for the most part.

Aleksandr sits brooding, as his fingers fly over his phone screen. He mutters to himself and stifles a groan. Today's news fucked up our plans. But the Romanovs always find a way to prevail.

I tap my computer monitor and pull up the video feed. Viktor is the first that shows on screen, followed swiftly by Kolya, Lev, Nikko, and the rest. \

"We have a situation." I quickly bring them up to speed.

"This morning, I got a call. Irina Smirnova was found dead, strangled in her sleep. Of course they have no fucking leads, but we know who was responsible."

Nikko scowls at the camera, his arms crossed over his chest. He's glistening with sweat and I can see the walls of his home gym behind him. Nicknamed "The Steel Serpent," Nikko's our head assassin. "Volkov."

Kolya finally breaks the silence. "Being engaged to you's a fucking death sentence."

Kolya, our group mastermind, served with my father in the army. Though younger than my father, he's older than I am. I respect his brilliant strategic mind.

Our laughter quickly dies because it's true.

He shakes his head at the camera, running his fingers through his short hair streaked with silver. "We don't have much time to arrange another marriage, Mikhail." Kolya's voice is grim. "If we hit that deadline and you're still unmarried, we know the consequences."

The destruction of our assets, the possibility of attack from our enemies, the potential threat they could use leverage against the few people that mean anything to us. Even my tribe of panthers isn't enough.

We're on the cusp of war if I don't have a wife, a war we're not equipped to win.

Kolya continues. "No one in our circles will agree to another arrangement, Mikhail. We'll have to find someone else."

I nod, stroking my chin as I think. The waiter brings our food and pours vodka into shot glasses.

"You have our support and protection, brother," Nikko says, his sober, earnest eyes meeting mine on screen.

I nod. "Thank you."

"We'll find you a wife," Aleks says. "Secretly, of course. We have a network of contacts and resources that can help."

The rest agree.

My phone buzzes with a text. I feel my eyebrows rise with surprise.

The timing couldn't be better.

Want to find out what happens next? Scan the QR code below to order your copy of *"Sovereign: A Dark Bratva Forced Marriage Romance"* now.

Fueled by dark chocolate and even darker coffee, USA Today bestselling author Jane Henry writes what she loves to read – character-driven, unputdownable romance featuring dominant alpha males and the powerful heroines who bring them to their knees. She's believed in the power of love and romance since Belle won over the beast, and finally decided to write love stories of her own.

Scan the QR Code below to receive Jane's Newsletter & be notified of upcoming new releases & special offers!

Be sure to visit me at www.janehenryromance.com, too!